THE DAEDALUS PROTOCOL

THANKS FOR SUPPORTING Na'Amat

JEFF SHECKTER

For the real heroes in my life.
My family.

"Now I am become death,
the destroyer of worlds."

- J. Robert Oppenheimer from
the Hindu Bhagavad-Gita

"How much more grievous are the
consequences of anger—
than the causes of it."

- Marcus Aurelius

PREFACE

Throughout the ages, humanity has fought a losing battle. Death is inescapable.

All cultures have prepared their loved ones for the afterlife in one way or another.

The ancient Egyptians buried their most exalted leaders with artifacts they deemed necessary in the afterlife. Their recently removed organs, embalmed for eternity, were left close at hand, ceremoniously deposited into intricate hammered gold and jeweled sarcophagi that signaled their regal status in the world to come.

The Greeks used a simple coin to aid the passage of their dead, known as Charon's obol. Loved ones would place 'obols' on the eyes of the dead. These coins were typically made of copper or bronze and were used as a measurement of weight for trading and as currency by the ancient Greeks.

Hades, god of the underworld, appointed Charon as the boatman to ferry souls from the world of the living to the underworld after they died. These two worlds were separated by the rivers Styx and Acheron. Charon would require compensation for taking these souls across the twin waterways, and as payment, the obols would be left on the eyes of the dead as payment for passage to the next world.

Even cultures that eschew adding anything to the deceased have their own rituals.

Jewish funeral rites entail washing, cleansing, and ritually purifying a body. It's then wrapped in a plain white shroud and the body buried as quickly as possible in an unadorned wood coffin. A humble departure back to the soil from which they first emerged.

Immediate family members say special prayers and engage in an intense week-long mourning period call Shiva. These rituals are said to elevate the soul of the departed in heaven.

Regardless of ritual or tribe, these actions are all done in preparation for the afterlife.

But what if death could be cheated? What if someone could choose to live forever?

Even those who have conquered vast empires or have become titans of industry all eventually lose their battle with life. There is no negotiation on the subject, no waiver. The game has been rigged since their first breath.

However, there are many stories of mystical healing waters with the power to give life itself. Drinking them, bathing in them. It was an elixir to fix all ills. Could people really live to be hundreds or even thousands of years old—as recorded in the Bible—healed of all disease and injury?

Does such divine nectar still flow somewhere now? Were its secrets and location lost through the passage of time? Or perhaps purposefully hidden away? To behold such power would make its possessor nothing less than a living god on Earth. Able to span an endless desert of time. Accumulating knowledge and wealth beyond measure. To remain sharp of mind and quick of limb for centuries on end. The power to heal and to kill. Millions would dutifully follow this mirage of a messiah.

It would stand to reason that an army, blinded by awe for their god-king, would quickly rise.

A benevolent ruler would be wishful thinking. Tyrannical rule from a superior class would be inevitable. Slavery and servitude would provide an endless cycle of torment and misery that would know no end.

Would this genesis-like elixir be a portent for eternal life, or the greatest weapon the world has ever known?

Was this ancient source of life and power lost forever, or had it ever existed at all?

PROLOGUE

417 BCE
Parthenon, Greece

He was a dead man.

The ancient warrior stood between the limestone pillars of the acropolis. The roaring flames below casting long shadows against the worn stone. His armor was all but destroyed. Blood flowed freely from the myriad of wounds across his ravaged body. It wasn't the heat from the flames that ignited his veins. Nothing less than the fate of humanity itself fueled his hurried ascent.

A blazing serpent of fire chased around the mountain below, its fiery venom devouring everything in its path. Broken limestone and ruin lay everywhere. The symphony of war roaring from every direction. Men with missing limbs and punctured flesh screamed hopelessly into the night. The wailing from grieving mothers and terrified cries from freshly orphaned children were nearly drowned out by the tormented agony of wounded and dying soldiers.

Odysseus allowed himself a rare moment to rest. His lungs screamed for air. Muscles across his body complained that they could be pushed no further. His mind, overwhelmed by the enormity of the task, took brief solace in the memories that had been seared into his brain. He thought back to happier times. He remembered the lush, rolling verdant hills that sprouted sweet dark grapes and an overabundance of fat, flavorful olives. Fields of wheat, pregnant with plump golden seeds, added an ochre contrast to the scene in his mind. Gardens of lavender painted the landscape an impossible royal purple while gently perfuming the summer air. Peace was even more plentiful than the produce.

A scream echoed from the madness below, bringing him back to the present carnage. The night was ablaze with the fury of conquest. He would not fail this last sworn duty.

Hector, Greece's finest marksman and Odysseus's most trusted servant, stepped from behind an adjacent column and approached. "Master, I beg of you. Return to the city. Without you, we'll have no chance to ge—"

Odysseus placed his bloody, bandaged hand on Hector's chest. No words were needed. The decision was made. It was far too late to turn back now.

"What if she couldn't flee in time? What if she was killed with the others?" Hector pleaded.

"She will arrive safely, my brother. The gods will it," Odysseus said with certainty.

"But what if…" Hector didn't want to finish his own sentence.

His brief rest over, Odysseus reached down to retrieve his sword. Fire and gore glinted in the night. How many lives had he taken for this? How many others fighting alongside him had been lost? Could anything be worth all this destruction?

Death seemed to be all he knew now. He could feel it clinging to him like dew on morning grass. He laughed aloud at this irony. All this death in order to bring meaning to life. He feared that no amount of joy could wash away the ocean of sorrow he was drowning in.

He kept his breathing slow and even, but felt precious time slipping away. Odysseus lifted his sword, twisting it in the moonlight. He was beyond exhausted, but they were so close to achieving their goal. He felt the tightness of muscle across the breadth of his back and shoulders. It wasn't from the heft of the Damascus steel in his hand. More likely from the growing concern that maybe she wouldn't come. Perhaps Hector was right, and she'd been lost to the carnage below. Even if his love had survived, was bringing her there resigning her to the same tragic fate?

Crack!

The sound of a twig breaking was like thunder to his ears.

Odysseus spun on his heel as he peered into the darkness, his keen eyes searching for shifting shadows and his ears straining for the familiar creep of footfall. Fires continued to rage below. Shadows danced and crept all around.

He and Hector quickly took cover behind a large marble boulder. Odysseus spotted a lithe form slinking through the darkness and watched as it crept toward their position. He raised his Damascus blade and saw Hector's bow already pulled taut against the advancing threat. As the form broke through the darkness, both men relaxed and lowered their weapons.

"Odysseus, thank the gods I've found you." The shadows receded, revealing a beautiful woman standing before them.

Odysseus pulled his lover into a crushing embrace, lifting her into his powerful arms.

"Ianthina, my flower, I was afraid you'd been lost."

"My love, the gods have protected me. I told you we would see each other again. Now put me down, we still have much to accomplish."

Odysseus could remember the first time he had laid eyes on Princess Ianthina like it was yesterday. Her long, dark hair and almond-shaped eyes shimmered like the deepest ocean. Flowers adorning her hair. Her body flowed beneath a silk robe that concealed her long legs, but at the same time, left little to the imagination. The scent of jasmine floated on warm tendrils of air as she passed, intoxicating all who were close. But the sadness behind her eyes, that's what he remembered more than anything. How could someone so beautiful, someone so loved and adored, emanate such a profound air of melancholy and misery?

It was only after she found Odysseus that she felt true happiness for the first time. The two quickly became confidants sharing stories and secrets. Sharing a bed soon followed. They had talked about marriage, and how many children they would have. Now all of that seemed like a fairy tale. *Would they even be able to survive the night?*

"Were you successful in securing the vessel, your highness?" Odysseus asked. He prayed that she had; otherwise, all this bloodshed was for naught.

Ianthina broke her gaze from his, glancing down at her feet. Odysseus feeling hope slip further away. It was only when she kneeled down to retrieve the satchel on the ground did he realize she had indeed been victorious in her mission.

It felt like the weight of the world in her hands. The secrets to the sands of time now lay in a simple copper enclosure. Still, she felt shame and embarrassment for this affront to the ethereal substance inside.

Its customary home was a chalice made from solid gold, adorned with brilliant, faceted jewels. That opulent bowl and its revered contents forever rested on its altar of intricately carved acacia wood covered in gold leaf and more jewels. Rumors abounded that it was a sacred relic from the gods on Olympus themselves.

Nothing in Greece was as valued or sacred.

The confused look on Odysseus's face prompted Ianthina to answer his unasked question.

"I placed the contents of the golden vessel into this plain copper shell. I knew those evil men would quickly notice if the golden chalice were missing from the altar. I left it behind to buy the time I needed to make my retreat. I pray that the gods forgive me for my disrespect."

"I will guard this with my life, your highness," Odysseus said as he took the simple copper pot from her grasp. His hand lingered on her slender fingers, pausing for a moment. "My love, you are as brilliant as you are beautiful, and your ruse worked just as you had hoped. You're now safe here with me, and my oath to your family is intact."

"Many have died to protect this, Odysseus, and many more will perish if we fail. The very fate of man hangs in the balance."

Hector remained silent, his eyes following the dialogue but saying nothing. The gravity of the situation pressed on all of them, but none more than his companions on this fateful night.

Odysseus secured the valuable cargo in a leather satchel and secured it to his pack. "We must leave immediately. We have a long journey ahead, and our enemies are at our heels." He knew this journey would likely see them both killed, but they had no choice but to try. Ianthina knew this as well, but remained her regal, stoic self.

"Be safe, my love," she said. "We will see each other soon. You will not die, and you must not fail. Return to me soon, General. That's an order from your queen."

"Zeus himself couldn't keep me from returning to you." Odysseus enveloped his future bride in his arms once again. His lips found hers and kissed them with passion fueled by their upcoming absence.

Her lips suddenly tore away from his. She shuddered and gasped as pain racked through her body. Ianthina went rigid before falling slack in his arms. He felt the impact of another object just before he spun her around, using his body and armor as a shield against this black-hearted assault. The bombardment ended and he drew back, dread already creeping through his bones.

Odysseus knew instantly that she was gone.

He felt an object that had no place in his beloved. Then a second, and a third. He knew the hardware well, sending thousands of them from the grasp of his own bow.

As he cradled his love in one last sorrowful embrace, Hector loosed a single arrow that caught Ianthina's stealthy killer in the throat. The assassin gurgled and spasmed for a few heartbeats as his life pooled out of him, finally collapsing like a ragdoll.

Ianthina's blood seeped through Odysseus's fingers. As he supported her back, he pulled free the shafts of the arrows that had pierced her body.

More arrows screamed overhead. Shouting from another group of pursuers revealed that their attackers were almost upon them. Steel-tipped shafts were chipping the limestone temple all around. The barking from the scent-hounds reverberated against the stone, the direction of the attacking hoard indiscernible in the night. They were out of time. Remaining even another few seconds at the temple ruins would mean certain death.

An unlucky shot slipped through the night sky, finding its way through Odysseus's shoulder guard, slicing deep into his heavily muscled arm. He winced when he broke the hilt of the arrow, leaving the tip embedded in his flesh to deal with later. Their pursuers were closing in fast now and would be upon them any moment.

Odysseus and Hector placed Ianthina behind a large block of marble, a thick wall of safety between her lifeless body and the onslaught of airborne lethality. She had fulfilled her duty to Greece and honored the oath she swore by forfeiting her life to protect this ancient secret.

Now she and her family were gone. All for this precious package. What could be worth so much loss? How could something so small contain such incalculable value? Something the royal family gave their very lives to keep from the evil that now waged war on them now.

While planning for the mission, Hector had tried in vain to determine the contents of this special treasure. He was sworn to secrecy about its very existence, and yet he had no idea what he was protecting. All he and Odysseus had been told by Ianthina was some cryptic riddle about it containing the blood of gods.

"There will be a time to grieve, but that time is not now. We must leave at once!" Hector heard Odysseus's words, but they were muted, his body numb. His queen lay dead in front of him. He had failed to protect her.

Hector looked up at his friend and mentor and saw the sense of loss and sorrow raging across his battle-hardened façade. He nodded to Odysseus and spun on his heel to retrieve his weapons, crouching to avoid the continued barrage.

Odysseus took Ianthina's face in his hands and kissed her raven hair one last time. He laid her down, then scrambled to pick up his sword. "Hector, we finish this now," he said through gritted teeth, every fiber in his body seething with anger.

Odysseus faced Hector and clasped his friend on the shoulder, both giving and receiving strength. Steeling their mutual resolve, they turned and vanished down into the darkness.

The smell coming up the mountain was a mixture of acrid smoke, seawater, and rot. The black sky merged into the deepest parts of the ocean somewhere out on the horizon. This celestial kiss was exposed only by the myriad of stars and the growing sliver of a waxing moon. The dock, which was still far below, came into view only after they cleared a thick growth of trees, although calling it a dock was now a wild exaggeration. While the destroyed dock looked deserted, the pair of seasoned warriors knew it could also be a trap.

Their escape route had always been fraught with peril, but the heavy blanket of darkness slightly improved their odds of escaping undetected, one of the few gifts the gods had bestowed to them on this suicide mission. Thin cloud cover further obscured the moonlight, casting shadows that danced along the terrain, concealing their movements.

Splinters of wood and detritus floated aimlessly, barely visible from the rocks behind which Odysseus hid. Abandoned and severed ropes were coiled in the shallow depths, appearing like eels waiting to strike out. Vegetation that only days before had grown above the rocks now floated silently by. Their sun-filled futures stolen for eternity.

This part of Piraeus, the ancient Greek seaside dock, had been home to the Athenian fleet and an important hub for merchant vessels. It was now reduced to skeletal ships and kindling.

Destruction and death lay everywhere. No structure was left standing. The foliage, once verdant and lush, was now ember and ash. The ruin spread like a cancer from the sea to the sky.

Their footfalls were silent; each step expertly placed to avoid betraying their presence. They passed sentinels twice during their descent. Thankfully, none were alerted to their presence.

The sound of lapping water told them they had arrived at sea level. Soft currents washed back and forth against the abandoned moorings that were now tilted at impossible angles, oblivious to their own demise.

The hardest part of their plan had been a success. But success was not a word Odysseus or Hector could fathom. Not with Ianthina lost forever. Her body, once anointed and attended by eunuchs and maidens, had been left discarded on the mountain above. Regardless of the outcome now, success was not a word Odysseus would ever think of using. Too many had died already. The contents of the sacred vessel still could not fall into the hands of the enemy.

The rendezvous that had been arranged prior should have been waiting for them already, but there was no sign of life anywhere. Had they come this far, only to have snared themselves? Maybe the rescue party had abandoned hope and left already. If his men already met the same fate as those on the mountain, Odysseus and

Hector would be trapped and outnumbered 100-1, their quest a failure.

Hector was the first to see it.

"Odysseus." Shock and relief washed over his face. "I see the signal. I'm sure of it."

Odysseus peered out to the sea, cupping his hands around his bleary eyes, willing his mind to see something, any spark of hope. After a long moment, he assumed it was just wishful thinking on Hector's part, but it flared again. Lightning on the water.

Hector grabbed his flint and struck it against his scabbard in response. Moments later, a skeletal craft emerged from the inky night. Through smoke and mist, it crept toward the shore as if the vessel itself could sense the dangers ahead.

"Masters, thank the gods that you made it safe. Your ship is ready around the point. The men are eagerly awaiting your return. The passage is clear," said a haggard looking man, piloting a feeble raft.

Odysseus thought back on all that had transpired to reach this point. Hope began to swell inside him. Their losses may not have been in vain after all.

The plan was to use this simple raft as an invisible escape to a larger boat anchored a few hundred yards offshore, still cloaked in darkness. From there, they would take a short trip to his other love, the mighty *Paralus*. His sacred trireme. The *Paralus*, was a sister ship to only one other like it in the entire fleet.

Twenty-nine oars strong, with ninety powerful men fueling its passage; their combined effort etching into the frothy ocean below. Her oars were sculpted timber trunks, each one skillfully shaped from a single fir tree and anchored to the frame with leather loops. The *Paralus* was built for speed and agility, and at over thirty yards long, she was also one of the biggest on the sea.

Being nimble on the water had won her countless battles. The ship could also accelerate and decelerate quickly. So prestigious was her pedigree that the *Paralus* was rumored to have transported none other than the Oracle of Delphi on her diplomatic missions.

Watching Odysseus sail the *Paralus* brought great pride to the Athenian fleet. The large bronze battering ram at the bow had been sculpted after its namesake animal. Massive, curled ram's horns protruded from the ship's prow, rearing up above the bow, as if to challenge all who sailed toward her.

Its eyes were black obsidian. No warmth or comfort would be found emanating from these dark orbs. This giant beast charged through the seas, carried by her massive white sails, and propelled by the muscles of mighty Greek oarsman.

Once Odysseus was aboard, he knew there would be no catching his elite crew. He was finally able to transfer his precious cargo to its intended destination.

As the raft pulled closer to the shore, Odysseus waded out into the murky sea to meet it. Saltwater burned the lacerations on his arms and legs as he made his way onto the rickety platform. Hector followed closely behind.

Upon closer inspection, it wasn't as much a raft as it was a loose collection of debris and bindings held together more by prayer and hope than anything else. *Would this deathtrap even make it to the next vessel?* It seemed they were proceeding from one peril to the next with increasing penalty.

Hector trailed his legs over the edge, keeping just his torso on the raft, afraid to fully board the platform for fear of the structure coming apart at the seams. Having them all splashing around would surely alert a patrol. If they were found floundering in the water like that, they would be as good as dead.

As the shoreline fell away behind them, Hector carefully re-balanced his weight on the tilting raft, making his way onto a large log that formed the port side. He let the raft settle and then worked his way into a seated position. Hector picked up a discarded board that floated by and started to paddle.

"We've made it, Odysseus." Relief washed over Hector's ragged face. "You honor all of those who have paid for this passage with their lives. The gods continue to shower you with fortune."

Odysseus felt himself relax for a moment. He grinned at Hector and was preparing to chastise his young charge for speaking of their good tidings prematurely when he felt his chest explode.

A feeling of bewilderment was quickly followed by an immense pressure, then a fire igniting in his core.

Waves of pain washed through him like the sea rolling beneath his blood-soaked perch. He watched through wide, frantic eyes as

Hector drew a dagger from his belt. He didn't flinch when it spun past his face, as if time itself slowed to witness this strange sight. His mind caught up with the action and processed the final macabre scene at once.

Hector's dagger protruded from the neck of the raft's traitorous captain. Metallic crimson glistened under the pale moon, his treasonous heart ignorantly pumping his lifeforce from his throat.

The sword that had pierced Odysseus's chest had found a gap in his armor just under his bicep. A crude fissure now separated the ribs on his right side. Blood poured from the mortal wound. The curved handle at the base of the Kopis sword jammed tight into his body.

Odysseus could see that Hector was trying to speak to him, but couldn't discern any meaning. He felt the weight of a thousand bulls crushing the air from his chest. His vision began to darken and narrow.

How could the treacherous actions of this insignificant actor be the undoing of such well-laid plans? Was this just a greedy opportunist? A Persian spy, perhaps? Or maybe just a simple fisherman left with no other option to provide for his starving children. Whatever the rationale for his untimely attack, Odysseus was bleeding out into the cold depths.

"Odysseus, don't move. Please tell me what to do," Hector pleaded with his dying friend.

Breathing was impossible now. Odysseus knew he was drowning in his own blood. There would be no recovery from his wound. His only solace was that he would soon be able to join his love, Ianthina.

"Remove the sword," he said as he forced air into his collapsing lung.

Hector reacted swiftly, pulling the blade from deep inside Odysseus's ribs. Stars shot in front of his eyes. His brain exploded with pain, transcending anything he'd felt in battle. Death approached quickly. As his mind was slipping into unconsciousness, Odysseus could think of only one thing: The elixir. They couldn't lose it. Not after all this time, after getting so close.

"Hector." Only a faint whisper now.

"I'm here, Odysseus." Tears welled in Hector's eyes. Would this night of loss know no end?

"Protect th…"

"I don't understand. I don't know what to do." Hector's voice was full of fear and despair.

"The elixir… it must not…" Odysseus's voice was punctuated by pained gasps.

Hector felt the warmth in his hands before he saw it. The copper orb that now rested in his palm was a foreign sensation in contrast to his soaked and chilled body. He stared down at Odysseus, taking the copper pot, slick with his mentors' blood.

"Hector, do not give…"

"Give what? Odysseus! Do not give what?" Hector begged.

No response came. This great warrior, this leader of legions, was now silent. His words would be reserved only for the gods now.

Hector was no more. Destroyed. His will and faith had been tested past their breaking point, his body, now a hollow shell. Devoid of emotion, absent of purpose. All this suffering and loss for a cheap copper trinket and its cursed contents.

The waters were still calm, their travels slowed by the lack of paddling, but the tide had slowly set their raft out to sea.

The larger skiff deployed to bring them to the *Paralus* was now less than one hundred yards away. It seemed to be coming nearer in a valiant effort to shorten the time and distance that Odysseus would remain unprotected. Little did they know their efforts were now in vain.

Hector just sat there, transfixed by the copper vessel. His mentor, dead at his side.

What did any of it matter now? The world he knew was gone forever. To return home would be certain death. Whether he perished here or there, it didn't matter. Hector burned to know what he had forfeited his life for. He knew to look upon the treasure was forbidden. The secret was protected by kings and gods. It wasn't meant for someone of his station.

He didn't care anymore. Hector grabbed the square seal on the top of the lid, but it wouldn't release. He could feel the material inside slosh around as he struggled. After trying a few alternate methods to remove the lid, he realized he needed to unthread the top from the base. This attachment method afforded the vessel a tight seal to ensure that none of the contents would be spilled in transport.

With the last turn of the top, Hector heard a faint click, and the lid released. A waxy paste rimmed the circumference of the chalice. Ianthina must have applied it to keep the vessel watertight. *Beauty and intellect in abundant measure*, he thought to himself. Admiration quickly turned to sadness at the thought of losing his queen.

The night hadn't brightened much. The moon still wore wisps of clouds around its thin frame. The stars seemed content to shine brightly in the dark sky, oblivious to the horrors below brought by the deadly night.

Hector gazed into the copper vessel. The liquid inside, this source of so much death, seemed to radiate without assistance from any external light source. It didn't have a color, per se, but glowed with a spectrum of colors. It was mesmerizing. Rich royal hues seemingly brought forth from the depths of the ocean. Aqua blues and azure greens twirling in hypnotic ribbons. Veins of light pulsed through the solution. A strange, sparkling sediment was suspended in the liquid. It swirled and danced, giving the shallow copper bowl the appearance of endless depth.

Never had Hector seen such colors, whether in nature or on an artist's palette. It was remarkable. He was transfixed as he watched the streams undulate and roll. Could it truly be the blood of the gods?

What had Odysseus been trying to tell him only moments before? Do not do what? Fail? Quit? Go forward? Why were the gods punishing him like this? What must he do now?

The clouds gave way for a moment, allowing the thin slice of moon to shine in all its waxing glory. As the flash of moonlight shone on the open pot, the elixir seemed to absorb it and reflect it back with even greater intensity.

If this is truly the blood of the gods, Hector prayed, *then I petition the ancient and powerful ones to help me now.*

Raising the pot above his head in both hands in prayer, Hector shifted toward his friend. He placed his arm behind Odysseus's neck and brought him close, then brought the copper pot, now alive with color, to his lifelong protector's bloodstained mouth. Hector repeated his prayer as he poured a thin stream of the liquid through his fallen brother's cold, parched lips.

He kissed his fingertips and pressed them to his friend's forehead. "I'm sorry I failed you." He laid Odysseus on his back, then swept his hand down across his face to close his lifeless eyes. Hector hung his head in his hands and wept.

He hadn't noticed the soldiers from the *Paralus* approach. How could he tell them that Odysseus was gone? How could he explain that he had failed at upholding his one sworn duty, to protect the General and Ianthina at all costs?

Hector felt the wooden beams spread slightly and then dip as Odysseus's loyal regiment pulled the makeshift raft to their own boat. Hector instinctively snatched the copper pot closer to his chest as he fell back, bracing his fall with his other arm. He was rolled to his right and found himself lying on the wooden planks, staring into the olive-green eyes of his dead friend.

Except he wasn't—dead, that is.

The two of them were frozen in their optical embrace until Odysseus broke the trance with a gasp like a newborn baby filling its lungs for the first time. The copper hue of his skin was fast returning from its lifeless waxy pallor.

Too stunned to speak, Hector crab walked backwards to the far edge of the skiff. Water soaked him as it splashed up through the rickety planks.

Hector had hoped that the elixir would, at best, ensure safe passage for Odysseus across the river to the underworld. Charon, the boatman, would certainly recognize the blood of the gods mixing within the body of this mortal, and guide him to his rightful place in the next world.

Who was this imposter cloaked in Odysseus's skin? A demon? A god? Surely not a man anymore. Hector had seen many men die in battle and had put his share of men into early graves, burying many of his own. He knew death intimately and was certain that the injuries his friend had sustained were fatal.

Rising onto his hands and knees, Odysseus struggled to understand what just happened. He moved each part of his body slowly and deliberately. It wasn't the stiffness of joints or pain that caused his trepidation. It was the opposite. He felt too good. Too alive. His wounds no longer bit with the sting of salt. In fact, the deep gashes and lacerations were barely visible. He thought the dim lighting was playing tricks on his eyes because he could have sworn to the gods that he saw his own wounds disappearing, leaving only healthy flesh, in less time than it would take to drink a large ale. The soreness in his back and shoulder which plagued him for years also disappeared. Smells and sounds enveloped him. His senses were heightened to levels he'd never experienced before. He rose to his feet, feeling taller and stronger than he could ever remember.

"What happened to me?" he asked, shaking the cobwebs from his head, trying to clear his thoughts.

"I gave— You died, but… you…" Hector's mouth hung slack, his eyes wide with fear.

Odysseus extended his hand to help Hector up from the sinking raft, but Hector recoiled in terror. "Hector, it's me! Why do you shrink from me, brother? Take my hand."

"Odysseus. How can it be? I watched you die."

Images came back in flashes. The assassination attempt, Hector's dagger killing the attacker, the fires that ravaged his home in the countryside outside Athens, the loss of Ianthina. It felt like Odysseus's head was going to explode. His heart ached with the sorrow of such loss that he feared it may tear in two. The copper vessel. The source of all this madness. Odysseus remembered it all. Like a raging river, his memory flowed back from the recesses in his mind, and everything fell into place.

Now he was the one gripped by terror. The realization of what had occurred was becoming frighteningly clear.

"What have you done to me, Hector?" His voice rose in panic.

"You were… dead. I failed you and our queen in this world. I begged the gods not to see that as your fault, but as my sin alone. I gave you the blood of the gods so that they may recognize you as one of their own when you crossed over. But now you have made the journey to the underworld and returned. You really are a god, Odysseus. Your foothold is in the heavens and on earth. Maybe everyone was right, and you are Heracles incarnate."

Hector bowed his head in reverence as he held out the copper enclosure, once again closed and secure, suddenly embarrassed to be holding such power with his bare and soiled hands.

Odysseus relieved Hector of the vessel and placed it in his satchel. How could this have happened? What cruel turn of fate had the gods decreed for his soul? Confusion and rage tore at Odysseus's countenance.

He raised his head toward the dark sky and erupted, his anger volcanic. Odysseus clenched his fists, nails biting into his palms. A guttural scream burst forth, shattering the night. His men watched this tormented soul vent his fury to the gods above. The echo of his madness carried across the water until the last of the air in his newly repaired lungs was expelled.

"I don't understand why you're not happy to be alive, Odysseus," Hector said as he stood up, eager to move to the rowboat and find safety aboard the *Paralus*.

"I had the power to save Ianthina in my very hands, Hector. I could have given her some of this!" He thrust the chalice toward Hector but never released his grasp. "I didn't know. I could have saved her. . . I could have saved her the whole time." His body began to shudder with sobs.

Hector regained his footing and embraced his friend. As Odysseus looked at him, Hector instantly saw the change.

"Odysseus, your eyes! They're glowing!"

The olive-green eyes that had stared lifelessly at Hector only a short while before now shifted in color. His irises rolled like mercury, firing rich blue and violet colors. A radiance seemed to illuminate from his eyes like an aura.

Hector immediately recognized the dance of impossible color and fire. He had seen it when the moon illuminated the contents of the jar. The elixir. It had the same luminescence, but now it was trapped in the mortal coil before him.

Before Hector could ask Odysseus what their next steps would be, the reinvigorated man answered with a determination that even Hector had not known his master to possess.

"We're going back to save Ianthina. Once she's safe and on the Paralus, we're coming right back with the entire fleet."

"We're coming back?" Hector was stunned. "I thought you were keeping the fleet back at a safe distance. What are you going to do?"

Odysseus climbed into the larger boat. "First, I'm going back to save our queen. Once she is safe, by the gods I swear, I'm coming back here to kill every last one of these bastards.

μέρος πρώτο
PART ONE

CHAPTER ONE

PRESENT DAY

Thirty minutes outside of London, England
January 8, 11:27 p.m.

The prisoner's wrists were bloody and raw. The coarse rope binding them caused the skin underneath to peel away, like someone had taken sandpaper to the joint. His bony hands were thin and weak, matching his emaciated frame.

How long have I been imprisoned? Marcus had lost track of the days and weeks entirely. The only thing he was certain of now was his impending death. How and when it would come were the only questions that remained.

His captors had beaten him within an inch of his life, all to discern exactly how he'd betrayed their order. In the time since his subterfuge was discovered, he was subjected to all manner of torture. This wasn't even what the government deemed "enhanced interrogation techniques." Those would be kind by comparison. They utilized sleep deprivation, constant bright light, loud noise, and waterboarding. The usual suspects. Afterwards, the power tools and scalpels were brought out. His body had been contorted into positions that no human was meant to bend. In between these inquiries, they beat him mercilessly. Sometimes the methods of torture were used in combination, all while subjecting him to an endless barrage of questions. The pain and fear inflicted was used to disorient him into revealing the secrets he held and those he shared.

But Marcus hadn't uttered a single word. He screamed and cried out during the sessions and sobbed uncontrollably after each atrocity was inflicted upon him, but he wouldn't break. He hoped they would finally believe him after enduring all he had and give him a quick death.

He was wrong.

He'd lost his front teeth during his previous beatings. When the last of them were knocked out, they came back for his molars with pliers. He'd blacked out after the third one was pulled from his shattered, bleeding mouth.

The tips of his fingers and toes had been abused or removed, often both. When the supply of digits expired, they moved on to his ears. The wounds were brutally cauterized with a branding iron to ensure he wouldn't bleed to death before disclosing the information they sought. His extremities were swollen and gangrenous. Agony consumed him. He was in and out of consciousness and could tell the end was near. The only thing he looked forward to was death itself. It was his beacon of light. An end to the agony. He hadn't eaten in weeks, and the water they gave him was foul. If the next beating didn't kill him, the infections that ravaged his body certainly would.

Marcus felt the stomp of boots coming for him, the vibrations in the floor rattling his thin bones. His eyesight was terrible. His orbital sockets had been fractured early in the beatings, leaving him with only a faint detection of light and rough shapes. Marcus's eyes were swollen shut most of the time anyway, not that there was anything for him to see in his putrid existence. His hearing was muffled due to ruptured eardrums and extensive tissue damage from the branding after they cut off his ears. This caused him to be in a constant state of vertigo because of the trauma to his inner ear. They spared his tongue so he could speak clearly when they finally broke him.

He perceived shadows and movement disrupting the light at the bottom of his cell door, the only source of light in his cell. When that was extinguished, he was left in complete darkness.

He didn't hear the squeak of the rusted hinges before the door to his cell burst open, and the shouting began. This was how his days started. The guards would ask their questions, and he wouldn't respond. They would beat and torture him, and he'd black out and wake up some indeterminate time later. This was his living hell, but it was almost over. He knew his body couldn't last out any longer.

Marcus was being guarded by two sadistic twins known as the Bough brothers. Each was a depraved and inherently evil individual. When working together, somehow their atrociousness grew exponentially. The fraternal twins stood at six feet three inches tall. Their faces were scarred and mangled from countless bar brawls. Their bulging guts were a testament to a lifetime spent drinking beer and gorging on fast food. Their muscles, while concealed under a thick layer of flab, were still sizeable. Both knew how to fight, one of the few skills they possessed. As such, the Boughs had been inflicting pain on others since they were little boys. Now they were being paid to be cruel. They'd finally found their calling.

Bough brother #1 released the leather shackles that bound Marcus to the cold stone floor. This wasn't to prevent him from escaping. He was too weak to stand, never mind run from what were certainly many armed guards. No, the restraints were only there to prevent him from killing himself and ending his torment too early.

Bough brother #2 picked up a large bucket of cold water and dumped it over the dying man, washing the grime, filth, and gore down the open drain in the corner of the room. He repeated the procedure until the naked man lying in the center of the room was free of his torturous residue and left shivering uncontrollably. A white gown was pulled over Marcus's emaciated shoulders as a chair was brought into the bare cell and placed against the wall opposite the door. The brothers dragged the pile of skin and bones to the chair and roughly seated him on it.

Marcus's head hung low, his chin and scraggly beard resting on his bruised and shattered chest. They tied his slim torso to the chair with a leather strap to ensure he wouldn't fall out and then exited the cell, flanking the door on either side.

The bright light from the hallway turned to darkness, and Marcus knew the devil himself had just entered his cell.

"Brother Marcus, you don't seem to be doing very well since I last saw you," the shadow from the door said.

How long has it been since he last visited? Marcus wondered. He'd completely lost track of time. It was more than a couple weeks, he knew that much. Maybe a month? Could it be longer?

He wasn't certain about anything anymore. But one thing he was sure of was that he wouldn't live long enough to see the man again, and Marcus wouldn't give him the satisfaction of thinking he'd been broken. His body may have been destroyed, but his dignity remained fully intact. He felt emboldened for the first time since his capture, his impending death coming for him like a warm embrace.

"Why don't you end your suffering, Brother Marcus? This isn't something I want to do, but believe me, I will not show mercy to those who are undeserving of it. You may think the worst is over, dear brother, but I assure you, we have only just begun."

"Don't call me 'brother,'" Marcus said, his voice raspy. "I have endured your worst. Death comes for me now, and you have not broken me. You think you're a god? You're not even a man." A violent cough shook his fractured chest. It was the first thing he had said to the bastard since the day they'd started torturing him.

"I admire your conviction, *Brother* Marcus," the man said with a sneer, "but I'm not done with you yet."

"There's nothing more you can do," Marcus said between pained gasps. "Daedalus will know everything soon. You'll never succeed now."

The man glared at the dying soul, a sinister smile creeping across his lips. He reached into his pocket and retrieved a small gun-like device. A glass vial was already threaded onto the top of the unusual-looking weapon. The liquid inside sloshed a brilliant blue. He stepped toward Marcus, pressed the tube to his chest, and pulled the trigger.

Pain like Marcus had never known coursed through his broken body and lights exploded behind his eyes. His head felt like it was going to shatter. His blood burned like molten lead. His heart began to race so fast that Marcus was certain it would burst. Seconds later, everything went black.

The mysterious man towered over the lifeless body, the injection device hanging by his side, the vial now empty. The Boughs remained at their posts, neither budging an inch without an instruction from their leader.

As Marcus began to come around, questions flooded back into his consciousness. *What happened? How long was I out this time?*

Marcus opened his eyes. Confusion and panic overtook him. New questions crashed into his brain. *How am I still alive? What new torture did they decide to inflict on me now? Which body part is missing? Why can't I move?* The cascading effect of the unknowns created even more panic and confusion.

Marcus raised his head and saw the wicked man standing over him. Then it all came flooding back. He remembered being shot with the madman's poison, and then... he couldn't recall anything. He strained against the leather that kept him bound, but he couldn't move. His eyes squinted against the bright light.

But something was wrong. Or rather, nothing was wrong. He could see. In fact, he hadn't seen so clearly since he was a small boy. The recent beatings had rendered him almost blind. The colors and clarity he saw now were so vivid that it startled him. Marcus gasped at the clarity of his vision. Breathing so quickly and deeply would have normally sent pain shooting through his body due to his multiple fractured ribs. Now he didn't feel pain anywhere. Marcus glanced down at his mangled hands to find that they too were now as healthy and strong as they'd ever been.

"I've explained to you already, I'm not done with you, Brother Marcus. I first came here to offer you mercy if you were willing to be forthcoming."

Marcus sat there, confused. *Why would he choose to heal me now?* He knew this madman was evil. Why relieve the suffering they had spent so much time inflicting?

"You see, you have made some grave errors in your thinking," the man continued. "You have rejected my merciful offer. You have insulted and slandered me. I hold the power of life and death in the palm of my hand. Who else other than a god could do so?" His voice rose in anger. "You dare insult me and tell me that I'm 'not even a man?'" He stepped close to Marcus. "I am to be the god of gods!" he shouted just inches from Marcus's face. "No one can stop me!" His voice echoed off the concrete walls, making the effect even greater.

"You say there's nothing more I can do to you, Brother Marcus? You have no idea of the power I possess. But now you'll see just what it is that I can do."

The rage that had twisted his face a moment before disappeared, replaced by righteous indignation. "I suspect you're wondering why I healed you. It wasn't mercy. Far from it. It was so that I could break you over again. And when you're about to die again, *dear brother*, we will meet like this again. I will heal you once more so that you know my power—and then I will break you again and again and again. You see, death will not be an escape for you any more than it is for me." With that, he turned to leave.

A terror and panic unlike Marcus had ever known overcame him. He knew exactly what he would be facing and was certain he could never endure it again. The only hope he had was that his suffering would eventually end. Now his living hell was to become an eternal living hell. He felt the life drain from him.

"I'll tell you everything. Please. You win. I'm nothing but your humble servant. Please have mercy on me. I'll tell you everything. Please, my master, let me confess, and then I beg of you to give me a quick and merciful death."

Marcus's former mentor stood in the doorway, his back to his captive. "Tell me," he said. "Everything."

After Marcus finished his confession, the leader of the Brotherhood smiled. "You see? That wasn't so difficult, was it? If only you'd done that earlier, you could have avoided so much suffering."

"Will you now give me a quick death?" Marcus asked, utterly defeated.

"Now? No. I told you before, you will get no mercy from me. You insulted me, you tried to sabotage my life's work. No, you do not deserve to escape my wrath."

"But I've told you everything. Please!" Marcus was in tears, pleading with everything he had.

The man looked at Marcus and then back to the two Boughs outside. "Start over again," he said. "Drag it out for a while this time. Really make him suffer. Let's see if there's anything else he knows."

The two sadistic brothers stepped inside. They hadn't shown Marcus an ounce of compassion during any of their countless beatings. With specific instructions to increase the brutality to a prisoner who was astonishingly unblemished, their bloodlust ran wild. A virgin canvas for their macabre art form.

"Let's have a little fun with him before he blacks out this time," Bough #2 said as he slid his thick leather belt off from around his waist, dropping it to the floor. "I'm going first this time."

Marcus struggled in his restraints. He almost broke free of his bonds, taking advantage of the loose wraps and his newfound strength.

"We've gotta keep him from bucking around like that. Do something," Bough #2 said.

Bough #1 picked the belt up off the floor and swung it around his head like a cowboy with a lasso.

Marcus watched the entire arc of impending pain descend from its apex all the way to the moment when the massive silver belt buckle crashed into his knee, obliterating the bone on impact.

The guttural scream that exploded from Marcus drowned out the laughter from the brothers as they slammed the cell door, and began their beatings anew.

CHAPTER TWO

Nassau, Bahamas
January 12, 6:13 a.m.

The ship's hull rested in powder-like sand under seventy feet of clear turquoise water. Its once watertight hold was now home to a multitude of tropical fish and corals. Shadows and light danced across the barnacle-encrusted portholes and onto the skeletal remains of this once seaworthy ship. Brilliantly colored fish darted in and out of every crevice and crack, looking for their next meal or seeking shelter from becoming one themselves.

Commander Gryphon Oake was running low on air. His dive computer was telling him he was getting close to his no decompression dive limit. He didn't think that he would need to be worried about getting "bent" on this dive, a condition in which nitrogen bubbles leached out from a person's blood, much like a soda bottle that had been shaken and opened quickly. The bends could happen to scuba divers who either stay down too long or come back to the surface too quickly—most often when both happened at once. Right now, he was concerned with the amount of air left strapped on his back. He'd started out with a less than typical 3,000-psi tank fill about 40 minutes ago, thinking it would be a quick dive. The reading from his air integrated module informed him that there was less than 200 pounds of pressure left. He figured that would give him a few more minutes until he would be completely out of air. The bends would soon be something to start worrying about.

When he glanced up from his rapidly blinking air gauge, now in full alarm mode, a flash of gray-and-white flesh swept by the windowless portal of the abandoned wheelhouse in which he found himself trapped.

A pair of large bull sharks had snuck up on his position while he was completing his early morning mission. Upon spying the two maneaters, he sought refuge inside the shipwreck, one of many scattered along the shallow reefs all over the seven hundred islands that made up the Bahamas. Unfortunately, each time he swam out of the wreck to surface, the bull sharks would dart in close, making his escape impossible. Gryph enjoyed diving with the Caribbean reef sharks, black tips, and other smaller shark species, but the bulls were not to be messed with.

What have you got yourself into now? This was supposed to be an easy search-and-recovery mission, and now you're surrounded by sharks and about to run out of air. Not your finest moment, Oake.

He checked on his precious cargo again, not wanting to lose it after coming so close to completing his objective. He watched his air dwindle even more while the two prehistoric predators circled his position. The largest of the two sharks was easily over ten feet long and would have tipped the scales at over four hundred pounds. The other, while shorter, looked even heavier than the first. A bite from either would likely prove fatal.

Movement by his flippers caught Gryph's eye as a large tiger grouper swam under the fissured deck floor below him. He grabbed his speargun and dove after his quarry, aiming his shot just ahead of the big fish's gills. The spearhead punched through the thickest part of the now convulsing fish and clear out the other side. He pulled back the retrieval line to bring the sixty-pound snack closer to him, sending a trail of blood undulating through the seawater. The reddish hue from the gore was distorted due to the depths he was at, giving the blood an alien green tinge.

As Gryph maneuvered the grouper inside the wheelhouse, his dive computer warned his air was down to under one hundred pounds. He felt the resistance increasing with each breath he took and knew his air was going to run out any second. He fastened a slipknot from some of the salvage line he'd brought down and placed it around the tail of the dying grouper, tying the other end to the barnacle-encrusted wheel at the center of the steering house. The sharks were circling closer and not retreating as far back as they were before.

Commander Oake removed a serrated stainless-steel dive knife from its sheath and slit open the belly of the brown-and-silver grouper, eliciting the final twitches of life from the fish before it went still. He positioned the flayed-open cavity toward the window he was previously stationed at and headed out the other side of the wheelhouse. Small bits of flesh and fluids seeped from the gaping wound into the water on that side of the wreck.

As he'd hoped, the blood and guts from the grouper sent the two bulls into a frenzy, both trying to get to the juicy prize just inside the vessel. Their massive size prevented them from getting their rows of razor-sharp teeth around the bleeding meal, creating the momentary distraction Gryph needed to make a break for the surface.

Moments later, he breached the water into the brightening day, careful to avoid splashing and attracting his foes from the deep. He stole a quick glance down to confirm the two beasts were still circling below. Relief washed over him seeing them both still frustrated at the wreck. A smirk played across his lips, clutching his well-earned prize in his grasp. *That was a bit too close for comfort*, he thought. His gauges confirmed his assessment. He was now out of air entirely. However, his mission was a success.

The chance of dying or being killed was something that Gryph had to accept as a possible outcome in his line of work. This time appeared to be no different, but it would have been beyond embarrassing to be done in by a couple fish.

He climbed up the steps and onto the teak deck of his rented forty-five-foot catamaran. The sound of the azure waters lapping against the twin hulls was the only sound he'd heard since climbing aboard. He laid down the mesh salvage bag and removed his scuba gear, ears alert for any disturbance, eyes absorbing and analyzing everything. The constant surveillance was a subconscious act now. Gryph was on alert all the time and had been that way for as long as he could remember.

He began to disassemble his gear and rinse the salt off his equipment by submerging it in a barrel of fresh water that he had set up onboard for just that purpose.

Gryph took in the picture-postcard view. Calm, clear waves undulating between shades of aqua blue and translucent greens rolled gently over each other. There was nothing but ocean between his boat and the horizon. The sun was still an hour away when he first dove into the water that morning, but it was out now, climbing quickly and burning off some of the humidity that lingered from the sweltering night.

He worked the kinks out of his back and shoulders. Joints popped, and muscles tensed and then relaxed. He was craving a cup of coffee. Strong and black. If he had a vice, that was it. Hot, fresh, dark coffee. He hadn't had a chance to make any before his dive, and his body was now requiring its caffeine fix.

He tried hard to push the thought of leaving this paradise from his mind. His next assignment, the most important of his life, was to commence in the coming days. This rare opportunity for R&R was something he needed, and had a hunch it would be a while before he'd be able to relax like this again. Gryph let the tranquility of the moment seep into his bones and calm his busy brain. The upcoming mission would require all of the skills and training he'd honed throughout his lifetime.

Commander Gryphon Aaron Oake joined the military on the morning of his eighteenth birthday. The US Navy put him through school, and it soon became evident he was born to be a soldier. He worked his way through the ranks as quickly as policy and proce-dure would allow. He applied and was accepted to the Navy SEAL program and always found himself at the top of his class, whether in warfare strategy, the obstacle course, jump school, or the firing range. No one was surprised when it was announced that he was leading the pack by the end of "Hell Week" either. The brutal sev-en-day period weeded out the best of the best from the rest. His superiors noticed how exceptional he was, even within a group of men who were all exceptional. They were the top one percent of the top one percent, and Gryph was the best of them all.

He'd been deployed around the world, earning the respect of both those planning his operations, and those who served on them. His leadership skills allowed him to attain the rank of SEAL commander faster than anyone in SEAL history, earning al-most every accolade and promotion the Navy and the SEALs could bestow upon one of their own. At thirty-three, he retired from active duty and was promptly recruited by the CIA as a field agent. Within a year, he'd attained Special Agent status.

Gryph completed his master's degree in psychology with the Navy at Annapolis and followed that up with a PhD at Quantico with the FBI, specializing in strategy and data analytics. He could speak more than five languages proficiently and was often called in to assist the government with profiling international criminals who were deemed more monster than man, and then devising the plans to capture or kill them.

The only thing more impressive than his intellect was his physical condition. His body was like granite, and his speed terrifyingly fast. Gryph's hand-to-hand combat skills were legendary in SEAL circles. Even with a prolonged absence from SEAL Team Six, his abilities were as sharp as the day he'd left. He spent a lot of time in the gym training, and it showed.

He'd been invited to the White House on a number of occasions to accept messages of deep gratitude from two different sitting presidents, even though much of his work could never be acknowledged publicly.

Gryph, as he was known to his friends and fellow SEALs, was about to head-up a new team in a world outside official military jurisdiction. He'd been given the opportunity to lead an elite group of experts with complete autonomy and was promised by his new handlers they'd spare no expense in equipping and funding their up-coming exploits. The totality of his life's work had prepared him to conquer this next challenge.

Gryph turned around after feeling the cool breeze from the air conditioning inside the boat flutter across his back and heard the slider door to the interior of the catamaran glide quietly along its rails. The rich aroma of coffee wafted out from the galley kitchen. His stomach growled with impatience spying the full French press steaming on the white marble counter. Two large mugs sat adjacent, waiting to be filled with the dark, delicious brew.

"Hey there, sunshine. I was trying to be quiet and didn't want to wake you," Gryph said. "I was planning to be back on board much earlier so I could make us some coffee and breakfast, but I ran into a little trouble. But it looks like you got a jump on it already."

The woman standing in front of him may have been more beautiful than the scenery itself. Her long, slender legs seemed to go on forever. A playful band of freckles danced across her sun-kissed face. Long blonde locks fell just past her toned shoulders. Her eyes were as clear and blue as the water on which they were floating.

Her delicate hands intertwined as she stretched and let out a satisfying groan. She was wearing one of his white T-shirts, with the words "American Dream" emblazoned across the chest in blue, although it fit her more like a mini dress than a shirt. Her long, deep stretch revealed her lithe form—and a little more as the hem of his garment rode up around her curvaceous hips.

Two quick steps forward, and she had her hands around his neck. Her lips found his as they shared a passionate good morning kiss.

Gryph had always been popular. The guys in his class growing up always wanted to be like him, and the girls always wanted to be on his arm.

"I got up shortly after you left and made us some coffee," she said. "It may not be as good as yours, but it's pretty darn good, if I do say so myself. There are some amazing looking mangos inside, too. I'll bring it all out here, so we can eat on the deck, okay?" She danced into the cabin without waiting for an answer.

As Gryph watched her head back into the galley to retrieve his first cup of the day, the sight of her toned, tanned body barely con-tained in his shirt was getting him hungry for more than breakfast.

"Are you sure you have to leave tomorrow, Ben? Can't you put off your meetings for another few days? Pretty please?" Her pout was more sexy than sad.

Gryph couldn't tell most people his real name, not outside the circles he worked in anyway. The woman with him on the catama-ran was no exception. To her, he was Ben Mayer, a wealthy VC fund manager from Canada. He often felt bad about the subterfuge, but he knew to bring anyone into his life full time would be putting them in grave danger. He loved the thought of settling down one day, but until this part of his life was behind him, these shallow, unfulfilling relationships were all that he had.

"I'm sorry, but it can't be postponed. Believe me, I'd love nothing more than to stay right here with you, but I really have to get back soon. We have all day today and tonight though, so let's enjoy the last day of the trip, okay?"

He could tell by her expression that she was hoping he would put his departure off a little longer. He had been hoping for a delay from his new boss as well, but none came, and it was unlikely that it would.

"Did you at least get what you wanted?" she asked.

"Yup. Even better than I was hoping for."

"Can I see?" She looked inquisitively at his salvage bag.

Gryph turned so his back was to her and loosened the drawstring at the mouth of the mesh bag. He reached inside and grasped the treasure he'd been searching for that morning, what he couldn't just leave down in the depths, what those sharks may have wanted, but that he wanted even more. As he spun back toward her, she screamed in horror.

"Those are so gross… and so big."

Gryph laughed. "And they're going to be absolutely delicious with butter and garlic."

He clutched the two massive spiny lobsters expertly in his hands, keeping the pincers away from his digits. He pushed them toward her like he was playing with terrifying puppets. She shrieked again and ran back into the galley.

Gryph put the tasty crustaceans into a cooler full of ice in preparation for the romantic dinner he was planning for their last night onboard. He rinsed his hands in the freshwater barrel and headed inside for his coffee. As he turned toward the door, he was stopped dead in his tracks.

The beauty in front of him was now holding a small plate of sliced mangos. Somehow, she had found it necessary to lose the T-shirt and was now standing in front of him stark naked, sucking on a slice of bright yellow, juicy flesh. The nectar squirted from the ripe fruit and splashed across her chest.

"Ben, this is so delicious. It's sweet as candy. You've got to try some."

Gryph closed the distance in a heartbeat. He snatched the last half of the slice from her mouth with his own, her tongue chasing the pilfered fruit into his mouth. The lingering sweetness dripped from both of their lips.

"You're right. These are incredible."

"Do you want me to make us some breakfast now?" she offered, wanting to get a jump on their day together.

"No, I think I feel like having dessert first," Gryph said, pulling her even closer.

"Dessert for breakfast?" she asked playfully. "What's on the menu?"

"You, baby. Just you." He tossed the plate onto the counter and then swept her into his powerful arms. She giggled and kissed his neck as he carried her back to their stateroom.

The coffee would have to wait.

CHAPTER THREE

Palm Springs, CA
January 3, 1:29 p.m.

"That's absolute bullshit! Kiss my hairy white ass." The echo from the onslaught of insults still hung in the air as the curved Samsung LED display exploded against the cinder-block wall. Bits of plastic molding and shattered glass flew in every direction.

"That referee is either blind or on the take. Crooked sonofabitch, motherfu…" Dallas fumed at the carcass of the Samsung monitor now in pieces by his feet.

He walked over to the rear wall and kicked the ruined display further into oblivion, spreading the destruction all around his computer lab. He bent down to retrieve the bulk of the useless screen and dumped it into a metal recycling bin with all the other victims. It was the third monitor that had met the same fate in as many months.

Dallas swiped his hand across his shaved head, wiping away the perspiration from his recent outburst. He'd gone bald right after high school and had been shaving his head ever since. He told people it was for convenience's sake, but at only nineteen years of age, he hated seeing his receding hairline and bald spot in the mirror each morning, so one day he'd gotten rid of it all. *You can't have a receding hairline if you have no hairline at all*, he'd mused at the time.

"How could the Cowboys suck so bad for so long? I just don't get it," said to no one in particular. His computer lab, or the *dungeon,* as he affectionately called it, contained enough bandwidth and brute computer processing power to make even the most well-funded universities envious. Unfortunately, it also bore more of a resemblance to a post-party frat house than a lab.

Discarded takeout food containers lay strewn across every available surface, some with half-eaten food abandoned inside, but most of them just stained and empty. A large KFC bucket was tipped over, revealing a graveyard of chicken bones.

Hundreds of feet of multi-colored cables snaked along the floor, terminating inside all manner of routers, hubs and switches. The steady hum from the army of cooling fans that were strategically placed to ensure the chips and circuit boards that Dallas assembled wouldn't overheat, cooled quietly in the background. The fans, in addition to their heat-dissipating functions, provided a white noise backdrop that Dallas found soothing while he hacked into the off-shore accounts of some very despicable people. He relished in relieving these greedy bastards of their ill-gotten gains and redis-tributing the proceeds to various sick children's causes across the globe.

These secret bank accounts were often traced back to high-ranking government officials, human trafficking rings, and on one occasion, the president of an EU country. But his favorite score was locating terrorists' slush funds. *Those assholes all have it coming*, he reasoned. It wasn't even about the money for him. He knew that someone, or a group of someone's, would likely lose their heads when they couldn't explain to their radical friends how their operating accounts had been emptied. *One less terrorist in the world is always a good thing*, or so he figured.

His phone began to vibrate and flash in its custom cradle. A long yellow data cable extended from the phone through the maze of circuitry at his feet that fed into a bank of digital switches, working harmoniously to keep his physical location secret. Once the line was secured by his software, he routed the call through to the speakers on his workstation. The large monitor on the wall in front of him would typically display the name, location, and other digital fingerprints lifted from the incoming call. In this instance, NO CALLER ID was the only information offered. *Burner phone*, he figured. He was hesitant to answer, but knew he'd have to pick up eventually. Nobody could hide forever.

"Lama, it looks like the Cowboys let you down again, huh?" the voice on the other end said. "You owe me fifty thousand from today's game and another hundred grand from your terrible picks last week. You need another hobby. You really suck at this one."

"Really, Doc? Do you have to be such a prick?" he asked his bookmaker. "Why can't you just take your money and shut your mouth?"

"I'd love to, Hayle," Doc said, reverting to Dallas's last name, "but for me to shut my mouth, you've got to pay up. Now, when am I gonna see my money? I'm running out of patience, and you're running out of time."

"Gimme a few days, and I'll fire off some crypto to you," Dallas said through clenched teeth. "It'll more than cover what I owe."

"Okay, but I'm not taking any more action from you until we're square."

"Yeah, whatever. You'll get your money. In the meantime, do me a favor and go fuck yourself." Dallas disconnected the call.

Dallas "Dali Lama" Hayle surveyed the post-game damage caused by his latest outburst. Quite ironic that he was nicknamed after the peaceful spiritual Tibetan leader as Dallas was neither peaceful nor spiritual, but could often be found praying during the last few minutes of most major sporting events. The few friends he had called him Dali or Lama. To everyone else, he was simply Dallas.

His last name was usually only used by the police, judges, or the prosecutors whom he found himself too often on the wrong side of. His bookie knew this too, which is likely why he chose to throw the *Hayle* moniker in with the others on their call.

That guy is such a piece of shit. I really need to find someone else to take my action, Dallas thought. Knowing the chances of that were highly unlikely. He'd burned far too many of those bridges over the years. It wasn't really paying the money after a loss that Dallas had an issue with. He just hated losing. It really affected him, almost like a physical ailment. It was that same drive that propelled him to the top of the hacking community. He would just keep working until the problem was solved. Dallas believed everything could be solved when given enough processors and power. He loved sports almost as much as hacking, but computers and code were his first love.

He also took comfort in the fact that he could always dip into some of the "bad guys'" accounts to offset his losses, if necessary. Technically, it was stealing, but he only stole from assholes. He was like Robin Hood, only sometimes he took a small cut. It was his own twisted way of manifesting goodness in the world. This somehow made sense to him, and he never lost a wink of sleep over it.

His phone began to vibrate in the cradle again. The same NO CALLER ID message flashed on the screen above.

"Now what do you want?" Dallas fumed into the speakers. "I said I'd get you the crypto soon enough. Now piss off." He was about to disconnect the call when the voice on the other end interrupted.

"Mr. Hayle? I'm looking to speak with Mr. Dallas Hayle."

"Who's this? How'd you get this number?" Only a handful of people had this private line.

"You may call me Daedalus. I'd like to speak with you about a certain Afghan warlord that you have recently taken quite a large sum of money from."

"Uh, yeah. I don't know what you're talking about. You have the wrong number, buddy." Perspiration was beginning to blossom on his bald head, before he even reached to disconnect the call.

"Mr. Hayle, I'm not looking to turn you in… yet." The caller paused after this last word, to ensure the threat was not lost on Dallas. "Nor am I asking that you return the funds you stole. I'm certain his handlers wouldn't take kindly to losing $4.2 million dollars of their blood money. I doubt very much if they're still walking this earth." Another pause, another veiled threat. "I hope that I now have your full and undivided attention, Mr. Hayle. I'd like to offer you a job."

"Again, I don't know what you're talking about. I don't know this Hayle guy, I don't know any Afghan warlords, and I sure as shit don't need a job." The confidence in his voice was increasing, but so was the concern in the pit of his stomach.

"Look at your monitors, Mr. Hayle."

Dallas glanced up at the screen on his wall as it came alive with data. Bank transactions and details from his own private accounts, along with the multitude of others that he'd hacked, ran down the multiple displays in neatly organized columns. Profile pictures of the crooks and terrorists whose money now resided elsewhere due to his skillful liberation stared ominously back at him.

"Your firewall protections were some of the most complex we've ever encountered. Please don't take our success at gaining access to your servers as a slight, Mr. Hayle. Our resources are unmatched. You never had a chance."

Dallas's fingers pounded instructions across multiple keyboards. The drone of the fans behind him increased in volume and pitch as additional banks of processors and microchips came online. *How is this possible? They have access to everything!* Cloud servers, his physical solid-state drives, all of it was compromised. He had been laid bare.

"Okay, you have my undivided attention," Dallas said as he continued to seek out the source of this disturbing intrusion. His fingers were flying, a blur over his keyboard.

"Mr. Hayle, as I said earlier, I'm not looking to turn you in to the authorities. I don't have any issue with the torment you're causing these bad men. However, I require your particular skill set for an undertaking I'm about to embark on and would appreciate your immediate cooperation and assistance."

"And if I refuse to help you?" Dallas asked, now conceding that his identity was blown.

"Then I'm afraid I would be inclined to disclose your location to any number of the groups you have stolen from. I assure you, Mr. Hayle, they would not be offering you anything but the edge of a blade once you're found. I believe my job offer is much more lucrative, although it also brings its own risks."

Dallas had been running a sophisticated tracing program on the line ever since the call came through. His back and forth with the caller was an attempt to prolong the conversation enough to complete the trace. It would normally track the caller's location in a matter of seconds regardless of where they were in the world. He stared dumbstruck at the results of his proprietary trace program. Somehow, this single call was originating from over one hundred different locations from across the globe—simultaneous-ly!

"Any attempt to locate my whereabouts by tracing our call will be entirely futile, Mr. Hayle. I am the proverbial needle in a haystack."

Dallas looked at the data on the screen again. His entire network was now under someone else's control. Anger and terror coursed through his veins. "You aren't really giving me much of a choice here, are you?"

"We all have a choice, Mr. Hayle. Some choices are just more difficult to make than others."

"Right. Well, the choices you're offering suck. How do I contact you once I make my decision?"

"You don't."

"How the hell am I supposed to find you, then?"

"No need, Mr. Hayle. We'll find you."

This guy is playing games now, Dallas thought. *I'm not letting some random asshole push me around.* He pushed the acid and fear back down into his gut.

"That may not be as easy as you think, *Daedalus*. What's with the goofy name, anyway? Big fan of the old-school Hercules cartoons when you were a kid or something?" Dallas loved giving nicknames to everyone he met. If he liked a person, which was rare, the nickname would typically be biting, but benign. If he didn't like the person, Dallas could get very creative. In this case, he thought the actual name was more ridiculous than anything he could come up with, so he simply chose to insult his new nemesis, hoping the brief bout of bravado would put the caller back on his heels.

"You may have hacked my network, but I'm logged in remotely, you schmuck. You have no clue where the hell I am, do you? Nice bluff, but I call." He was going to show this Daedalus guy that he wasn't someone who would be easily intimidated and just roll over.

"Find you?" Amusement tinged the digitized voice. "Oh, I think I'll manage just fine. In fact, I have a car waiting outside your door right now, Mr. Hayle." Dallas could almost see the grin on Daedalus's face. He checked the surveillance camera covering the front of his building and saw a white Lincoln Navigator parked directly in front at the curb. A giant of a man was standing by the passenger door, waiting for him to come out. *How did I end up so royally screwed?* he wondered.

"That was pretty presumptuous of you, Daedalus," Dallas said in a more respectful tone. "What if I hadn't agreed to come along and help?"

"It all comes down to choices, Mr. Hayle. I was betting on you making the right one for a change."

Dallas sat there for a moment, stunned. "Shit. Okay. I need a few minutes to put a bag together."

"Excellent choice, Mr. Hayle. I very much look forward to working with you." The line went dead.

"Great. The Cowboys lose again, my bookie is up my ass, I'm being blackmailed by strangers, and now I have to get a fucking job. Could this get any worse?" Dallas said as he shuffled begrudgingly out the door.

Little did he know that this was the best day he was going to have for a long time.

CHAPTER FOUR

Boston, USA
January 31, 2:30 p.m.

D r. Aliyah Tzion tugged her navy-blue down-filled jacket tighter around her shivering body and pulled the thick scarf farther up around her face until her hazel-green eyes were barely visible under her icy, frosted lashes. The weather in Boston had turned ugly, an infamous nor'easter—a cyclone of freezing air coming in from the Northeast Atlantic—had descended over the area, bringing bone-numbing temperatures and over two feet of snow to the New England area in the past thirty-six hours.

A heavy blanket of white powdery snow covered the walkways and rooflines of the Georgian-style buildings for which Harvard University was famous. The snow was everywhere and still falling hard.

Lonely wood benches and empty steel bike racks gave a skeletal feel to the abandoned courtyard at Harvard Business School. The sun, snow, and low cloud cover above created an opaque blanket of light that seemed to smother the landscape rather than illuminate it.

The last of the professors who had been brought in for Dr. Tzion's lectures were headed back home to ride out the storm. Her arrival at the school was the only reason they dared to venture out in the blizzard. The rare opportunity to meet with the famous doctor was not something the professors would allow any amount of inclement weather to interfere with.

Aliyah had been vigorously pursued by the acclaimed business school for years to assist them with formulating a new negotiation curriculum module for the school's MBA and PhD students. Her background in hostage negotiation and her sharp analytical mind were the reason the prestigious school had sought her out. She was renowned in academic circles for her brilliance in many mathematical pursuits, game theory being her specialty. This specific knowledge was something Harvard was hoping to harness and pass along to its students and faculty. She'd come a long way from her humble beginnings.

Her mother had passed away from complications after giving birth to Aliyah. Her name, which means "exalted" in Hebrew, was the only gift bestowed upon her by her dying mother, other than Aliyah's life itself.

Her father soon found himself ill-equipped to raise a little girl by himself. He'd tried to provide Aliyah with all the love and attention a little girl needed, but fell short in both. The loss of his beloved wife seemed to have drained the capacity to love from the poor man. He never remarried, and Aliyah couldn't recall him putting in any effort to try find another suitable match.

Her father tried to find things that he could use to bond with his little girl, and as such had taught her to play chess when she was only five years old. Aliyah loved it, partly because of the patterns and math associated with the game, but more so because it provided a rare opportunity to spend time with her father. Within a short period of time, though, their games would be over in a handful of moves. She tried to let him win in a futile effort to extend the time they spent together, but he always saw through the charade. It didn't take long before he lost interest altogether. He could hardly put up a defense, much less a convincing win. She'd earned her grandmaster status when she was fifteen. Her father hadn't played her, or anyone else, since.

Learning fueled all that Aliyah was in life. She had known she was different ever since she was a little girl. Numbers and patterns fascinated her. She would work out massive calculations in her head just to test herself. She played such little solitary games to keep herself occupied in her sad and lonely home.

The absence of affection created a vacuum that she filled with knowledge. Books were her means of filling the emptiness inside. She read anything she could get her hands on. Her voracious appetite for learning allowed for her to finish high school by age fourteen and receive her undergraduate degree two years after that.

Her pair of master's degrees in molecular biology and mathematical optimi-zation theory were completed mere days before she'd joined the army.

Aliyah served her two mandatory years in the Israeli military, submitting to the draft on her eighteenth birthday. She was fast tracked early on for the officer training program and excelled when accepted. Upon her successful completion, she was assigned to the Mossad anti-terrorism and biological warfare unit.

Her military-sanctioned IQ test scores ranked somewhere north of 150. Genius level.

Eleven years later, on her twenty-ninth birthday, she had retired from active duty while earning dual PhDs from the Technion Institute of Technology, Israel's equivalent of MIT—the other Ivy League school just up the Charles River in Boston, just a short walk from where she now stood.

Having grown accustomed to solitude because of the lack of friends her age growing up, coupled with the emptiness she felt at home, the swarming mass of humanity in the army was a foreign and uncomfortable environment those first few weeks of basic training. However, it didn't take long before she found friendship and support within the small platoon she now thought of as her surrogate brothers and sisters. The military was the family she never had, but always craved.

It must be forty below, she thought. She glanced down at her Hermes Apple watch, a luxurious treat she bought herself on her last birthday. It was -25C according to the weather app. With the windchill, it felt even colder.

Even if she chose to run, which the icy conditions and her current choice of footwear prohibited, she would be late to rendezvous with her new colleague. She had been instructed to meet him at Harvard Square, which was on the opposite side of the Charles River from the Harvard Business School. From there, they were to depart for Logan International Airport and on to their final destination.

Aliyah rushed from her last meeting in Tata Hall, the famed Business School's new state-of-the-art teaching and student dormitory facility. The warmth and ease in which she had been crossing under the school's large campus utilizing its labyrinth of tunnels had long since dissipated. She was now hurrying on foot across the Charles River via the long arching expanse of the John Weeks bridge. The route would normally be much quicker than ordering an Uber. The rideshare cars would typically be stuck in bumper-to-bumper traffic for the short run across the Charles, taking two or three times as long. However, the frostbite setting in on her face made her question the logic of her decision.

During warmer seasons, dozens of students could be seen rowing up and down the scenic waterway, flanked by gaggles of fit coeds running along its wide banks. Now only snow and ice floated downstream beneath Aliyah. No one was on the water or the bridge; everything was deserted because of the storm.

By the time she arrived at the pub, her toes were numb. She could hardly feel her fingers grasping the dark iron handle affixed to the heavy wood slab door. It wouldn't budge when she tried to tug it open. *Locked?* she wondered. They couldn't be closed. She could smell the food and grease aromas wafting from the kitchen exhaust. The heavy smoke was lost in the gloomy whiteout all around. She tried the door again, pulling much harder this time. The door began to budge, inch by inch, scooping up snow that continued to jam against the base of the door. The icy obstruction in the entryway would continue to grow as the powder fell.

She stepped around the pile of snow that was accumulating behind the door and slipped inside the restaurant. A gust of cold air slammed the door behind her with a wet slap as she was assaulted by a blast of warm air blowing from the space heater perched above the empty hostess station. She moved closer to the heater, unwound her scarf from her face, and let it hang over the shoulders of her snow-covered parka. She rubbed her hands together to restore circulation, unable to feel her fingertips anymore.

Aliyah cast a glance across the room and spotted her contact standing by the bar. She had not yet met the man she was there to see. Her new employer, a man she knew only as Daedalus, told her he was building a team for a sensitive undertaking that had worldwide implications. Daedalus had selected all the operatives for the team, and they were now assembling for the first time. It was the first opportunity Aliyah had to meet any of them.

She knew very little about the person she was meeting that afternoon but wasn't concerned that this was any kind of threat or setup. The contact wouldn't be there if he hadn't already been vetted from up on high, but she was eager to find out as much as possible about her new teammate. All that Aliyah had been provided was a short bio and digital photo sent via an encrypted message.

Phil Wu looked just like the file currently displayed on her watch. Asian male, six feet one inches, long black hair, medium build. With no one else in the restaurant due to the storm, the picture really wasn't needed.

"Dr. Aliyah Tzion," she said as she reached out to shake his hand. "But please, call me Ali."

"Phil Wu. Pleasure to meet you, Ali," he said and extended his hand to hers.

"Do you want to see a menu or are you just here for drinks?" a petite waitress asked, having seemingly appeared from out of nowhere.

"Menus would be great, thanks. Do you mind if we take that booth over there?" Phil asked, pointing to a small table beside a roaring fireplace. The vantage point also provided him with a clear line of sight to the front door and quick access to the rear exit just a few feet away. "I'd love a large hot chocolate, please."

"That sounds like heaven, Phil. Make that two, please," Aliyah added.

As the pair settled into their booth, Aliyah noticed that Phil's eyes never stopped scanning the room, even though they appeared to be the only people there.

"Are we expecting company?" she asked. "I thought it was just us."

"Nope. We're not expecting anyone else. Just ensuring it stays that way." Phil always made it a habit of keeping his back to a wall whenever he could, keeping as much of his environment visible and exits easily reachable, just in case.

Aliyah removed her coat and allowed the heat from the fire to warm her frozen limbs. Their hot drinks came after a few minutes. She warmed her hands around the large ceramic mug and sipped it carefully. She wasn't sure if she'd ever tasted anything so satisfying. She felt the sweet concoction radiate warmth from deep inside her belly as she drank it down.

The waitress suggested the daily special, featuring deep-fried fish and chips and French onion soup as a side. They both ordered the same thing, not for simplicity's sake, but because it happened to be a legit favorite for both. They laughed at the odd coincidence and made idle chitchat until their server returned. The food was hot and plentiful. They fell into an easy conversation, and before long, they felt like they had known each other for ages.

"I'm sure you've received the same limited brief on me as I did on you," Aliyah said between forkfuls of crispy fish and steaming, cheesy spoonful's of rich broth. "But your expertise was listed only as logistics, personal security, and transportation. What's that all about? Seems kind of cryptic."

"It's quite simple, actually. I do my best to keep everyone on time and secure the tools we need for the job. Like I explained to you earlier, I've also been training and teaching kung fu my entire life, and, as such, I'm able to provide security as needed."

"And the transportation?" Aliyah asked, trying to encourage more dialogue from her new teammate.

"Oh, I drive. Pretty fast too," Phil said with a wink.

They each began to fill in the additional blanks on their respective expertise. With each new revelation, a clearer picture formed in Aliyah's mind. The various skill sets being brought together seemed much less random. She was looking forward to meeting the rest of the team and slotting those puzzle pieces into place. Phil hadn't met Daedalus either. Their new boss was still very much a mystery.

Their server cleared their empty plates and bowls. The lack of food on the dishes was a clear sign that the recommendations had been spot on. They declined refills and desserts. The bill came, and the customary banter of who would pay the tab ensued. Phil emerged victorious, and Aliyah went on record assuring she would pick up the next one.

They bundled up to head back out into the snow and on to Logan International Airport. The thought of braving the cold outside sent chills down Aliyah's spine even before being exposed to the actual frigid temperatures.

"So, Phil," Aliyah said as they made their way to the exit, "we discussed a lot of specifics and details over lunch, but I didn't ask you what made you want to join this team."

"Probably the same thing that made you join."

She stopped and turned to Phil and as they reached the door. "Really, what's that?" she asked.

Phil pushed the door open, exposing them to the blizzard outside, then glanced back over his shoulder. "I was told we only had one mission to complete, I found it pretty hard to turn down."

"I still haven't been told what our objective is. What did Daedalus tell you the mission was about?" Aliyah asked.

A serious look set deep into Phil's face. "To save the world, Ali. We're here to save the world."

CHAPTER FIVE

New York City
February 1, 8:45 a.m.

A black-and-gold Sikorsky S-76C helicopter, often referred to by its other name, the Black Hawk, raced along the edge of the Hudson River affording the passengers clear views of the Manhattan skyline to the left and Jersey to the right. The pilot announced over the intercom that the area they were passing over was the exact same spot that Captain Sully famously landed a commercial airliner on the Hudson River, saving everyone on board. The helo's nine-seat configuration allowed for a greater number of passengers than the military's standard four-seat configuration. The supple, cream-colored leather seats and gold-inlaid accents that adorned the sound-dampened cabin stood in stark contrast to the utilitarian black and gray typically found on the gunships.

Crystal glasses were nestled securely in their place. A digital screen above the bar was anchored to the wall that separated the luxurious cabin from the pilots. Another screen was placed across from the first, giving all the passengers an unobstructed view of whatever was being displayed on the devices.

Chief Petty Officer William (Billy) Kivahudajak, was known to his brothers-in-arms as "Chief" or "Billy K" because of his obnoxiously long last name, was seated in the left seat of the Sikorsky cockpit. His father's family hailed from Tibet, his mother from the Dominican Republic. Both parents were short and slight of build. How their son grew into the mountain of a man he was, no one knew. His whole life he had been head and shoulders taller than his friends, outweighing them by two to one on average. His light mocha skin, an even blend of his parents, made his green eyes stand out even more. His mixed race gave him an interesting look, one that many though was boyishly handsome as he was growing up, but the time that Billy had spent in the sun and sand had weathered those good looks, and the scars on his face and body that he'd accumulated over his illustrious career as a SEAL had all but ruined the chances of anyone calling him for his close-up. The large scorpion tattoo that stretched from his enormous chest all the way up his neck kept most people at bay. He preferred it that way, being on his own. *People are generally a letdown*, he'd said aloud so often it was almost a mantra.

The pilot, seated to his right, a young recruit named Solomon (Solo) Daniels, was peering through the windshield, focused on the task at hand.

The helo shifted slightly as Solo banked the bird to the left. They were soaring at 90 mph at just over 1,200 feet. They crossed over the west side highway toward midtown Manhattan. "We're about two minutes out," Solo said to the passengers in the cabin behind him.

Chief nodded in approval to the young pilot. The storm that had chased Dr. Tzion and Phil from Boston to New York was providing the same turbulent air that now buffeted the aircraft. Solo had deftly maneuvered the Sikorsky through the early morning skies, providing his guests with only a few moments of discomfort. Solo felt in complete control when he flew, whether it be helicopters or airplanes. The huge Navy SEAL seated next to him, watching his every move from the corner of his half-closed eyes, did more to unnerve him than any weather system. He knew that a recommendation from the big guy would go a long way toward securing his future with the group for which he was now auditioning.

The top floors of a few of the new skinny 'pencil' towers that were sprouting up all over Manhattan looked like they were floating in midair, their bases obscured by the thick cloud cover. The instruments and radar on the helicopter were best in class, and the poor visibility provided little issue for the advanced navigation technology the Black Hawk had onboard.

The elevation fell away as Solo began his final approach,. With the clouds now above them, the entirety of the world-famous skyline came into focus. He was asked to provide a short scenic flyby of NYC at the request of one of his guests before they set down at the heliport on West 30th Street. While it would have been quicker to set down on the roof of the building to which they were headed, landing a helicopter on a building in New York had been banned since 1977 due to one of them crashing into the Pan Am building (now called the Met Life building). There had even been renewed calls as of late to ban all flights over New York City entirely to ensure the safety of the pedestrians below, but those flight paths were still open for now.

With their brief flyover sightseeing tour complete, Solo settled the craft on its skids and powered down the rotors at the designated heliport by the river. A white Lincoln Navigator and matching Audi RS7 were idling in the distance.

Aliyah shuddered at the thought of getting out of her comfortable, heated seat and back into the cold. She was sure that even the short run to the waiting vehicle would bring a quick chill to her bones.

Phil seemed to enjoy every minute of the flight. Their quick detour was his idea. Even the mild turbulence they'd experienced left him unfazed. The cold didn't seem to bother him either. His entire persona was relaxed. The arms of his aviator-style Prada sunglasses rested comfortably above the Air Pods he had been listening to during their short flight. He was wearing a black puffer jacket, color-matched Gucci track pants, and a pair of retro Jordans. *The dude dresses like he stepped out of a GQ fashion shoot*, Aliyah thought. Phil looked as comfortable as could be.

He had told Aliyah over their meal in Boston that he had a weakness for sneakers and seemed a bit embarrassed when he confessed to the number of pairs he owned. She almost choked when he told her he stopped counting after 150. She had a hunch he knew the real number and made a mental note not to get down on herself the next time she went shopping for shoes. Some retail therapy would be order after she returned from this assignment.

"All right everyone, let's get moving," Chief said from the front. The speakers in the rear cabin relayed this message clearly. He turned to Solo. "Thanks for the lift, kid. Smooth as a baby's ass. I'll be sure to let the boss know." The massive SEAL extended his hand for a fist bump. When Solo's knuckles met the soldiers, they looked like a small child's by comparison. Billy K's hand was a gnarled mess of scars and bone. Solo couldn't imagine the facial destruction that would ensue after getting struck with the weight and fury of his right cross.

Chief heaved a large green duffel bag over his shoulder and exited the chopper. Seconds later, the rear doors opened, and the remaining two passengers poured out, both of them instinctively ducking under the slowing rotors, and headed straight for the waiting vehicles.

"I'm taking the Lincoln. I gotta make a stop on the way, but I won't be long," Billy said. "I'll be there in time for the official kick-off." That was the most he had said to either of them after his initial introduction that morning.

Chief tossed the key fob for the Audi to Phil. "Address is already programmed into the GPS," he said as the giant climbed into his Navigator. "Key cards and access codes for the, uh… *office* are inside the car too. See you soon."

Phil unlocked the car with the remote, and he and Aliyah slid inside. They closed the doors, and both let out simultaneous smiles, albeit for very different reasons.

"Bless the soul of whomever decided to keep this warm for us, and look," Aliyah said, smiling, "they turned the seat heaters all the way up too. I'm still defrosting from Boston."

"I have to admit, I'm feeling a lot of love for the person who left us this whip, too," Phil said with an even bigger grin. The almost 600 hp beast of a car could do 0 to 60 mph in just over three seconds, and with its advanced traction control, it stuck to the road like glue even in the wet and icy conditions like New York was offering them at the moment. He spotted the metal-studded tires while walking up to the vehicle as well as the bullet-proof windows and wondered why they were needed. He kept that thought to himself, though, not wanting to spook Ali.

"Ready?" he asked. Phil grabbed the carbon-fiber paddle shifter behind the leather-wrapped steering wheel, punched the accelerator, and launched out of the heliport like they were being chased by a demon. The car started to spin out, but the computer-controlled traction ensured the wheels stayed on course.

"Whoa, that's really fast! We're not even out of the parking lot yet!" Aliyah yelped, her nails digging into the door handle. The sudden acceleration fired adrenaline through her body.

"The GPS says we're twenty minutes out with little to no traffic," Phil said as if she hadn't said a word. "We lucked out this morning. Looks like a lot of people are staying in today. I bet I can do it in ten." He flicked the paddle shifters under his fingers. The car roared forward, and the buildings became a blur. The weather had indeed kept most people at home, allowing him to race down nearly empty streets and barren sidewalks that were trod upon by only a few weary, frozen pedestrians. Aliyah closed her eyes, hoping that not looking would be less terrifying. It didn't help.

"You weren't kidding when you said you drove fast," she exclaimed as they rounded a corner way faster than she thought the car or slippery roads would allow. She wasn't sure if he was doing it on purpose, or if he really drove like that all the time. She made another mental note never to eat right before driving with Phil. To that end, she was glad she had skipped breakfast. The ride would have been unbearable otherwise.

"Twelve minutes," Phil said, sounding slightly dejected as they pulled up to the entry of the private parking garage. "I'm sure we could've made it ten minutes flat, but I'd have to drive much more aggressively. I didn't want to shake you up too much this early in the morning."

Aliyah wasn't sure how that was even possible. She felt lucky to be alive. "Well, we're here ahead of time," she said as they rolled to a stop at the first security checkpoint. She was eager to get out of the car. "We may as well go inside."

Two giant steel bollards, each easily three feet in diameter, blocked the way into the subterranean parking structure. On either side of the mammoth security towers rose even taller concrete walls that were almost as thick as they were tall. The silent sentries provided an effective means of preventing vehicles of any size from crossing the threshold unless authorized to do so.

Phil tapped the matte-black NFC security card that Chief left for him onto a sleek metal box, finished in the same black material. The card had no identifier other than an ornate letter D embossed in silver on one side. When the microchip embedded in the plastic got within inches of the access device, a green check mark flashed from the depths of the featureless black metal box. The check mark faded and was replaced with a virtual keypad. Phil entered the digits that Chief left for him into the digital keypad and sat back. Only then did he notice the numerous cameras mounted on the walls surrounding them. Phil also spied a small reflective lens on the black box that was likely a camera, recording his interaction with the inanimate guard.

His code was validated, and the reinforced steel pillars slid swiftly and silently away, allowing the RS7 access to the secure parking area. They drove down three levels and through an additional key card access point, identical to the first. The second stop utilized smaller bollards than the street-side entry, but would be equally effective at keeping anyone without the proper credentials out. One more rotation around the spiraling geometry, and they were finally ushered into a narrow, dimly lit lane, facing an apparent dead end.

Looks of confusion washed over their faces. Had they missed another entry somewhere?

Just as Phil was going to slip the transmission into reverse, a light flicked on ahead, illuminating a large concrete frame at the far end of the parking structure. A large vertical seam, invisible a heartbeat before, grew wider. Harsh LED lighting blazed from the interior of a massive elevator cab poured out. The opening was large enough to accommodate their vehicle and at least three others. The Audi rolled over the threshold with barely a bump. Once clear, the doors slid quietly shut. The elevator interior had no buttons or controls that they could see, but a screen displaying a digital *down* arrow indicated they weren't done with their descent. The pressure in their ears popped as the elevator cab dropped farther away from their entry point.

When the elevator reached its destination, the doors parted in front of them to reveal another parking area. It was like the one they had just left, but this one had a more sterile feel. It was much smaller as well. Two rows of overhead lights popped on as their car rolled off the heavy-duty lift, its massive doors already closing behind them.

The motion-activated lights above laid a path toward a solitary glass box. It was the only other structure on that level. No other vehicles were in sight.

Phil turned the Audi off with a touch of a button. "This is such a beautiful car. I can't wait to see what she can really do," he said as they got out. *Pings* and *ticks* could be heard coming from the engine as it cooled from its morning workout, sounding much louder in the confined space. A passenger elevator and requisite exit stairs could be seen through the steel-and-glass enclosure. The overhead emergency signage gave off a greenish hue that added to the clinical feel of their environment.

The same card reader greeted them at the entry to the passenger elevator. Four cameras peered at them through smoked out domes, each providing a different vantage point. Undoubtedly, their every move was being watched and recorded. They entered their credentials, and the pressure seal on the door hissed open. *There's definitely no sneaking into this place*, Aliyah thought.

As she stepped into the elevator, she noticed there were no buttons to press. Phil placed the NFC card onto the matching symbol embedded into the elevator wall. The door closed silently as they began their second descent.

Aliyah admired the yellow onyx floor on which she was standing. It was the only warm color she'd seen since they passed through the heavily guarded gates. She watched the arrow on the wall cascade downwards in ripples of green LED.

"Green lights, golden floors," Aliyah said. "Inspired color scheme. I feel like we're walking on the yellow brick road on the way to the Emerald City in Oz."

"I think you may be right," Phil said, "and I can't wait to meet the wizard."

The elevator came to a stop, and the doors parted. They both stood there in awe, their mouths hanging open.

"Uh, Dorothy, we're not in Kansas anymore," was all Phil could think to say.

CHAPTER SIX

390 feet below New York City
February 1, 9:30 a.m.

The cavern standing before them was immense. The roof soared over a hundred feet above their perch. About the size of a large aircraft hangar—a stadium hewn from solid rock. The bright lighting rigged high above cast its illumination all the way down to the flat-black metal grating that covered every inch of the ground level.

Warm currents of air rose and fell across the massive enclosure. The breeze carried a scent from the rock that stretched in every direction. The earthy smell and warm air reminded Aliyah of the nights she spent in the desert during her military training in Israel. She loved being in the mountains just after the sun went down. It was when the heat of the day began to recede; the sun admitting temporary defeat to the darkening sky. The absence of light out in the desert allowed the stars to shine brighter than she'd seen anywhere else on Earth. The cave's roof even sparkled like her memories of those desert night stars.

Metal catwalks and stairs meshed to create a perimeter around the cavern, allowing for the movement of people and equipment at multiple levels throughout the structure. Mechanical lifts moved metal crates and all manner of equipment along the intricate web of steel and cable. The support staff—or any people, for that matter—were curiously absent.

A small army of robots of various sizes and configurations moved crates along the floor while others conducted autonomous operations at multiple stations throughout the vast expanse.

A deep voice rang out in the cavernous space. "Dr. Tzion, Master Wu, welcome to what I affectionately call, the Workshop."

Phil and Aliyah both turned to see their host, the elusive Daedalus, finally make his way around the corner and walk onto the platform on which they were standing. He looked to be in his late fifties or early sixties. He stood well over six feet tall and looked like he kept himself in excellent shape for a man even half his age. His salt-and-pepper hair and matching beard gave him a refined, sophisticated look.

Aliyah leaned in close to Phil as Daedalus approached. "He kind of looks like George Clooney," she whispered.

"You should tell him that," Phil said, trying not to laugh.

Phil's face turned serious, and he greeted his employer with a slight bow. "Thank you for the opportunity and the invite. This is quite the impressive operation you've put together here. And please, call me Phil. Only my students call me Master."

"Phil, it's an honor and a pleasure to finally meet you. I am known simply as Daedalus. And before you ask, no, that isn't my given name, but any other that I give you would be just as false. I've kept my identity concealed behind the Daedalus façade to ensure my work is kept safe from the people hell bent on my death and destruction. We can get to all of that later once we dive into the mission details because, ultimately, that's why I've gathered you all here.

"Sorry if I made you uncomfortable with the 'Master' formality before, but as an eighth-degree kung fu black-belt and someone who has taught all over the globe, you certainly have earned the title. I didn't want to be disrespectful. I've been studying martial arts my entire life and am always looking to gain a unique perspective. I would very much like to learn from you too, if we get the opportunity. Your dedication to your craft has earned my deep respect."

Phil was taken aback by the humble attitude and sincere sentiment. Most powerful and successful men he had worked for loved to peacock and assert their alpha side when given the opportunity. There was definitely something different about Daedalus. Phil hadn't heard much of anything about their mysterious benefactor before—none of them had, actually—but he had a captivating presence. It was more than charisma; he had a positive vibe about him. Phil was already a fan, and he'd just met the guy.

"Dr. Tzion, I hope the trip in from Boston was okay for you?" Daedalus asked.

Aliyah's mind flashed back to the blizzard in Boston, the turbulent weather in the airplane to New York, the chopper ride that morning, and Phil's race against the clock on the drive over. "It was fine," she said. "Happy to be here, sir. And please, call me Aliyah—Ali for short."

"Very well… Aliyah. It's an honor to have you with us. Your recent utilization of game theory to predict the interaction of bacteria and viruses during mixed infections models is fascinating. Having such a brilliant person on this team is a gift to us all. I've also been an avid student of mathematics for most of my life. I love numbers, as I'm sure you do. The order to it all. The power and potential they contain. Actually, I was hoping you'd be able to assist me with an equation of sorts that I've been having some difficulty with for a while now—once you're settled in and acclimated, of course."

Aliyah felt her face warm at the compliment. Not many people outside her field knew of, never mind understood the ground-breaking work she was close to completing. She was accustomed to people trying to disprove her theories or play "stump the genius," like she was some kind of parlor trick. It was nice to have someone who just wanted to listen and learn.

"I look forward to our conversations, Daedalus." Aliyah smiled, appreciative of his transparency and warm demeanor.

As Aliyah's mind filed away the compliments and pleasantries from the introduction, her mind subconsciously processed all the data it had been ingesting since the doors first opened to the Workshop. She kicked herself for not seeing it sooner, but the spectacle of the Workshop and finally being able to meet Daedalus had momentarily distracted her normally rapid-fire observations. The people, places, and names all fell into place at once.

"Daedalus, the Workshop. I get it now. Very clever. When do we get to see the labyrinth?" she teased.

"You put that together rather quickly, Aliyah," Daedalus said.

Phil looked between her and Daedalus, confused as to what he was missing. "Uh, does anyone want to let me in on what it is you're all talking about?"

"Greek mythology, my friend," Aliyah said. "The Daedalus of lore was said to have been the son of Athena, the goddess of wisdom, warfare, and handicrafts. He was a master inventor and tinkerer of the gods and the one who famously fashioned wings for his son, Icarus, who, as the story goes, flew too close to the sun and fell to Earth when the wax bindings on his wings melted. Most of Daedalus's creations were made in his Workshop. The labyrinth I jokingly referred to was an elaborate structure he created that was meant to trap the beast known as the Minotaur, a half-man, half-bull creature. Since we both just met Daedalus—and we're standing in the Workshop—I thought I'd ask where the labyrinth was."

Phil nodded slowly in understanding. Daedalus smiled with something akin to pride. "I feel very much like a kindred spirit to the legend of Daedalus," he said. "I love to invent and solve complex problems and puzzles. Due to the sensitive and secretive nature of what we do here, as I mentioned to you earlier, I've found it beneficial to conceal my identity from those who wish to steal and destroy what we have created here. I felt the name Daedalus was very apropos and the Workshop just evolved from there, even if it is a bit of a cliché. For the record, there really is a labyrinth in here too." Daedalus chuckled in embarrassment. "In fact, it's where you'll be spending most of your time. I hate to disappoint, but it doesn't contain a Minotaur. However, I'm sure there are other things you'll find equally surprising."

Phil wondered what this guy could possibly have concealed that would more be surprising than a half-man, half-bull hidden inside a cave a mile under New York City.

"Are all the other members of the team here yet?" Aliyah asked.

"Almost. Our computer expert has been here for a few weeks already. He's been busy getting our network up and running after becoming acquainted with some of our proprietary technology. You'll both meet Mr. Hayle soon. Commander Oake arrived last week. The others should be here within the hour. Come, let me give you a quick tour while we wait."

Daedalus led them down a long concrete and steel ramp. Miles of cables and mechanical piping were strapped to the sides of the walkway in neatly organized rows. They made their way down the snaking metal path, then rounded the corner at the end of the ramp, arriving at what appeared to be the main entry point for the maze of catwalks and lift stations.

Walking down to the floor level gave Aliyah her first real look at the technology in which they were now enveloped. It was even more impressive up close. The juxtaposition of the high-tech equipment with the rough and raw natural environment made the whole thing feel surreal.

Phil's face also betrayed the incredulity of the spectacle. While the exact nature and purpose of the equipment in front of him was far beyond his understanding, it didn't take a genius to determine that this technology was something far more advanced than most people knew existed. *It's like something out of a Batman movie*, Phil thought. He couldn't help but wonder if Daedalus would turn out to be a real-life Bruce Wayne, seeing as he already had a version of the bat cave in his possession. At that point, nothing would have surprised him.

"Where exactly are we?" Aliyah asked, gazing at the soaring roof above them. "I mean, it's obvious that we're deep underground, but I didn't know places like this were found under New York."

"This location is one of a kind as far I know, Dr. Tzion, and I've been searching for a very long time. You see, the geological formation below New York City is made from extremely dense rock, making the ground incredibly strong and very stable. It's this unique geology that allows the massive skyscrapers in New York to be built so large and so close together. What you're standing in, is a rare pocket we found in that geology. Think of it as a giant bubble trapped in the rock formations below the city."

The pair looked at the soaring heights above their heads in awe and trepidation.

"The top of the Workshop structure is almost four hundred feet below New York, measured to the top of the bubble, and drops another two hundred and ten feet to the floor we're standing on. The rock above the cavern also seems to have thickened when it originally formed, creating the cavern's irregular shape, providing us with a roof structure that can withstand pretty much any kind of attack. Even a direct nuclear strike on Manhattan wouldn't penetrate this far down. It's pretty incredible what mother nature can sculpt."

"I'm not sure if I feel safer that we're protected by all this," Phil said as he swept his arm over the sight in front of them, "or terrified because you've already worked out the calculations in case someone may want to come at you with a nuke. What exactly have we gotten ourselves into?"

"Nuclear strikes are too much for me to deal with before I've even had a cup of coffee," Aliyah said. "Can we please continue with the tour? I'm anxious to know what all this is being used for."

"Yes, of course, Doctor. I just wanted you both to know that we are very safe and quite secure down here. Some people are fearful of being so deep in the earth—images of trapped miners and such. I just wanted to quell that fear now, although it doesn't seem as if I've done a good job of that. We'll review the details of the facility when the team is all together. I'll also provide you all with the schematics of the Workshop for your reference and orientation. As to the specific research we're conducting, well, I'm afraid that isn't something we can just gloss over quickly. But I'm happy to answer any other questions you may have thus far."

Disappointed that she would have to wait a little longer for the specific reason they were there, Aliyah took the opportunity to ask about something that she had noticed as soon as they stepped off the elevator. "Daedalus, what's that sparkling material spread across the roof of this cavern?"

Phil hadn't noticed that detail until Aliyah pointed it out. The cavern's roof and walls sparkled like diamonds as the light from below danced across its surface. Aliyah also spotted what appeared to be a thin metallic webbing that hung close to the roof. It was almost invisible against the dark rock above. The black mesh was betrayed only by a white light perched atop a massive crane that soared above everything else in the cavern; otherwise, she would have missed the mesh completely. The crane was the tallest structure in the Workshop by far, but there was something very different about it. It seemed to be shimmering, almost like heat waves in a mirage, but it wasn't sparkling like the roof. It was something else entirely.

"The type of rock that makes up the majority of the Workshop is called Manhattan Schist," Daedalus said. "As I said earlier, it's this type of rock that gives such great foundational strength to the New York area. The refraction of light that you're seeing on the roof is caused by the natural presence of white mica and quartz within the bedrock itself."

"And the black mesh up there?" she asked, pointing to the upper elevations.

"Wow, that's quite impressive, Aliyah. Most people miss that entirely. The "mesh", as you called it, serves a dual purpose. First, it acts as a layer of protection—an early warning system, if you will—against any rock fragment that may break loose and fall. Even a small rock falling from that height could irreparably damage the equipment below. If it landed on a person, it could be fatal."

The newcomers shared nervous glances.

"No need to worry," Daedalus said. "We've also deployed autonomous robot spelunkers to take preventive measures to ensure that nothing comes crashing down. If we do detect anything coming even remotely loose, they deal with it before it becomes a problem. You know the old saying, 'an ounce of prevention.'" He didn't bother to finish the well-known proverb. "I've been down here for quite a while, and the system has worked flawlessly."

"How exactly does it work?" Aliyah asked.

Daedalus smiled like a proud father and pointed to the black mesh high above. "Our unique webbing design is really just a series of interlacing hexagons that can expand, and contract individually or collectively as required. The mesh is constructed entirely out of the nanobot technology I have developed here. These microscopic creations have been fashioned from an amalgam of experimental metals and synthetic polymers that are all being managed in real-time utilizing our proprietary AI system that I've affectionately named… ICARUS."

Daedalus reddened when he saw Aliyah smirk at the mention of his operating system's name. His penchant for Greek mythology was looking more obsessive by the minute, even to him.

"It's like having a team of geologists who never tire," he explained. "They survey and protect the area from any harm from above twenty-four hours a day, all without any additional human instruction."

"Are you saying this net is being held together, or rather, is actually made up of tiny robots all guided by artificial intelligence?" Phil was stunned. "No offense, sir, but that seems like an overly complex solution to a relatively easy problem. I've seen safety nets catch boulders that have rolled all the way down a mountain toward the highway while driving the switchbacks up in the Rocky Mountains. If the nets used there can stop such massive rocks, why not use something similar? I'm sure it would be a lot simpler, and I'd suspect a lot less expensive, too." Phil hoped he hadn't offended his new boss, but this looked like an extreme case of overkill.

"Ah, very true, Phil, but that brings us to their second purpose." Daedalus grinned. "While the nanobots create a protective physical barrier above, they also act as a digital mesh network across every inch of my Workshop. They create an electromagnetic field that rewrites and bounces any incoming signals back to their source, making the Workshop appear to be made of solid rock to anyone using ground penetrating radar, sonar, etcetera. They've also been programmed to block all unauthorized communication frequencies from penetrating this Workshop. It's nothing short of a hybrid physical and digital fortress, and the culmination of the research and development we've been working on here. Many contractors and builders use those types of GPR devices for construction purposes all over Manhattan when surveying the soil and bedrock conditions for new buildings. We'd prefer not to alert them to our presence."

Aliyah and Phil both glanced up, recognition of what was suspended above them now starting to sink in.

"The mesh structure is also self-regulated and self-healing. It moves instinctively to protect whatever it's been programmed to protect. In this case, it's a simple expansion and contraction of the hexagon webbing in order to catch a stray rock that may suddenly come loose. From a rock as small as a grain of rice to boulders larger than a Sherman tank, it can catch them all. The system intuitively adds strength and support to any area that needs it, by sending an army of bots to the site, like blood platelets pumping to a wound to clot it. The size of the rock is almost irrelevant. The ICARUS AI just directs the appropriate number of bots to where they're needed.

It's a fairly simple task for such an intelligent cohesion of code, but we're pushing the envelope with much more intricate and complex structures every day. ICARUS learns continuously and keeps the bots on task and *alive*, so to speak. It's highly experimental, but we're nearing the end of our testing phase, and things are performing as planned, if not better."

Phil and Aliyah glanced nervously at each other for the second time when Daedalus mentioned the word *alive* when describing the nanobots.

He caught the look and smiled to lighten the mood. "Relax, it's not going to evolve and take over the world like in a Terminator movie. It's simply programmed to learn and modify its size and structure to keep itself online and on task. Now that I say it like that out loud, it does sort of sound like a Terminator movie." He laughed at the irony. His two new recruits didn't share the humor, but smiled politely.

"Are the nanobots being used to assist with the structural integrity of that huge crane over there?" Aliyah asked, staring at the spire that pierced the heights above. The crane's surface seemed to shimmer with an even greater intensity the closer they got to it.

"We don't use the nanobots to 'assist' with the structure, per se," Daedalus said. "The crane is made up entirely from nanobots, just like the webbing. Here, let me show you something incredible."

The group stepped back to get a better view of the gigantic tower looming above them. Daedalus pulled a device the size of a smartphone from his coat pocket and typed in a string of commands. Small red lights began to flash across the cavern floor, delineating a wide arc at the crane's base. Once they were all standing safely out-side the ring of lights that identified the perimeter of the restricted zone, a metal plate which only moments before had surrounded the crane's base began to open wide, receding into a mechanized floor system. A hidden hollow channel in the floor received the large metal plates, revealing a deep pit located at the base of the tower structure, less than forty feet from where they were standing. A loud klaxon rang out, and a moment later, Aliyah felt the hairs on her arms stand on end. Long wisps of Phil's jet-black hair danced on invisible waves of static as an electrical charge filled the air. The smell of petrichor wafted up from the pit like steam from a kettle.

"Take a look at the top of the crane," Daedalus said, pointing to the top of the tower.

Aliyah and Phil were mesmerized. It was like watching an intricate matrix of dominos fall. The individual pieces were far too small to discern, but the cumulative effect looked as if the mighty crane simply began to dissolve from the top down. One moment it was there, the next, the crane had disappeared into the pit.

Daedalus's guests stood in awe of the spectacle that had just witnessed. Apparently, nothing in the Workshop was as it seemed at first glance.

"That's not even the best part. Watch this!" Daedalus winked and turned his attention back to the device in his hand. After entering another set of instructions, the process repeated itself, but this time in reverse. The nanobots ascended from the pit as the air buzzed with a high-pitched whine. Moments later, the crane began to materialize from the pit below. The titanic structure was once again soaring above them where there had been a void just moments before. When the process was complete, the room fell silent. The electrically charged scent still lingered, the only remnant of the process they just watched.

"Okay, that's the coolest thing I've ever seen, and I've seen some pretty cool stuff in my life," Phil said, still in shock.

Aliyah just stood there, slack jawed, still too shocked to speak. The mathematics involved in such an intricate dance between man and machine was mind-boggling.

"Shit, I just missed the crane trick, didn't I?" a deep voice said from behind them. They all turned to find Chief approaching. "I love that thing. So freaking cool."

"Chief, I'm glad you've arrived safely," Daedalus said. "Phil, Aliyah, I know you all met on the flight over. You'll all have a chance to get reacquainted, so let's continue the tour later this afternoon. We should meet up with the rest of the group now that everyone is finally here."

Chief discretely handed Daedalus a thin silver briefcase that the mysterious man accepted with a nod. Aliyah wondered if that was the errand the big Navy SEAL had to run when they all left the heliport.

The group headed toward a set of glass doors that were embedded into the side of the rock face less than twenty yards away. Daedalus explained that the doors led to another large cave system within the giant cavern. No idle chitchat was made on the short walk over as the two newcomers took in as much of the surrounding spectacle as they could. Their heads were on swivels, not wanting to miss anything before heading inside.

Daedalus explained along the way that he named this area the Labyrinth due to the maze-like topography created by the numerous cave openings which were accessible deeper into the system. "Because the Labyrinth is the most secure structure inside the Workshop, it's where I've located our headquarters and base of operations," Daedalus said as they made their way toward the bunker within a bunker.

As they got closer to their destination, Phil increased his pace until he was walking in stride with Daedalus. "You never had a chance to answer my question from earlier."

"I'm sorry. What question is that?" Daedalus responded.

"About being attacked."

Their dialogue was interrupted when the four of them reached the doors to the Labyrinth. Chief glanced at his boss. A look of concern spread across the SEAL's face in response to Phil's words about being attacked. He'd have to ask Daedalus about it later. It was the first he heard of any sort of attack. Chief took one last step forward and pulled the aluminum handle to open the door for the group. Cool air from the interior spilled out into the warm cave.

"Ladies first," he said, gesturing for Aliyah to lead the group inside.

"Chivalry isn't dead after all. Thank you, Chief," Aliyah said as she crossed the threshold, only then aware of how warm the cavern was as she walked into air-conditioned comfort. Truth be told, she'd rather be too warm down there versus freezing in the temperatures outside above. Chief followed Aliyah inside, and the door closed quickly behind him, leaving Daedalus and Phil alone to finish their conversation.

Phil placed his hand on the door handle, but didn't make a move to open it. "The question I have is, well… should I be worried that someone may be trying to come after you with a nuke or anything like that? I work here now, or I'm about to anyway, and if some-one is hell-bent on attacking you, then for all intents and purposes, they'll be attacking me, too. I'm not entirely comfortable with peo-ple I don't know coming after me with that caliber of weapon. I'm just trying to keep it real with you, sir."

Daedalus nodded as he took a moment to collect his thoughts. "It isn't the threat of a nuclear bomb spiraling down from the sky that keeps me up at night. I'm terrified of something far more le-thal. Something that even the strength of this mighty structure and my vast resources can't be sure to defend against. It's the reason you're here. In fact, it's the reason you're all gathered here now. But whether you choose to be part of this team or not, the danger we face will be inescapable for anyone on Earth, regardless of lo-cation. At least here you have a chance to stop it."

Phil glanced back at the vast expanse and enormity of the Work-shop and then back at Aliya and Chief waiting on the other side of the glass. "Okay, let's get to work."

CHAPTER SEVEN

The Workshop, NYC
February 1, 11:00 a.m.

As the group walked through the natural stone cavern, Daedalus continued with his guided tour. He explained that even though the smaller caves were made from the same impenetrable rock as the giant dome above, he had also fortified the Labyrinth with additional security measures. Doors and digital locking mechanisms had been installed throughout. The opening and shutting of various openings and exits in the smaller caverns created an unlimited combination of escape passages for the team. These could also be fashioned as dead ends for anyone who dared intrude, as unlikely as that scenario was. Any cave without a secondary exit could easily become a vault or a prison with the simple opening or closing of a door.

The group assembled in a complex control center that seemed to be tracking data from all over the world. Satellite feeds playing on giant digital screens covered the rocky backdrop. Daedalus gestured for the group to walk a little deeper inside. A massive table hewn from the very rock they were standing on was centered in the space. Sleek black leather chairs were placed evenly around the massive stone. Metal trusses were suspended like a halo over the table. The little flecks of quartz and mica in the stone sparkled across the table's surface.

Above them, data and power cables snaked through the voids in the truss structure. Faint baby blue and white LEDs colored the modular system suspended above them, giving the aluminum halo a soft blue glow. Clips and fasteners kept the wiring neat and organized, while still allowing easy access for any upgrades or repairs. Larger white LED floodlights were secured at the corners, illuminating their entire meeting area. Large TV screens hung on all four sides of the halo, although they were all currently switched off.

Aliyah and Phil saw two other people seated at the table whom they hadn't met yet. One rose to greet them. The other stayed seated and continued working on his laptop, either ignoring them or oblivious to their presence.

"Aliyah, Phil, it's my pleasure to introduce you to Commander Gryphon Oake. Commander Oake will be leading the team on this and any of our future missions," Daedalus said as Gryph walked toward the pair. Phil and Aliyah had read the impressive bio on the military man with their original briefs. By all accounts, he was a living legend.

"Please, call me Gryph. If I'm going to have to ask you to put yourselves in harm's way—and unfortunately, I may have to—we can drop the formalities if that's okay with you two."

Phil and Aliyah smiled and nodded. It seemed that egos had been checked at the door, and everyone was there to do their part.

"Works for me, Gryph. Good to meet you. Please, call me Phil."

"Hi. I'm Aliyah Tzion. Nice to finally meet you, Gryph. My friends call me Aliyah or Ali or both." A fresh round of smiles and greetings were exchanged.

The last member of their team remained anonymous until their host interjected, clearing his throat. "And this is Mr. Hayle. He's our resident technical expert on, well, just about everything with a power button, it seems. His talents with computers, programming, and circuitry know no bounds."

Dallas looked up briefly, ignoring the compliment. He took in the sight of Aliyah and Phil standing there, and flicked his chin up an inch, expending the least amount of effort possible to acknowledge the pair. "I'm Dallas," he said, then returned to his work.

"I guess he likes things informal too," Phil said to Aliyah and Gryph. The three of them shared a smirk at Dallas's expense.

"You actually caught him on a good day," Gryph said. "He's pretty intense, that one."

"Please everyone, take a seat," Daedalus said.

All six of them made their way into the high-back black chairs. Aliyah noticed that Chief and Dallas shared a subtle acknowledgment of some type, realizing they must have been introduced beforehand.

"I'd like to thank all of you for coming," Daedalus began. "I know each of you are very sought after for the unique talents and perspectives you bring to your respective fields. I want you to know how much I appreciate your willingness to work on such an important project with such little notice and information."

Dallas scoffed a little too loudly when Daedalus said the word *willingness*. A stern glare was shared by the two, but Dallas quickly acquiesced, and Daedalus continued without missing a beat. "Much of what I am about to tell you will come as a shock. I expect you will have many questions and likely many more when you get those answers."

Daedalus reached into his breast pocket and brought out a small device. Aliyah recognized it as the one he had used to control the nanobot crane earlier. The touchscreen lit up as he entered new instructions onto the smooth glass. The truss-mounted OLED TV screens which had until that point been dark, powered up. The overhead lighting dimmed automatically to enhance the image coming from the monitors.

Graphic images of dead cattle strewn throughout an open field assaulted their vision. There was no end to the sickening sight. It was a sea of carnage. The dead beasts must have numbered in the hundreds. The pictures started to shuffle. Tighter shots of the livestock showed that while most animals had no visible wounds, some had been ravaged by the scavengers that always lurked near death and disease. Something had caused the entire herd to die right where they grazed.

"We've taken some recent samples from the areas you're seeing on screen and confirmed that it's the same thing plaguing each of these sites. We thought that would be good news for us at first, knowing what we're looking for. But there's no good news with this pathogen. After the first few locations were brought to our attention, we immediately went to work on a containment strategy, to keep this pestilence from spreading to the surrounding areas."

Daedalus continued the narrative as he cued up another slide-show. Even though each location was from a different part of the world, the message was universal. This killer, whatever it may be, was no longer contained. Scenes with snow-covered peaks morphed into images of flat prairie pastures. Heavily timbered areas flanked by gentle streams gave way to images of rolling hills and seas of golden grain. It was a simple but concise pictorial representation of livestock habitats and crop-growing locations from all over the world. Each environment was vastly different from one the others, but they all shared the same macabre element. Death lay everywhere. By the time the last slide was presented, the list of animals affected grew to include sheep, goats, poultry, horses, and most other domesticated farm animals.

"Gryph, can you please explain what you've seen on the satellite imagery," Daedalus said. The slide changed again, and the group stared at a landmass from space. As the image zoomed in closer, it showed acres upon acres of pasture that was brown and dead. This was in stark contrast to some of the other areas visible in the picture, which were either deep green or golden yellow. More images were shown, all of them revealing the same menacing issue.

"These shots were taken over North America, Russia and India five months ago," Gryph said, cycling through the different areas as he spoke.

"It must be some kind of pathogen in the fields or groundwater," Aliyah remarked, the gears already spinning in her brilliant mind. It was becoming more obvious why her vast knowledge of viral and bacterial biology was needed on the team.

"It does appear that something out there is killing whatever it encounters," Gryph said. "Daedalus found the same organism at each of these sites. It's the only common denominator."

The image changed again, and this time, a video began to play. An unknown person was outfitted in protective clothing complete with a large, specialized hat. An ultra-fine white mesh spilled over the brim of the hat, keeping the wearer's head and face protected. The dislodged the top of a white wooden box which stood no more than four feet tall and was roughly half as wide. Not that it was required, but the bright yellow bee logo on the side of the box was a dead giveaway they were looking at a beekeeper and his hives.

More of the white boxes were stacked in the background, but at least half a dozen could be seen in the current frame of the video. The apiarist finished removing the lid from the hive and signaled to the off-screen cameraman to come closer. The image shifted to the interior of the hive itself. The apiarist pulled out a "honey super," a shelf supporting the honeycomb inside the hive, holding it nearer to the camera, providing a close-up of the wooden insert.

There should have been a flurry of activity inside the hive and all over the supers themselves. The honeycomb should have been saturated with delicious golden sticky honey being attended to by busy little bees. But all the hives looked the same. Dead. Deserted. There was only a smattering of bees in some, but for the most part, they were entirely abandoned.

"Some of these pictures and videos were taken this past summer at various locations around the globe," Gryph said. "To make matters worse, we're not seeing these as isolated occurrences. Rather, all these things are happening at the same time all over the planet. As you can see, the devastation, while limited in scope and breadth, is absolute once this sickness takes hold."

"Why isn't this stuff killing everything in its path?" Chief asked. "It seems to just stop dead in its tracks." All heads turned to the huge Navy SEAL, who had remained quiet until then. "I also noticed that this dead grass is always in the middle of a field or forest. It's never on the edges or near the roadways. Why does it just pop up in the middle of a field each time? It's almost like someone dropped a bomb or something." By the looks on the faces around the room, it seemed they had all missed that subtlety.

"Look at Billy K with the big brain. I guess you're not two hundred and fifty pounds of ugly *and* stupid," Dallas said, finally deciding to join the conversation.

Chief glared at Dallas and sat taller in his chair, making his immense frame seem even larger.

"Take it easy, ya big ape, and clean out your ears. I said you weren't ugly *and* stupid," Dallas said. "You're just ugly." Dallas snickered.

Billy started to get out of his seat.

"Gentlemen," Gryph said, raising an eyebrow as everyone's attentions snapped back to the images on the screen. The new set of slides were on the other end of the magnification spectrum. An enlarged image taken from a microscope showed a tight grouping of elongated translucent pale green cells. Tiny, hair-like appendages ran around the circumference of the organism. Deep yellow organelles floated inside. "We've discovered this organism at all of the dead zones, regardless of whether it was insect, animal, or plant."

Phil raised his hand. "Excuse me, dead zones?"

"Right," Gryph clarified. "The dead zone is how we've been referring to these affected areas. We've measured and recorded numerous data points from each site. We brought the samples back here to study just recently and—"

"Uh, guys," Aliyah said. "I'm sorry, but I believe there's an error with the magnification scale shown on your slide. It makes no sense. This is obviously a bacterium we're dealing with, not a viral contagion or chemical agent. The organelles and plasmids in the cell are clearly evident. However, the scale shown from the scan calculates the width of the cell to be…" Aliyah referenced the screen in front of her. "Zero point nine two nanometers in length. That's impossible."

Gryph smiled and nodded.

The three other men at the table hadn't even tried to hide their confusion. Phil looked to Chief to see if he was following, but he didn't notice because he was looking at Dallas for the same reason. Dallas unwittingly answered them both with a shrug.

"You're correct about the classification," Gryph said. "It's definitely a bacterial cell and an incredibly tiny one at that. This was the anomaly Dr. Tzion was finding problematic," Gryph added, but the three men still looked lost. "The size of this bacterium makes it very unique. It would be small, even for a virus." The confused looks staring back at Gryph told him he needed to provide a lot more context. "Viruses are much smaller than even the smallest bacteria. So small, in fact, that they're measured in nanometers, not microns. That's one thousand times smaller in scale. This bacterium is unlike anything ever discovered. We're not sure how this is possible, but you can see it for yourself. We've also run multiple diagnostics and recalibrations on all our equipment, and everything checked out. We shouldn't be seeing what we're seeing—but there it is."

Everyone went back to looking at the images glowing above them. The threat loomed even more ominous despite its diminutive size.

"So, that's what we're here for? To contain and kill this bug?" Chief asked. "Can't we just spray it with insecticide before it spreads any further?"

Daedalus rose from his seat. "There's an element to this particular organism that makes your suggestion impractical." Heads turned to the secretive man who had assembled them all and waited for him to continue as Gryph took his seat next to Aliyah. "Chief recently brought me the results from the latest samples retrieved from areas in the midwestern United States. Unfortunately, they have confirmed my worst fears. The bacterium has been identified there too." Aliyah's mind flashed back to the silver briefcase she'd seen Chief give Daedalus earlier. "What's even more concerning is that these bacteria haven't gone dormant in the samples we retrieved from the frozen ground."

"So, why don't we don't we kill it along the lines of what Billy Big Brain here just suggested... except without sounding like it came from a third grader?" Dallas asked.

Chief ignored the jab. "Why wouldn't killing it solve the problem?" he asked. "What could be worse than allowing it to spread worldwide? You've already told us it'll kill whatever it infects." The way he saw it, dead enemies, microscopic or not, rarely caused further problems.

Daedalus stared at the battle-hardened soldier. "Because no matter what we've tried, they just won't die."

CHAPTER EIGHT

Awhite Dassault Falcon-8X transoceanic jet cruised high above the thin clouds almost three hours outside London. The air at 42,000 feet was thin, and they hadn't encountered any turbulence since they'd left Mumbai nearly five hours earlier. The reduction in wind resistance at that altitude allowed the business jet to attain speeds of over 700 mph, even faster with a tailwind. The winds were in their favor and shortened the trip by almost an hour. Not that spending additional time onboard was any kind of hardship. Appointed with cream-colored leather seats, thick chocolate carpeting and highly polished wood accents that complimented the warm tones. The aircraft had the ability to cross the Atlantic without refueling, yet it felt as warm and cozy as a private study in an opulent home. Gourmet meals were prepared for the flights, and the finest scotches, wines, and cigars were placed onboard to be enjoyed at any time.

Basileus ensured that he had a new flight attendant on board each time he flew. He'd been using the plane much more frequently as of late, but typically, it was only a few times a month. If he was forced to take to the sky, he would only do so in luxurious fashion. The plane was a necessity in his line of work. The sixty-five million dollars he'd spent on it meant nothing to him. His wealth now measured in the tens of billions, distributed throughout the globe. All of it totally untraceable, yet under his full control. The flight attendant on this voyage was an exotic-looking Brazilian with a face beautiful enough to adorn the cover of any fashion magazine.

It was obvious she worked hard on her body, too. From what he could see so far, it might even be more impressive than her face.

Early into the flight, Christina, as the Brazilian's name tag read, poured Basileus a generous portion of a rare forty-year-old Macallan scotch and shortly after brought him his four-course meal. He finished his food, downed the last of his scotch, and felt his eyes grow heavy from the combination of the two. Basileus completed the final review of the documents outlining the vast holdings of the German fertilizer company he'd just acquired. An Indian shipping company purchased a few hours before, expanded his reach even further. Satisfied he finished enough work for the night and seeing as he had a few hours left before they landed, Basileus decided to make his way to the master bedroom at the rear of the plane, requesting that a cigar be brought to him.

Christina arrived at the door holding the cigar, clipper, matches, and another glass of scotch neatly arranged on a sterling-silver tray. The room already had an ashtray, which she'd placed on the nightstand prior to takeoff. She always tried to anticipate what her clients would want next and strived to deliver it before they asked. She balanced the tray in her left hand and knocked on the door with her right.

"Come," came the reply from behind the door.

"I've brought your cigar, sir. A Monte Cristo number two, as requested. I also poured another Macallan in case the desire arose." The tall brunette stood in the doorway, presenting the items on the tray.

"Bring them here. Christina, is it?"

She walked inside and put the cigar and accessories beside the ashtray. Basileus was seated on the bed with his shirt unbuttoned, his back against the headboard, and his muscular chest and chiseled midsection on full display. The TV on the opposite wall showed some news channel, but the volume was off. The glow from the television screen was the only illumination in the luxurious suite.

"You're really quite stunning, Christina. And if you don't mind me saying, you smell absolutely delicious."

She smiled warmly at the compliment. "That's very kind of you to say, sir. I can see you keep yourself in excellent shape, too. Is there anything else I can do for you before we land?"

"Yes, since you asked. Why don't you close the door and get undressed? Keep me company for a few hours."

The shock on her face made it look like she'd just been slapped. She opened her mouth to protest, but Basileus spoke first. "Look, we can go through this yes/no charade for a while because you think it will save you some measure of dignity, so you can look at yourself in the mirror without feeling quite as guilty tomorrow, right? But you don't have to feel guilty, you know why?"

She shook her head but didn't say anything.

"Because everyone is guilty of something, Christina, and who am I to judge?" He reached into the nightstand cabinet and pulled out a small orange box with a brown bow wrapped around one side. "As a token of my appreciation for the care and attention you've provided me so far."

She'd been his flight attendant on the original outbound trip from London to India, but Basileus was busy with calls and pressing work matters and had all but ignored her. She took it from him with her delicate hands and perfectly manicured nails.

"Hermes?" she asked, though she already knew it was. She opened the box to find a silk Hermes scarf and a pair of white earrings. Her wide eyes bore the same shocked look from earlier—but for altogether different reasons.

"Thank you very much, sir. You're far too generous. Please allow me to show you *my* appreciation." She closed the door behind her and began to undress. It only took a moment until she was wearing nothing but a small black thong. She was even more gorgeous than he imagined.

Christina climbed onto the large bed and inched toward him, reaching up to undo the last few last buttons on his shirt. She didn't notice Basileus smiling at the pretty scarf hanging halfway outside the orange box she left on the pile of clothes she'd been wearing a minute earlier. He almost laughed out loud thinking that Christina would go through her entire life thinking she was wearing genuine Hermes pieces, having no clue that the scarf and earring set he'd just given her could be bought for twenty bucks on the streets of Mumbai.

A boy no older than ten had approached his car peddling the fakes while he was stuck in traffic on the way to the airport. Basileus remembered the harsh lessons he endured on the streets when he was a young boy and, as such, wanted to help the poor kid out. He figured the trinkets could prove useful at some point, so he took five of them without negotiating the price and gave the kid a crisp hundred-dollar bill and sent him on his way. He had no idea the payoff would come so quickly.

Basileus snapped back to the present when he felt Christina tug his belt through the loops of his pants. The Amazonian was all over him, eager to show him just how appreciative she could be, but was no doubt looking to see what else was up for grabs before they landed. Maybe she could make something more of this chance encounter. He was incredibly handsome and had a body that belonged on the cover of *Men's Health* magazine, plus he was obviously fabulously rich. She'd much rather travel on such jets than work on them. Basileus knew exactly what she was thinking, having seen that look many times before. It was why he asked for a new flight attendant every time he flew. They were always the most eager to please the first time they had the opportunity.

A short time later, the plane was making its final approach to London City Airport, known for its VIP service and proximity to the heart of the city. Basileus had showered and changed into fresh clothes and was settling back into his seat. Christina had departed the room twenty minutes earlier to prepare the cabin for landing.

Basileus knew that his bodyguard, Dima, who was also head of his security, would be waiting for him at the airport having tracked the flight the moment it took off from India.

Basileus pulled the air phone from the pocket located on the side of his seat. He had a strong signal throughout the flight, compliments of the jet's satellite connection, but he'd been occupied in his suite until recently. He called Dima, who picked up before the second ring.

"I'll be landing shortly. Were you able to secure the additional warehouses?"

"Yes sir, we secured all the property you asked us to. Everything is on schedule. We'll be ready to forward the deliveries within the week."

"Excellent. Everything went well in Mumbai and Germany, too. They'll ship the seeds tomorrow. If all goes according to plan, we should be able to start full-scale distribution in the coming days. The fate of the world is in our hands, Dima. We need to be ready when the time comes."

Dima beamed with pride. He worked hard for Basileus over the years and had put his life in danger countless times, all to show his boss how loyal and dedicated he was to him and to his cause. It was nice to know his efforts hadn't gone unnoticed.

"Thank you, sir. I'm forever in your debt. I'll let you know the second I hear anything."

Basileus hung up and returned his phone to the side pocket of his chair. Christina came back to where he was seated carrying a small bottle of soda with a lime wedge. A simple white card with her phone number was also discreetly placed on the tray. She kept her distance when he was on his call, affording him privacy, now that he was off the call, she was up close and personal again.

"Do you need anything else before we land, sir?" She had tied the colorful scarf around her neck, and her earlobes were now adorned with the famous H monogram.

"No. I think you've done all you could have to make this flight as enjoyable as possible for me."

"Thank you. I very much enjoyed my time with you as well, sir." She turned and walked toward the front of the aircraft to take her seat. She looked over her shoulder and smiled before she sat down and buckled in for landing. He smiled, but not at her. She couldn't see him anymore anyway.

He wasn't smiling because he was on his sixty-five-million-dollar jet drinking forty-year-old scotch and smoking fresh Cuban cigars. It wasn't even because he had duped some starry-eyed gold-digger into sleeping with him for a twenty-dollar fake. Basileus was smiling at the thought of the other four orange boxes stowed in his travel bag. He chuckled at the image in his mind. Maybe he'd break his own rule about having a new flight attendant on his next trip. Christina was a firecracker, and she'd done everything in her power to show him how appreciative she was. He figured maybe next time he could interest her in the box set.

CHAPTER NINE

The Workshop, NYC
February 1, 12:08 p.m.

"What do you mean they won't die?" Aliyah asked, a look of deep concern furrowing her brow.

"Well, maybe I should clarify my statement. There's nothing I've found yet that is capable of killing the organism that wouldn't also sterilize the soil and destroy anything planted in it for the foreseeable future," Daedalus explained. "This peculiar bacteria seems to be attacking the root system of the plant. It looks to be feeding off the nutrients and starving the plant, or it's injecting some kind of toxin into the roots. Maybe both, we just don't know yet. That's one of the reasons you were chosen, Dr. Tzion, to lead our biological pursuits. We also found trace amounts of alcohol in the affected areas, but much of it may have evaporated before we ran our tests, so the exact concentration is anyone's guess."

Dallas looked up from his laptop. "So? What's the big deal if we gotta torch a couple of farmers' fields? Scoop up the old dirt, truck in new dirt, plant some new carrots or some shit like that, problem solved."

Chief was about to comment on the primitive tone and detail Dallas had just outlined in his proposed solution but didn't want to give him the satisfaction of knowing that his previous hack on him even registered.

"The problem with that idea, Mr. Hayle," Daedalus said, "is that this organism doesn't stay at the surface. It spreads across the kill zone but also reaching deep down into the soil. The ground has been sterilized to such an extent that replacing the affected soil over any significant area would be next to impossible and certainly not practical."

"I don't understand," Phil said. "I thought you said this was contained for now. Why wouldn't replacing the diseased soil be a possible solution?"

"If this were to remain isolated, and we only had to remedy a few locations, we could do exactly that. However, if this were to spread through the midwestern states, the breadbasket of America, the problem would be insurmountable. Same thing goes for the prairie provinces in Canada and the grain belt in Ukraine. The amount of remediation would be too large of a problem to fix. Everyone would be looking for the same soil, nutrients, and fertilizers at the same time. There just aren't that many resources to address such a widespread problem all at once."

"But that's not the real problem, is it?" All eyes once again turned back to Aliyah.

"How can that not be the real problem? Sounds pretty fucking terrible to me," Dallas remarked.

"Because this organism will kill the crops at the root level, rendering the surrounding soil sterile," Aliyah said. "Based on what we've just been told, that's not a problem that can be fixed in months or even years."

"Yeah, I heard all that before," Dallas said. "Why isn't that our big problem, though?"

"Because long before we have to deal with the soil replacement issue, we'll have a far bigger problem to address." Gryph noticed Dallas was going to interrupt with another question, so he held his hand up and hurried to conclude his explanation. "If this spreads as quickly as we think it can, it will devastate the planet's food supply. There won't be enough grain or rice to feed the people of the world, nevermind the grain and grass products the livestock industry relies on. Farm-raised proteins would disappear. Red meat, poultry, eggs, dairy—they'd all be wiped out in weeks, leading to a worldwide famine. The crops in the ground would die before they could be harvested, and the soil wouldn't be able to grow anything for who knows how many years. There's no time to prepare or stockpile anything; it's already started. If this bacterium were to spread around the globe unchecked, billions of people would die from starvation within the year. I've worked alongside the UN in Africa on previous missions, and I've watched as adults and children starved to death. It's a terribly painful way to die. I can't even begin to comprehend what that would look like on a planetary scale."

"Okay, I take it back. That's much fucking worse," Dallas said. "We need to do something, tell someone in the government, or let people know through the media. People need to take precautions, stock up on food and shit." He was now pale and looked panicked, the severity of the problem finally registering.

"No, the last thing we want is for people to find out," Gryph said. "If this organism spreads beyond our control, there's nothing that can be done anyway. The famine would last for years and, unfortunately, we wouldn't last long enough to fix the problem. If the public were to get wind of this, it would cause panic in the streets. You saw how people hoarded toilet paper and basic supplies during the pandemic when there was no need. Can you imagine how dangerous things would be if governments told people the world was about to run out of food? It would be madness. Riots, looting, and much worse would ensue. The fabric of society would unravel as people got more desperate. I imagine it wouldn't look much different from one of those post-apocalyptic zombie shows."

Everyone sat with that sobering thought for a moment.

"So, what was it exactly that killed the animals?" Aliyah asked, bringing the group's focus back to the problem at hand. "You've demonstrated that there are numerous ways this organism could be killing the plants. Have you figured out if the substance is toxic to animals, or are they only dying after ingesting the infected grasses and grains?"

"Hey, guys, what are we calling this thing?" Dallas asked. "Is it a poison or a toxin now? There are far too many nouns for me to keep straight. I don't understand half the shit you guys say anyway, and I'm likely not paying attention to the other half. I've got my own problems to deal with, not that anyone cares. Anyway, we should call this thing something badass, like the Megadeath Bug or, wait, how about something funny, like Tiny Bastards? You know, keep it light and airy. We could say, 'Have the Tiny Bastards spread again? Or have we killed all the Tiny Bastards yet?'" he said, laughing hysterically at his own joke. Gryph's psychology expertise told him this was just an attempt to mask the fear Dallas was feeling. Gryph didn't hold it against the computer genius though. It wasn't every day that someone found out the world was on the verge of annihilation.

"We're not calling this organism Tiny Bastards," Aliyah said, shaking her head while trying to suppress a laugh. "I don't think Super-death Bug would instill much hope in people either. If word got out, that is." Dallas was a crack-up, and the break in the doom and gloom was a welcome respite.

"For the record, I said Megadeath, not Super-death, but you're the scientist, so whatever you think is best." He smiled, and for an instant, Aliyah saw a thaw in his frosty exterior.

"Okay, we'll compromise a bit, Dallas. Let's stick to your earlier suggestion—and call it a toxin. It's a noun, it's simple, and ultimately, this kills whatever it touches. If that's not the bullseye description of a toxin, I don't know what is."

"Well, I'm glad that important issue is settled." Gryph was losing the battle to keep a straight face, partly because Dallas really was a funny guy, but also because he was happy with the way the team was coming together. The group had just received word that the vast majority of humankind was in imminent peril, yet they all seemed to take it in stride. He thought it much better that they laughed and joked to reduce the stress than succumb to the pressure and fear that such news could bring.

"Getting back to Ali's question about the cattle, we're not sure if the toxin itself is killing the cattle or if it's the grass they feed on that's poisoning them. We're hoping Ali's molecular biology expertise can help us answer that."

"Daedalus, you said earlier you hadn't found anything practical that could kill this toxin," Aliyah said. "Have you determined what exactly it is about this bacterium that protects it from commercial pesticides or the use of antibiotics?" She knew there were numerous strains of bacteria that were becoming resistant to all known antibiotics. Superbugs were what they were being called. Was this a new strain or possibly a variant of an existing one?

"The previous research team was working on that very question," Daedalus said. "I believe they made some progress with the biology, but were wrestling with the issues that the diminutive size of the toxin presented, more so than the toxicology of the specimen itself. We did, however, notice something extraordinary when we were examining the samples. Let me show you."

Daedalus retrieved his small tablet once again, and a moment later, the screens suspended above the group bloomed to life, displaying a video of the microscopic toxin under slightly less magnification than the static image of the single green-and-yellow cell they were just shown. The shot showed seven or eight of the cells moving aimlessly around under the microscope's field of view.

Aliyah stared at the screen, then back at Daedalus. Her eyes were wide, face full of confusion. Daedalus nodded as he watched her process the sight. He could almost see the gears turning behind her pale green eyes.

"That's impossible." Aliyah's voice was almost a whisper. She tilted her head to the side, as if changing the orientation would somehow give her additional perspective. Her face was bunched up in confusion as she focused on the slow-moving cells.

"And yet, there it is," Daedalus said, his eyes fixed on the screen. "Like I said, Ali, it's all very extraordinary."

"Uh, sorry guys, again, I'm totally lost. Those little blobs up there…" Dallas pointed to the monitors. "They're just swimming around. I'm no scientist, but I didn't see them attack anything, and they didn't grow bigger or replicate or change at all. Why are you all freaking out? She looks like she just saw an alien screwing a unicorn." He nudged his head in Aliyah's direction. She didn't seem to notice or care; her eyes fixed on the video.

"The fact that they're *just swimming around* is what's freaking me out," she continued. "Honestly, I'd be less shocked if I saw the unicorn. Let me explain, guys. As we pointed out earlier, this toxin is smaller than any known bacteria. That alone is incredible, and an entire field of biology could be dedicated to it. Anyway, to view something that small, you have to use an electron microscope. Electron microscopes use electrons instead of a beam of light to view a sample under magnification. They can also view objects a thousand times smaller than even the smallest bacteria. Another benefit to using electron microscopes, is that they also provide a much more detailed picture than traditional microscopes. With me so far?"

Nods around the room prompted her to continue.

"The major downside to using these microscopes is the inability to view living cells. The electrons used to create the scan destroy the sample as the image is created. To make it even more inhospitable, all of this is taking place in a vacuum chamber. That's how the electron charge is contained and focused."

She paused to ensure everyone was tracking with her before she continued.

"Gentleman, what we're looking at here is an organism that can exist in a vacuum, be bombarded with electrons, and somehow still survive! And it happens to be smaller than any other known bacteria on Earth. It's obvious now why traditional methods of eradicating this have been ineffective. I've never heard of anything like this, nevermind seeing it up close."

Aliyah's last sentence hung in the air as everyone absorbed the details of her impromptu science lesson.

"Something must be protecting that cell," she said. "Maybe some type of external membrane we haven't seen before. If this type of cellular protection could be harnessed, it could lead to new treatments in disease, and in, well, everything. It would open up a new world of targeted medicine. 'Game changer' isn't a strong enough term."

"I'm looking forward to having you get to work on answering those very questions," Daedalus said. "We have a lab set up here with every piece of equipment you'd ever hope to have and a few proprietary pieces of our own that I think you'll find helpful in your research."

Judging from what she had seen so far, Aliyah was certain he'd be true to his word.

"The one thing I haven't heard any real discussion on yet is how, or where, this started," Phil said. "Also, do we know yet if this is a naturally occurring type of thing, or was it manufactured somewhere?" It was the first thing Phil had said for a while. He too had been too unnerved by the dangers facing the planet.

Daedalus took his seat and sighed. "The answer to that question brings us full circle to the reason I put this team together. I'll leave it to Commander Oake to elaborate further."

Gryph took the cue to resume the narrative. "The one thing we know for certain is that this toxin was engineered. This isn't some random freak of nature. Unfortunately, we don't know where it was created, nor do we have any confirmation of why it was deployed. Yet."

"Why would someone want to develop something that would wipe out most of humankind?" Chief asked. "That wouldn't benefit anyone unless they're just into some new kind of crazy. Maybe our bad guy has a Thanos complex." He was a huge Marvel movie fan and was referring to the villain in the movie who tried to erase half of the living beings in the universe with magical stones with the snap of his fingers. "Gryph and I have had a lot of experience with the type of assholes who get off on killing others for kicks, and we've faced the worst of the worst." Aliyah and Phil looked surprised when they found out that Gryph and Chief had a shared history. "They're either in it for the money, or they're extremist lunatics. Destroying the world doesn't sound very profitable to me, and this is way too complex for your local terrorist yahoos to dream up. Like the doc said, she's never seen anything like this, and I'm sure she's seen it all. No one cooked this little bug up in some rogue lab in a cave in the desert."

Something mentioned earlier was still bothering Phil.

"Gryph, I'm not sure why you're saying we don't have any confirmation that this was purposefully deployed. This was no accident. We've seen almost a dozen locations all over the globe where Daedalus found this toxin, and there's no apparent connection between the different locations. These guys knew what it would do after the first time they deployed it, and they sure as hell knew after the fifth or sixth. They're up to something, and it's not going to be good."

"I've got a question for Daedalus too," Dallas said, piling on. "You mentioned all this previous study and work you completed a few times now. I've been here a month, and until two weeks ago, the only person I saw in the Workshop was you and this big gorilla." He hooked his thumb over toward Chief. "And then he showed up a couple days after." Dallas pointed at Gryph. "Then the rest of you showed up." Dallas swept his arm in an overly dramatic arc, encompassing everyone at the table. "What I don't get is, where are all the people who did that work before us? When I got here, all the servers and drives were in dire need of some TLC. It's like everyone just went home and didn't bother coming back." This was the first bit of history on Daedalus or the project the newcomers were getting. Aliyah wondered how much of it, if any, Gryph knew already. "And it's not like they've come back since, either. So, Daedalus, what's really going on? We have a right to know."

Daedalus could see Gryph was about to come to his defense, but signaled that he would address the inquisitor himself. It wasn't that Gryph was in the dark. In fact, he'd been fully briefed prior to accepting the assignment—including the details that Daedalus was about to reveal. He also understood why their benefactor would want to deliver this sensitive piece of information himself, so he sat down and waited for the story to be told.

"I had an extremely loyal and brilliant team working tirelessly on researching the origins and biology of this... toxin. Many of them spent their entire post-doctorate careers helping me develop the nanotechnology you saw earlier, among a myriad of other projects. It was almost an accident, discovering this deadly bacterium. We were fortunate enough to be looking at everything at that infinitesimally small nano scale for our research already. We had the right tools and the right people at the right time. We also had a very capable security detail that was, and still is, bolstered by various branches of the US government. Some of it official assistance, some less so."

Curious looks went around the table. Dallas then realized that Daedalus must have marshaled the brute computing force of a group like the NSA or the CIA to break through his firewalls to track him down. He could out-hack nearly anyone, but no one was better than the NSA.

"So, we're really part of a secretive government agency? Some black ops shit. I knew it!" Dallas shouted.

"No, Mr. Hayle. We don't work for the government. They do, however, ask us to assist them in matters where we have some unique insight and abilities."

"Oh, I see it now. That's very informative, sir. Really clears things up. Very detailed explanation. Good chat, thanks."

Daedalus closed his eyes at Dallas's sarcasm and continued with the story of his previous research team. "I had reassigned everyone from their tasks at the Workshop to focus exclusively on the toxin. I split the group into three teams with the intent to retrieve samples from the infected sites in Canada, Russia, and China. We sent along a standard security detail with each team. These security details, while armed, are generally used for travel and logistical services and to keep any locals from amateur kidnapping attempts, theft, or simply meddling in our affairs. Remember, we're primarily a scientific organization, not military, regardless of our ties to some in the sector. We've always taken measures to protect what we have created vigorously, but they've rarely been deployed."

Daedalus sent a few image files from his mobile to the screens above as he spoke.

"My entire team in China was ambushed. They'd made camp a few hundred feet from the edge of the dead zone, and sometime during the night, they were attacked. I was to meet them the next day." He paused briefly and reflected on that horrible day. "We found the two perimeter guards at their posts, their throats slashed. The tents were torn to shreds by fifty-caliber rounds, based on the brass casings left at the site. The people inside, the team I sent there, never knew what was happening in those last moments of their lives." Daedalus looked off into the corner, as his eyes lost focus. The enormous toll the loss of his team had on him was palpable.

"I keep telling myself that it was over quickly, that most of them didn't wake up when they were under fire. Deep down I know that's probably not exactly true, but the alternative is too horrific for me to think about." He snapped back out of his self-induced trance. "By the time we made it to the site, it was too late. There were no survivors. We tried in vain to reach the teams in Russia and warn them as soon as we discovered the carnage in China, but no one answered our calls. We called in an emergency evac and had special ops teams at both locations within hours of our discovery in China. By the time they arrived at the other sites, they found the same bloodbaths we did."

The group around the table was deathly quiet. They could see that even now Daedalus was deeply wounded by the loss of life under his watch.

"I've dedicated every hour of my day to hunting down the animals who murdered those innocent people while they slept. Immediately after we discovered what happened, I sent some ex-special force's soldiers across the globe to find the killers. I called in a few favors and secured the assistance of some assets in China and Russia, as well. They would never allow US forces to operate on their soil—regardless of the immense favors they owed me. Both countries had lethal strike teams, assigned by their handlers for this mission to assist me. I was promised only the very best would be sent. We located some of the people involved in each of the three countries where the attacked took place, one group just hours before they were about to board a merchant ship and disappear. We managed to capture and interrogate a few, but none of them were of much use. Just a bunch of hired mercenaries, too far down in the food chain to know anything of real value. Those who fought or resisted were killed like the dogs they were."

Daedalus spat on the floor. Even the memory of those vile men was a bitter taste in his mouth. "I'll never forgive myself for allowing it to happen. They weren't prepared to go into battle; that wasn't the world they lived in. It was an unfair fight and one that I have vowed never to lose again. The next time we face this enemy, we'll all be in a much better position, simply because we know they're out there this time around."

"Hold on. Lemme get this straight," Dallas said. "We're all second-string replacements for the people who were brutally murdered during the last job you sent them on. If that's really what's going on, then I'm—"

"That isn't the case at all." Daedalus pounded the stone table and stood up tall, taking in the group with a penetrating stare. "The team we had here were like family to me, and their loss will haunt me for the rest of my days, however long that may be. With the exception of two of them, none of those souls had any training in combat. They were engineers and PhDs, not sergeants and captains. Their research and contributions will live on. I will make certain of that."

The gaps in the story were narrowing, and it didn't look good. The challenge they faced wasn't just the impossible task of quickly discovering a way to kill a bug that was somehow engineered not to die, they also had to do it while being hunted by an enemy who was trying to destroy the world for some unknown reason and obviously had no issue with killing anyone who got in their way.

"Each of you were handpicked because of various meritorious acts you have performed in the past as well as your unique skills and knowledge. A person's actions speak louder than anything. Please don't think for a moment that I view any of you as replacements or less important in any way. Each of you brings tremendous value individually, but together your skills complement each other perfectly. You really are greater than the sum of your parts, and I can tell you with certainty that the talent and experience in the group I see before me is better positioned for success than any team I have ever assembled."

"I had never even heard of Daedalus until a couple of weeks ago, but I've known Gryph a long time now," Chief said. "We served in the SEALs together and stayed close even after he decided to jump into the alphabet soup." Referring to the jumble of letters and acronyms that plagued the intelligence industry, he gave Gryph a toothy smile before he continued. "I don't want to blow sunshine up his ass, but Gryph is a legend in SEAL circles. One of the greatest to wear the uniform. A born leader. I'd follow this guy to the end of the earth and back. And to be honest, I've done it once or twice already. If Gryph is leading the charge, I'm all in. My boy Oake here will get the job done." Gryph was trying not to acknowledge the kind words, but the flush in his cheeks betrayed him.

"Well, I think it's clear why I'm here now, and even though this is uncharted waters, much of my research can be applied to this problem," Aliyah said. "And even though I'm not sure what each of our roles is yet, I promise you that if we need to get somewhere quickly, our friend Phil here will get you where you need to go faster than you ever thought possible." She said with a smile.

Phil smiled at the compliment, relieved she was able to make light of the death-defying ride she'd endured earlier.

"I know I'm here to be the master of all things digital, and I also know I'm the best there is, so good job, Daedalus. Seems like you really did put together a rockstar team." That was as close to an unsolicited apology as Dallas was going to give.

"I'm relieved and grateful that you all now realize you have been chosen not as a last resort, but as our best hope to prevent this apocalypse." Daedalus was satisfied that they could finally see the situation for what it truly was.

"I'll be working on locating the source of the toxin in the hope that it leads us to the head of the snake running this operation," Gryph said. "Aliyah will focus on the characteristics of the toxin itself and do reconnaissance work at some of the affected sites. We need to understand what's causing the livestock to die before this situation gets worse. Dallas will be supporting the communications and tech for all our missions. Phil will be providing logistical support, transportation, and security details. Chief will support ground ops, weapons, demolition, and excavation... if required. We can on some additional support staff as we get rolling if need be, but we need to stay small and remain nimble for now. Don't forget, there are people out there looking to put us in the ground. Keep your heads down and your eyes and ears alert. Any questions?"

Aliyah raised her hand, and Gryph nodded in her direction. "What are we planning to do if we find the... what did you call it? The 'head of the snake?' We may be too late already."

"We have no choice but to try. There are too many lives at stake not to do everything in our power to stop this from spreading. Again, we can't really call outsiders for help on this. News like this can't be contained in this day and age, and if this were leaked to the public, the damage would already be done. It would be chaos and anarchy overnight. Even if we're able to contain the toxin, the fallout from the civic unrest and panic would be catastrophic. I'm afraid it's just us for now."

"You know, you didn't really answer Ali's question," Dallas said. "About what we'll would do, ya know... to the snake."

Daedalus jumped out of his chair, startling everyone around the table. "I'll tell you what we're going to do. We're going to squeeze the head of this snake until it tells us how to stop its venom from poisoning the planet." His voice was seething with vengeance. "Once its deceitful tongue has spilled its secrets and has no further use, I'm going to chop its fucking head off!"

"Sheesh. Take it easy, Dracula," Dallas said, holding his hands up in mock surrender. "That works just fine for me. One less bad guy in the world, the way I see it. This asshole seems to be a major league douche anyway. You won't see me shedding any tears for him."

The rest of the table turned to Aliyah. After all, it was her question that was being answered, and no one knew what she thought of Daedalus's outburst. "Why are you all looking at me?" she asked. "I agree with Daedalus. Whoever is behind this, they're way past evil and need to be put down. Permanently."

Gryph was happy to see the team had aligned philosophically. The monsters they were after had no qualms about killing innocent people and had developed a pathogen with the ability to destroy most, if not all, of humanity. They weren't looking for justice in a court of law. Their brand of justice would be swift and severe.

"Looks like we're in complete agreement here. Unless there's anything else, let's get settled in. We have a lot to accomplish, and time is not on our side."

"Just one thing." Chief turned to Daedalus. "Are any of those new weapons you were telling me about ready yet?"

"Follow me, Chief" Daedalus said with a wicked grin. "You're going to love this."

CHAPTER TEN

The Labyrinth
February 5, 5:36 a.m.

Gryph carefully walked toward the tall cylindrical white towers perched above the electron microscope. Any slip up in his footing would cause irreparable damage and waste the product he had worked so diligently to concoct. A few strides later, he found himself standing over the hunched figure at the base of the machine.

"Good mor—" was all he could get out before Aliyah jumped back with a shriek, the wheels under her chair rolling effortlessly until she stopped the momentum with her foot on the stone floor.

Gryph anticipated the oncoming collision and got the scorching hot liquid out of the way just as Aliyah moved, saving them both from a bad burn. Gryph's years of training helped hone his cat-like reflexes. Those skills saved his life more times than he could remember, and was relieved they'd helped him avoid this mini disaster too.

Aliyah stared back with wide eyes as everything started to register.

Gryph was standing with his arms out wide, carrying a cup of steaming coffee in each hand. He also bore a shocked look on his face which was melting into relief.

"Uh... good morning, Ali. Thought you could use some coffee," Gryph said while lifting the two cups as a visual explanation for his intrusion.

Aliyah hadn't heard him approach, having been engrossed in her work. The smell of the coffee didn't register before and was just now wafting across her nostrils. "Geez, you scared me half to death, Gryph."

"Sorry. I wasn't trying to sneak up on you. I figured you would have heard me coming a mile away with my boots and all. Anyway, I thought you could use a fresh cup before the briefing this morning." He placed the hot beverage on a small portable steel table a few feet away.

He's right. I should have heard him coming, Ali thought, but she was beyond exhausted. The last week had been grueling. She'd only taken a few power naps the past couple days, and the lack of sleep had finally caught up to her. She wasn't even sure she'd been awake when Gryph first walked in. Ali caught herself nodding off a couple of times while working into the early hours of the morning already, but knew time wasn't on their side, even though she had been making great progress. Ali wanted to keep the momentum going, but was finding it hard just keeping her eyes open.

"You must have got an early start this morning. Getting some last-minute prep in before you present to the team?" Gryph asked.

Aliyah pushed herself back from the workstation she'd been at for the past eighteen hours. "I wish. I haven't really left since I got here yesterday. I just need a hot shower and some of that." Pointing to the cup of coffee that Gryph had brought in.

The rich aroma from the pair of steaming mugs filled the room. Aliyah rolled her shoulders back and straightened her spine, working the stiffness out of her back. Tiny pops and cracks escaped her joints as she reached up and stretched. She stifled a yawn and scooted her chair over to the table to get some much-needed caffeine into her bloodstream. She took a tentative sip, smiled, and followed it with a larger gulp, feeling the deliciously bitter liquid sink into her belly. "I think this may have just saved my life. Bless you." She exhaled deeply across the top of the mug and took another sip.

Gryph laughed. "No problem, sorry about the scare. What were you working on? Find anything that could help us?" He didn't want to get his hopes up or make it seem like he was putting any more pressure on Aliyah than she was already under.

"I wish I could tell you that I had a eureka moment, Gryph, but it didn't come last night, I'm afraid. We've made a lot of progress this week though, but a few things still defy all explanation.

We can get into it in more detail when I present my findings to the team in a bit."

Gryph knew she was running on fumes and didn't want to press her for the details before she was ready. "Is there anything you want that Daedalus hasn't provided? I'm sure he can get whatever you need to accelerate the process. I'm happy to push him on your behalf."

"No, that's definitely not the problem. In fact, I don't understand how he's even in possession of some of the equipment he has in this lab, to be honest. Some of the technology here is a decade or more along in development than anything I've ever seen. Like this microscope, for instance." Aliyah waved her hand at the black control console that contained an array of buttons, switches, and more than a few joysticks at the bottom of the white telescoping metal casing.

"What do you mean? You're telling me that he has better stuff in this cave than the labs at Quantico and Langley, or even your research labs at Technion in Israel? I would've thought you got to play with the best money could buy."

"That's just it, Gryph, there's nothing better out there anywhere. On my recent trip to Boston, I was invited to tour a brand-new research incubator that just so happened to be developing the next generation of electron microscopes. My research in virology requires extensive use of that extremely sensitive equipment."

Aliyah's reputation in the scientific community had given her VIP access to the latest and greatest technological advancements in her field. A recommendation from her could help secure funding or open the doors to labs and universities looking to purchase the equipment or license the technology further.

"During the tour of the incubator, I was shown images they had recently processed with their new experimental electron microscope. They achieved a resolution that got down to within half the width of a hydrogen atom. There's nothing else even close to that level of resolution in the market. It's truly ground-breaking technology. Or at least I thought so. I was told it would be years before it would be available for commercial use." Aliyah scrolled through her phone to show him some pictures she took of her visit to the lab in Boston for some additional context.

"So, let's tell Daedalus that we need this one-of-a-kind super scope. I'm sure he'd—"

"Gryph, the scope I'm using here is running magnifications ten times more powerful than the experimental one I saw, maybe even more. It makes Boston's look obsolete by comparison. And it's not just the microscope either. Nearly every piece of equipment in this lab is far more advanced than its counterpart in the world outside this Workshop. There's equipment in here using technology that's still theoretical as far as the rest of the world is concerned, and yet here it's already fully developed and operational."

Gryph nodded. "I don't doubt that for a minute based on everything else I've seen around here, too. He's shown me some advanced weaponry using tech I've never even heard of before. Next level shit. Even if you're right, doesn't that provide a huge advantage for us in finding a solution?"

"Don't get me wrong, it's been an immense help. There are things that we discovered in days that would have easily taken months or years anywhere else. It's all a bit surreal though. Also, the work done by the previous team was impeccable. I get how replacing them would be next to impossible. Many of them were geniuses in their own right. Having them working together here, collaboratively, without any red tape or politics, with an unlimited budget... I can see how they managed to get some of this going, but still..." Aliyah couldn't get over the technology that Daedalus had running in the Labyrinth. "I'm going to grab a not-so-quick shower and try to feel, and look a little more human. I'll see you at the table at seven bells." She took the rest of her coffee with her as she headed toward the door.

"Okay, sounds good. I'll run some more coffee through the press before you start. It'll help keep you on your toes until you get a chance to lie down for a bit, which I highly recommend you do ASAP." Gryph had been making coffee with a specialized gravity press for himself and the team all week. He appreciated truly good coffee and shared his passion for the bean with everyone. The group really loved their java too, but more for the effects of the caffeine than the taste, and had proven that they would drink whatever quantity was provided. As of late, he felt more like a part-time barista than their Commander.

"I'm not sure if they have an employee-of-the-month program here, but if they do, you have my vote, Gryph." Aliyah laughed over her shoulder as she walked back toward the residences that Daedalus had provided for them. That little perk was a surprise to them all. Daedalus told them they were free to live anywhere they chose, but preferred that they all stay onsite, knowing there would be many late nights followed by many early mornings. Having the option of staying at the Workshop was a much more efficient use of everyone's time.

What they hadn't been expecting were the unique amenities that had been incorporated into the stone cavern. Each residence was a singular offshoot of the Labyrinth. There looked to be over a dozen completed residences of varying sizes they already identified on the schematics that were provided as part of their onboarding. Prior to Daedalus developing and finishing the dwellings, each residence was, in essence, just a simple cave-like structure. Over fifty individual pods had been mapped throughout the Labyrinth. The micro cityscape spread under the vastness of NYC and was invisible to everyone above thanks to the nanobots lining the dome.

The average size of each residence was just over a thousand feet. Some were over twice that size, and the smallest was just under eight hundred feet square. Each had its own unique shape and topography. Some had soaring cathedral-like ceilings, while others boasted two-level structures. Much of the surrounding rockwork was infused into the design element of the residence, giving them all a unified theme but their own characteristics. If the Four Seasons had a subterranean hotel, it would have looked very much like what had been created in the Labyrinth. Each unit had a full kitchen, private workspace, bedroom, and a luxurious bathroom. It had been developed with expansion plans in mind. The current team would barely put a dent in the total capacity. The Workshop and the Labyrinth were massive structures to be sure, but in overall scale, they were nothing but little bubbles in the rock under a tiny part of a very large city.

The team was beyond delighted when Daedalus told them to pick their favorite residence and make themselves at home. Dallas had been relegated to the smallest residence since he'd arrived ahead of the team, but was now being offered a chance to relocate.

It was the first time anyone saw him happy and smiling, however short the effect may have lasted.

Each person on the team selected their residence based on their personal tastes and preferences. The first room Phil walked into featured massive natural stone arches that peaked high above the floor. The surface of the wall on one side of the room was punctured by colorful rock-climbing holds, and the opposite wall offered only natural handholds in the rock face used in free climbing. Free climbers didn't use ropes or anchors, just chalk, skill, and courage. While not a professional climber, Phil could free climb as well as traverse vertical faces with ropes. He couldn't pass up the opportunity, so he staked his claim right then and there.

Aliyah had picked a residence across the hall from Phil. She didn't care which one she ended up in. Each room she'd seen was as gorgeous as the last, so she just chose the closest door to where she was standing. The balance of the team occupied the rooms directly adjacent to each other. By the time everyone had picked their spot, the group found themselves in a tight cluster together.

With one exception. Dallas decided that instead of taking a spot directly beside the team, he would make the most of the opportunity to upgrade. The largest residence shown was about forty-five hundred square feet and was situated at the far end of the wing from where the rest of their rooms were. It was now *Chez Lama,* or so the sign on the door stated in Dallas's messy scrawl via an oversized yellow post-it note, affixed haphazardly to his large wooden door.

The distance didn't make any logistical difference to them. Dallas's "remote" location was less than a thirty-second walk from the rest of the team. Aliyah told Phil and Gryph in confidence that she had a feeling Dallas didn't really want to be there. Phil suggested that it was Dallas's lone hacker persona and that he was just there to do a job, not make friends. Plus, the fact that he was there in the first place spoke to his character, even if he came across as an asshole most of the time. *It's not like Daedalus held a gun to his head*, he thought. Everyone else seemed to relish the opportunity, but Aliyah thought that Dallas seemed like he always had one foot out the door. *Time will tell.*

It was a few minutes before 7 a.m. when Aliyah made her way to the massive stone table where they had been meeting regularly for their updates throughout the week. Everyone was there already, anxious to hear what she had learned. The smell of coffee wafted up from the table. Steaming cups were being passed around when she joined the group.

"Thank you." She said, accepting her second cup that morning, "I didn't get much sleep, to be honest. There were a few things I couldn't wrap my head around. I wouldn't have slept much even if I tried—and believe me, I did. I decided to work the problem from a different angle, and I think I may have found something. I have more work to do, but it could be a solid lead."

Aliyah glanced back at the table and saw everyone focused intently on her conversation with Daedalus. She typed something on her laptop bringing the screens above the large stone table to life. With all the group had absorbed over the past week, it seemed impossible they'd only been there for such a short period of time. It already felt as if they were long-lost friends who'd been reunited after some time apart, but were now simply catching up with each other and falling into old routines. The level of comfort and camaraderie they already felt belied the brief time they had spent with each other.

"I'll start off bringing you up to speed on my latest findings. As you know, I've spent the last week examining this organism in as many ways as I know how, and a few that I didn't even think were possible." Aliyah took a deep breath. "We've all been told that this toxin somehow kills all the vegetation it touches, yet we can't kill it. Something was also killing the livestock in these affected areas, and we weren't sure exactly what was causing that either. Those were the first questions I set out to answer after the previous group was… lost."

Any time that the murdered scientists had been mentioned over the course of the week, it had reminded them of the additional threat they faced. Aliyah wanted them to focus and not be distracted by things they couldn't do anything about.

"Because of the exceptionally hard work put forth by everyone to date, I think we are now able to answer those questions and possibly a few more, although in some cases the answers may raise new questions of their own." Aliyah streamed an extremely close-up image of the toxic bacterial cell from her laptop to the screens above.

"I still cannot express how incredulous the size of this cell is on its own. I wondered at first if that's what was making it so difficult to eradicate, and while its size does complicate the issues we face, I don't believe it's the size of the organism itself that's causing the devastation we're seeing. In fact, I'm almost certain I know what's killing these crops and animals now." Ali could see they were all anxious for her to reveal the secret, so she continued without pause. "Size aside, the cellular structure and features of this organism are quite unremarkable except for one thing, but it's a big thing, and I'll circle back to that soon. At first glance, the cell membrane, nucleus, mitochondria, and cytoplasm all appear to be normal." Aliyah used her trackpad to highlight the structures on screen as she gave her dissertation. "If you weren't made aware of the infinitesimal size or the devastation the alcohol was causing to the crops and animals, these little guys would have likely gone undiscovered. I couldn't figure out what made them so deadly or the unique feature they exhibited that made them impervious to our efforts to kill them. It didn't occur to me until last night that it might've had something to do with the actual makeup of the cell itself. Something Daedalus said to us a few days ago has been floating around in the back of my mind. He told us that together we were greater than the sum of our parts. It took me a while to make the connection, but it makes perfect sense." Aliyah could see that some of them didn't quite follow the analogy, so she backtracked a bit.

"There was nothing about the cell that should have made it so rugged. No unusual appendages or organelles were visible, but thanks to the gear Daedalus has provided, I was able to look closer than anyone would have thought possible."

Daedalus smiled at Ali's comment. He knew she was aware that the equipment in the Workshop was beyond state of the art.

"You remember how shocked I was when we first saw the video of these cells surviving inside the vacuum chamber under the electron bombardment. Well, it turns out I have a bit of good news on that front. When I inserted new samples of the toxin into the vacuum chamber and observed them again, they did, in fact, live for a while and again withstood the harsh environment, but after a few minutes, all the cells in the sample died. I ran this sequence a few times, then retested the toxin's cellular structure after they were removed from the chamber and placed back into ambient pressure. In every one of the tests, the toxin never recovered. It died."

"Wait, you really found a way to kill them?" Dallas exclaimed. "Way to go, Doc! That didn't take you long at all. Now we can finally get the hell out of this cave."

"That isn't a viable method to kill them, Dallas. It was just a bench experiment. We can't put a farmer's field into a vacuum chamber, but it did prove they aren't invincible. Gryph and I explored additional methods of attacking the toxin. During one of our first attempts, we utilized a few of our own nanobots to pierce the toxin's cellular membrane and extract some of the cytoplasm for further sample. Remember, the cytoplasm is the fluid inside the cell. Think of it like the blood in your body. While not a perfect analogy, it's close enough for this explanation. Let me show you."

Aliyah changed the image on the screen, and a single toxin cell was displayed on the monitor. "Dallas helped me program the bots to form a nano-sized collection device to retrieve a sample of the cytoplasm, and that's when everything started to fall into place."

She switched to the next slide in the presentation. "When the nano-needle punctured and tore open the cell membrane and began the extraction, a strange reaction occurred that released an unidentified compound from every component of the cell. An 'all for one and one for all' type of approach, if you will. Within seconds, this mysterious compound repaired the portion of the cell wall that was damaged by the needle. During this repair, we observed another fascinating occurrence. The compound released by the cell gave off some form of bioluminescence during the healing process, and once the repair was complete, everything stopped glowing. The cell was completely normal and as healthy and whole as it was before we'd punctured it."

"How could this cell produce bioluminescence?" Chief asked. "I thought that just came from plankton and marine organisms." He had his chin resting on his massive fist in a contemplative pose. He looked like a swollen version of Rodin's 'The Thinker'.

"Puh-lease," Dallas said. "Like you have any idea what the hell bioluma-whatever is. Stop trying to impress the pretty lady by acting all fancy. You're not her type, Billy boy. I'm sure she's restricted her dating pool to the same species. You're still a caveman." Dallas snorted.

"Bioluminescence is caused by a molecule called luciferin which glows when it's exposed to oxygen," Chief continued, ignoring the interruption. "It's found in plankton, algae, and some marine creatures like jellyfish, giant squid, and anglerfish. Want me to go on?" The stunned look on Dallas's face was answer and satisfaction enough.

Billy K laughed. "I've been a Navy SEAL Chief for well over a decade, buddy," he said, addressing Dallas. "You may have heard of us. We go scuba diving and jump out of planes while we hunt down bad guys, and sometimes get to blow shit up. If it can be seen on a dive, I've seen it before."

Gryph and Billy K had done hundreds of deep-water dives together, many of them night dives. Special LED lights and waterproof night-vision goggles were used on such nighttime missions. It was common to see various types of bioluminescence in the water when an animal or plant with the luciferin gene was activated by their dive lights. When the underwater lights were turned off, the animal or plant would continue to glow, much like the glow-in-the-dark hands and markers on a watch.

Dallas went back to his sulking when he saw everyone trying to suppress smiles and cover fits of laughter with fake coughs.

Aliyah ignored the chuckles and answered Chief's question. "I'm not sure if it's caused by the same type of bioluminescence you've seen in the ocean, Chief, but the glow reminded me of exactly that. Anyway, we removed the cytoplasm from a few of the cells to run some tests, and we should have some preliminary results on that sometime this week."

"Ali, you said you made some headway on how this was killing the crops as well?" This question came from Daedalus, who had a concerned look on his face. Aliyah had noticed the change in his countenance after she finished her summary on the protective nature of the bacterium and the conversation about the bioluminescence.

"Yes, sir. I solved that part of the puzzle late last night."

This was good news and not something anyone at the table was aware of yet. The group was silent, not wanting to miss any of the information Aliyah was about to divulge. Even Dallas was paying close attention.

"This bacterium may have initially been designed and engineered with noble intentions, but I think one variable turned it into the deadly cancer that it's become. I'll get to that in a moment, but let me explain exactly what the toxin is doing that's causing the crops to die."

Dallas held up his hand. "Can you try and dumb it down for the rest of us non-scientists and resident marine biologist SEALs? No mumbo-jumbo. Pretty please with a nanobot on top."

She nodded and smiled. "Sure, no problem. It's really quite a simple answer anyway. They're dying from alcohol poisoning. It stands to reason that when animals ingest the infected grasses and feed, they also succumb to the effects of severe alcohol poisoning."

"Hold on," Dallas said, "you're saying these plants and animals are getting so wasted that they die?"

"Well, I don't think they're getting drunk per se, but I'm pretty certain they're dying from acute alcohol poisoning."

"Wow. I've gone on some benders that could have killed a cow, but yeesh. This one time in Vegas, me and these three strippers were doing shots and—"

"No one cares about your drinking exploits, Dallas. Will you stop interrupting and let her finish?" Chief had saved them all from what he was sure would be a NSFW story.

"Fine, whatever. Your loss. It was an awesome story. You don't deserve to hear it anyway." Dallas folded his arms over his chest and went back to sulking.

"Anyway," Aliyah continued, "I think this could've originally been developed as a novel approach to dealing with the parts of the plants that were to be discarded or destroyed, known as 'plant litter.' Many farmers burn off parts of their field to get rid of unwanted hay, roots, weeds, vines, and so on. This also helps keep diseases in the soil in check. However, the downside to this practice is that it causes significant air pollution, releasing smoke and particulate into the air. The fires themselves have been linked to many rural vehicular deaths as visibility plunges to near zero when the smoke drifts over the roadways. Respiratory illnesses and eye irritation are also commonly reported. It's an unhealthy practice for the planet and the people living in close proximity to where the burn is occurring. Unfortunately, it's a standard practice in the farming business and isn't likely to change anytime soon."

None of the team had any significant farming experience, so most of this was new to them.

"The bacteria may have originally been engineered to break down these plant litter by-products, as opposed to having to burn them. In theory, the bacteria would accelerate the plant litter decay rate, providing essential nutrients back to the soil, acting as a natural fertilizer. The unique trait this bacterium provided was the production of ethanol during this decomposition process. This grain alcohol—ethanol, as it's more commonly known— could be captured and used as biofuel or used for a wide range of fuel additives. It could even be used in products like hand sanitizer."

"How did something with such great potential turn into the monster we're facing now?" Gryph asked.

"The original design would likely have encapsulated the bacterium in some type of biodegradable shell, depending on the format. It would be a different formulation depending on if it was meant to be mixed into the topsoil, inside the seeds themselves or via some type of fertilizer. Each version would be formulated to dissolve at the proper time in the growth cycle and activated by specific PH levels, moisture content, or a host of other conditions. Basically, it could piggyback off anything that would eventually be planted in soil or used in the process of growing crops. However, the toxic variant we've been dealing with was engineered to take hold at the root level, so the entire plant would be at the mercy of its effect."

Aliyah brought another slide to the screens overhead. This time, it wasn't a picture of the bacterium or animals. The display featured a few charts and some startling figures.

"When the process is in full bloom, the cells do exactly what they should do, and they're very efficient at it. Unfortunately for the crops, they're too good. The bacteria produce ethanol at a concentration of approximately fifty parts per million, which may not sound like a lot, but just one part per million is fatal to any type of plant life. We chose a wide group of grains and grasses to test our hypothesis and observed the same result in all twelve samples. Each subject produced a lethal amount of alcohol at the root level of each plant. There was no way any of these plant species could survive in such a harsh environment. This infection would have the same effect on the roots that watering the plant with rubbing alcohol would. It would wither and die almost immediately. The damage irreparable. Any questions so far?"

Everyone shook their heads. Chief shot Dallas a look before he could even open his mouth to crack a joke.

"Whoever designed this originally must have counted on the bacteria dying off when the alcohol concentration reached a certain level, figuring it would snuff itself out so that the next batch of crops could be planted safely," Aliyah said. "It would have been quite an elegant symbiosis if it happened as they hoped it would. Unfortunately for all of us, this cell seems to be resistant to high concentrations of alcohol and almost everything else we've tried. There are some extremely toxic chemicals and some radioactive compounds we used that caused the cells to die, but adding these to our groundwater and food supply would be like eating farm fresh produce from Chernobyl going forward."

It didn't take a scientist to understand what she was implying.

"The real problem we're facing here, is that this toxin stays in the soil and doesn't die off. It feeds off any and all organic material and continues to produce alcohol as part of its cellular activity. For all intents and purposes, anywhere it finds something to feed on, it will devour it, and in doing so, salts the earth with a lethal dose of ethanol. All the vast microbiology that is found in healthy soil is destroyed. And it doesn't stop killing. Ever."

"Can't the farmers plant some new seeds? Maybe engineered against alcohol poisoning?" Phil asked. "And what about the dead animals we saw?"

"Even if we were to design and produce new soils or seeds— which could take years—they would be infected as soon as they began to grow and sprout. I think the animals are immune to the toxin itself, but the food they eat continues to produce alcohol, especially during their digestion, and eventually proves fatal. The cell seem to hold up well in the stomach acids of these animals, so the process goes unchecked. I also suspect that is what caused the beehive collapse we viewed earlier in the week. The pollen on their bodies could carry traces of the toxin too. The bees may have been unwitting culprits in spreading this. That's my working theory so far, but it's still early on."

"Ali, you've made incredible progress in such a short amount of time. Thank you!" Daedalus said. "I look forward to reviewing the details of your tests. Please let me know if you need anything to expedite your work."

"Thank you, Daedalus, but I think I have everything I need. I know this toxin can be defeated. We just need to discover the method before it's too late."

Everyone got up and took turns thanking Aliyah for the clear and concise presentation. She really had made a lot of progress in just a few short days, and they were all hoping the velocity of their problem solving continued at such a torrid pace. Before returning to their duties, the team used the impromptu huddle at the end of Ali's debrief to bring each other up to speed on their respective pieces of the puzzle.

Gryph remained seated at the table. He'd been looking in Daedalus's direction when Aliyah was making one of her points earlier on in the presentation. He was listening intently to Aliyah, while simultaneously watching his boss for any sort of sign that would give him additional insights into how much Daedalus really knew about what was going on.

Gryph happened to be an excellent poker player finishing deep in the money at three World Series of Poker events. He'd almost made it to the final table a few years back, but lost his chips to the eventual winner. He'd gone all in with a pair of kings but lost when a king came on the river, giving him three of a kind but also completing his opponent's straight. The last card knocked Gryph out of a tournament that he thought he'd have a real chance to win. He'd made the right move and had the man beat when he went all-in after the flop. He read the subtle body language change and calculated the other man's breathing rate by watching his chest rise and fall. Oake knew he'd just been unlucky that hand, but his observations had been spot on.

Those same observational skills told him something Aliyah had just said, upset Daedalus greatly. Gryph set out to determine exactly what it was.

CHAPTER ELEVEN

Downtown London
February 5, 8:06 p.m.

Basileus climbed into the backseat of his white Rolls Royce Phantom. The 560 hp luxury beast purred silently in the rain. The only other passenger in the rear of the vehicle was his body-guard, Dima. The driver sat silently behind the smoked-glass par-tition which afforded the two people in the back complete privacy.

The two men had met almost a decade earlier. Basileus had killed a man who tried to double-cross him during a weapons deal at the docks in London. The man he killed had snared Dima's sister, along with countless others, in his human trafficking racket. Basileus and his forces seized all the trafficker's illicit assets after killing him and his lackeys. The metal shipping container containing the weapons he purchased also held a few men and over two dozen women. Human trafficking was something he wanted nothing to do with. Not because of the morality of it all, it just wasn't as lucrative as his other ventures.

The report came back that not even half the women survived the treacherous journey. Two of the men survived but were in rough shape, having limited access to food or water for what was likely weeks. Basileus ordered his mercenaries to give the captives some food and drink and let them find their way back to whatever shitty life they had before. The bodies of the dead and injured smugglers that Basileus and company had dealt with were loaded into the con-tainer with the corpses of those who hadn't survived the original trip. He ordered his men to take the shipping container out to sea and scuttle it to the ocean floor. The smugglers they bound and trapped inside would have one more agonizing experience before their lives were snuffed out forever.

When Dima's sister was able to contact her family and tell them of her ordeal and benevolent savior, Dima made the trek to London, sought out Basileus, and pledged his loyalty as an eternal sign of his gratitude. The former soldier had no country worth fighting for, nor any other job prospects. The combination of the two, provided the requisite motivation to offer his deadly skill set to someone who might be able to provide him with a better life. He hadn't left Basileus's side since. Loyalty, he learned, was something that his new boss demanded—but also rewarded in equal measure.

"Tell your men to head back to the estate," Basileus ordered, as he dialed a number on his phone. Dima relayed instructions into his own mobile. A moment later, the two black Ducati sport bikes idling in front of them pulled away from the curb. The riders wore matte black bulletproof jackets and helmets, their HK MP5 submachine guns were barely concealed at their sides. The driver of the Rolls followed the bikes into traffic. The balance of Dima's security team followed them all in a large Mercedes SUV.

"Have you completed the last of the acquisitions?" Basileus asked the person on the other end of the line.

"Yes. We've executed the documents with the last of the holdouts this morning, sir," came the reply.

"Very good. See to it that we integrate our product into their supply immediately." Basileus ended the call without waiting for any acknowledgment.

The overcast skies and steady rain didn't look like they would let up anytime soon. The bikes stayed out in front as the convoy made its way through downtown London and out toward the English countryside.

Basileus looked at his reflection in the darkened glass. Even with the deep tint to the privacy screen, his thick, black hair and strong, chiseled jaw were indicative of a man in the prime of his life. He ran at least five miles every day, often using this time alone to clear his thoughts, feeling meditative despite the exertion. Basileus kept his physique hard by lifting weights, and the muscles he developed gave his body a deep V shape. However, if his brain were considered a muscle, it would be the strongest in his body.

He absorbed everything that happened around him. A man with his power and position would always have people trying to ride his coattails or stab him in the back. He was acutely aware of both.

The gloomy look outside matched the dismal mood Basileus found himself in since learning he'd been betrayed a few weeks earlier. One of his disciples had turned their back on Basileus and his brethren, exposing them all to the one person who could ultimately unravel his well-laid plans.

"Dima, have you heard anything back about our other problem? I cannot allow anyone to interfere when we're so close."

"No, sir, I'm sorry. This man that you've had us looking for is a ghost, but we won't stop until we find him… and kill him. I promise you that." Dima had no choice but to admit to his failure. He knew better than to lie.

"Keep searching, Dima. I'm not asking you to chase after a ghost. He's very much real and very much alive. Our former associate has already confessed his betrayal. While Brother Marcus wasn't privy to all that we were working toward, the knowledge he did possess would prove disastrous to our efforts if he was able to locate this Daedalus person."

"We do have a lead on a computer hacker who may know something," Dima added, hoping to improve his standing with this tidbit of information. "We're still trying to locate him. He owes some money from a gambling debt to one of our outfits, but has recently gone underground. He's probably lying low while trying to raise the cash he owes. Typical of these degenerate gamblers. When he comes up for air, I'll find him and make him tell me where Daedalus is."

The look on Basileus's face expressed his skepticism.

"Sir, Daedalus's team was no match for us before. They—"

"No match for your team? I seem to remember you losing almost a dozen men that day, Dima, or am I mistaken?"

Dima's eyes shot to the floor. "Well, yes, that's true, sir." His face flushed. "But we also eliminated his team. You were pleased by that, remember?"

"Four people, Dima. You lost twelve to kill four? And one of them was a female scientist. Not even a soldier." The volume of his voice rose. "They got too close last time, and you were barely successful in protecting the test sites. It's true that the loss of life on their side was much more damaging to them than our losses were to us, but you still failed to kill Daedalus. He and his team are too close. I can feel it. They have contacts in governments and militaries around the globe. We cannot let this continue unchecked."

"Basileus, I thought the Brotherhood had connections to the highest levels of government. Even presidents and prime ministers bow down to you. How can this person wield so much power? Who is he?"

"That is a question I will have an answer to shortly. My contacts know of him only as Daedalus. It's an alias, of course, but his group, unbeknownst to me at the time, has been thwarting a few of my other business dealings over the years. Once he is stopped though, no one will stand in my way. This is what I'm paying you to do, Dima—to find him. Now do your job." Basileus turned to the gathering storm outside, feeling his own storm brewing deep inside.

Dima looked after all matters of security for Basileus and, as such, handpicked all his own men. Basileus only knew a few of the guards, preferring to deal only with Dima whenever possible. Everyone else was anonymous and disposable as far as he was concerned, and as such, Basileus seldom bothered to learn their names. They had a tendency to die early and often. Remembering them, now or posthumously, seemed pointless to him.

He did happen to remember the name of the pair of guards watching over the prison cells below his castle. The Bough brothers. Sick, sadistic, and twisted was how Dima first described them to Basileus when he tasked him to find new jailers for their secretive prison. Conveniently, both guards went by their last name. This, and their demented, cruel behavior, was likely the only reason Basileus had cause to remember the brothers Bough.

"I won't let you down this time." Dima's voice had lost all its previous swagger. The muscular soldier looked over at Basileus, but the man didn't turn back around from his thousand-yard stare out the window.

"I hope not, Dima. Failure at this juncture would be unforgivable." The veiled threat was delivered in no uncertain terms.

The two of them sat in silence for the rest of the drive, with the same thing on their minds—killing Daedalus.

CHAPTER TWELVE

The Labyrinth, NYC
February 6, 10:01 a.m.

During the past week, Daedalus had introduced Gryph to many of his clandestine contacts in the intelligence community. Over just a few days, it was made clear he had connections to the leaders of all the G7 countries, plus China, Russia, Saudi Arabia and a few select others. Each of those leaders had advised their senior-level operatives and intelligence directors to provide whatever Daedalus requested, no questions asked. In turn, Daedalus provided state-of-the-art solutions to some of their most complex problems and some exclusive personal favors for the kings, princes, and presidents who ran them.

He used the elixir on only the rarest of occasions and only for his most important *clients.* His most meaningful exchanges were with leaders who agreed to forfeit a war for a sip. Others offered their kingdom, even their own life, to save the life of another they loved. Almost always their children.

The last time he parted with any of the elixir was over fifty years ago. In that case, it was to cure the leukemia plaguing the daughter of a former Soviet leader. She'd recovered immediately, and Daedalus had earned the unwavering loyalty from an eternally grateful parent. A deal for an effective cure had been struck prior and, as promised, the Berlin Wall came down a few months later. He coordinated this momentous event with then President Reagan, who used the opportunity as a victory lap for the USA and its triumph over communism. Daedalus had once more proved his irreplaceable value to Washington.

Such stories of Daedalus were not uncommon in the halls of power-brokers and decision makers across the globe. Information like this was passed down through the countries' successive leaders as an *emergency use only* contact. The lore and legend of Daedalus was enough of an inducement to secure fierce loyalty. The technology, healthcare breakthroughs, and military solutions he provided to these countries earned the respect and fidelity of those who made the big decisions and those who truly ran the government behind the scenes.

This quid pro quo, only available to those at the highest levels of power was known as invoking *The Daedalus Protocol.*

Daedalus was the cavalry, and he always came through when called upon. He had a gift for maintaining a delicate balance and distance, even when working on both sides of the same conflict. He knew better than to try and be judge, jury and executioner.

Each of these covert government conversations were conducted over highly encrypted communication lines that Dallas had recently upgraded. He assured Daedalus they were untraceable, and no known system on Earth could eavesdrop on the conversations.

Internationally, Gryph now had support from Mossad in Israel, MI6 and GCHQ in Britain, FIS and SVR in Moscow, the MSS in China, and more. He'd met with Daedalus's contacts on the US intel side first and even recognized one of them as a mission director from a hostage-rescue team that Gryph led a few years back. The operation they'd conducted was off the books, so neither man even slightly acknowledged the previous acquaintanceship when introduced by Daedalus, but there was no question that each man recognized the other. Gryph remembered him as a very effective director and was happy to have the highly talented agent as his contact.

Chief walked into the comms room as Daedalus was walking out. He and Gryph were finishing a conversation with a new ISI contact in Pakistan. The ISI was the Pakistani equivalent of the NSA and the CIA. Chief had been participating in some of the secure conferences throughout the week as well. He'd had top-secret security clearance for years. All the cloak and dagger secrecy was nothing new to him. Gryph trusted him with his life and knew his friend Billy K would never divulge anything that would put his team or his country in harm's way.

The call ended, and Chief knew Gryph had another country under his belt. "Bro, if Daedalus really has access to the dark corners of all these foreign agencies and can operate around the world with the full support of damn near every nuclear power and a few of the up and comers too, he could very well be the most powerful man on the planet. And he basically just introduced you as his heir apparent, which makes you a very important dude."

Because of the stories Gryph had recently learned about, he wasn't surprised that these foreign intel representatives were falling over themselves to offer him whatever assistance he asked for and kept reiterating their unwavering support. Caller after caller informed Gryph that the same gracious offer that was extended to Daedalus was now being conferred to him as well. If he required anything, all he had to do was ask.

"I wouldn't go that far, Chief," Gryph said, trying to downplay the significance of his involvement, but Billy K was right, as crazy as it sounded. After introducing Gryph to these power players, they all pledged their support to him as readily as they had to Daedalus. The enormity of that had yet to sink in. "But you're right in saying that the connections and information he has access to is astonishing. I know at least two of the contacts he introduced me to yesterday have direct access to the Oval Office on a daily basis. I've worked with one of them before, and she's as high up the food chain as they come. I've even heard her name mentioned as a possible candidate for secretary of state." His denial was only strengthening Chief's case for the influence Gryph now wielded.

Gryph was impressed by Daedalus's ability to command such deep allegiance from a group of countries that had warheads pointed at each other for decades. He confessed to Gryph earlier that he was instrumental in de-escalating more than a few situations which were leading to terrible wars that no one needed to suffer from.

"It's always good to have friends in high places, and this dude seems to know them all. I'm just glad we're on his side," Chief said, always looking at things from a tactical perspective.

"That's the thing, Billy. I'm not sure who or what the other side is yet. That's what we need to figure out, and fast."

The toxin was primarily affecting crops, and that would be their starting point. Gryph had cast a wide net early on, looking for anything that stood out in the biotech farming space. Things like recent land sales near any of the infected sites, or unusually large movements of fertilizer, soil, or seeds. He didn't know exactly what he was looking for, but he knew something out there would lead him to the truth. Dallas had deployed his newest AI engine to comb through an enormous number of records and databases, both public and private, to identify any anomalies, or revealing any kind of pattern in the chaos. If they found a few clues, they could pull at any of the common threads. The task would have been impossible without the next-level cyber intelligence that Dallas had them plugged into. The sheer amount of data they had to analyze would have taken multiple lifetimes without the assistance of the AI now processing all of it at quantum computing speed. Dallas was like a kid in a candy shop in awe of the computing power Daedalus had amassed for him to use.

One of Dallas's early hits identified a location on the other side of the world that showed some unusual activity, unfortunately, nothing as promising appeared since. Gryph and Chief planned to catch up with Dallas a little later that morning to see what his system had uncovered. They'd been tracking some unusual purchase activity in the agriculture sector in India and were hoping to catch a break.

India and Pakistan were two countries that had been shooting at each other non-stop for years, and Gryph knew that the best dirt was always dug up by someone's enemy. Since he now had universal access to a myriad of intelligence groups, he figured he'd go directly to the source, which, in this case, was Pakistan. Because of their ongoing conflict, Pakistan always had their ears to the ground in India and vice versa.

"We should call Fatima at ISI," Gryph said. Lt. General Fatima Noor had been introduced to him earlier in the week. From what Daedalus had told them, she outranked everyone but the director of the ISI himself. "Hopefully, she's been able to track down the purchaser of those two trucking companies."

Gryph was referring to the AI's recent search results that flagged the sale of two of India's largest long-haul agricultural trucking firms to an undisclosed third party. Even more interesting was that both sales were completed within two days of each other, and the purchaser had gone to great pains to obscure their identity behind multiple shell company transactions and offshore bank transfers.

Chief had seen firsthand Gryph's amazing ability to see correlations between seemingly unrelated events. If he thought he saw smoke in India, he was sure it wouldn't be long until Gryph found the fire, but he still wasn't sure what his friend was so focused on.

"What makes you so sure there's a connection between trucking in India and the toxin?"

"It's not the transactions themselves that were bothering me, however odd they were. It's that the purchaser was going to great lengths and considerable expense to hide their involvement. Why hide behind a complicated matrix of corporate entities if you're just completing a routine acquisition? In my experience people who go to great lengths to stay hidden are doing so for a reason. This may amount to nothing, but the sale of these companies creates a combined trucking fleet with routes reaching every corner of the country. One of their largest truck yards is only fifty miles from the infected site in Ludhiana. Take all those coincidences together and add the level of secrecy the entire transaction was completed under, and I'd say it's as good a place as any to start."

Chief nodded. "It never ceases to amaze me that you figure that kind of shit out when everyone else is blind to it. Even ICARUS missed it."

"Thanks, Chief, but I've seen what that quantum computer can do, and it's pretty incredible. Don't forget, it found the suspicious transfers to begin with. There's really no substitute for the human imagination, though. Those machines are great at analyzing massive amounts of data, and they never tire or make mistakes, but they're still just circuits and silicone. Nothing even comes close to the power of the human mind."

"That's not entirely true, Commander Oake." The men turned to see Daedalus and Dallas entering the communication center. "It's true that the generally accepted belief is that AI and quantum processing power have yet to achieve the same problem-solving logic and aptitude of the human brain. However, the realm of quantum computing and advancements in artificial intelligence may have not only closed that gap but even left their biological counterparts in the dust."

The news surprised Gryph. Although he wasn't a computer scientist, he'd heard from reliable sources that the human brain was still far more advanced than any machine. "I was told by one of the NSA's best and brightest that we're still quite far off from the singularity." He was referring to the moment when computers become self-aware. Some would argue that they gained consciousness, others even said the machines had a digital soul.

The CIA had contracted Gryph out to the NSA on more than a few occasions as part of the inter-agency cooperation policies instituted after 9/11. The CIA would lend assets like Gryph to the NSA and receive intel in exchange. Of course, no agency revealed everything they knew. Knowledge was power, and each of the alphabet agencies thought their organization was top dog.

"Director Oake, you obviously are well versed on the subject," Daedalus said, "but the singularity has come and gone. Computers have already made that leap, although to be fair, not many. You saw it on full display inside the Workshop. I explained to you all that my nanobots ran autonomously from the ICARUS AI once given instructions. What you may not have realized is that the AI itself is autonomous from me. Now don't get me wrong, I'm still in full control. I ask ICARUS to complete a task, and the AI computes the most efficient method and executes it using the bots. It's essentially a digital brain attached to an unconstrained body. There are obviously numerous safeguards in place to avoid any unintentional consequences." Billy and Gryph glanced at each other with a look that said, *I've heard that before*. Daedalus could read it in their eyes as plain as day.

"I've watched all the movies and read all the sci-fi books that you have. ICARUS isn't some kind of Skynet." Daedalus's mention of Skynet—the name given to the artificial intelligence that achieves singularity in the *Terminator* movie—was exactly what Chief had in mind while listening to the exchange.

Dallas finished connecting his laptop to the overhead screens and took a seat. "Okay, I'm ready now," he said when the image on his laptop sprang to life, oblivious to the conversation going on in front of him.

"We can get back to the debate later, Commander Oake," Daedalus said. "Something arrived this morning that we need to examine right away. Dallas, can you bring these two up to speed, please?" At that moment, Phil and Aliyah walked in, each carrying a stack of reports.

"So, what are we all looking at this morning? Did Dallas's engine find something new to look into?" Phil saw the cables running from Dallas's laptop to the ports under the monitors and made the assumption. He and the hacker had been getting friendlier over the week, and Phil had been receiving regular updates along the way.

"Actually, Dallas was just about to get into that. Good timing on your part." Daedalus signaled for Dallas to start.

"So, I went for a walk to this coffee shop just around the corner this morning. There's this smokin' hot barista who works there. Her name's Luna, and she's always wearing these super-tight tank tops…"

He realized the group was staring at him oddly. Aliyah was smirking. Chief had his eyes closed and was shaking his head.

"Anyway, I was walking back here with my coffee in hand, but I had my head down because it was windy outside and cold as balls out, uh… sorry, Doc. I mean, it was really cold outside."

Dallas had been trying to tone down some of his more colorful expressions when Aliyah was around. Phil had asked him to clean it up a bit, and Dallas reluctantly agreed. He wasn't sure if Phil had a thing for Aliyah, but they both had been nothing but nice to Dallas since they'd first met, so he had agreed to at least try.

"I barely left the café, when some dude jumps out from behind a tree. Lemme tell you, he scared the shit out of me and almost made me spill my coffee. So, I was like, 'What the hell, man? You scared the shit out of me!' And he was like, 'You need to get this to Daedalus. It's a matter of life or death!' And I was like 'Whoa, that's a bit dramatic, bud, and also, how do you know about Daedalus?' because you're all secretive and mysterious and shit, ya know?" He nudged his head toward Daedalus as he said that last part, as if the team needed the clarification.

"Anyway, I reached out to take the package, and the guy basically threw it at me, again almost spilling my coffee and then just ran off. Before you ask, no, I didn't get a good look at him. He was wearing a mask and scarf and a big parka with a hood. He might have had a British accent, but I can't be sure. Anyway, I came down here, looked inside the package, and found a single USB drive. No note or instructions. I scanned the USB in my lab for viruses and to see if there was any type of tracking device embedded inside, but it was clean. I should have realized the tracking beacon was kind of a waste of time, since they practically dropped it off with me at our front door. Anyhow, I was about to check the files for the first time now."

The USB plugged into his laptop had less than one gigabyte of data, spread across three separate folders. The first one contained shipping and transport manifests from ports all over the world. Gryph noted the locations shown on some of these documents matched areas where the toxin had already been found. The second folder contained several dozen pictures. Dallas scrolled through them quickly. Most were crop and livestock related, similar to the death and destruction they had seen in their welcome video. The third was a single video file. Dallas clicked on the file, and it began to play for the group.

An image of an old man wearing a dark robe came into focus. A deep hood covered his head, casting shadows across his face. "I pray this message reaches the ears of the man known as Daedalus. My name is Marcus Davies. I belong to an ancient order that has, for centuries, possessed a great power. I assure you that I am not some simpleton who has been misled by a false prophet or succumbed to the trappings of a cult. Believe me when I tell you that the leader of this order has power unlike any on Earth. The power of life itself. I have done many things in my life that I am very ashamed of and have accepted that I will have to atone for those sins in the world to come. I pray that I can gain some measure of favor with my creator with the good that I am attempting to do now, even though doing so will seal my fate. I have walked this earth for over two hundred years. I have seen people at their best and at their very worst. I must warn you—"

"Hold on a minute." Dallas stopped playback. "Did this coffin-dodger just say he's over two hundred years old? I mean, he's old, but over two hundred? Gimme a break. He's just a nut job."

"We can talk about all of that after the video ends. Put it back on," Gryph said, a hint of aggravation in his voice. He wanted to hear the rest of the old man's story, even if it seemed ridiculous.

Dallas complied without protest for once, and the playback resumed.

"—that our leader, a man who calls himself Basileus, has gone mad. He has commenced plans to wreak havoc across the globe and wipe out ninety-nine percent of the planet's population. He believes humankind has become too toxic for the planet and needs to be eliminated in order for the earth to heal itself and move on from its time dominated by man. I've stolen all of the files that I could find pertaining to this plan, but no one, not even the most-trusted members of his inner sanctum, are aware of all the pieces to this puzzle. Basileus is ruthless and brilliant—a dangerous combination. I fear he'll be successful in committing the greatest mass murder in the history of man."

The team hadn't taken their eyes off the screen for a moment. If they had, they would have noticed the blood had drained from Daedalus's face, staring wide-eyed at the screen, his mouth agape.

"I don't know who this Daedalus man is. Some say it is a group, not a person. Others say he is more shadow than man, always working behind the scenes. Someone spoken of but never known. I only know of his name because Basileus and his men are hunting for him. I overheard them say Daedalus was the only entity who could stop them from completing their plan. I hope and pray this message reaches him in time and that they were right about his chances of stopping Basileus. If Daedalus fails, the world is lost." The old man reached forward in the video to turn the recording off, and the screen went dark. No one moved or said a word for an uncomfortably long time.

"Like I said, this guy is a total nut bag. Power over life? Two hundred years old? Pshhh, whatever," Dallas said. "Let's get back to work and leave the fairy tale shit to some other loser who wants to go on that wild goose chase. The guy who gave this to me isn't the guy on camera. I know that for damn sure."

Gryph frowned with concern. "Someone must have tracked you to that café, Dallas. How else would they know you're connected to all of this?"

"No clue. I went there earlier in the week to send my bookie some crypto to pay off a debt I owed. I used an internet café 'cause I didn't want to use the signal from the Workshop, so I used their terminals instead. Not gonna lie, I may have gone back a few times to chill with Luna too. She's totally into me now."

"Did you contact your bookie directly from the café or just send the crypto?" Gryph had a feeling he already knew the answer.

"I had a couple of quick Zoom calls with him. Had to convince him to take my action again, 'cause I was a bit late with the last payment. I actually forgot about the debt 'cause I've been working my ass off down here. He wouldn't take my phone call, so I figured a Zoom may be better, and he answered. I won my bet too, in case anyone's interested. Thanks for asking."

The looks he got told him that no one cared about the wager.

"I think they may have traced the IP back to the café, or saw something on the video call that gave away your location," Gryph said.

"To Basileus? No way. It was a Zoom call to my bookie. How would they track that? I knew him long before I got caught up in all of this."

"I'm not sure how they did it," Gryph said, "but that's the only thing that makes sense, as far-fetched as it seems. If Marcus knew where to send us this message, then Basileus would know, too." Everyone let that terrifying thought sink in.

Aliyah looked at Daedalus to ask him if he knew anything more about Basileus or his thoughts on how the package found its way to Dallas. However, she didn't get to ask either of those questions because Daedalus looked terrified to his core, like he'd seen a ghost or worse. Now the only question she wanted an answer to, was why.

CHAPTER THIRTEEN

The Labyrinth
February 6, 10:49 a.m.

"Daedalus, are you okay?" All eyes turned to Aliyah when she asked the question, then back to Daedalus. The color had yet to return to his face when her question snapped him out of his trance.

"It can't… I've searched, but…" Daedalus was stammering, his eyes darting around. "Please excuse me." He spun in his seat and hurried out of the room.

"Okay, if that freaky-deaky display didn't send alarm bells off for the rest of you then I don't know what will," Dallas said. "He definitely knows something. Gryph, you should go find out what it is. He's not gonna tell us, but he may spill his guts to you. People seem to do that with you." It was true that people opened up to Gryph largely because of the behavioral techniques he'd learned from the CIA. He had become so proficient he'd been asked to teach the course during his last few years at the headquarters in Virginia.

"Based on what I just saw, Dallas, I'm not so sure he'll tell me anything. In fact, I'm not so sure he knows the whole truth either. He was in shock, that's for certain, but there was something else in his expression. He was also confused, scared almost. But I agree with you, the best way to prevent this toxin from spreading is to chase down any lead we have, and I think our biggest one just ran out the door."

Gryph found Daedalus just outside the doors to the Labyrinth. He had only managed a few steps after exiting the glass doors leading to the Workshop. He was leaning against a massive rock wall, eyes closed, the back of his head resting on the cool stone. He didn't move or open his eyes to look at Gryph as he approached.

"I'm sorry for the way I reacted in there. I guess that didn't really inspire much trust or confidence in me," Daedalus said, finally opening his eyes. "I'm sure you all thought we were listening to the ravings of a lunatic on the video we just watched. Some of the claims Marcus made would undoubtedly make it hard for anyone to believe what he was saying."

"To be honest, Daedalus, his claim to be more than two centuries old was a bit tough to swallow. He didn't strike me as the type of guy to speak in metaphors, so that statement still must be reconciled. We don't have any time to waste here, and I don't want to go on some wild goose chase, as Dallas put it, so if you know something, you really need to tell us right now."

Gryph let the weight of his comment hang for a moment before continuing. "You brought us here because you trusted us, and we're all putting our lives on the line to help you. I think you owe us a little more transparency. What secret can you have that's worth more than the lives of eight billion people?"

Daedalus remained still. The pause allowed him to process everything he'd heard in the video, upending everything he thought to be true. Daedalus knew he had no choice. He needed their help to stop Basileus, and hiding information from them would be counterproductive to that effort.

Daedalus pushed off the wall to face Gryph. "You're right, Commander. If we're to have any hope in stopping this madman, all of you need to hear the truth, as hard as it may be to believe. Let's head back inside. I'll try my best to explain. I'm warning you now though, you may have a difficult time coming to grips with all of this when I'm done."

The two men made their way back through the glass door that led to the Labyrinth. Gryph was even more curious than ever. He figured Daedalus would deny any knowledge of what Marcus was talking about in the video. He was pleasantly surprised to hear that his boss did actually know something about this, and would divulge the details to the team momentarily.

Daedalus and Gryph found the group still seated where they'd left them minutes before. They were analyzing a few of the files and pictures from the USB drive up on the screens. Even with the distraction caused by Daedalus's sudden departure, the team wasted no time getting to work with the new information. The group was surprised when he and Gryph walked back in so soon after leaving. Gryph took his seat, and the group turned to Daedalus and waited for him to speak.

"I feel I owe you all an explanation, and hopefully I can shed some light on the statements made in Marcus's video. What I'm about to tell you, I haven't told anyone in over four hundred years."

"Excuse me? I must not have heard that right," Dallas said, vocalizing what everyone else was thinking. "Did you say four hundred years?"

"Yes, you heard correctly. Please, everyone, let me finish before you ask anything else. I think I'll answer most of your questions if you give me the opportunity, but as I just cautioned Commander Oake outside, much of what you hear will seem impossible at first. All I can promise is that it's the truth. I have physical proof if you still require convincing when my explanation is finished."

The group was unsure what to make of the initial four-hundred-year-old claim, but they were eager to hear how the incredible remark could be true and discover what possible proof Daedalus could offer to support such a fantastic claim.

Daedalus took a deep breath and then began to tell a story that he hadn't told for centuries.

"How many of you know the story of the Jewish people's Exodus from Egypt in biblical times?"

"Holy shit. If this backstory starts a few thousand years ago, I'm gonna need more coffee." Dallas laughed at his own joke as he reached for another cup. Daedalus hadn't even made it more than one sentence into the story before he was interrupted. The dirty looks Dallas got from around the room told him no one was in the mood to joke. "Sorry, go on," he said, reddening. "I'll shut up now."

"It's the story told of the Jewish people who were led out of Egypt by their Prophet Moses after being enslaved for hundreds of years. Moses secured their release only after God struck the Egyptians with ten plagues. Moses led the Jews into the desert on the way to their promised land of Israel, but Pharaoh changed his mind about setting them free shortly after they left and chased the Jews to the edge of the Red Sea. The Bible states that God split the sea for the Jews to walk through, while keeping the Egyptians at bay with a wall of fire on the other shore. Once the Jews were safely through the sea, the fire keeping the Egyptians from attacking disappeared, and the entire army gave chase once more. As soon as Moses saw all the Egyptian chariots and soldiers were within the confines of the two towering walls of water in the sea, he lowered his staff, and the walls of water collapsed. The entire Egyptian army, the most powerful fighting force on Earth, was drowned in an instant, and the Jews were finally free."

"I used to watch that old Ten Commandments movie around Easter time," Dallas said. "I loved that movie. It played on six different channels for a week. Charlton Heston was an awesome Moses. I'm totally following along for once." He said proudly, before stopping himself. "Sorry, I'll shut up again."

"The caravan of Jews was said to have been comprised of 600,000 adult men over the age of 20 adding up to a grand total of over 2.4 million people, when including the women and children before and after receiving the Ten Commandments. The Bible tells of many miraculous things that happened to, and protected them during the forty years they spent exposed in the desert. Can you imagine having to provide food and water for over 2.5 million people in a barren wasteland every single day? They left in such a hurry that they took nothing but the clothes on their back. But not only did they not perish, they actually thrived. The Bible recounts that they were an extremely fertile people and expanded in numbers rapidly. It's also written that no woman suffered a miscarriage, and no one took ill while they were wandering the desert in all that time. The miraculous source of food the large nation relied upon was known as manna. This superfood fell during the night and was collected by the Jewish people each morning."

Daedalus had been directing his attention between each of the people at the table ensuring they were following the story. Each of them had an intense look on their face. Dallas was also following along, likely conjuring mental images from the movie to supplement Daedalus's narrative.

"Some accounts say the manna could taste like anything you wanted it to, but the more widely accepted biblical description was that it tasted like wafers fried in honey. Its appearance was said to be like white dew on the ground, and people would collect it fresh daily. They were warned not to keep any overnight or it would become wormy and foul. In the sacred Jewish texts, it's written that after consuming the manna, one wouldn't produce any bodily waste products. It was a perfect food, absorbed entirely by the body. It provided everything a person needed to live."

"I know this story well," Aliyah said. "I was fascinated by the stories in the Torah. I read it many times when I was growing up. A lot of what's written in those texts are more than stories. They provide the fundamentals for almost all democratic legal systems, among other social structures we take for granted today. It contains more wisdom than people give it credit for."

Daedalus smiled. He was glad Aliyah had an extensive background in this area. He assumed she had some exposure to her heritage when he recruited her, but the confirmation was a welcome bit of news.

"Something must have happened to the Jewish people out there in the desert that allowed them to survive and grow in number and ward off all sickness and finally arrive intact in the land of Israel some forty years later," he continued. "There's no *natural way* for that to have occurred. There were too many people and not enough resources to keep everyone alive for even a short while, nevermind forty years. I believe the manna was the reason for this miraculous turn of events."

"Okay, I've been a good boy and have kept my mouth shut— more or less," Dallas said. "I listened to your story, and I'd like to ask a question if I may."

"Yes, of course. What is it?" Daedalus said.

"How the fuck does that explain your claim of not telling this story to anyone in four hundred years? You seemed to have left that part out." He looked at Aliyah. "Sorry about the 'fuck' part, Doc."

"I'm getting to that now, Mr. Hayle. I wanted you to understand the 'backstory,' as you put it, *before* I asked you all to take that leap of faith. Let me get back to our story in the desert, and things will start to come into focus. The manna was available for many of the forty years the Jews were wandering their circuitous route through the Sinai Desert, but I believe there was something unique, something very special about the manna that appeared for the Jews on those first cold desert mornings away from bondage. Moses knew this miracle stood out from the myriad of others that he and the nation of Israel had witnessed while fleeing their Egyptian taskmasters. I think the manna provided some type of supernatural healing for them. Remember, they would have been severely malnourished at the time. They had been beaten and broken during the long years of servitude and slavery. I think they woke up one morning, and all evidence of wounds suffered during those years of abuse were gone. The manna must have provided a strong, concentrated prophylactic dose when they first ingested it, something that stayed with them and protected them for years to come."

Aliyah raised her hand, and he nodded her way.

"I don't understand how you could possibly deduce that there was a special initial batch of manna that was different from all the others and attribute that to a specific moment on the timeline from two thousand years ago. Very little is written about the manna in the Bible other than some of its basic characteristics like size and color. The Scriptures say it appeared white like frost and was small like coriander seed. That's all straight out of the Old Testament, but I've never read that there was a difference in the potency of the manna or differences due to when it fell. How can you say these things with such certainty? And that's aside from the fact that you're basing your entire premise on ancient scriptures that may just be metaphors and hyperbole anyway."

Although Aliyah was Jewish, she learned later in life that both her parents had once been observant Jews. After the death of her mother while giving birth to Aliyah, her father had lost his faith. Aliyah often wondered if God was real, and if he was, why he had taken her mother and left her with a broken father when she was so little. She had no interest in pledging allegiance to an entity who had wronged her so early on in life. She devoured the Talmud and other Jewish texts not because she felt a need for God in her life, but because they were colorful stories and provided deep insights into humanity. It was for those reasons alone she read them and, in some cases, had grown to love them.

"I'm almost there, Ali, I promise. Just a few more moments of your patience." Daedalus took a deep breath and continued. "I believe the positive effects of the manna became apparent to Moses right away. He would have felt the effects in his own body. It's also written in the Old Testament that a portion of this manna was put away for safekeeping shortly after it first began to appear. That's why the manna that fell during those first few weeks or months had healing properties. However, I don't think the manna they collected later had the same effect."

"You kind of answered the timeline question, but what makes you think this manna stuff lost its mojo later on?" Chief asked.

"It's pretty simple," Daedalus said. "The entire generation that left Egypt died out before going into Israel. The Bible recounts that it was the punishment for the Jews worshipping the golden calf while waiting for Moses to come down the mountain with the Ten Commandments. But make no mistake, it says the entire previous generation died out before going into the Promised Land. Only their children were allowed to enter. Scholars agree that by this point, the manna had long since stopped falling. If the manna in the later years didn't provide healing effects anymore, the Jews either built up an immunity to it, or the manna lost the trait somehow. That's how they survived for so long in the harsh desert and remained so healthy all those years. This special healing manna only fell at the start of their journey—it was unique. That's my theory."

"Great! But are you going to get to the part where you're four hundred years old before we're all four hundred years old?" Dallas asked. "This story is taking forever, and I'm not sure we're any clearer on what the hell this trip down Exodus Lane has to do with anything. Can you hurry it up a bit? I gotta take a leak really bad. I've been sitting here for a while now and had two cups of coffee before this one. My back teeth are floating."

"Dallas, give it a rest, man. Let the guy finish," Chief said. "I have a feeling he's about to drop the bomb on us soon."

"Fine, finish. I'll just sit here and piss myself while he tells us a story that starts with frickin' Moses and runs till now. He's still on the Moses part, if you hadn't noticed. But yeah, sure, go ahead. Keep telling your long-ass, go-nowhere story. Don't mind me."

Daedalus was used to such outbursts by now and let it slide. "Stories have been passed down through the ages that date back as far as the ancient Greek and Roman empires. Elements of these stories have been retold in the gospels and were later twisted into legend and myth by many others. These stories tell of an elixir so powerful that when drunk, would make a man immortal, heal him completely, and give him eternal life."

"Are you talking about some kind of fountain of youth story?" Phil asked. He'd been engrossed in the dialogue all morning. He was a Buddhist and wasn't aware of many of the Old Testament details they were debating, but the conversation still fascinated him.

"That's exactly what I'm talking about. Many legends describe these healing waters. Although, the actual source of power for the elusive fountain has rarely been discussed. I believe the manna which first fell is the original source of this fountain, which really isn't a fountain at all. I think portions of this manna have been stolen over millennia and scattered throughout the globe, giving whoever possesses them its restorative powers."

"Even if that's true, Daedalus," Gryph said, "which, by the way, is a huge leap, why was it referred to as the fountain of youth, and why the legends about living forever? You said this elixir would heal people if they were hurt or sick. How do you infer from that, that it bestowed eternal life?"

"Very good questions, and there's one straightforward answer. Are you familiar with the theory that the signs of aging and, ultimately, death itself aren't just the natural effects of getting older but that aging is a disease we have yet to diagnose and treat?"

Gryph pondered the thought before shaking his head.

"There are many things pointing to exactly that," Daedalus continued. "Humans succumb to heart failure, dementia, kidney, and liver failure because those vital organs wear out over a lifetime of use and abuse. Some people's lifestyles accelerate that deterioration, but in most cases, the human body simply wears out because our ability to create healthy, young cells stops. But what if it didn't? What if a person could repair the damage to their body at a cellular level? If cells stayed healthy and were repaired in real time, they would never wear out, right? A compound that would protect the cell by continually healing it could potentially allow someone to live indefinitely. Nothing would cause their body to deteriorate 'naturally' anymore. Of course, any significant trauma would still cause the person to perish from their wounds if these special properties couldn't heal the person quickly enough."

There was no turning back now, and Daedalus steeled himself for the conclusion. "I know much of what I've told you seems improbable at best, but there's something in that toxin that I've seen before. I knew it for certain when Aliyah poked through the cell wall and it started glowing. When Marcus admitted he was as old as he was, the final piece of the puzzle slid into place. It makes perfect sense to me now as to why we couldn't figure out how it was so resilient against anything we used to weaken or kill it."

He took a sip of water and swallowed hard. "I think Marcus was telling the truth when he said he was over two hundred years old. I believe this Basileus character that Marcus spoke of in the video, is in possession of this ancient elixir and has used it as an additive to the toxin."

"What do you mean?" Dallas asked.

"Aliyah will have to run a comparison between some more samples to be certain, but I think the toxin has been infused with the healing effects powered by that ancient strain of manna. It's protecting the toxin by providing continuous repair to the cellular structure to keep the organism safe from alcohol poisoning. When we pierced the outside of the cell, the cytoplasm leaked out, and the cell repaired itself when we saw it glowing. Maybe it's more vulnerable at some point in that process. We need to look for any other potential weaknesses."

Gryph ran through a few scenarios that would make sense based on this new information. He tried hard to stay objective when solving a problem and not capitulate to his own internal bias because this seemed like sheer lunacy to him. "Are you saying you think Basileus gave some of this elixir to Marcus in exchange for something? Maybe to dangle a carrot to keep him dedicated over the years? Promise him a few more sips to keep him loyal for another lifetime?" It was Gryph thinking out loud this time. "This was all okay with Marcus until Basileus decided to put an end to the world as we know it. He said he regretted a lot of things he did. It doesn't sound to me like that Brotherhood of theirs has been up to any good."

"I'm not sure about the motivation or the dynamic inside that group, but your suggestion makes sense," Daedalus said. "There are a lot of possibilities to consider. It's usually greed or fear that keeps a person hostage to another. I'm sure this truth isn't too far off from either, or both."

"Okay, maybe the third time's the charm," Dallas said, standing up. "For the life of me, I still can't understand why you won't answer my damn question." His voice began to rise in volume. "You said you hadn't told this story to anyone in four hundred years. Those were your exact words. I'm not letting you off the hook, buddy. Stop dodging my question. What did you mean by that? Just fucking tell us already!"

Daedalus slammed his hands on the desk and jumped to his feet. "I'm your answer, Dallas! My very existence is your proof!"

Billy and Gryph both jumped up to put some mass between the two overheated men, but more to ensure Dallas didn't do anything stupid out of rage. Phil had moved quicker than all of them and took a position closer to Daedalus, neither defending nor opposing him, but expertly positioned to control the situation.

"I told you before that I would provide proof of my story if I hadn't convinced you, and obviously, I haven't done a good enough job yet. I don't know how it's possible, but I think Marcus was given the elixir to drink at some point in his life. I could see it in his eyes. I've only seen that look in one other person's eyes in all my many years on Earth, and only when I look in the mirror."

"I don't understand. What look?" Aliyah asked. "Why would you and Marcus have anything in common? You said you've never seen or heard of him before."

"It's true. I've never laid eyes on Marcus until now, but I'm sure we both have the same ancient source of life coursing through our veins. I have consumed the elixir, just as I know he has. I have been protecting it for centuries. I am far older than even Marcus claims to be. You wanted proof. There it is."

"Okay, let me see if I've got this straight." Dallas was too calm. Everyone knew where this was going.

"This ought to be good," Phil muttered to the trio beside him.

"You want us to believe you're actually some super old dude, except you look like a guy who walked off the set of some CrossFit infomercial because you've been dipping into a private stash of some ancient cake from the time of Moses, which coincidentally has super healing powers. That's why you look like you do, because your cells repair themselves all the time, so you never get old because aging is really just a disease, and your magic juice cures all diseases, including age." Dallas took a deep breath. "Then this Marcus guy drank some of that ancient Kool-Aid too, and you know this because you saw something in his eyes that none of us noticed. You also have that glowing eye thing, but we can't see yours either. And then some other asshole, Basila-something gets a hold of this mythical first-round draft pick manna, not the junk from the later rounds, and uses it to develop a toxic with bacteria smaller than anyone has ever seen before, designed to wipe out mankind by killing all the crops and cattle to starve-out the planet, but we have no idea why that is yet. Oh right, and because he already started spreading the toxin, we could already be too late to stop him. And all of that, in some fucked up way, makes sense, except for the part where you need to be more than five hundred years old to make the story work. Do I have that about right?"

Daedalus looked directly at Dallas. "Dallas, my friend, I couldn't have said it better myself." He began to laugh. It was subdued at first, but a moment later, he was rolling with laughter. He felt a huge weight had been lifted from his shoulders. The burden of carrying the secret alone for so many years was finally released. He was overcome with emotion. Daedalus wiped the tears from his eyes with the back of his hand; from crying or laughing, he wasn't sure.

"I'm glad you think that was funny, too. I'm legitimately relieved. For a minute there, I thought you actually expected us to believe that load of horseshit."

"Dallas, I wasn't joking. I was laughing because I've wanted to tell so many people my secret through the years. Until now, I had kept my oath to take the secret to my grave. And who was it that I finally gave in to? Who got under my skin so deeply that I cried out the secret I never even dared whisper before? The one and only

Dallas 'Dalai Lama' Hayle. Let me tell you," he said, pointing at Dallas, "Karma has a sense of humor."

"That still leaves us at an impasse, *old man.*" Dallas smiled at his insult. "For this little story of yours to make sense, you still need to prove that you were around and kicking in the thirteen hundreds. Otherwise, pay me the money you promised me, and let me off this ride. I'm finished with crazy town."

"Okay, Dallas, fair enough. Come with me. In fact, let me show you all something. The Labyrinth doesn't just contain the residences, labs, and communication center. There are many rooms that aren't shown on the schematics you reviewed earlier. The caverns go much deeper into the rock than the maps suggest." Nervous looks were shared all around.

"I've been collecting rare and important artifacts throughout my time on Earth and have dedicated my life to protecting them. These hidden caverns are the safest vaults on the planet. They had to be, as they now hold some of the greatest treasures the world has ever known. What you're about to see hasn't been viewed by anyone but me for centuries. At the end of the tour, you will have no doubt left that everything I've told you is true."

Daedalus walked over to a nondescript portion of the wall in the corner of the cavern. He pressed his thumb to a seemingly random spot on the stone, and seconds later, the giant slab that had been indiscernible from the rock face pivoted in place, revealing a hidden passageway leading deep into the rock. The group gathered around the opening, their curiosity propelling them forward. Daedalus saw Dallas trying to peek into the area beyond the rock, but it was too dark to make out any details in the shadows.

"Go ahead, Mr. Hayle. I'm excited for you to get your proof," Daedalus said while extending his arm toward the secret entrance.

"No way I'm going in there first. Age before beauty, dude. How do I know you're not just going to lock me up in one of your little jail cells now that you've spilled your secret?"

Daedalus smiled. "I'd be lying if I said the thought hadn't crossed my mind once or twice, but this is no trick."

Their host rushed through the opening. They could hear his laughter echoing off the stone walls as they crossed the threshold, the door swinging close behind the group. Motion sensors at the door triggered a switch, and a series of overhead lights flickered on. It took a moment for everyone's eyes to adjust to the light, but once they did, the sight in front of them provided a significant down payment on the proof Daedalus had promised them.

"You're all looking at the greatest collection of knowledge the world has ever known."

"Holy shit! This place is huge," Dallas said. "There must be thousands of artifacts in here. It just goes on forever. Where'd you get all this stuff? It's gotta be worth a fortune!"

"Originally, this all came from Egypt, although long after the time of Moses."

Ali's hand flew to her mouth when the realization hit her. "It's not... This can't be..."

Daedalus smiled broadly. "Welcome to the Library of Alexandria."

μέρος δεύτερο
PART TWO

CHAPTER FOURTEEN

London, England
February 6, 7:33 a.m.

Basileus pulled himself from the icy pool and gulped the fresh cool air into his aching lungs. His skin felt like he was being pierced by a million tiny daggers, his exposed flesh tingling in the warm ambient air of the pool deck. A faint odor of petrichor energized the air. He loved the natural, fresh thunderstorm scent the ozone gave off. His private pool used an Absolute Ozone system instead of chlorine, keeping the water sparkling clean. The ozone generator did a far better job than the harsh chemicals that were still used in most pools.

He'd just finished his daily swim and was in the cool-down period of his workout, which also happened to be the same way he started each day, in a cold plunge pool. The cold-water immersion therapy numbed the nerves that surrounded joints and muscles, causing the body to release endorphins and hormones. The combination of these entities reduced inflammation and alleviated muscle and joint pain. Cold therapy was also known to increase the production of antioxidants, boost the immune system, and make people more alert. The godfather of the cryotherapy movement, a man named Wim Hoff, was one of the few people on Earth whom Basileus actually respected.

He looked forward to the cold-plunge sessions and the invigorating feeling after rising from the icy pool, likening it to being reborn each morning. Basileus would sink into the pool, slowing his heart rate and focusing on the air in his lungs. It calmed and centered him. He'd trained his mind to push through the pain from the ice-cold water on his exposed skin and suppressed the urge to panic when his lungs were almost empty. None of it registered as pain to him anymore, only as a sensation to compartmentalize and manage. The cold-water training taught him how to turn off any pain he was feeling by using the same intense focusing techniques. Shaolin monks were said to be able to reach a state of transcendence through meditation, without requiring the cold-water shock to help focus their energy, their Chi. These monks had legendary abilities to concentrate and ignore pain. Their feats of walking across hot coals or lying on a bed of nails while concrete was broken over their bellies, only to walk away unscathed, were world renowned.

"I have the bankers from Geneva on the phone for you, sir." Dima had been standing on the pool deck while his boss did his laps and cold plunge. Dima handed him the burner phone. Basileus stood there, a towel wrapped around his waist. His large, defined six-pack abs and broad chest expanded and contracted as his breathing returned to its normal cadence. There was rarely a time or a place Basileus would be as vulnerable as he was in the water. He would not be carrying any weapons and would have no place to hide if someone stormed in. He would be a sitting duck. Having Dima literally watch his back while he torpedoed through the water allowed him to focus on other matters as he swam.

Basileus pushed away from the edge of the pool deck. He listened to the chatter on the other end of the call for a few moments before taking himself off mute. The financiers on the other end were engaged in some small talk while they waited for him. The timer on his phone showed they had been waiting for over ten minutes. Good.

He didn't apologize for keeping them waiting. The bank was making an obscene amount of money from this deal. They could cool their heels for a while. He was sure they had already made grand plans on how to spend their newfound fortune. At worst, he was giving them a few more minutes to savor the possibilities.

"Gentleman," Basileus began, "I hope you received the funds I wired to you."

"Yes, sir. We can confirm that this most recent deposit brings your total cash balance to three billion US dollars exactly. We have charged your account our agreed upon fee of $150 million. It has been a pleasure doing business with you, sir. Your money is safe with us, and, as promised, we have ensured it's untraceable. The additional information you requested was sent by encrypted mail. If you require anything else, our firm is at your service."

"That will be all for now, gentleman." Basileus ended the call and tossed the phone to Dima, who deftly snatched it out of the air, removed the battery, and tossed the remains into the pool in one fluid motion.

"We need to review the documents the bank sent over. It better be everything I've asked for, considering the grotesque fee they charged. Not that it'll matter in a few months. There won't be a banking system for them to run anyway. The constructs of man will have already begun to come crashing down. Make sure you get a copy of the files they sent to Brother Sanchez right away. He'll be able to use the untraceable funds to ensure our products are distributed to each of the areas we have designated. Once my beautiful seed takes hold, nothing will be able to stop us."

Basileus walked toward his grand bathroom, which was adjacent to his pool. "Inform the Brotherhood that I want to meet with them at Chambers in an hour. I'm going to shower and dress. We'll walk over together when I'm ready."

"I'll set it up now." Dima went to work on his phone to ensure everyone would be in attendance.

Basileus had created a fortress for himself. His main residence was set far back into the woods of his hundred-acre estate, nestled securely into the English countryside. The location was still close enough to London to make a short trip of it should he need to go into the city to conduct any of his affairs. Most of those who worked for him lived on the property in small groups of cottage-like houses that were sprinkled throughout the vast grounds. Multiple layers of security had been designed into the master plan. Cameras surveyed every inch of the main house, and many more were hidden in the woods. Lookouts were placed in tree stands, like hunters stalking their prey. Invisible in the branches above, sentries swept their sniper scopes in continuous arcs, looking for any unfortunate souls foolish enough to violate their perimeter. The "No Trespassing" signs were plentiful and unmissable. If ignored, it would be at the interloper's peril.

Another building was situated one hundred feet from the main house. The rectangular structure was more beautiful than all the others. It measured sixty feet long and half as wide, boasting temple-like architecture, with high walls and Solomonic columns. The edifice was known as "the Chambers," and it was where all meetings were held. Basileus rarely allowed anyone into his personal home, despite its palatial size. Dima was a rare exception, something the bodyguard took great pride in.

Basileus finished showering and changed into a pair of black pants and a white button-down shirt. A silver letter H adorned his belt buckle, but this Hermes accessory was the real deal. The fakes were for his playthings. His own possessions were always authentic. He met Dima under the covered walkway which led from the main house to the adjacent stone building where most of the Brotherhood had already gathered. The two men walked in silence. Dima knew his employer despised small talk. He kept quiet unless he needed direction or Basileus instigated the conversation. As the men walked inside, Basileus wasted no time.

"Thank you all for coming," Basileus said, as the golden doors closed silently behind him. The gilded room was the Chambers' inner sanctum. Dima was allowed inside, but was posted by the door for security purposes. He was not allowed to participate as he was not a member of the Brotherhood, at least not yet, though he was hoping that would change soon.

Basileus made his way to a large, elevated chair at the midpoint of the room, ascended the three large marble steps at its base and settled into what was essentially a marble throne. He looked down at his followers, the Brotherhood he'd created. The eleven men wore identical black, hooded robes, and stood against a curved railing that separated them from Basileus's lofty position, both figuratively and literally.

"I have confirmed that our final shipment of seeds and fertilizer has reached our last three distribution hubs in Europe. This order should be all we need to infect the top one hundred grain and produce farms on the continent. Success is within our grasp, my brothers. We cannot let our guard down. Not even for a moment. There are those out there who would call what we are doing madness—or worse, only thinking of saving their own skin. Do not be dissuaded when the time comes to turn our backs on the last dredges of this wretched civilization. We must protect the planet at all costs, and you will all be greatly rewarded for your efforts."

The group of men in front of him nodded, their faces somber. No one was joyful to finally execute what they had spent the previous twenty years planning, yet none of them would waiver from their commitment to see it all through to the end. The fact that they'd all been offered a drink from Basileus's fountain of youth as a reward for their loyal service had a lot to do with it. But one of them had a change of heart, betraying their order and putting everything they worked for in grave danger. Basileus would visit Marcus again soon and pry loose the last few details from his deceitful lips.

The one known as Brother Samuel stepped forward and handed Basileus a thick file. "Here are the customer lists and land holdings summaries that I have completed for South America and Mexico. The seeds and fertilizer have been distributed all over those countries as well. We are only awaiting your approval to commence delivery to their farms. Everything you have asked of me has been completed." He said with a raspy voice and thick Spanish accent.

"You have served the order with honor for many years, Brother Samuel. You have earned your place in the world after man and your ascension to my new kingdom."

Samuel positioned himself at the base of the marble throne and kneeled, remaining silent with his head bowed.

Basileus reached for Samuel's arm and pulled it up toward him, exposing the inside of Samuel's wrist. He rose from his throne with Samuel's arm still firmly in his grasp, and looked out to those in attendance. "Fate has decreed that the heavy burden to save our world and ultimately save man from himself must fall upon us. The blood of many will be on our hands. We spill it to save what has always been and to protect what is yet to come."

"To save what has always been, and to protect what is yet to come," the Brotherhood repeated the mantra in unison.

Basileus lifted a golden scabbard that had been resting on its own ivory pedestal beside his throne. The sword had been supported on a pair of giant wings fashioned from intricately chiseled marble. The detail in the carving was so lifelike, the wings looked light enough to take flight, though they must have weighed over a hundred pounds each.

Basileus drew a golden blade from its matching sheath and raised it over his head for all to see.

"Be witnesses to my power and see that I honor my word. Brother Samuel, receive my reward for your loyalty."

Basileus brought the blade down and ran its razor-sharp edge along the length of Samuel's forearm until it passed through the veins in his wrist, severing both the radial and brachial arteries. Without immediate medical assistance, he would bleed to death in less than two minutes. He wiped the few drops of blood from the blade on the sleeve of Samuel's cloak, returned the blade to its sheath, and placed it back in its cradle.

He watched as Samuel remained in place; his arm raised high above his head. The life force from his body flowed down the marble steps in rhythmic pulses of crimson, but he did nothing to stem the flow.

Basileus grabbed the amulet hanging from his neck on a thick gold chain. The craftsmanship was magnificent. A royal-blue sapphire the size of a small egg had been hollowed out by a master jeweler and fitted with an ornate golden top. The gem produced a soft glow, as if a small, lit wick floated inside. Basileus carefully removed the top, revealing a thin needle forged to the underside of the lid, acting as a handle of sorts. The tip of the golden spike had been submerged deep into the heart of the glowing sapphire and the powerful contents its hollow cavity contained.

Samuel's skin paled and turned gray. His arm remained raised, but it was dropping and shaking as the seconds ticked by. The periphery of his vision began to darken, and felt himself slipping away.

"Who, other than a god, can bestow such gifts?" Basileus roared. Then he plunged the top of the amulet into Samuel's lacerated arm. The golden spike penetrated his skin inches from the incision that the golden dagger had opened only a minute before.

Basileus placed the golden top back on the glowing stone and twisted it in place to secure it to the chain. He looked down at Samuel at the very moment the bleeding man lost consciousness. The others all wore looks of confusion and revulsion.

"Do not look away, brothers. Man was created from earth and will eventually return to it, but it is not time for Brother Samuel to make that journey." Basileus covered him with his robe and placed his hand on top of the wounded man's head. "Give Brother Samuel a few moments."

The group huddled in a semicircle. Not even a whisper was shared between them. Dima realized he had been holding his breath while watching the lifeless body on the ground.

The singular focus in the room was their wounded brethren. The group's inner core had seen and heard of many examples of Brother Samuel's loyalty over the last forty-plus years that he had worked for Basileus. He had been recruited when he was twenty-four after being discharged from an illustrious career as a killing machine for the army. He'd given the best years of his life to Basileus, and now it was time for his reward.

The figure sprawled at the base of the stairs began to stir. Samuel pushed up slowly from the stone and raised his head to see Basileus standing over him. The color returned to his face as he felt the strength flooding back into his body. He brought himself to a sitting position and took a moment to catch his breath and get his bearings. Samuel saw his fellow brethren gasp as he turned to them to assure them he was okay. One of the brothers fainted and was caught under the elbows by the men on either side. The others just stood there, slack jawed.

Samuel rose to his feet and grabbed Basileus by his outstretched arm. "It's true. You really are a god." Samuel kissed Basileus's hand. "I promise to serve as you build your new empire, my king." He kissed his hand again before releasing it. Basileus smiled and nodded in acknowledgment.

For the first time ever, the group had witnessed the mythical transformation firsthand. The brothers knew Samuel was over seventy years of age. The hair on top of his head had long since fallen out, and all that remained were wispy white strands growing wildly from the sides and back of his wrinkled head. The dark bags under his eyes and deep creases that crossed his face looked like the intersecting lines of a map, all of them earned as mementos from a long, hard life. He walked with a limp after taking a bullet to his hip from a previous mission for the Brotherhood.

But the person who stood before them was no feeble old man. The person who had risen up from beneath the cloak was neither bent nor broken, neither old nor gray. The man who they knew as Samuel was young again. The wrinkles and lines had already begun to fade and seemed to continue receding right before their very eyes. The wound on his arm was now only a deep pink scratch. He stretched his back and found he could stand ramrod straight without any pain. The sagging skin around his neck had already tightened, as muscles formed and hardened everywhere across his body.

"All hail Basileus!" one of the brothers said. It was the first sound any of them had uttered since witnessing the miraculous rebirth.

"All hail Basileus!" they shouted in unison.

Basileus smiled. The final phase for his conquest of the world had begun.

CHAPTER FIFTEEN

Inside the Labyrinth
February 6, 12:18 p.m.

"I've never claimed to be an expert on ancient history," Phil said while taking in the impressive repository, "but wasn't the Library of Alexandria destroyed a couple thousand years ago? And, um—again, not an expert here—but I seem to recall it being in Egypt, not New York."

"Daedalus, if there was ever a collection that looked the part, this would be it, but I have to agree with Phil here. Wasn't the knowledge and history from that ancient library lost centuries ago?" Aliyah said.

Aliyah was very well read on many different cultures and their histories. The Greeks and Egyptians were two of her favorites. "If these really are authentic, this treasure trove of artifacts would be worth… It would literally be priceless. It would be the greatest archaeological discovery in the history of the world." Aliyah had to slow down her own excitement. She knew better. This couldn't be the famous collection. "Even if some of these date back to the time when the Library stood, there's no way anyone could verify these artifacts from the actual Library of Alexandria. The chain of custody was broken long ago. In any case, it's an incredible collection. May I take a closer look?"

"Be my guest. The area under the golden abacus structure over there may be of particular interest for you. It contains all of Archimedes' master works and some unfinished equations he was working on when he died." Daedalus pointed to what looked like a new-age metallic gold sculpture twenty feet from the entrance. The timeless relic served as a manual calculator and stood over six feet tall. Twelve golden rods ran vertically inside a thick jade frame. Rows of onyx orbs were organized in perfect columns, each spaced evenly beside another. The ancient counting machine was obviously not built for actual use, the precious metals being incredibly heavy and cumbersome to use. It must have been built long ago as an homage to the purest science of all, her favorite. Mathematics.

"Archimedes was known as the father of mathematics," Aliyah said. "He was a Greek mathematician, physicist, engineer, and inventor; one of the most brilliant minds of his time in an era that boasted heavyweights like Socrates, Plato, and Aristotle. Discovering even a single page from one of his original manuscripts would be an incredible find in and of itself. A collection containing his entire life's worth of calculations and personal notes would be a find beyond imagination." Aliyah couldn't resist the urge and hurried over to the giant mathematical edifice to sneak a peek at the documents purportedly stored there.

"The Library of Alexandria was attacked over the course of hundreds of years, losing precious knowledge to the ravages of these senseless raids," Daedalus said as he brought the group further into the collection. "I led an effort long ago to safeguard the knowledge and artifacts from future theft and destruction. I've continue to provide that protection until today."

"Gimme a break, man. Who the hell can trace their family tree that far back?" Dallas asked. "Is this stolen art from the Holocaust? I saw a movie about that before, Monument Men, I think. It was pretty good. Anyway, you're a real piece of shit if you're keeping the stuff your Nazi grandpa stole." Dallas lowered the volume of his voice like he was telling a secret. "Also, and I'm just putting it out there, so don't judge me, but I know a guy who buys this kind of stuff. Pays top dollar too. If you want, I can—"

"No, that won't be necessary, Mr. Hayle," Daedalus said. "And I assure you, my collection has nothing of the sort within these walls. I have accumulated artifacts and treasures from all over the world and added to this repository of knowledge. I hoped that one day humanity would realize that the true value of these ancient scrolls was for the genius they contained and not for their fundraising usefulness to museums or bragging rights for some private collector. People have always been afraid of what they don't understand

and intrinsically fear changing the status quo and commonly held beliefs. I realized this early on and made what now seems like a prophetic attempt to safeguard as much knowledge as possible for future generations. Although, I admit I never envisioned it would have to be protected and concealed for so long. But as Dallas alluded, even as recently as eighty years ago, the Nazis recklessly burned sacred Jewish texts in bonfires all over Europe. Those artifacts and the irreplaceable knowledge they contained went up in flames, lost forever. Unfortunately, we haven't really progressed much over the last three thousand years as a species."

"For the record, I was just joking about the black-market connection thing," Dallas said. "I knew you wouldn't steal things like that. Bad joke. Didn't mean any offense."

"That's alright, Dallas. None taken," he said. "The collection you see before you has been in my possession for almost two thousand years. This iteration of the Library of Alexandria contains even more information than it had at its peak. I continued to add to it as the sands of time passed by. The wisdom of many different civilizations and cultures are represented here now. Several of them were lost prior to my protection, but nonetheless, I've been successful in recovering large caches of those missing documents. I spent years pouring over these texts. There is knowledge contained in those ancient scrolls that answer some of the most existential and eternal questions people have." He let the weight of that sink in. "The Library had to remain secret until humanity matured enough not to misuse the power found in those volumes. I fear that time has run out anyway, but maybe, hopefully, we can find something in here that would be helpful in buying us—and the world—a little more time."

"This is for real, isn't it?" Gryph asked. It didn't seem like Daedalus was exaggerating or speaking metaphorically. "As insane as that explanation is, it does answer a lot of other questions I've had. With the lifetimes you've experienced, you could easily forge relationships with every government on Earth. The wealth you could acquire would be unfathomable." Gryph paused to contemplate for a moment. "Except you'd have to remain hidden. You would stay young while everyone else grew old around you. You couldn't conceal that for long. That must've been an incredibly lonely existence."

A visible sadness shone in the old man's eyes, "You're correct, Commander, but I pray my sacrifice has not been in vain. I've kept this repository intact until what may be humanity's final days on Earth. If we're unable to stop the toxin in time, we must ensure this collection is preserved for the civilization that rises after we're gone. Hopefully, they'll be better stewards of this knowledge than we were."

"Hey, which section has the thousand-year-old scroll that's going to tell us how to kill a bio-engineered toxin?" Dallas asked as he rifled through some of the parchments.

"Mr. Hayle, you must treat these items very carefully," Daedalus said sternly. "Most of these scrolls and papyrus haven't been touched in centuries. My library has much better temperature and humidity control now than during the thousands of years that preceded it. Unfortunately, many works have been lost to decay and the effects of time. However, the vast majority I've kept here are in very good condition despite their age. I'd like to keep them that way, so again, please be gentle."

Dallas carefully picked up a large piece of parchment with an inked image of a clock on it. The intricacies of the gears and the details on the drawing were mesmerizing, leaving Dallas speechless. He didn't take his eyes off the image until Daedalus walked over and carefully took the diagram from him, placing it back on the table. "That particular drawing was hand drawn by none other than Hipparchus, an ancient Greek astronomer and geographer who lived around the second century BCE. He's also famous for being the founder of trigonometry, but what may be of particular interest to you, Mr. Hayle, is that the design you see drawn here was the blueprint for the world's first computer."

"This is a design for a two-thousand-year-old computer?" The drawing took on an even greater significance in Dallas's mind.

"Incredible, isn't it? They found one on a shipwreck in 1901 and named it the 'Antikythera Mechanism' after the island of Antikythera near which the shipwreck was found. It was used as a navigational device and as a timepiece tracking the phases of the moon and the position of the planets relative to Earth. This early astronomical clock was said to be accurate to within one day every five hundred years. It was also capable of so much more than just tracking planets, much has been written on those capabilities here. I even have the prototype, which was built from the very design you're looking at now, and one of the most complex Antikythera-type mechanisms ever created. I store these and other one-of-a-kind relics in a separate area of the Library."

Dallas had no idea any computing technology, even in primitive form, had been around for so long.

Phil, Gryph, and Chief had also been listening to the informal dissertation Daedalus was giving to Dallas about the origins of the computer and the drawings. Aliyah was still busy examining the Archimedes section.

There was, however, an inconsistency that was bothering Gryph with respect to the overall arc of advancement in technology. He wondered if Daedalus had an answer for that, too. "If they had designs for these incredible machines two thousand years ago, how did we slip into the dark ages afterward? It seems like everything peaked early on, then faded away."

"I heard that's what all of Billy's girlfriends say about him, too. Peaks early and fades away." Dallas burst out laughing as if funnier words had never been spoken.

Chief chuckled too. He had to give Dallas credit. The guy had great comedic timing, even for an asshole.

"You're right, Commander. Things did indeed take a turn for the worse. It was on the heels of this first wave of enlightenment that the dark ages began. Many of the greatest thinkers, designers, engineers, and philosophers were brutally murdered for their new teachings or for simply being on the losing side of never-ending wars and conquests. The illumination and advancements they brought to the world of science and math weren't seen again until the fifteen hundreds. Those early years of death and destruction were when I first began to protect all of this." Daedalus gestured at the treasures that lay before them. "And for that very reason."

Aliyah walked back to the group, who all were still gathered near the entry, with an incredulous look on her face. "There's a three-volume set over there that was written by Archimedes. *The* Archimedes! I did a quick online search and was able to match some of the writing found in previously authenticated works to the books I saw here. The first volume I found was an expanded version of what's known as the Archimedes Palimpsest. It's the most important source of diagrams that the world had from Archimedes. The book in here is like the deluxe extended version. There are hundreds of handwritten notations in it, too. I can't believe this!" she said excitedly.

"You said it's a three-volume set. What are the other two volumes about?" Phil asked. "Anything interesting there?"

"That's the most amazing part. The other two books are both master summaries of his work. Both books deal with mathematics and time and space in a way I've never seen before. It's like an entirely new field of study. Even stranger, when I was reviewing the books, out of the corner of my eye, I noticed a glowing sphere hovering above a golden tablet. I checked closer and saw it wasn't connected to any type of power source and didn't seem to be giving off any heat either and gold isn't magnetic. It's very beautiful though. Any idea what its purpose is, Daedalus?"

"Ah. That special piece actually produces and consumes its own power, but its true purpose is as a communication device. I've never been able to harness its unique energy signature or decipher the messages it generates. I've tried many times to figure out how to make it work - but have yet to succeed. Maybe you'll have better luck with it than I have. It's probably the most powerful item in the entire collection."

"What was it supposed to do?" Chief asked. "You know, before you found it. You said it made its own power. Is it some kind of weapon?"

"To be honest, Chief, it was probably the most powerful weapon humans have ever possessed, but not for the reasons you think," Daedalus said cryptically. "This was the most powerful weapon in the world because it could predict the future. The last person to be able to use this orb successfully was Pythia, the Oracle of Delphi, almost three thousand years ago."

"What could she do with it that made it so special and powerful?" Dallas asked.

"She claimed she could interpret its messages and peer into the future. The emperors of ancient Greece wouldn't make any decisions without consulting her first."

"I watched a show late one night that was talking about all these crazy conspiracy theories," Chief said. "This billionaire went on and on about myths regarding ancient electrical technology, too. Something about the pyramids and wireless power even way back then. But based on what Ali and Daedalus just told us, I guess it's not much of a stretch. These guys also said there was ancient information hidden in the pyramids about the location of Atlantis, aliens, and those kinds of things. You got any of that in here?"

"A considerable amount of the Library is dedicated to those topics. You may be surprised by how simple the answer is to many of them, but I promise you'll never be the same again once you learn some of those truths." Daedalus didn't elaborate further.

"It's aliens for sure!" Dallas blurted. "I'll bet anyone here three to one odds right now that he's going to tell us he's really an alien, and the world has already been invaded. C'mon, any takers?"

"Sorry to disappoint you, Dallas, but I'm human, just like you. Well, maybe not *exactly like you* anymore, but I was born to a normal mother and father. Albeit a long time ago."

"Oh. Okay. No bet, everyone. You snooze, you lose." Dallas dusted his hands together as a "no deal" sign.

"This whole place is legitimate, isn't it?" Ali said, more of a statement than a question. "This really is the long-lost Library of Alexandria. The story of the manna and healing elixir, your timeless existence, it's all true?" She couldn't believe the words that were coming out of her mouth.

"Yes, Dr. Tzion, it's all true. I give you my word. I swear everything I've been telling you is the truth. I couldn't risk exposing the Library's existence prior to this, but we have never before been this close to the precipice of global extinction. If we fail to stop the toxin, we need to ensure that all of this remains protected for the next era of civilization. I need to know that you'll protect this with your lives if anything happens to me."

"I can't speak on anyone's behalf, but you have my word that I'll do everything in my power to stop the toxin from taking hold,"

Gryph said. "We'll do whatever is needed to ensure this collection is safeguarded for future generations."

"I'm definitely down. Fast cars, Black Hawk helicopters, evil scientists, plots to destroy the world. You couldn't pry me from this if you tried," Phil said as he rubbed his hands together, itching to get started.

"Did you just hear yourself, bro?" Dallas asked. "You just described the worst possible scenario. This mission is likely going to get us all killed, and yet here you are, dancing around like some six-year-old on Christmas morning. Why the hell are you being so upbeat? You were the one who was most worried about getting nuked or attacked when you first got here, remember? The toxin is even worse than all of that, except now you've gone all Rambo?"

"What can I tell you? I like our odds. Isn't that your thing?" Phil said jokingly.

"C'mon, Dallas," Gryph said. "We're the good guys, and the good guys always win."

"I agree. I'm in too," Aliyah said, crossing her arms over her chest.

"I go where Gryph goes," Chief said.

The five of them stood at the entry to the Library, looking intently at the one remaining member of the team yet to pledge his support to a lifelong mission to preserve the ancient library at all costs.

"Daedalus, if I agree to this mission, protocol, or whatever it's called - it's on one condition," Dallas said.

"What's the condition?"

"If I make it through all this, I get to keep the picture that Hippowhatever guy drew of the first computer."

"Dallas, if we're successful in defeating the toxin, and you make it through this, not only will I give you the picture, but I'll even throw in the original prototype."

Dallas saw massive dollar signs flash in his head and grinned a toothy smile. "Then you've got yourself a deal."

The Daedalus Protocol was a go.

CHAPTER SIXTEEN

The Labyrinth
February 9, 7:11 a.m.

"Morning, Ali. How'd you sleep?" Phil asked, walking out the door of his residence and seeing her closing her own behind her.

"To be honest, I didn't really sleep much at all. I didn't leave the lab until late, but then I couldn't shut my brain off, so I just tossed and turned. I'm running on fumes. How about you?"

"I slept okay, but I had the craziest dream last night. You guys were all in it, too. It was so vivid, but it was really out there. Daedalus was this ancient guy, literally hundreds of years old. He said he had the real Library of Alexandria secreted away here with all these incredible artifacts and books inside." Phil shook his head. "Like I said, it was nuts."

Aliyah stared at Phil. The smile she had worn when she greeted him in the corridor moments before evaporated into a genuine look of concern for her new friend.

"Bahahaha. I'm just messing with you. I know it's real." Aliyah rolled her eyes and affectionately punched Phil in the shoulder. He laughed. "It just sounds so insane when you say it out loud, doesn't it? But it is what it is."

"You had me second guessing myself for a moment there. I was hoping you were right, and this really was all just a bad dream."

"I'm just looking forward to getting out of here and doing something productive," Phil said. "I know we've had a lot to catch up on, and I've absorbed more about nano and biotechnologies in the past week than I ever thought I'd want or need to know in my lifetime, but I'm going stir-crazy just sitting around knowing the toxin is spreading out there somewhere. What were you working on last night? Find anything that could help us?"

"Not really. It was strange. I was working in the lab, waiting on some test results from the cytoplasm samples I took from the toxin. I really wanted to find out how the cellular repair mechanism worked and how and why that strange bioluminescent reaction comes into play. I had received some preliminary data earlier in the evening, but the sample I used must have been contaminated because the results made no sense at all. I stayed up recalibrating everything with Dallas late last night and verified that the new sample we used was pure and uncontaminated, then I re-ran all the lab work again and tried to catch a few hours of sleep while it processed, but I just couldn't get into a deep sleep."

Phil could understand why she was so tired and yet unable to get any rest.

"I'll be able to catch a power nap a little later on," Aliyah said to reassure him, as if reading his mind. "I want to be back in the lab when the results come in. Let's get going, funny guy. I'm anxious to get my answers and then hopefully some rest."

The two of them covered the short distance to the comms center in under a minute. They knew Gryph had beaten them there before they even walked in. Aliyah inhaled the dark roasted aroma. "Mmmm. It smells so good in here. I'm in dire need of a caffeine fix. It's a borderline medical emergency." He knew Aliyah was exaggerating, but only slightly.

"Yeah, I walked by here a few times last night and saw you burning the midnight oil," Gryph said. "I figured you could use some of the high-octane stuff when you checked in. I made a fresh pot and left it on the counter over there. Enjoy." Gryph pointed to the tall clear carafe across from him. "By the way, Dallas got a head start on everyone for once. He was here before five o'clock this morning and has been babysitting your lab ever since. He's already three cups deep."

Aliyah recounted again, for everyone this time, how Dallas stayed up with her to review the readings from the tests and confirm the error she received from the first results wasn't due to a computer glitch or an AI hallucination. Dallas was adamant the computer systems were working perfectly, and they both concluded it must have been the sample.

"He actually stuck around to keep me company long after we determined the computers were working fine. I think the thought of getting that Antikythera prototype and original drawing really motivated him."

"Listen, as long as he's helping us stop the toxin, I couldn't care less what his motivation is," Chief said. "I'm just glad he's cooperating more. The little guy is starting to grow on me. He's funny as hell, but I'll deny it if you guys say a word about it to him."

Aliyah laughed. "I won't say anything, I promise. Let's see if the results from last night's run are complete." She steered the group under the stone archway that separated the communication center and the biolab. All the Labyrinth workspaces were configured in a spoke-and-wheel formation. The communications center where they'd entered was the central hub, everything else branched off from there.

"Looks like the gang's all here. Just in time, too. I could use a refill. Which one's mine?" Dallas asked, looking at the group, each person holding a steaming cup of Gryph's own magic elixir.

"I brought you one. Settle down, cowboy," Chief said and handed Dallas a cup that he had brought to the table with his own. "We heard you were in early helping Ali, so I figured I'd grab one for you. No big deal."

Dallas took the cup from Chief and gulped down a mouthful. "Damn, this really is good. Thanks, Billy boy. And Gryph too, obviously."

Aliyah and Gryph hadn't stopped with the rest of them for the impromptu coffee break. Instead, the pair hurried into the lab, eager to learn the results from Ali's most recent analysis, leaving the balance of the team to relax for a few minutes while they got their first coffee fix.

"Ali told us you two were up late recalibrating the sensors and ran diagnostics on the AI engine. That must've been a lot of work," Phil said to Dallas between sips.

"Yeah. Total bitch."

"What?" Phil exclaimed, almost doing a spit-take with the coffee in his mouth.

"No, the work was a bitch, dude, not Ali," Dallas said. "She's awesome. We figured the sensors must've lost their calibration or something, but she kept going on and on about some element not being recognized or some shit like that. I was too tired to understand it all. I just wanted to make sure I wasn't going to get blamed for slowing us down, so I stuck around for a bit to make sure it wasn't any of my stuff and then went to bed. I just tossed and turned, though. Couldn't sleep a wink. Too much late-night coffee maybe, so I decided to come in early and triple check that everything on my end was still kosher. So far, so good. If the results are still messed up this time, it's not on me."

Aliyah and Gryph were huddled together inside the lab, engaged in a hushed conversation over a monitor adjacent to the electron microscope. By the look on Ali's face, she'd discovered something very concerning.

"This is maddening. I checked the sample for contaminants and ran sensor calibration tests before we started this series. Dallas had all his systems dialed in, too. There must be another explanation. It's impossible!"

"What's impossible?" Daedalus asked. He'd just walked in and joined the larger group before heading toward where Aliyah and Gryph were conferring.

"I need to run tests on another set of samples. There must be another reason for this."

"A better reason for what, Aliyah? I think I'm still a few steps behind. Please bring me up to speed." The rest of the group had just made their way into the lab and crowded in to listen. Everyone was eager to hear about any new developments.

"Before I give you all a possible explanation, let me give some background on what I'm talking about here." Aliyah brought up a video of the toxin on the computer. "I've been extracting some of the cytoplasm from the cells using this next-level nanobot technology that Daedalus has here in the Workshop. It's incredible tech, by the way, but we can talk about that later. Anyway, I extracted some of the toxin's cellular fluid, as you can see on the video." Aliyah started the playback, and the image zoomed in on a single nanobot extending what looked like a giant spear deep into the cell. The magnification was incredible, and the details were crystal clear.

Just like the previous times that Aliyah punctured the cell wall, the cytoplasm and cellular structures began to glow. Unlike last time, however, she had the nanobots tear through the cell membrane until all of the cytoplasm leaked out from the organism, not giving it a chance to repair itself. This resulted in the complete destruction of the cell. "You can see the moment it happens right here." The video showed that, as the glowing cellular fluid poured out through the opening in the cell wall, the intensity of the glow diminished until it was extinguished entirely.

"We had the nanobot capture a cytoplasm sample after the initial puncture, just as the bioluminescence first presented itself. I wanted to discover and isolate the compound responsible for the cellular repair and determine if there was a weakness in its design that we could exploit in order to neutralize it."

As of yet, Aliyah hadn't revealed anything shocking. "When I ran the glowing material through the mass spectrometer, the results came back as inconclusive."

"The mass spec is the machine that identifies compounds and chemical properties, right?" Phil asked.

"Exactly," Aliyah said. "I guess you really were paying attention this week."

"Okay, so the ninja here gets the gold star from the teacher," Dallas said. "I didn't know we were going to be tested later. I would have taken notes."

"Ali, what did you mean by 'inconclusive?'" Daedalus asked, ignoring Dallas as usual.

"That's just it. The machine couldn't analyze the element from the cytoplasm. This state-of-the-art mass spec machine couldn't identify a single compound from the glowing toxin. The elements they're composed of don't even show up on the periodic table. Dallas ran the compounds through his AI engine, and it couldn't find any relationship between this glowing compound and any other substance known to science."

Phil had been taking crash courses on science from Ali. This latest discovery conflicted with what she had previously told him. "How can that be, Ali? You told me before that everything is made up from some element on the periodic table, or some combination of them."

"Yes, you're right again, Phil." Aliyah shot Dallas a look warning him to keep his mouth shut, this time he obliged. Aliyah was smart and beautiful but also ex-Mossad, and Dallas knew she'd have no problem kicking his ass. Satisfied he wasn't going to interrupt, she pressed on. "These elements are at the core of everything on Earth. They're the building blocks that everything is made from, and this machine couldn't recognize a single one of them in the sample."

"Sorry, I'm still not sure where this is leading," Daedalus said.

"To be honest, sir, me neither. I didn't know what I expected to see when the first set of results came back, but I wasn't prepared for unknown elements. I figured there must've been an error in the program or some contaminant affecting the sensors, and the 'unknown element' message was just the way the system reported the glitch. As I told you before, Dallas checked his end of things, and I checked mine, both were error free. We recalibrated the entire system and reran the samples overnight. I just checked the results from the second series of tests and they're still displaying the same error message."

"What Ali and I were discussing when you all came over," Gryph said, "were the possible reasons for getting these strange readings. The instruments are still calibrated, and Dallas already triple checked that this isn't a software or hardware issue. I asked Ali the same thing that Phil just did. If everything on Earth can be traced back to one of the one hundred and eighteen elements listed on the periodic table except this glowing nano-organism, then maybe the simplest answer explains it easily. The organism we're dealing with isn't from here."

"Whoa, whoa, whoa, what do you mean, 'not from here?' Please don't tell me we're talking about outer space now." Dallas rolled his eyes and let out an exasperated sigh.

"I had the same initial reaction you did, Dallas," Aliyah said. "I think the exact words I said to Gryph were 'maddening' and 'impossible.'"

Gryph sensed something in Aliyah had shifted while she was presenting the results from the second set of tests. "You said that you had a similar 'initial' reaction. Have you changed your mind about the possibility of it being extraterrestrial now?" Gryph was a master at noticing such adjectives and unpacking their significance in real time.

"I need to think it through some more before I can declare whether we're dealing with an unknown substance that is of extraterrestrial origin," she said. "I'd like to exclude several other possibilities first. But if it is, in fact, not from Earth, it would explain why we can't identify it on the mass spectrometer."

"Okay, I think that brings me full circle. This is when I walked in," Daedalus said. "I promised you all full disclosure before, and I believe I've demonstrated that by admitting my lineage and revealing the existence of the Library of Alexandria to you. Only a select few have been through these walls throughout my time here. The brilliant minds that I gave access to it used the knowledge and artifacts found here to discover major breakthroughs in science and medicine. Professor Hawking, the renowned theoretical physicist, made the journey here despite his disability. I was able to show him some star maps I found in the oldest archives of the Library. I carbon dated the astronomical maps and they pre-dated ancient Egypt by thousands of years."

"And this is relevant to us today because?" Dallas was quickly losing his patience due to lack of sleep and the ongoing conversations about space germs and talk of ancient Egypt again.

"Because, Mr. Hayle, these maps showed constellations that have only recently become visible using powerful telescopes. These star maps are as accurate as any taken by today's large-array telescopes. Except there was no way for ancient people to have seen it. Someone or something else provided them with that knowledge."

"Daedalus, is there anything you've discovered down here that could definitively prove alien existence?" Gryph asked.

"If you're referring to little green men or the more popular gray version, as they're known, with the big black eyes and such, no. I have seen nothing in here that proves their existence one way or the other. There are some drawings in the Library that depict beings that fit the typical description of aliens to some degree, but they also contain many other mythological creatures and images of man-gods that often took odd forms. These alien characters could just be another one of those examples, or they could be the real thing. There are very few illustrations or references to them in the

Library. In my opinion, there likely would be more historical records for such an important discovery. But I'm not naïve enough to think that the answers to every question lie inside the Library."

"Just to be clear," Gryph said, "There's no confirmed record of any kind of 'Close Encounters'-type moment stashed away down here, but is there anything you have in the collection that contains an unexplainable phenomenon like this? Maybe that'll give us a place to start."

"That's the right question to ask, Gryph, and the answer is yes. There's a lot in here that's unexplainable. I can also confirm that there are life forms out there we can't begin to understand."

"Hold on, man!" Dallas said. "A minute ago, you said there was no proof of aliens in the oldest and largest library mankind has ever known, and then a second later, you're confirming there are other life forms out there. Pick a side, buddy. I think you may be going senile in your old age."

Daedalus laughed. "You may be one of the funniest people I've ever encountered, Mr. Hayle."

"You need to get out more because I wasn't kidding. What kind of crazy talk is this now?" Dallas asked.

"I told you the story of the elixir and how it healed and has kept me alive all these years. But what I haven't told you is how this powerful substance came into existence. I believe that it may answer at least part of the questions we face this morning. I haven't told anyone this, and as I told you earlier, I promised someone long ago that I would take this secret to my grave. If we're successful in our mission to stop the toxin, you must all swear to do the same."

Solemn nods were given in response. Daedalus rested his gaze on Dallas.

"What? I won't say anything. Scout's honor. I'm all ears, Gramps."

"I really don't have much of a choice but to take you all at your word, it seems, and only because what I'm about to reveal to you is pertinent to the problem at hand. You all recall the story of the manna we spoke about before. Scientists and biblical scholars have been looking for possible explanations for the manna for quite some time. A few scientific theories have been brought forward to explain this phenomenon. Some have posited that it was a specific type of lichen called *lichen esculentus*. Lichens are generally composed of a fungus and algae that bind together to act as a single organism. The lichen esculentus can grow to a height of six inches right on the desert floor and is still found in the Sinai desert to this day."

"You think it was the manna? That's what kept everyone alive for forty years, the lichen growth?" Gryph asked.

"Actually, no. One of the more popular theories, though, and the one I think is most probable, is that the manna was really the cocoon of a parasitic beetle known as the Trehala. It can still be found growing in the Sinai desert to this day. This Trehalose cocoon is a white crystalline carbohydrate made from two glucose molecules. It's highly nutritious, with a protein content of over thirty percent. A recent chemical analysis showed that it contained a mixture of three basic sugars and pectin. That would also explain the stories from the Bible that said it tasted like cake fried in honey due to the natural sugars it contained. The Bible also says it would turn wormy if it was left overnight, so fresh collections happened every morning to avoid infestation. If the manna was truly these spent cocoons, it stands to reason some of the larvae could have easily been mixed-in with the empty cocoons and hatched in people's baskets and bowls. Maybe that's why the Bible included the warning about keeping them overnight."

"I heard that story growing up, but I'm seeing this in an entirely new light," Aliyah said. "I discarded all those miracles as folklore and metaphor long ago. Now you're giving me reason to think that parts of it could have happened in a literal sense. That's a lot to process."

"What I'm about to reveal to you now may not make it any easier, I'm afraid. I think it was the Trehala cocoons the Jewish people found during those first days and weeks in the desert that gave them the ability to remain healthy. It would have been the first time they would have seen this type of cocoon because the entire populace was locked behind the mighty gated cities of ancient Egypt for hundreds of years prior. The Trehala would have been plentiful in volume and a very welcome treat for a weak and starving nation.

"If the beetles are still around today, wouldn't they have the same healing properties as they did back then?" Aliyah asked.

"I alluded to this answer earlier when you asked why I thought the special regenerative qualities of the manna were not found in later years. I believe that sometime during the first days of the Jewish people fleeing into the desert, the Earth was bombarded by a meteor shower. I think some of these meteorites were carrying our mysterious organism, and were deposited on Earth when the meteorites broke through our atmosphere, crashing to the ground. I suspect some of the meteoric debris landed in close proximity to Trehala beetles, as they both covered wide swaths throughout the desert. Its healing properties would have been transferred to the larvae, and by association, the cocoons. The Jewish people then ate this literal heaven-sent superfood, keeping them healthy and thriving in even the most inhospitable conditions."

"That would also explain how the cells managed to stay alive in the vacuum chamber of the electron microscope," Aliyah said. "They were conditioned to that extreme environment, possibly travelling billions of miles, over millions of years in the cold vacuum of space. They would have had to evolve to survive. Maybe the deep cold of space protected them like some sort of cryogenic hibernation state. When they were finally warmed up after landing on Earth, their internal restorative properties kicked in and brought them back to life. I've read extensively about organisms put in suspended animation and then brought back from the dead. It doesn't seem to work in complex systems like human beings, though. Tardigrades, for instance, are tiny marine creatures that can be brought back to life after being frozen, dehydrated, boiled, or even put into a vacuum chamber, and they return to normal once put in their regular environment. I know what you're thinking, but they don't have this bioluminescent cellular repair mechanism. I checked. They're just incredibly durable creatures," she said with a laugh.

"That's a good theory, Ali, and I bet it's not too far off from the truth, but I must correct you on something," Daedalus said. "The elixir, whatever its origin, cannot bring people back once they're dead. It can repair a person at a cellular level, but once a person's life force is completely gone, the elixir has no effect. It has the power to bring someone back from even the very brink of death. Without it, I would not be standing here today. Once someone dies, though, they are lost forever."

Daedalus looked away from the team, recalling memories from long, long ago. He quickly forced himself back to the present and to the problems at hand. He knew this wasn't the time for personal reflection. He cleared his throat and continued his hypothesis. "The seventh plague that befell Egypt was the plague of hail. This wasn't just a severe hailstorm, though. This heavy biblical hail fell to the earth, but burst into flames when it hit the ground."

"I just googled that verse," Aliyah said, reading the text from her computer. "'The Lord sent thunder and hail, and fire ran down to the earth. And the Lord rained hail upon the land of Egypt. There was hail and fire flashing continuously in the midst of the hail, very heavy hail, such as had never been in all the land of Egypt since it became a nation.'"

"Sounds like a pretty decent description of a meteor shower to me," Chief said. "You think that was the one which gave the beetles their superpowers?"

"I don't think anyone could ever prove that, but I think it supports the theory that there was meteoric activity very close to the same time as the departure of the Jews from Egypt," Daedalus said. "Meteor showers can occur over a few days and, in some cases over a period of weeks, or months. Whatever the real source of the manna was—lichen, cocoon, or something else—it likely became infected by this organism from the meteor shower. The contaminated food source then passed its healing properties along to whoever consumed it. It very well could have been a one-time event, and the Jews were lucky enough to stumble upon it at the right place at the right time."

Gryph offered another possibility. "When the meteor showers concluded, our special little hitchhikers were no longer falling to Earth, and the cocoons were relegated back to simple, sweet protein snacks. The effects of that early dose kept them healthy for some period of time in the wilderness. That would also explain why the manna that fell in later years didn't have the same effect. It wasn't really the manna providing the healing properties. It was really the short window of exposure to the meteor shower early on. Daedalus told us the first batches of manna were the only ones that mattered. If he's right about the meteor shower, the rest makes sense, as odd as it sounds."

Daedalus nodded. "I'm quite sure this miracle organism didn't come from Earth. We've all seen it moving under the microscope, and we know it's alive. By virtue of that alone, it means it's an extraterrestrial life form. Like I said to Dallas a moment ago, it may not be little green men, but I'm certain it came from somewhere out there." Daedalus looked up at the cavern roof, but everyone knew what he meant. "I hope this information helps you with your examinations, Aliyah."

Everyone started to get up from the table and back to their stations, but Dallas remained seated, wearing a defeated look. Daedalus sat down beside him. "What's wrong, Mr. Hayle? You look even more sullen than normal."

"I just can't believe it. You really are who you say you are. It's all true, even the meteor part. As batshit crazy as it all sounds, it makes the most sense to me now, too." He looked directly at Daedalus. "I'm sorry for not believing you before."

"That's okay, Dallas. I know it's a lot to digest, and I realize I didn't give you much of a choice when I recruited you. My previous computer expert, an incredibly brilliant woman, was killed in the ambush that took my previous team. I had to ensure our systems and information remained secure. I was under attack and couldn't allow the Library to fall into the hands of these evil men. I needed to secure someone right away, and you were the perfect fit. I wasn't honest with you when we first met and gave you an unfair ultimatum. I owe you an apology. I give you my word I won't lie to you anymore. I really do need your help, but you are free to go whenever you choose."

Dallas contemplated everything Daedalus said. "I appreciate the apology and the offer to let me go, but there isn't any point in leaving. I'd be just as screwed as the rest of the world if we can't stop the toxin. I'll stay on as long as you need me."

"Thank you. I appreciate it very much."

"I think I also might have a way we can find this Basileus asshole."

"How do you propose to do that?" Daedalus asked, a hint of surprise in his voice.

"Easy," Dallas said. "By using me as bait."

CHAPTER SEVENTEEN

London, England
February 8, 11:11 a.m.

Blood and gore pooled at Basileus's feet. His hands were swollen and sore. He had just returned from visiting Marcus deep in the bowels of his castle. The man hadn't coughed up any new information, but Basileus was still wary his old friend was holding out. He beat the excommunicated captive within an inch of his life before giving up on the brutal interrogation. He was scrubbing the remnants of that "conversation" from his skin beneath a scalding-hot shower.

He stepped out of the massive steel-and-glass shower and slipped on a pair of black pants and white V-neck T-shirt that hugged his well-defined physique. He walked out of his large dressing area and made his way to the kitchen, where he found Dima waiting for him.

"I have some good news from my contacts in the States," Dima said, happy to report the positive development. "I think we have a lead on Daedalus's location."

Basileus tossed the newspaper he was carrying onto the counter. "Tell me."

"We intercepted an interesting conversation from the hacker we were following. He was having coffee at a cybercafe we were watching in midtown Manhattan. Lucky for us, this guy likes to run his mouth. He told the chick who owns the place that he was really a James Bond type spy working for some super-secret government organization and that he's saving the world from a food virus. It's our guy for sure."

"How do you know he's connected to Daedalus? Maybe someone else has learned of our plans. It could be that he's working for a different organization, maybe even the US government itself. If this hacker said he worked for the government, maybe he was telling the truth. This could be disastrous for us, Dima!"

Basileus was growing very concerned. He knew that even the best laid plans were often thwarted at the last minute. He didn't want to leave anything to chance when he was this close.

"No, I wouldn't worry about that, sir. After we wiped out Daedalus's first team at our test sites, I put word on the street looking for any information on where I could find him. I didn't hear anything until last week. Like I said before, he was a ghost."

Dima had numerous contacts in the criminal underworld. Basileus was wealthy beyond imagination and spared no expense on security. Dima made good use of this capital by hiring only the best and paying them top dollar, too. In a world where there was no loyalty, Dima managed to amass a loyal following of thieves, snitches, and thugs who would do anything to keep themselves in his good graces, and his money flowing.

"The guy's name we're tracking is Dallas Hayle. He's some kind of computer whiz. Also has a big gambling problem. He's in deep with a bookie of ours who runs one of our underground casinos. The bookie was getting impatient with Hayle and started to apply pressure to collect. He said Hayle gave him some story about working for this super-rich Daedalus character, and he was getting a huge payday from him for some work he was doing, but he just needed a little more time to finish his job and collect. The bookie told me he remembered Daedalus's strange name, me asking around about him, and called me right away. I guess Hayle must have been super paranoid and would only make calls from the café. I got the name of the place from the bookie. He saw the name of the cafe stenciled on the window in the background during a Zoom call. Since we know what Hayle looks like, I've had my guys rotating in and out of the café ever since. They have digital microphones to listen in on this idiot's conversations. That's where my guys were positioned when he started running his mouth. I don't think he's government. I think he's just a computer geek in way over his head."

Basileus took a deep breath and tried to slow his rapidly beating heart. He would crush these meddling fools once and for all. "Excellent work, Dima. You've done well." Dima was bursting with pride, but he did his best to play it off as just another completed assignment.

"Was your operative in New York able to track Hayle back to Daedalus's base of operations?"

Dima had already asked his men that very question but received the same disappointing news he now had to deliver. "No. Unfortunately, he wasn't able to follow him. My men were hanging back a fair distance to ensure Hayle wouldn't notice the tail after he left the café. By the time he got out and across the road, Hayle already ducked between buildings. When my guys made it to the alley, Hayle was gone. He must have slipped into one of those adjacent buildings or realized he was being followed and found a way to shake them loose. I'm not sure."

Basileus contemplated this information for a moment. "Have someone check the title registrations and leases on every unit in every building within two blocks of that alley. I want to know exactly who the occupants are. If you find a shell company, pierce the corporate veil, and tell me who really sits behind it. Make sure to keep a couple of men posted outside that coffee shop twenty-four seven. If he shows up again, I want to know where he goes."

"Yes, sir. I've already instructed my team to take up their previous position across from the coffee shop. I also posted someone in the alley undercover, dressed as a homeless person camping out behind the buildings where they first lost him. Trust me, if he comes back through there, we'll be able to follow him all the way to Daedalus."

"Very good, Dima. Remember, it's better that he guides us to Daedalus first, then kill him. For now, instruct them to just observe and remain unseen."

"Yes, sir. Those were the instructions I gave them before I came here to deliver this news to you."

"You have always proven yourself loyal, Dima, and you've been instrumental in assisting me with completing these final tasks. I know you're anxious to join the Brotherhood, and your time is coming soon, I promise. Once our cleansing seed takes root throughout the world, and you bring me Daedalus's head, I will bring you up into the Brotherhood, and you and your progeny will be the princes of my new world for lifetimes to come."

"I won't fail you, Basileus. You have my loyalty until my dying breath."

"I know you won't fail me, but back to the business at hand. Explain to me how we're getting the seeds across the border, the crossings have never been more scrutinized."

"I've taken care of the border crossing issue already," Dima said, "The senior officer who controls the night shift at the Port of Le Havre in France is someone we own. This guy has a sick thing for little boys. We have enough dirt on him to ruin his pathetic life twice over. He'll do whatever I say. As soon as our shipment arrives, he'll guarantee that our containers will be unloaded onto flatbed trucks and given priority clearance. I have all the paperwork processed for the drivers and customs already."

The seeds and fertilizer Basileus was distributing awaited their final delivery to locations all over the world. Brother Marcus was responsible for the distribution of the seed and fertilizer throughout western Europe, but that portion of the operation fell into disarray when Marcus went rogue. Dima took advantage of the opportunity to prove he was capable of more than just protection and asked Basileus to let him take over where Marcus left off. Basileus knew he couldn't bring anyone new into the fold at such a late stage, so he agreed to give Dima the opportunity to finish coordinating the rollout of the containers filled with his deadly seed, and he had to admit, Dima had done a meticulous job thus far.

"Have the brothers all arrived in the Chambers yet?" Basileus asked.

"Yes, sir. I told everyone to expect you at noon. We can walk over now. Everyone is already assembled and waiting for you."

Dima and Basileus walked the familiar path from the main residence to their temple and found all the brothers awaiting his arrival. He took his seat on the large marble throne in front of the Brotherhood and appraised the robed men in front of him.

"My brothers, for the last hundred years, humans have been expanding their deadly footprint across this magnificent planet. The last few generations have exploited the resources of our beautiful world and have left her scarred and polluted. The damage caused by global energy companies drilling and fracking for oil and gas would take decades to repair if they stopped all activity today. But they're not stopping; they're only increasing their lust for this black gold. The lumber and mining industries have taken chainsaws to the very lungs of our delicate world." He paused, and murmurs of agreement swept through the men in attendance.

"The seas are rising in coastal areas. Hurricanes and tropical storms are growing more intense each season. It seems we have a 'storm of the century' every other year now. Wildfires have been raging unchecked through California and Western Canada. Marine life is being decimated by overfishing, and the number of fish returning to their hatching grounds to spawn has dwindled to almost nothing. They are poisoning our planet, our very home!"

The volume rolled through the group, louder now. The anger and resolve rising from the chatter was palpable.

"How many more species need to go extinct because of people's ignorance and malice? The air is so toxic in Johannesburg, Beijing, and Chile that long-term exposure can bring on respiratory distress and often causes irritated eyes and sinuses. This is what passes as 'fresh' air in much of the world today. We would never sit idly by if another species was attacking the planet the way that humans have. This butchery must end now!" Basileus smashed his fist on his throne's marble armrest, then stood.

The Brotherhood jumped up from their seats, fists thrust high in the air while they cheered for their great savior, Basileus. They were saving the entire planet for generations to come. What pursuit could be more noble? Basileus raised his hand toward his devoted congregation, and they quickly settled back into silence.

"We must face the difficult truth that, left unchecked, the human race will continue its destructive ways, and our planet will suffer irreversible consequences. The sacrifice that this generation will make will go down in the annals of history as the rectification that is essential to ensure the continuity of life on Earth for the next millennium. I have secured the expertise required to ensure that the world's nuclear reactors, hydroelectric dams, nuclear arsenals, power grids, and other pieces of vital infrastructure will be well attended to throughout the period of time that society devolves into chaos, madness, and finally, eternal silence. The footprint of humanity will shrink from just over 8 billion to just under fifty million people, or so our calculations project. That will be more than enough to repopulate the world responsibly. The reduced demand in consumption from such a small number of citizens will allow the planet to heal and restore itself from the damage we have inflicted. Pollution will be all but eliminated. The next era of our species would be powered by renewable energy and with genuine care and concern for our home. I will restore balance to nature. A fresh, clean world will rise with my new design." Basileus stood. "The Earth will be reborn, and I will be its king!"

Cheers erupted again, even louder than before, echoing in the marble chamber. Even Dima found himself on his feet, cheering, an outburst that normally would be frowned upon due to his lack of official ascension to the Brotherhood, but everyone was swept up in the fervor of the moment until Basileus silenced his loyal followers once more.

"Each of you and your immediate families will be royals among mere mortals. The power of eternal life that flows in my veins will one day course through yours. You will live a multitude of lifetimes as a reward for your loyalty today." He looked at Brother Samuel. The others in attendance followed Basileus's gaze until they too were all staring at Brother Samuel. The man who only two days earlier stood in the same spot as a weak old man appeared to look not a day over thirty. The shirt he was wearing below his black hooded cloak barely contained his powerful arms and massive chest. Thick brown hair flowed from his head. His bright, clear eyes met the stare of each of his brethren. A warm, generous smile revealed sparkling white teeth.

"Believe what he says, my brothers," Samuel said. "I gave my life to our cause and have been given a mind and a body eclipsing anything I had before."

"All hail Basileus!" came the thunderous reply. Although he was on the outside of the Brotherhood for now, Dima knew exactly what had just happened. There was no mistaking it. He was witnessing nothing less than the birth of a new god.

CHAPTER EIGHTEEN

The Labyrinth
February 9, 9:29 a.m.

Aliyah felt herself growing more comfortable with the explanation that Daedalus had given her. The outrageous claims actually filled in a lot of the puzzle. She refocused her investigation toward analyzing the genetic makeup of the nanobacteria now that she knew the equipment was working properly. Aliyah initiated a flurry of tests across a multitude of machines throughout the Workshop laboratory, and most of the team kept clear of the whirling dervish she'd morphed into. Gryph was assisting as best he could, having spent countless hours in a lab during his days with the CIA and FBI. Aliyah welcomed the extra pair of experienced hands and a colleague that she could bounce theories off, as new facts came to light. Gryph certainly had a knack for piecing together disjointed bits of data into a cohesive picture, but there wasn't much to go on yet.

Phil watched Aliyah buzz around the lab, attending to various machines and analyzing data from the samples she was testing. He saw Gryph working the gamma ray and X-ray machines that Aliyah introduced Phil to earlier when she toured him around, explaining the purpose, advantages, and disadvantages of each device.

"I'm gonna get out of here and get some fresh air. I can't keep sitting around watching everyone else doing something productive," Phil said to Dallas. "We're out of coffee, and I'm not about to embarrass myself and brew up a pot for everyone after drinking the stuff Gryph's been making. I'll grab something topside and maybe a quick bite. It's not like we can order Uber Eats down here. Might as well make myself useful." He stood up and stretched his back and rolled his shoulders. Pops and creaks released the tension from sitting for so long.

"I'll go with you," Dallas said. "I watched Ali do a bunch of these experiments last night. It's like watching paint dry. I have no desire to watch her do it again. And besides, I know a great place to go for coffee and pastries. Also, the girl who works there is totally into me."

It took a lot for Phil not to burst out laughing, but he remained in control. "Happy to have the company. I'm dying to see what your girlfriend looks like."

"Screw you, Bruce Lee. What's that supposed to mean? You don't think I can get the hotties? And by the way, I never said she was my girlfriend."

"I didn't mean to insinuate anything. I'm sure she's a lovely girl. Chief is busy with Daedalus somewhere, and everyone else is in the lab. Let's head up. I'll buy."

Dallas grinned. "Magic words, my friend. Let's roll." The two of them walked back through the length of the Workshop until they reached the elevator that would take them to the underground parking structure a couple hundred feet above their heads. After walking through the ground level exit, they found themselves under a cloudy sky that cast a grayish pall above the two buildings that straddled the alleyway in which they now stood.

"Geez, it's colder than a witch's tit out here," Dallas said as soon as they left the shelter of the steel and concrete building, exposing the pair to the biting cold air.

"You said the coffee shop was only a few minutes from here, and it's really not all that bad out. We'll be there in no time, plus you'll get to see your girlfriend." Phil wasn't sure if his mini pep talk worked or if Dallas just needed the additional motivation to get out of the cold, but they both picked up the pace and found themselves at the door to the coffee shop a few minutes later.

The sign above the door said *Bytes Internet Café*. Their logo, a cute little digital mouse perched beside a computer screen displaying a multi-colored coffee bean, was splashed across the windows. Phil reached the heavy oak door first and pulled it open using the large brass handle. Dallas walked through first, rushing inside to get away from the cold. Phil followed, and the heavy oak door swung shut behind them.

The aroma of cinnamon and roasted coffee rolled through the little shop on currents of warm air. An old man sitting in the back corner of the café had just finished the last sips from his cup and began wrapping up his partially eaten sandwich to take home, his head bobbing to the jazz tune playing overhead. Other than a couple of other loners, the café was relatively empty.

"Well, if it isn't my very own Jason Bourne." The greeting came from a petite woman with tattooed *sleeves*, running up her arms and blonde hair that ended in bright green tips. She appeared from the kitchen and slipped behind the long counter that ran the length of the café. The only break in the long solid oak countertop was a curved glass cooler full of sandwiches and delicious looking pies and cakes. Even more baked goods sat under acrylic domes by the register.

"Hi, Luna," Dallas said. "You're looking gorgeous, as always." She smiled at the compliment and blew him a kiss.

Phil looked at Dallas for an explanation to the Jason Bourne comment. Dallas winked at him. "I may have exaggerated my skill set a bit. Just roll with it, bud. She's crazy hot, and I think I might have a chance with her." Phil sighed and followed Dallas over to the register.

"Morning, guys. What can I get for you?" Luna asked. "We have a chai tea latte and cinnamon bun special on this morning, if you're interested." The two men looked at each other, shrugged, then nodded in unison.

Phil paid the bill in cash and left a very generous tip. He took a table off to the side that gave him a view of the entire coffee shop. The old man in the corner left while he and Dallas were placing their order, leaving the rear of the café free for them to speak privately.

"What'd I tell you, man? She's a total smokeshow, huh?" Dallas was watching his make-believe girlfriend prepare their drinks at the bar. Her back was turned to them, and Dallas couldn't peel his eyes off her toned legs, wrapped in tight-fitting black skinny jeans. She had a fit, athletic body, like a dancer. Ballet, not pole.

Luna also had numerous piercings adorning her lips, nose, and brow. Her ears carried enough hardware to set off an airport metal detector from five feet away. Phil wasn't really into that look and figured she'd be even more attractive without all the steel and neon. But he had to admit, with or without it, Luna was stunning.

"She's very pretty, Lama. I can see why you like her. I just can't understand why she likes you, though. I guess it makes sense since you're, like, James Bond, or was it Jason Bourne? My bad."

Dallas glared at Phil and then burst out laughing. "So, I embellished a bit. Sue me."

Phil was worried Dallas could get carried away trying to impress Luna and inadvertently divulge information that could jeopardize their operations. "Just be careful about what you say. The team before us was murdered. Don't forget that."

"It's not like I told her all the details about Daedalus or the Workshop. She just thinks I'm a little more dangerous and mysterious than you all do. Who am I to argue? Besides, I need all the help I can get." He laughed again at his own expense, and Phil couldn't help but join in.

"You guys seem to be having a good morning," Luna said as she brought them a tray with two steaming drinks and a pair of large sticky cinnamon buns topped with a ridiculously decadent amount of cream cheese icing. "Usually, Lama here is all grumpy when he walks in. It takes at least half a cup before he cracks a smile for me. I've never heard him laugh before. I was beginning to think he didn't know how."

"I've told you about the line of work I'm in. It's just hard for me to let my guard down, Luna. Danger could strike at any minute. I can't allow myself to get distracted, even by someone as beautiful and sexy as you. Too many lives are at stake." He layered it on thicker than the icing on his cinnamon bun.

"Mm-hmmm." She eyed him suspiciously. "I'm not sure if you're telling me the truth or totally bullshitting me, but I think it's cute, and you're sweet. Enjoy the tea. Let me know if you need anything else." Luna winked at Dallas before she left the table and walked back behind the pastry display.

"See? I told you she was into me." Dallas was grinning from ear to ear.

"'Danger could strike at any minute?' It's a good thing I didn't have a mouthful of this chai tea when you were talking to her, or I would have choked. Those may have been the cheesiest lines I've ever heard, man. I was cringing over here. I'm not sure how she found that sweet and cute, but I think you're right. She really does seem to like you."

The door to the coffee shop opened and closed, bringing with it a burst of cold air and a new customer. A larger man in a heavy trench coat walked over to the register.

"Hi! Welcome to Bytes. What can I get for you? We have a chai—"

"Four large coffees, black. To go. And maybe one of those sticky buns." He thumbed a finger toward the pastry under a glass dome, then placed a twenty on the counter. "Keep the change."

He took a seat near the register while his drinks were being prepared, directly across from where Dallas and Phil were sitting.

Luna entered the drink order into the POS system. It was already shaping up to be a lucrative morning for her. The old man had left her ten bucks on his small meal. Dallas's cute friend Phil just gave her a very generous tip when he paid, and now this guy, rude as he was, had left her more than a few bucks on a quick and simple coffee order. The weather as of late had caused foot traffic in her café to dwindle to almost nothing, and her tips followed suit. She put the change from Trench Coat's payment into her tip jar and turned around to finish the order.

Dallas went back to admiring the backside of his neon-green-tinged infatuation as she poured the coffee into to-go cups. Phil, however, secretly kept his eyes trained on Trench Coat from the moment he'd walked in. He brought the warm cup of chai to his lips and took a sip, but his attention never broke away from the man who'd just sat down across from them.

The direct line of sight may have been the only reason he noticed the stranger's iPhone surreptitiously taking photos of them. Dallas hadn't noticed, oblivious to everything except the back pockets of his caffeine-slinging señorita. Phil didn't let on that he saw any of this stealthy intrusion. He casually took another sip while the mysterious man did a quick review of the images. Apparently, they hadn't captured anything satisfactory because he lowered his arm and tried once again to get a better picture. There was no mistaking it for anything other than a clear attempt at subterfuge.

"Hey there, friend. If you want a picture, just ask politely. No need to be sneaky about it," Phil said loudly.

The man stood up and walked toward them, looking much larger close up than he did when he first walked in. Phil's comment and the sudden movement caused Dallas to snap back to reality. "Phil, what the fuck is going on?"

"I'm not quite sure myself. This fine gentleman was taking pictures of us for some reason. I was just explaining to him that if he wanted a snapshot, all he had to do was ask. Seems like this is some kind of headquarters for your fan club." Phil spoke calmly and acted like this was all still perfectly normal and friendly.

"You must be mistaken, guys. I wasn't taking pictures of anyone. You likely misunderstood something you saw. Sorry for the confusion. I've gotta get going. Have a good morning." The big man turned and headed back toward the door at the front of the café.

"Sir! Excuse me. You forgot your coffees." Luna placed the four cups that were nestled into a cardboard tray on the counter beside the cash register. Trench Coat ignored her and kept walking toward the exit.

Phil leaped up and took off down the perimeter of the café. In three quick strides, he covered the length of the room and reached the front door before Trench Coat was even halfway there. "Like I was saying, if you wanted a picture, all you had to do was ask. However, the flip side to that gracious offer is that you can't just take pictures of me or my friend without permission. If you have no issue showing me your recent shots, we can put to rest whether you have photos of us, or not."

"I think you better go into the kitchen. I have a feeling things are going to get ugly," Dallas warned Luna as he directed her back behind the counter.

"Should I call the cops?" she asked, already very aware that something bad was about to happen.

"No, we'll handle this. Keep the cops out of it for now. Now please get back there and stay out of sight. I don't want you to get hurt." She leaned over the counter and kissed Dallas on the cheek, then disappeared into the kitchen. Dallas stayed by the register, keeping an eye on the events unfolding at the front of the café.

Trench Coat tried to move around Phil, but he extended his arm and held out his palm, signaling for him to stop. "I'm sorry, sir, but I can't let you leave with those pictures."

The big man opened his trench coat to reveal the butt of a gun secured in a shoulder holster. "Move away from the door. I won't ask again." Any illusion of this being a misunderstanding was now shattered.

Phil shuffled his feet and settled into a wide stance, creating a low center of gravity. He whipped his long black hair so that it fell to one side, rotated his palm until it faced upward, and flicked his fingers toward the man in the universally understood "come and get some" gesture.

Trench Coat rotated back to deliver a thundering right hook aimed to take Phil's head clean off, but Phil easily blocked the meaty fist with his forearm and simultaneously clamped onto his attacker's arm, putting him into a wrist lock. Phil twisted the man's arm behind his back and effortlessly pushed him headfirst into a heavy wood table. The big man splashed over the top and was slow to get up. A huge gash had opened above his eye, dripping rivulets of blood down his face.

Phil gave him a pitiful look. "This will go a lot easier if you just hand me your phone. I might even give it back to you after I delete the pictures you took. Now tell me why you're actually here, and who sent you. In that order."

Trench Coat wiped the blood from his face with the sleeve of this jacket, dropped his shoulder and charged at him.

There were a multitude of options that Phil could execute against such a short-range attack. It was simply a matter of deciding which one he felt like using. He could sidestep the oncoming attack and use Trench Coat's momentum against him by throwing him headfirst into the solid oak door that lay only a few feet behind where Phil was standing. He was also in perfect position to land a devastating snap kick to the man's jaw. That little maneuver would break most of his teeth and knock him out cold. The resulting facial trauma from either maneuver would have Trench Coat sipping meals through a straw for months. He opted to let the man crash into the door. A serious head or spinal injury was also likely, and Phil would barely have to touch the guy. He'd let Trench Coat do all the damage himself.

Phil reached out and grabbed the charging man by the collar, spun on his heel, and watched him sail toward a painful impact with the door, but at the last second, the oak portal opened, and Trench Coat went flying harmlessly outside. The man who pulled open the door still had the brass handle in his grasp, wearing a look of bewilderment that quickly dissolved into something more sinister. He reached for the matte-black gun hidden under his jacket and jumped through the threshold.

This new combatant was even bigger than Trench Coat. These guys were obviously being fed a healthy diet of protein and steroids and spent a lot of time in the gym. The man with the gun landed a few feet to the left of Phil after he breached the doorway. The kung fu master reacted before the guy could even raise his weapon. Phil took a huge stride to the left, launched himself into the air, and exploded outwards with a flying sidekick that caught the man square in the chest and sent him crashing through a handrail and into a heap against the wall. He felt the attacker's ribs snap when his foot made contact.

Phil prepared to deliver a follow-up strike, but the man wasn't moving after receiving the bone-crunching blow. One or both of his lungs had likely been punctured, and Phil took the opportunity to scoop up the guy's gun from the floor.

Phil checked to see if it was loaded and found a single round in the chamber and ten more in the clip. These guys were not messing around. He lifted the weapon for Dallas to see. "Dallas, come get this gun, then grab his phone and check to see if he has any ID on him. Maybe we can find out why and how these guys were tracking you."

"I know why they were looking for me, bro. Daedalus and I were hoping they would be here sometime. I was the bait, but Chief and Daedalus were supposed to be here when it went down. We just talked about it this morning. They must have already had this place staked out. Holy shit! I would have been a sitting duck." Dallas said, letting that sink in for a second. "By the way, that flying kick was crazy! You're a bad motherfucker, Phil Wu. You wrecked that guy big time!"

Luna came back out front to investigate the cause of the crash. She hopped over the counter and slid into position beside Dallas to get a better look at the action. He could understand the look of shock on her face when she saw Phil standing near the door, pointing a gun at an unconscious man lying against the wall.

"Dallas, c'mon, grab the gun and search this guy." Phil needed someone to keep watch while he secured the front of the café.

"No way, bro. You're closer. Besides, I have to protect Luna." Dallas was a whiz with a keyboard, but guns weren't his thing, and this entire scene was way outside his skill set. Dallas turned to Luna. "I could have done the same thing, you know, but I wanted to stay back to make sure you were safe. He's just showing off. He's not my boss or anything."

"Dallas!" Phil barked. "I need somebody to keep this gun on that guy, now. Please." Phil was calm but losing patience and, more importantly, precious seconds.

"Give it to me. I'll do it. It's my café anyway." Luna took the gun from Phil and moved around to get a clear line of sight to the man on the ground.

"I'm going to check on our friend who went flying out the front door a minute ago. I'll only be gone a second. By the way, do you know how to use that thing?" Phil motioned to the pistol.

"For sure. I've been shooting my whole life." Luna appraised the matte-black weapon. She racked the slide back, took note of the chambered round, then released the slide. "It's a Glock. Model 22C. Uses forty-caliber ammo. The safety is built into the trigger. Just point and shoot. This model has additional porting. See those little openings at the top of the barrel? They disperse the ultra-hot gas released from the powder igniting much faster than a typical barrel. It reduces the kick and makes for a more accurate shot. Go get that other guy. I'm good."

Phil saw her take up a textbook shooting stance a couple of yards from the guy with the busted ribs, who was still out cold. Feeling confident she had things under control, Phil ran out the door looking to see where Trench Coat had run off to.

CHAPTER NINETEEN

Bytes Internet Café
February 9, 10:29 a.m.

Phil burst out of the coffee shop in pursuit of the first attacker, but didn't have to search very far. He spotted a pair of large, serious-looking guys charging across the street toward the café. Horns honked from angry motorists forced to brake and swerve to avoid the men, who were running against the flow of traffic. Trench Coat was standing on the sidewalk beside the café, motioning furiously for his compatriots.

"Hey!" Phil shouted at the trio, who were now all assembled on the same side of the street. "You guys should all come back inside. I think your friend might need some medical attention, and I still need to see that phone."

Trench Coat reached into his jacket and pulled out a Glock matching the one Luna was holding inside the café, but with one glaring addition. He had a box-shaped suppressor threaded onto the end of his barrel. Phil knew that anyone who was concerned with the noise their gun made was likely planning on using it. Silencers weren't for show. Phil read the embarrassment and hatred in Trench Coat's eyes and dove back toward the doorway just as the muzzle flashed, the first shot sailing wide. Phil grabbed the large brass handle and pulled the heavy door open, ducking behind it just as the next volley of shots were fired. Phil heard a round sizzle through the air right next to his position, followed by another that struck the heavy door. Bits of wood splintered around him. He risked a peek and saw the three men running toward him. He ducked back around the door and pulled it closed behind him.

"We have company. You two head out the rear exit now. I'll hold them off and buy you some time, but it won't be that much of a head start. So, get moving." Phil flipped the rugged steel deadbolt into place and secured the locking pin at the top and bottom of the door before jumping the counter and disappearing into the kitchen. When he emerged a few moments later, he saw that neither Dallas nor Luna had moved. "What are you two still doing here? Get going!"

"I'm not running away with the only gun we have and leave you here to fight a three-on-one battle," Luna said, and started toward the front of the café with her weapon trained on the door.

"How did you know there were four of them?" Phil wasn't sure how she could have seen the other two attackers outside.

"The guy just ordered four large coffees from me. We've seen two of these guys so far. One's still knocked out over there, and one flew out the front door. That means there are three more outside, but still just one of you. Pretty simple math."

Phil was surprised she put all that together under the stress of the events happening around them. She had a "my way or the high-way" attitude, just like Dallas. He could see why they got along. He peered over Luna's shoulder at Dallas as if doing so would induce him to try and change Luna's mind.

"Don't look at me, bro. I told her we should listen to you and leave. We can't have civilians getting hurt and all. She won't go. What do you want me to do?"

A succession of gunshots rang out. Bullets slammed into the lock and splintered part of the doorframe. Heavy boots pounded into the oak door, trying to break it free.

When Phil came out from the kitchen, he was carrying a selection of the largest, sharpest blades he could find.

"Phil, I don't know who taught you how to fight, but haven't you heard the old adage not to bring a knife to a gunfight?" Dallas asked. "Literally."

"Sometimes you have to make do with what you have. I think I'll be just fine with these." He was carrying an eight-inch chef knife in one hand and a pair of smaller knives in the other. A large thick metal cleaver was tucked in the small of his back.

Someone pounded on the door so hard that it shook the entire frame. "Another blow like that and they'll be through," Dallas said.

The largest of the men outside reared back and pounded his massive boot directly above the door handle, breaking the lock on impact. The door cracked and twisted in place, but not fully free of its hardware. The locking pin on the bottom right of the door was still latched in place, causing the upper portion to twist inward, but the base stayed secure.

A heavy black boot pounded the door again. The big man attached to the other end was attempting to slip through the narrow opening at the bottom of the door. Phil grabbed the size-fourteen foot, wrenched it to the side, and compressed it against his own leg. The big man tried to struggle as Phil pulled the man's knee back at an angle it was never meant to bend. He heard the joint pop and saw it buckle inward at a grotesque angle. All the ligaments and tendons supporting the man's knee were torn to shreds. Screams of agony erupted from the newly crippled man, sticking halfway through the doorway.

Busted Knee instinctively reached for his injured leg, and when he did, Phil grabbed the Glock from his grasp. He did a quick check to confirm the gun was loaded. Three shots left in the clip and one in the chamber, that would do for now. Busted Knee was hauled out from the entry by his buddies on the other side of the door. As soon as he was pulled clear, a new barrage of shots blasted through the broken doorway. Everyone in the coffee shop dove for cover. Sparks flashed as bits of plastic and wood exploded from the computers and flat-screen monitors that were perched on the tables for patrons using the cyber café's services. The domes covering the cookies and pastries along the countertop shattered, raining shards of glass everywhere. The cooler exploded when a round pierced the curved front face.

"Are you guys okay?" Phil yelled over the echo of the dying gunfire.

"We're good," Dallas said. He was lying on top of Luna, shielding her body with his own from the glass and debris that was flying through the air. He was more than happy to stay right where he was.

The daylight filtering through the broken doorway suddenly darkened with the silhouette of a new invader. Phil crouched low and to the left of the shadow at the door. He saw the figure raise his arm, aiming his gun at Dallas and Luna's position by the register. Phil gripped the tip of one of the smaller knives and flipped it toward the threat at the door. He followed that strike with the larger eight-inch blade, launching both projectiles in quick succession. The smaller knife caught the man in the forearm, causing his grip to fail and weapon to drop to the floor. The large chef's knife also found its mark, catching the man deep in the neck. His eyes went wide as he wrapped his hand around the handle protruding from his throat. He panicked and pulled the blade free, causing blood to spurt from the wound. He'd bleed out and be dead on the ground in less than a minute, not that leaving the knife in would have saved him, but it may have bought him a few more seconds of his pathetic life.

Trench Coat was standing behind the man who was bleeding to death at the door. He didn't see what had transpired because of his obscured vantage point and couldn't understand why the guy standing at the threshold wasn't moving in for the kill. He was even more baffled watching the man drop to his knees, falling flat onto his face. A dark pool of blood began to spread around his head as soon as it came to rest on the floor. The ghastly sight distracted Trench Coat just long enough for Phil to raise the Glock he'd stripped from the guy bleeding out in front of him. He pulled the trigger, and a fine pink mist erupted from the back of Trench Coat's head and into the parking lot outside, adding a splash of color to the grayness of the day.

Dallas and Luna got up and rushed toward the front of the café. "Holy shit! Who are these guys?" Dallas said, staring at the body bleeding all over the floor, then shifted his gaze to the dead man outside. He and Luna had both seen Trench Coat's head explode when Phil shot him.

"I think it's safe to say these were some of Basileus's thugs," Phil said. "They may even be part of the same team that took out the previous scientists from the Workshop." He had no proof of this, but he was hoping that his actions avenged those who'd been savagely murdered. "Let's grab their phones and get the hell out of here." Sirens could already be heard in the distance. Phil moved through the fractured doorway to confiscate the phones from the men outside and maybe have a quick chat with Busted Knee, who was still moaning in the parking lot.

A deafening gunshot echoed inside the café right behind Phil. He spun around to see Luna with her arms extended straight out. A wisp of smoke trailed from her gun's barrel. He saw a small red stain on the chest of the guy from the floor with the broken ribs, growing larger by the second. A small silver revolver dangled loosely from his hand; a backup gun no one had checked for.

Luna looked terrified. "He… He was going to shoot you. I saw him pull the gun from his jacket… and then he raised it up to shoot, and… it all happened so quickly. I just reacted." Dallas walked over and gently took the gun from her grip. Her eyes were as wide as saucers. "Oh my God. I just killed him, didn't I?"

Phil didn't bother to answer the rhetorical question. Instead, he ran to grab the phone from Busted Knee. He went over to the whimpering giant on the ground and took his phone and used the facial ID feature to unlock the phone and made a mental note to keep the screen active, so it wouldn't go back into locked mode. He tried in vain to get any additional information from Busted Knee, but all he could utter were profanities between heavy bouts of sob-bing. Phil wasn't going to get anything useful from him before they had to leave, so he just kicked the guy in the side of the head, knocking him unconscious. Phil figured he was doing the guy a favor. At least in that state, his knee wasn't bothering him. Also, it was highly doubtful he'd wake up and request backup anytime soon, giving them more than enough time to get back down into the Workshop and figure out what the hell was going on. Phil came back inside and ran to the rear of the café. "Luna, do you have se-curity cameras actively recording in here?"

"No, just a normal alarm system with door and motion sensors. No cameras." She said apologetically.

Phil collected all the guns and knives they'd touched and wiped them down with a rag, before leaving them with the bodies near the door. "Dallas, we have to get out of here now and back down into the Workshop."

"I'm coming with you guys. There's no way I'm staying here." The fear on Luna's face was turning into a very determined look.

"I'm sorry, Luna. We can't take you where we're going. Lama and I have to get out of here and off the streets right away. Just stay here until the police arrive. Tell them whatever you want, but you can't come with us." Phil turned to his partner. "Dallas, we have to go now!" The sirens were getting much closer. The coffee shop would be swarming with police in a minute.

"No deal. I just killed a man to save your life, man." Luna was on the offensive now. "Like I just explained to you, I have no cameras to prove what happened in here. I'm also not waiting for the friends of these guys to come back and grab me next week, thinking I can lead them back to you. I've seen enough movies to know that places me square in the role of 'expendable bimbo.'" She made the air quotes sign around the derogatory moniker. All the fear she had felt before was gone, replaced now by steadfast determination. "I'm coming with you guys. There's no point in saying 'no' again either. I'm just going to follow you anyway, and maybe I'll flag down a cop if you try to ditch me or make it too hard for me to tag along."

"She has a point, Phil, and like you said, we have to get out of here now. I can't get pinched by the cops again." Dallas said, eyes darting to the door, as anxious as any of them to leave. If it meant Luna had to come along, all the better. He also knew he would have a better chance facing Daedalus's wrath if Phil had also agreed to bring her with them versus Lama making the decision alone.

"I guess we don't have much of a choice then, but in any event, I want you to know that I very much appreciate you taking that shot back there, Luna. You saved me, and I'm forever grateful." He turned back to Lama. "Dallas, we're going to have a lot of explaining to do when we get back."

The three of them slipped out through the café's fire exit at the rear. Phil took the lead as they sprinted down the alley behind the café, but he was inexplicably running in the direction of the oncoming sirens.

"Why are we heading toward the cops? Aren't we trying to get away?" Dallas asked, already breathing heavily from the exertion.

"I have an idea," Phil answered vaguely, "but we have to hurry. Our window of escape is closing fast."

The group continued down the alley and made the first left turn they could, which had them running back out toward the busy street, directly into the path of the police cruisers that were closing in. Covering the thirty yards to the large intersection and making one final left turn, they were now walking back toward the internet café. The circuitous half-loop route brought them around from the backside of the building to the front, but it appeared as if they were now walking toward the action, not away from it.

The first police cruiser sped past them and screeched to a stop in the parking lot in front of the café. A few seconds later, another cruiser pulled in beside the first.

"Phil, what the hell are we doing?" Dallas asked. "We're trying to get away, not arrested."

A third police car slowed as he approached the trio, chirped the siren, and pulled close to the curb they were standing on. The officer lowered his window. "Listen up, everyone. We've had reports of shots fired in the area. I'm going to have to ask you to clear the vicinity immediately. It's for your own safety."

"Wow! That's crazy. Thanks for the warning, officer," Luna said. "Let's just head back the way we came, guys." They changed direction and jumped into a yellow taxicab rolling down the side street toward them. Phil had the driver roam up and down the street of Midtown until he was certain they weren't being followed. Twenty minutes later, they exited the cab and walked the last five minutes to their private parking garage, descending deeper into the earth until they were safely inside the Workshop.

"I'm not sure how our boss is going to react to you being down here, and I'm also not sure how *you're* going to react when these doors open," Dallas said, wanting to warn Luna. "I just wanted you to know I think you're badass and amazing, and, uh, well, some of the things I told you before may have been a bit of an exaggeration. But some of the things—"

Dallas, you're cute, but I know you're not a super spy," Luna said. "I just thought you were really sweet, and your stories were very creative. But a secret base, plots to destroy the planet, advanced technology? Did you really think I'd fall for all that? I really do enjoy your company and talking to you, but I didn't think any of it was real."

They reached the Workshop level, and the elevator doors opened. Luna turned her attention from Dallas toward the spectacle beyond the door and froze in place, seeing the immense cavern and soaring rock formations spread out before her. Her jaw dropped. It didn't happen often, but Luna found herself speechless.

"Like I was saying," Dallas said, continuing his disclaimer, "some of the things I told you about are even crazier than you could possibly imagine."

CHAPTER TWENTY

The Labyrinth
February 9, 11:15 a.m.

"No matter which piece of equipment I've used, the results have either come back inconclusive or unknown." Aliyah was getting incredibly discouraged. The last couple of hours hadn't revealed anything substantive despite all her efforts. "Here I was thinking I could find some weakness in the organism we could potentially exploit, and I can't even get a simple chemical analysis back." She and Gryph had been working at breakneck speed all morning, trying to glean any insights into the incredible healing compound found in the manna, yet nothing seemed to reveal the makeup of the mysterious substance.

"You may not be able to figure out what makes this thing tick just yet, but you've learned a lot. Maybe it would help if you stopped focusing on its composition and focused deeper into its behavior or maybe analyzed the sequence of events when it deploys its defense mechanisms? Let's try attacking this from a different angle. We keep getting stumped trying to figure out what it is. Let's focus on what it can and can't do." Gryph didn't have the robust molecular biology background that Aliyah possessed, but his analytical mind-set could often find alternate routes to solve complex problems.

"Just start with what you know, and build from there. You've figured out a lot more than you're giving yourself credit for. Remember when you told me earlier in the week that talking about a problem out loud helps you process information? Let's give that a try." Gryph wiped down a whiteboard fastened to a nearby wall and picked up a dry-erase marker and waited for Aliyah to start.

Aliyah knew he was right, getting frustrated would only cloud her thinking further. Maybe a change in tactics would reveal some insights that had eluded her thus far.

She drew a deep, cleansing breath, held it for a beat, before slowly releasing it. She let the confusion and stress out with the long exhalation. Now centered, she started fresh.

"Okay. We know the cytoplasmic gel inside the manna cells contain an unidentifiable type of healing compound that keeps the host cell alive and healthy, even in the most extreme conditions," Aliyah said. "Assuming Daedalus's cosmic origin hypothesis is correct, this protective attribute also explains how it survived in the harsh, cold vacuum of space. We also know that this specimen is smaller than any other type of bacterial cell ever discovered."

Gryph jotted down these disparate facts in point form on the board as she identified each piece of information.

"Let's drill down on the repair response mechanism for a minute. We all observed the cell repairing massive trauma to its own structures in real time when the nanobot pierced the cell's exterior membrane. Every distinct part of the cell began glowing in unison, not just the damaged area, and somehow the process completely repaired the wound that our puncture caused. However, we've also seen the scope of damage cannot be too great. It seems even the manna has a limit to what it can repair, which means it's not invincible, and that's very good news for us." Aliyah let the thought hang in the air for a moment. Maybe she could stop this thing after all. "Once an organism dies, even the manna's healing properties can't reanimate it. During my initial tests, we induced only minor to moderate damage to the cell, and after each of those minimally destructive routines, the cell achieved a complete repair. It was as if our probing hadn't caused any damage at all. During the most recent series of tests, I was much more aggressive with my tactics. You were here when we watched the nanobot tear apart the cell membrane faster than the manna repairs could be made. Once all the cytoplasm had leaked out, the organism died almost immediately, that would also confirm another of Daedalus's statements."

"Which statement is that?" Gryph asked.

"That the manna can't bring back the dead. I guess that means we've figured out a potential means to eradicate it. We could program the nanobots to seek out and destroy the toxin utilizing the same method, but I'm not sure how feasible that solution would be in a real-world deployment. I don't understand the technology powering Daedalus's nanobots or how many we have access to, but it's definitely something we should discuss with him next time we meet." Gryph made a note on the board for them to review the nanotech limitations and quantities available for their use.

Aliyah resumed her summary. "We also know the toxin Basileus engineered is using the manna cells to protect it from all types of conventional perils, whether herbicides, pesticides, or anything else we've thrown at it. During any attack on the toxin, the protective manna cells jump into action and repair the damage. This protective attribute must also be how the toxin keeps itself safe from the lethal amounts of alcohol it releases internally, while at the same time protecting itself from any external threats to kill it, too. It's quite ingenious. But that would also mean..."

She paused her discourse and once more slipped into a contemplative, distant stare. Gryph remained silent, not wanting to interrupt her train of thought. Then Aliyah snapped her fingers. "That would mean the toxin on its own could likely be killed by conventional methods. It's the manna cells providing the defenses for the toxin, not the alcohol production. Without the manna's preservation, the rest of the cell would likely be extremely vulnerable. I would suspect the high concentration of alcohol it releases would kill the host organism within minutes of exposure."

She glanced at the whiteboard, using the visual cues to keep her focused and moving forward. "It's the bond between the two we need to focus on. Specifically, how to break it. I'm sure it would've taken countless attempts to engineer this fragile cellular connection. As I admitted to you before, I can't even begin to determine what elements the manna is formulated from, but someone much smarter than me was able to manipulate it enough to combine it with the toxin." The defeatist tone began to creep back into her voice.

"You've only had a week to investigate this unique biology and look at all this information you've already uncovered. Keep it going, you're on a roll." Gryph didn't say it just to give her a confidence boost. He really felt they were making great progress, and

Aliyah was on the verge of shaking something loose. He could feel it.

She smiled. "Alright. If someone figured out how to combine these two life forms, then I'll focus on how to sever that bond. I should have realized earlier that a more effective approach would have been to focus on disrupting the relationship between the toxin and the manna."

"That's a great idea, Ali, and it makes total sense too. This organism is only as strong as its weakest link. But maybe..." Gryph paused, "What if getting the manna cells to combine with another organism isn't as difficult as you think? It might be possible for us to harness the power of the manna cell like Basileus did. We could combine it with a design of our own, engineered specifically to attack the toxin. Like fighting fire with fire."

"Hey! I think I actually have a few options we can pursue to that end. But even if I could get the manna to bond with another cell successfully to create an antidote—which I'm not sure we can do—we would still have a major problem that I'm not sure we can get around."

"What's that?"

"Each time we try to extract the cytoplasm from the toxin, the organism resists the intrusion. You saw how the cytoplasm glowed brighter as the damage being inflicted on the toxin increased. It must sense when it's about to die, and utilizes all its energy in a last-ditch effort to protect its host. The insurmountable problem we're facing is getting a pure sample of the manna cell for us to experiment with. Once the manna cells have bonded with Basileus's toxin, they die when the connection is broken. That's why we can use the idea of separating the two entities to destroy the toxin. Without a pure source to power our antidote, we can't even begin to test your theory."

"Damn, I missed that. But I think you're right. We'll need a pure sample for our test. I truly think we're onto something, here. Even assuming you could engineer something that would break the cells apart, we couldn't bond our antidote to anything but an original manna cell. Unless..." Gryph's eyes lit up. "What if Daedalus has some more of the manna secreted away in the Library somewhere? He told us he ingested some of it in the past, but he never mentioned if he had any more. Maybe he has to take it on a regular basis to stay young and healthy, and might have more that we can use to bind…" Gryph stopped and held a finger to his lips. He was sure he'd heard someone call his name, but now… nothing. Aliyah hadn't heard anything and was looking at Gryph quizzically. Then he heard it again.

"Gryph, Chief? We got a problem?"

The door to the lab burst open. Gryph reached instinctively for his gun and realized he didn't have it on him. They never carried firearms in the Labyrinth. He made a mental note to change that policy. Fortunately for everyone, weapons wouldn't be necessary for this particular intrusion. Dallas thundered through the swinging door. Phil trailed a few yards behind looking quite concerned, though he didn't seem nearly as agitated.

"Gryph, Ali. Holy shit! You won't believe what just happened to us." Dallas's face was red and sweaty, his eyes were dazed, and his breathing, shallow and erratic. He was coherent, but clearly in a state of shock. Gryph and Aliyah had seen it countless times on the battlefield. The adrenaline high soldiers felt kept them moving, but it would fade quickly, and the effects of shock would eventually creep in.

"We just got into a huge gunfight at the coffee shop. We're okay, but we left a few dead guys back there. We barely got out before the cops showed up."

"Hold on, Dallas. You got into a gunfight and shot someone? And where's 'back there?'" Gryph wasn't anticipating such a brazen attack on the team. This caught him totally off-guard. He'd been focused on microscopic cells and theoretical problems for so long, it took him a second to adjust to the contrast between the ethereal lab issues and the fact that Dallas just admitted to killing someone. He quickly gained his bearings and transitioned into tactical mode. "Take a breath and tell me exactly what happened."

"Phil and I were grabbing a coffee a few blocks away, and this guy who came in supposedly took pictures of us on the sly and tried to escape. Phil jumped in the way to stop him from leaving, then the picture taker's buddies showed up, guns blazing, but thirty seconds of *Enter the Dragon* later. . ." Dallas thumbed his finger toward Phil, referencing the famous Bruce Lee movie, "and the whole gang was lying around dead or broken."

"Okay, I'm going to assume you've never seen any of them before. Did you have a chance to check them for ID once they were down?"

Phil stepped forward. "I checked each of them, they were all clean though. No ID. No credit cards. I found an iPhone on one of the attackers and checked the contents as we drove around after the fight to shake any possible tail we may have picked up. I'm certain we weren't followed back here."

"That's great, Phil, but hacking into an iPhone is next to impossible. We may not be able to access the data it contains, but we might be able to lift a print from it and run it through a few agencies and see if we get a hit."

"You still may be able to lift a print, but I've handled it a bit since taking it," Phil said. "I figured we'd all want to take a look once we were back here safe, so I unlocked it before we left, using the face ID feature from the dead guy who was carrying it. I kept the screen active until now. I also switched the auto-lock feature off. I didn't want to take a chance that it would lock us out." Phil held the device out toward Dallas. "I'm sure you can hook this up and see if there's anything useful on it."

Dallas took the device from him, careful to touch it as little as possible. "That was smart. Good thinking, bro. Let me just check something quickly." He swiped at the screen for a second. "We're lucky. The 'Find my iPhone' feature is disabled, or they could have tracked us here."

"Shit, I didn't think of that at the time. Sorry about that, Gryph." Phil felt terrible that his negligence could have led the killers back to the Workshop.

"Phil, you brought us the only lead on Basileus we have. Don't be sorry. This phone could have very valuable intel on it. We need all the help we can get."

"Just one more thing. Who's that, and why the hell is she down here with us?" Gryph pointed to the tattooed stranger standing behind Dallas. Luna was still wearing the incredulous look that hadn't left her face since taking in the sight of the Workshop for the first time.

"Oh, right. Everyone, this is Luna." Dallas set the iPhone down carefully and began the introductions. "Luna, this is, uh… this is the Daedalus crew." She waved to the group in a single, slow sweep of her heavily inked arm.

"Hi, guys," was all she could manage to get out. Luna's focus was on the miraculous array of equipment spread throughout the lab. Her mind was still processing the recent spectacle and enormity of the Workshop, and she'd felt uneasy on her feet ever since stepping off the elevator.

"It's nice to meet you, Luna," Gryph said with a warm smile. "Would you mind excusing us for a moment? I need to speak to my friend Dallas here privately. If you'd like, there's some coffee over there. Help yourself. We won't be long."

Luna walked over to the coffee station and poured herself a cup. Her hands hadn't stopped shaking since she pulled the trigger in the café. Once she was out of earshot, Gryph stepped close to Dallas. "You two must have a very good reason for exposing the Workshop to that woman." Gryph remained composed and didn't want to come across as accusatory, but this was a serious breach of protocol.

"We didn't have a choice, Gryph. Phil and I told her we couldn't bring her, but she said she'd follow us and even threatened to go to the cops if we tried to ditch her. Ask Phil if you don't believe me."

"He's telling the truth, Gryph. What he didn't tell you is that Luna literally saved my life and likely Dallas's too. One of the thugs I put down in the fight got back up and was going to shoot me. Luna used a pistol I wrestled away from one of Basileus's guys and put the guy down for good." It hadn't hit Phil how close he'd come to getting shot until saying it out loud.

"Even with that," Dallas said, "I told her we couldn't bring her with us, but she wouldn't take no for an answer. The cops were screaming down the road toward the coffee shop and Basileus's guys were anything but subtle. If we stayed behind to argue for even a second longer or tried to leave Luna behind, we would have been busted for sure."

Dallas and Phil pinballed back and forth, describing a few more of the details from the attack.

He asked only a couple of questions and was both impressed and relieved when Phil told him they'd wiped down all the weapons and surfaces they'd encountered, and that Luna confirmed the coffee shop was devoid of security cameras.

"Okay. I'm glad you guys got back here safely. There doesn't seem to be much you could have done with Luna except to bring her down here where it's safe. Those guys would have come back looking for her and, most likely, you and Dallas as well."

"That's what I told them." All eyes turned to Luna, who was standing behind them with a steaming cup of coffee in her hands. "By the way, this coffee is incredible. Kudos to the brew-master."

"Yeah, that's Gryph. He gets that a lot. Commander Oake is the top dog around here. He's got a magic touch when it comes to coffee," Dallas said. Gryph nodded once and smiled in recognition of the compliment.

"Sounds like you've had an eventful morning," Gryph said. "I'm sure Phil expressed his gratitude to you for your heroic efforts earlier. Allow me to extend my heartfelt appreciation as well, for keeping our team safe. I'm sure firing that weapon wasn't an easy thing for you to do."

"To be honest, it was easy. Like a reflex. That's what scares me. I knew he was going to shoot Phil and I couldn't just stand there and watch. I had to do something. I've been around guns all my life and have been shooting since I was a little girl, but I've never even aimed a gun at a person before. That's a cardinal sin for any responsible gun owner. And now, the first time I did it, I pulled the trigger and killed another person." Luna grew somber and hung her head, her eyes welling with tears.

"Hi, Luna. My name is Ali." She placed a gentle hand on Luna's shoulder. "You did the right thing. If you didn't shoot him, he would have killed all of you, especially if he was prepared to shoot Phil in plain sight of you and Dallas. People like that are trained not to leave witnesses. I'm so sorry that you had to experience such a traumatic event. If you need to talk to someone about it, I'm here for you."

"Thanks, Ali, I think I'll be okay. I appreciate it." She took another deep gulp of Gryph's coffee. "You really think they would have tried to kill all of us if I didn't shoot him?" The team responded with a resounding *yes*, which seemed to give Luna a measure of comfort. She stood a little taller, and some of the worry she carried on her face began to fade.

"Luna, those guys back there were grade 'A' assholes, and they came in looking for trouble, not the other way around," Dallas said. "If it wasn't for you, we'd all be dead right now. We owe you big time. Phil and I especially."

"Thanks everyone. I appreciate you guys getting me out of there. Sorry if I was being a bit demanding back at the café but I knew I couldn't stay there alone." Luna drank down another delicious mouthful. "Can you answer a question for me?"

"That depends on the question you ask," Gryph said.

"I've already figured out we're deep underground because I felt my ears pop a few times in the elevator on the way down. I've lived in New York most of my adult life and have never heard of anything even remotely like this existing under the city, which means you're either some secret government agency like Dallas told me or some rogue group that's obviously very well-funded. I can tell you're the good guys. If you weren't, you would've left me up there or killed me. I know I've unofficially met you all— Ali, Gryph, Phil, and, of course, my Dali-Lama." She pointed at each of them as she said their name, like confirming a roll call. "But really, guys… who the hell are you?"

"I was about to ask you the same question."

Luna turned to see the source of this new voice. She froze in place, and her eyes went wide with fear as she stared down the barrel of the gun Daedalus held mere inches from her head.

CHAPTER TWENTY-ONE

The Labyrinth
February 9, 11:44 a.m.

"Whoa! Holy shit! Daedalus, put the gun down. She's cool. She saved our lives this morning." Dallas was freaking out, seeing the gun pointed directly at Luna.

Luna had instinctively put her hands above her head, dropping her coffee mug, spilling the last dredges of her coffee onto the stone floor. Daedalus took a step back and slowly lowered his P226 Sig Sauer. The gun was the official sidearm of the Navy SEALs and widely known as one of the most accurate pistols ever made, although considering how close he was, accuracy wasn't an issue.

"Would someone explain to me how this unauthorized civilian made it to the inner sanctum of my Workshop?" Everyone could tell Daedalus was not happy about the intrusion.

Gryph relayed the events of the past hour pertaining to Luna and the attack from who they assumed to be Basileus's henchmen. Daedalus looked at Luna a few times during Gryph's debrief with shock and admiration as the details of the attack and their subsequent escape were explained.

When Gryph finished with the rundown of the morning's event, Daedalus extended his hand to Luna in gratitude.

"Thank you for your heroic actions," he said. "Without your intervention, I fear... Well, let's just say that we're all beneficiaries of your bravery. Losing my team at this stage would have consequences you couldn't begin to imagine. I'm sorry about pointing my weapon at you earlier. I'm an extremely cautious man, and sometimes that places me in uncomfortable situations. An unfortunate necessity, I'm afraid. Please accept my sincerest apologies."

"I understand. It's okay, don't feel bad about it. I already had a gun pulled on me once this morning. You're a little late to the party if you wanted to scare me." She smiled at her little joke. "Seriously though, it's a lot to process, and it's not even noon yet. This is all still quite surreal, to be honest. I was just acclimating to the incredible sights down here before you walked up. This place you have here, Mr. Daedalus, is something else."

"You're handling all of this surprisingly well. And please, just call me Daedalus. Feel free to stay with us for as long as you wish. I would highly recommend that you remain here until we know exactly what, and who, we're dealing with. However, if you'd like to leave, I'll have Phil take you back home at your convenience, and he'll arrange for a private security detail to protect you for as long as you wish."

"Thanks, Daedalus. You're very kind. If it wouldn't be too much trouble, is there a quiet place I could lie down for a bit?" Dallas looked up from the recovered iPhone he was working with. "Yeah, for sure, Luna. You can chill out in my room. It's only a short walk through there. I have the biggest one down here, actually." Dallas pointed down the hallway to the residences in the Labyrinth. "I'll take you there and get you settled in."

"That's a kind and generous gesture, Dallas, but Luna is my guest down here," Daedalus said. He turned back to Luna. "I wouldn't think of asking you to share quarters with anyone. I have plenty of space available for you to call your own while you're with us."

The excited look on Dallas's face quickly dissolved as he realized his ploy to get Luna into his room had been thwarted. "I'll have Dallas show you to your own room, and then we'll *all* give you some time and space to decompress from this morning's events." He gave Dallas a look to emphasize his point. "When you're feeling up to it, I'm sure Dallas would like to give you a more in-depth tour of the facility."

"That would be great. Thank you again, Daedalus," Luna said. "You're too kind." Dallas puffed up once again upon hearing that last instruction. He could have sworn he saw Daedalus give him a wink when Luna responded favorably.

Daedalus pulled out his mobile controller and entered a few keystrokes. "Luna, I've unlocked the two vacant doors near Aliyah's room. Feel free to choose either one of them. Dallas will show you the way. Once you have a chance to rest up, I'll arrange to have Phil take you to your home to pick up any necessities you may need over the next few days."

"This place gets even more incredible each minute. Thanks again, everyone. Show me the way, Lama." Luna looped her arm around Dallas's, bringing a huge smile to his usually dour expression. The two of them walked off toward the residence wing of the Labyrinth, leaving the rest of the team in the lab.

Daedalus turned to Gryph. "Keep an eye on her. I'm not a very trusting type."

"I understand, sir. Neither am I."

Daedalus addressed the rest of the team. "It's been quite an eventful morning. I believe we're all up to speed on the attack in the café. Thankfully, everyone is safe."

He nodded to Phil in appreciation.

"Have you made any headway with the toxin, Dr. Tzion?" Daedalus asked.

Ali relayed the working theory, in which, separating the two compounds from each other would render the alcohol-producing bacteria defenseless against even conventional herbicides. In fact, without the manna cells' protection, they would almost certainly die from their own lethal dose of alcohol. The cells would snuff themselves out without additional intervention. Ali's assessment that reverse engineering the toxin could take months or longer. Time they didn't have, and without any guarantee that any of it would work in the end. Aliyah had reached the critical point in her summation and wasn't quite sure how to broach this delicate subject. She opted for the direct approach and used her roadblock in the lab as a springboard into her next question.

"The problem we face, Daedalus, is that we can't test that theory without a sample of the original elixir. We can't use a sample from the toxin because the elixir attached to it loses its restorative effects once it becomes unbonded. I do seem to recall you telling us that you'd consumed some of it a long time ago, even offering it to secure the relationships with those high up in some governments. Respectfully, sir, we need to ask if there's any left that we can examine and use."

Aliyah's request hung uneasily in the air. Daedalus remained silent for an uncomfortably long stretch. Gryph knew they'd probed close to the deepest, darkest secret their mysterious benefactor kept hidden for centuries. He wasn't sure how much Daedalus would disclose, but was prepared to push if necessary. This threat was much bigger than any one man, regardless of pedigree or lineage.

"There are things at play here that I cannot explain yet myself. The story of my life casts a long shadow because of the elixir. It has healed and extended my life on many occasions throughout my time on Earth. However, the last time it crossed my lips was over one hundred and twenty years ago. I've dedicated my research during the twentieth century to the examination of the elixir, and the reason I developed the nanotechnology in the first place. It's only been within the last fifty years that any meaningful testing could begin. Technology has come a long way as of late, but I was in the dark for an eternity."

Gryph sighed. "Damn! We were so close."

Aliyah was utterly confused by the sudden outburst. "Gryph… Sorry, I don't understand what happened. What do you mean, 'we were so close?'"

"The elixir. There isn't any left." Gryph looked at Daedalus when he spoke.

"What led you to that assumption, Commander?" Daedalus asked.

"Wait. Is Gryph right? There's nothing left?" Aliyah asked in a desperate tone.

"I don't think Daedalus has made any more headway in reproducing the elixir than you have, but I bet he's been trying for a long time," Gryph assumed. "Like he said, it's the reason he developed the nanobots and the advanced equipment you've been using here in the first place. You said yourself some of this gear is a decade or more advanced than anything you've seen before. If he created all of this to study the elixir, it would mean that all conventional methods had failed."

Gryph turned to Daedalus. "Ali's been stumped ever since running her first series of tests. Inventing the breakthrough technology that went into designing and fabricating these nanobots would be a monumental feat of engineering in and of itself. If that was the easier route, then the secrets of the manna have yet to be unlocked." Gryph saw a coy smile on Daedalus's face, which he didn't quite know how to interpret yet. He wasn't sure if Daedalus was amused because he was right on the money, or way off the mark.

"Also, I don't think you were the first one to think of utilizing the characteristics of the elixir to combat the toxin," Gryph said. "Daedalus would have figured out a way to harness the power of the manna cells for an antidote if there was an opportunity to do so already. I think he brought you here to find a path to success that everyone else, including Daedalus himself, had missed."

Aliyah looked to Daedalus for any indication that Gryph's assumptions were correct, but she saw nothing, just the same smile he had earlier.

"And one last thing," Gryph said. "The question Daedalus asked Ali just now was, 'Have you made any progress with the toxin?' He didn't ask if you made any progress with the elixir. That's because he had already long since exhausted every method under the sun and came up empty. Even with the benefit of all this incredible technology he's developed, Daedalus hasn't been able to replicate the original. I hope I'm misreading the situation because it's pretty damn bleak, but that's how I see it."

Daedalus was about to answer when Chief entered the lab with Dallas. They were in the middle of a loud and animated conversation growing steadily in volume as the pair approached. Dallas was still relaying the events at the café.

The big Navy man strode up and took a position beside Gryph, clapping his friend on the shoulder. "What's up, everyone? Sounds like I missed all the action. Heard Phil kicked some serious ass this morning, too!" Phil acknowledged the compliment with a modest shrug.

Chief told everyone he'd been working through the night with Daedalus and had left with him early that morning as the events at the café unfolded. When he got back, he went straight to his quarters to grab a shower. It was only after leaving his room that he saw Dallas escorting a girl he hadn't seen before into the residences beside Aliyah's room. Dallas already brought him up to speed on the gunfight, but hadn't discussed Aliyah and Gryph's progress with the toxin. Gryph quickly summarized why they needed a pure sample to defeat the toxin and ended with his somber assessment that there may be none left.

"Although, I think we're finally about to get some clarity from Daedalus on the elixir and its availability." Gryph motioned for Daedalus to provide the answer he was about to give right before Chief and Dallas had walked in.

"I knew it was a good decision to have you to lead this team, Commander Oake. You have an incredible ability to get to the crux of an issue even when provided with scant details. I hope those skills continue to expedite our search for an antidote."

Daedalus wasted no time once Chief, Gryph and Dallas took a seat.

"Commander Oake was correct when he deduced that I have no more of the elixir in my possession. Unfortunately, he was also correct about my lack of success in attempting to replicate it. Long ago, I learned that it couldn't be diluted without losing its healing effects, and I've tried everything, believe me. I spent the last two decades developing new technologies and advancing theoretical notions into working models, but they all ended up being wasted efforts to unlock its secrets. The vessel that once held the elixir is now empty. I originally programmed my nanobot-AI system to analyze the interior of the jar for any trace of the manna cells that could be salvaged. I was able to recover a limited amount, but not enough to provide me with its life-extending benefits. The little bit left behind, I used to study and test. But everything I had was all used up in that futile effort."

Gryph was disappointed to hear their plan to get hold of a pure sample seemed impossible, but was pleasantly surprised that Daedalus was being so open and direct. He too must have realized the time for keeping secrets had long since passed.

"However," Daedalus said, "I'm convinced that using the elixir and ICARUS together gives us the best chance at preventing the toxin's spread. It would also give us the time we need to track Basileus down and ensure something like this never happens again."

"I don't understand," Aliyah said. "If you haven't figured out how to replicate it by now, we're certainly not going to be able to do so in a couple of weeks. And like you said, there isn't any more elixir anyway. I don't know if we should expend any more time or effort on that approach, as promising as it may have been."

The excitement building in anticipation of a breakthrough had briefly energized the team, but Daedalus's news deflated those hopes, and the mood in the room reflected their imperiled state. Everyone wore a gloomy and defeated look except Daedalus, who sat back with the same placid look that Gryph and Aliyah had spotted earlier on in the conversation.

"You seem to be taking this setback better than the rest of us. Is there something we're missing here?" Gryph asked. He knew they were up against insurmountable odds, but he couldn't figure out why his boss seemed unbothered by the fact that their only working theory relied on getting a pure sample of the elixir, one that he admitted he no longer possessed. Then the answer to his own question flashed in his mind.

Gryph pointed at Daedalus. "You're not upset because you know where we can get more of the elixir, don't you?" He felt a combination of hope and adrenaline surge through him. If they could get a supply of the elixir, he was sure Aliyah could come through with an effective antidote.

"Commander, believe me when I tell you that I'm still very much concerned with the toxin and the challenges we face in defeating it. But yes, you're right. There may be a way for us to acquire a meaningful quantity of the elixir. If anyone ever had a chance to succeed in that sensitive recovery mission, it's the team I see before me."

"If there was another source of the elixir, why didn't you pursue it earlier?" Aliyah asked.

"I decided long ago that when the day finally came, and the elixir ran out, I would finally allow nature to run its course and put an end to this strange journey that fate has bestowed upon me. Before I die, we must rid the world of Basileus. He's been lurking in the shadows for far too long. I cannot allow him to weaponize the elixir. There's no telling what will happen when the toxin upsets the delicate balance of nature. It could prove fatal to more than just his intended human targets. It could destroy the planet's entire ecosystem."

"If we don't know who this guy is or where we can find him, how are we supposed to strike his position and recover the elixir?" Chief asked.

"We don't necessarily need Basileus to be our source for the elixir, even if he's somehow gained access to it. It's possible he may have exhausted his own supply while using it to produce the toxin," Daedalus said.

"Okay, so where exactly do we go next?" Chief asked.

"There is only one place I know of that can provide the quantity of elixir we'll need for the antidote. However, gaining access to it will be extremely difficult. This last source has been left unmolested for thousands of years. If it was already discovered, the world would have heard of it."

"This new source, where is it? Do you have a map or a lead that we can get moving on right away?" Gryph asked. "We don't have much of a choice but to go after it, and the clock is ticking."

"It isn't so much a lead or clue that I can offer, but I can direct us to the last known reference and location. Also, just to be clear, we're not going to be searching for the elixir." This last statement drew confused looks. "Our mission is to recover the *source* of the elixir—the original manna itself. That is what will power our antidote. More specifically, the same manna that was exposed during the meteor showers on those first nights of freedom the Jewish people experienced in the desert." The sentiment on the team shifted from confusion to outright disbelief.

"How the hell are we supposed to track down a bunch of magical kosher crackers that may or may not have existed forever ago?" Dallas asked. "If that's our grand plan, then we're totally fucked." His assessment may have been a bit crude, but the rest of the team was thinking the same.

"The location of the manna has been disclosed for millennia, Dallas. It's been written in plain sight for thousands of years. Anyone with a copy of the Old Testament knows where the last remnants were stored," Daedalus said.

"I don't profess to be a biblical scholar," Aliyah said, "but I don't recall an 'X marks the spot' treasure map buried in any of those ancient texts."

"Take an earthenware jug, and put a full Omer of manna into it," a voice behind them said. "You should place it before the Ark of God, to be preserved for your generations to come… and Aaron deposited it in front of the Ark, to be preserved."

All eyes turned to see Luna had ventured back into the lab, offering a verbatim quote of the relevant passage.

"It's the second of the five books of Moses.. The Book of Exodus, chapter sixteen, verse thirty-three, in case anyone wants to double check for accuracy, but you're wasting your time. I know I'm right. The room and the bed were incredible, but I'm still too wired to sleep."

"You certainly are full of surprises, Luna," Daedalus said, breaking into a wide smile. To say that the rest of the team was amazed would be an understatement.

"See? I told you she was great." Dallas was embarrassed by his own PDA and blushed a light shade of pink.

"Aw, Dallas, you're so cute," Luna said. Upon hearing her sweet sentiment, he turned fire engine red.

"Bible study was the other pillar of my life growing up," Luna said. "My dad would take me to Sunday school, and afterward we would head over to the rifle range and discuss what I'd learned from the pastor. 'God, guns, and rock 'n roll' was the doctrine in my house, in that order too. Why exactly are you guys looking for references to the biblical manna? Please don't tell me you're seriously thinking about trying to find some."

"As crazy as it sounds, that's precisely what we're going to do," Daedalus said. "As to the question of *why*, well, that's something I'm not able to disclose to you yet."

Luna simply shrugged her shoulders and didn't press for any further explanation. She assumed Daedalus would be more forthcoming later, and if not, she'd see if Dallas would let her in on what was happening. For the moment, she was just happy to be safe and hidden away from the people who'd attacked the café, and she didn't want to rock the boat. The setup down here was better than anything she had four hundred feet above.

"Based on the verse that Luna recited," Gryph said, "it would seem the original jar of manna was packed away for future generations and left with the Ark of the Covenant. If that's truly the case—"

"Wait, wait, wait. Are you talking about the Ark from the Indiana Jones movies? Like Raiders of the Lost Ark, except the real one?" Dallas asked, stunned.

"Unless you know of another one," Daedalus said. "With access to the original manna, we can run our tests and harness the larger, undiluted quantity needed for use in the antidote." The team saw the logic in the plan, as ambitious as it was. Luna looked even more confused than ever but refrained from asking any questions.

"Just to be clear," Chief said, "we're now shifting to a search-and-recovery mission to locate—I can't believe I'm saying this—the Ark of the Covenant which holds the actual Ten Commandments. And if by some miracle we find this treasure—which, by the way, has eluded everyone who has been searching for it since the day it was hidden—we're hoping the jar of manna left with it, is still there for us to find?"

A few sideways glances were shared between the skeptical bunch. Daedalus merely nodded. "Yup, that's right, Chief."

Ali jumped in. "Many commentaries passed down from time immemorial say the Ark was hidden away by King Yosheahu somewhere in Jerusalem right before the destruction of the Second Temple. Finding it would be one of the greatest archaeological discoveries ever. As Chief said, treasure hunters and scholars have been searching in vain for millennia. While I'm sure that using the original manna would give us the ability to engineer an antidote to defeat the toxin, I think actually finding it would be impossible. It was hidden away to ensure it would never be found. I'm not sure how you think finding the most precious artifact on planet Earth is a reasonable 'plan A.'"

Aliyah read extensively on the history of the Temple Mount growing up in Israel and visited the Western Wall more times than she could count. She and her friends in the IDF also participated in guided tours of the Old City Tunnels in Jerusalem. She knew it was a fool's errand, and wasn't going to let anyone waste the precious little time they had left.

"I'm prepared to do whatever it takes, but we don't have time to search the globe for a treasure that's been lost for an eternity,"

Gryph said. "Like Aliyah mentioned, it was hidden by the king somewhere so it couldn't be found easily. Why do you think you can just lead us to it now?"

"Because, Commander Oake, I was the one who helped him hide it."

CHAPTER TWENTY-TWO

42,000 feet above the Atlantic Ocean
February 10, 7:29 p.m.

The lights in the luxurious interior of the Boeing Business Jet were dimmed after they'd finished dinner. Aliyah was reviewing some lab results on her laptop while she stretched out on a soft, butter color leather sofa in the center of the expansive cabin. Dallas, Luna, and Phil were seated near her at an adjacent table, talking quietly amongst each other. They finished topping up large crystal glasses with generous amounts of Don Julio 1942 tequila. Luna was drinking mint tea. Chief had moved into one of the chairs at the front of the parlor and was snoring loudly. Being in the service taught him many things, chief among them, "Eat when you can, and sleep when you can." Billy already put away copious amounts of the delicious gourmet dinner that was served onboard. With his belly full, his next mission was making the most of his sumptuous lay-flat seat. He was out the instant his head hit the pillow.

This version of the BBJ 777-8 wouldn't be available for purchase for at least another year, but Daedalus had managed to procure an advanced prototype from Boeing to complete some of his own modifications on the final build, with the assistance of some of his friends at various Defense Department contractor firms. Offensive and defensive weapons capabilities were some of the unique enhancements that Daedalus added to the plane. The DoD and Boeing completed much of the work under the guise of prototyping weapons systems for the next generation of Air Force One.

The 5,100-square-foot interior and twenty-foot-wide cabin gave its lucky passengers the feeling they were living and dining in a five-star hotel, belying the fact they were doing so at an altitude of

40,000 feet. The 8,700-mile range allowed the aircraft to fly non-stop between any two points on Earth. The gorgeous jet wasn't just opulence and range. The 105,000 pounds of thrust her twin GE9X engines provided propelled the luxury craft through the skies at over 700 mph. Their current flight plan showed takeoff to touchdown from New York to Tel Aviv would take just under nine hours.

Gryph checked in with the pilots, and they'd confirmed the skies ahead looked smooth. If anything, they would pick up a bit of time flying with the jet stream, not against it. These powerful winds blew from west to east in the upper troposphere at speeds of up to 275 mph, aiding anything flying in its currents. The jet departed at 4:00 p.m. for the nine-hour flight and had been airborne for just over three and a half hours. He calculated that they would touch down at Ben Gurion International Airport in Israel around 8:00 a.m. local time the following day.

Commander Oake took in the sight of his team in front of him. Everyone seemed calm and peaceful. He recalled the near pandemonium that broke out in the lab when Daedalus told them he was part of the group who'd secreted away the Ark of the Covenant over two thousand years earlier. Everyone immediately started shouting and pointing, trying to talk over one another. Daedalus just stared back silently until everyone quieted down. He disclosed that the process to locate and gain access to the Ark would require multiple steps, none being easy. The final location of the biblical prize was protected by a staged approach to prevent someone from accidently stumbling upon the artifact. The only specific piece of information Daedalus offered was the location of their first stop—Israel. He promised to explain in greater detail when they were underway.

Daedalus said nothing more. He simply turned away and exited through the hidden door leading to his ancient library. The stunned silence after his abrupt departure lingered for only a moment. Gryph took charge, immediately instructing Chief and Phil to put together a logistics package for the team for the flight over to Tel Aviv the next day. He asked Aliyah to gather whatever portable equipment she thought her mobile lab would need, assuming they succeeded in recovering the manna. Dallas was given similar instructions for technical and computing gear.

The previous night, Dallas told Luna that the team had to leave the next morning on matters related to the attack on them at her café, and wasn't sure how long they'd be gone for. He had been under strict orders from Daedalus not to reveal anything about the actual reason for the upcoming mission or the danger posed by the toxin, making their conversation that much more difficult. To say the lethal barista wasn't receptive to the idea of staying behind would be the understatement of the year. She stormed away from Dallas and straight to Gryph, who was holed up inside the lab. She protested and, in a highly animated manner, informed him that she wasn't going to be abandoned in the Labyrinth until who knew when and was adamant that she wouldn't go anywhere near her apartment, security detail or not.

Gryph figured since she already knew of the Workshop's existence and heard them speaking candidly about the manna, not to mention that she'd killed someone to save them, it wouldn't be such a bad idea to keep her close. Luna came in useful more than once already, and she couldn't divulge their secrets if she was traveling with them. Also, Dallas seemed to be more cooperative anytime Luna was involved. He was their digital backbone, and if Dallas was focused and engaged, it boded well for them all.

Gryph explained to everyone that Luna wouldn't be deployed into any part of their active mission but could assist Dallas on board the massive jet. They'd recently learned that Luna was a technical whiz in her own right. The internet café destroyed in their gun battle was all she had left to show for her life savings, now laying in a splintered ruin. Insurance would pay for the repairs, but she was done with grinding out a living slinging espresso and bandwidth. Luna informed the group that she was a seasoned network engineer and programmer and well read on a wide variety of subjects. It didn't take long for everyone to see the logic in bringing her along, and just like that, Luna became an official member of the team. The secrecy and vetting process normally required seemed a bit redundant at that point, even to Daedalus. They were mere days or weeks from the beginning of global devastation. If they failed, there wouldn't be anyone left to keep the secret from anyway. If they succeeded, she would have earned her stripes. Baptism by fire.

The team gathered the equipment and provisions required for the rushed departure with the skill and efficiency their combined years in the field taught them. Weapons, lab equipment, and hard-shell cases of all sizes filled with a wide assortment of technical gear were all packed and ready by the next morning. Gryph was pleased with the speed and execution of their mobilization. If Daedalus came through on his end, he was sure his team would be successful on theirs.

"Have a drink with us, Gryph. You like tequila?" Dallas offered up a tall, slender brown bottle.

Gryph, who'd been lost in thought, looked up when Dallas waved him over. "If you're pouring 1942, I'm definitely in. I'll take it neat though, no ice please." Gryph loved tequila, and the Don Julio onboard was one of his favorites.

"Oh, you're a tequila snob. I can respect that." Dallas poured two fingers' worth of the pale-yellow spirit into a crystal glass and handed it to Gryph. The three men clinked the thick crystal.

"L'chaim," Dallas said. "I figured since we're headed to Israel and all." Luna rolled her eyes and laughed. A fresh chorus of "L'chaim" ensued. She got up to pour herself a fresh cup of tea.

The traditional Jewish toast and the clanking sound of crystal prompted Aliyah to pop her head up above the sofa to see what she was missing out on. She'd been reading the same lab reports multiple times, hoping something new would jump out at her, but nothing had. She must have nodded off.

"What's a lady got to do to get a drink around here?" she asked with fake annoyance.

"I'd be happy to remedy that situation, Doc. What can I grab for you?" Phil asked.

"I'll have whatever any of you guys are drinking. As long as it's not tequila."

Luna laughed.

"Uh, any second preferences, Ali? That would be strike one, two, and three over here," Phil said.

"If you've all decided to move past wine, then I'll have a scotch, please. Neat. I'm sure there's a bottle of something old and smoky somewhere onboard this gorgeous jet."

Phil went back to the bar in search of a bottle just as Daedalus came back into the main cabin. He'd left the group before they even finished dinner. It was the first time any of them had seen him since.

The aircraft's crew had been instructed to retire to their own section of the plane after serving dinner offering the team the ability to discuss the mission in private. No one had a chance to get into any details since they departed. Once airborne, their time was first occupied by the customary grand tour of the massive jet and a detailed schematic review of the various military upgrades installed on the aircraft. Once the tour was complete, they returned to the parlor, where everyone found a comfortable place to occupy until dinner.

The sumptuous evening meal was prepared by a Michelin-star chef in the plane's gourmet kitchen, another unique feature of the next-generation jet. They ate in a separate dining room adjacent to the parlor on a gorgeous honey-colored maple table which sat ten people comfortably. Each area of the plane was finished to perfection. After dinner, they made their way back to the parlor and settled into their comfortable places once again. Chief was still snoring when Daedalus sat down beside Gryph.

"I think it's time we discuss what we need to accomplish on this first part of our journey," Daedalus said, finally willing to provide the details he promised. "But I don't want to be the only one at the table without a drink, so let's fix that first." As if on cue, Phil walked back in with a bottle of Macallan Fine and Rare sixty-year-old scotch.

"I hope this works for you, Ali. It seems kind of old, but I'm sure it's still okay to drink," Phil joked. The bottle of Macallan was similar to one Sotheby's had recently sold for $1.9 million, but Phil figured if they had it on board, it must be to drink. "In fact, I'm switching to scotch now too." He poured generous amounts of the deep amber liquid for himself, Aliyah, and Daedalus.

"Someone should wake up sleeping beauty since the gang's all here." Dallas picked up a pillow and tossed it at Chief's head. He snatched it out of the air an inch above his face, the fabric never making contact.

"Gotta be quicker than that, Lama." Dallas was thoroughly impressed with the big man's cat-like reflexes, not that he'd ever tell him. "That little nap was such a great idea," Chief said. "Tip of the hat to you, Daedalus. I didn't know planes this opulent even existed. I've even been onboard Air Force One a couple times, and this baby puts her to shame. It's like we're flying in a hotel. You definitely win the prize for having the coolest toys. What did you name this bird?"

"I'm glad you approve of the accommodations, Chief. Her name is *Hera*, named after the Greek goddess of flight. As you all learned earlier, she's as lethal as she is beautiful. Designing her was a labor of love." Daedalus looked around the interior fondly. He knew every inch of the magnificent jet. "Now that we've all had a chance to eat and relax a bit, and I have my drink, I'd like to explain to you what it is we need to do when we land in Israel," he said. "The path to the Ark can only be revealed using a series of five ancient keys. Each one unlocks the location to the next in the chain and so on until the final key is uncovered. That last key will open the doorway to the hidden place containing the Ark."

Dallas took a sip of his tequila and set the large, crystal glass down. "Oh, that's a relief. I thought this was going to be a hard mission. We just have to find five keys that have been hidden since biblical times. In five different places too, I assume. And we're on the clock. Good luck with that." He picked up his glass and finished the shot.

"Actually, Dallas, we'll only have to explore three different locations, and we only need to find two keys. I'm able to offer us quite an advantage in that regard. While I don't know the location of the Ark itself, I do know the location of the third key in the chain. We don't have to search for the first two to gain access to the third. That puts us almost halfway there before we even start."

"I thought you said you helped hide the Ark. Now you're saying you don't know where it is?"

"I told you all that I helped hide it, and I did. But it was an elaborate scheme requiring a great deal of care and planning. Remember, the Ark was supposed to remain hidden until the end of days. That isn't something that could be accomplished without help. I played my part in hiding it, but King Yosheahu of Judah was the one to seal the final door and secure away the Ark."

"Okay, so where's the third key hidden, and where do we need to take it once we have it?" Gryph asked.

"The third key in the chain is buried at the tomb of Adam and Eve. Once we retrieve it, we need to take it to the Vatican. After that, I haven't a clue, literally."

Dallas burst out laughing. "What the hell, man? Are you shitting me right now? Each step into this crazy world of yours gets weirder by the day. It's never simple with you. How exactly do we find the graves of Adam and Eve? We're talking about the original fig leaf couple, right? The story with the snake and forbidden fruit?"

"Yes, Dallas, that's exactly who I'm referring to. Their burial location isn't a secret. In fact, many people pray there every day knowing full well who is entombed below."

"Me'arat HaMakhpela," Aliya said. "He's referring to the Cave of the Patriarchs. It's located in the old city of Hebron. The English translation means 'cave of the double tombs.' The forefathers of many religions and their respective wives are buried there, as well. Many ancient texts record it as the final resting place of Adam and Eve. I remember going there once when I was a little girl with my father, and the story he told me. We peered down through a grate in the floor located directly above the caves, and he told me that way deep down inside, at the very end of the caves where Adam and Eve are resting, you could still smell the fragrance of apples wafting up from the Garden of Eden. He only told me the fable the one time, but I still think of it every time I smell apples." She smiled at the memory and wasn't sure why she shared it, but she felt comfortable around her new friends, and it just came out naturally.

"Okay, so maybe finding them will be easier than I thought," Dallas said. "Where's this Hebron place? The Israelis must have such an important place locked down tight."

"Hebron is in the West Bank and has long been under Arab control," Aliyah said, "it's not safe for us to just waltz in. Most tours to the site arrive via armored buses with armed escorts onboard to protect the occupants. The site is also one of the holiest sites in all of Islam. Abraham was the father of all Arabs too, so an arrangement was made in the late 1960s to leave the site under Arab control, as they also had a vested interest in keeping it safe. The Jews have exclusive access to the site for Jewish holidays, and the Muslims have exclusive access for their respective holidays. The rest of the time it's a strained relationship, but the Arabs have done a great job keeping it secure. The recent fighting makes visiting there even more dangerous than normal."

Aliyah was referring to the well-known ongoing conflict in the region. The fighting all but eliminated any issues they would have with tourists and crowds at the site. The papers they were traveling on gave them diplomatic immunity and would expedite any traditional customs and immigration bureaucracy. Representatives from the Israeli State Department received orders from on high to accommodate Daedalus and his group with anything they needed and to give them VIP status. Though the papers would mean nothing to certain Arabs guards if they were caught in the tombs.

"I've done a lot of work in this part of the world," Gryph said. "While Hebron is no place for a Sunday stroll, it's not an active war zone right now. Billy K and I were in the thick of it daily in Afghanistan and Baghdad for years on end. This is Aliyah's backyard, so I know she's comfortable here. We'll have no problems getting inside, and I doubt the tomb is heavily guarded at night. We're likely to run into a local or two, at most. The guards are there as a deterrent to thieves and to keep the homeless from using it as a shelter. Everybody in the area respects the sacred location. Plus, we're not going to be stealing anything. We're putting the key back right where we found it when this is over. If someone in the future needs it, it'll be right where it's supposed to be."

"I would suspect your assessment of the security at the mosque is accurate, Commander," Daedalus said. "However, we won't need to gain access to the tombs from the prayer rooms above. There's a hidden tunnel leading into the lower of the two caves that make up this ancient tomb. Once inside, we'll be able to retrieve the key I placed there so many years ago."

Gryph was happy to hear they had a backdoor to expedite the retrieval of the key, but he knew things weren't going to be as easy as Daedalus made them out to be. They never were. "Where exactly do we find the entrance to this tunnel?" he asked.

Daedalus closed his eyes and thought back to the night he'd hidden the key away. He remembered it raining hard, making his work even more perilous. He had been exhausted from climbing through the mud and loose stone. Lightning flashed against the sky in angry streaks. Even though centuries had passed, he could still clearly remember the events of that fateful night.

"There's a small cemetery on the southeastern side of the tombs. A secret tunnel connects the cemetery to a hidden fissure at the rear of the caves. A large stone mausoleum in the corner of the graveyard has a false floor inside that will lead us to the caves without alerting anyone inside."

"We should keep the size of the team at the caves as small as possible," Gryph said. "We'll need a few lookouts to keep the local security contingent off our asses. It seems at first blush that this'll be a simple recovery mission, but we all know to be prepared for anything. We have one shot to recover the key. If anyone suspects an intrusion, they'll lock the place down tight for the next week or two, and we're dead in the water. No margin for error on this one."

"I know where the key is hidden inside the tomb. We'll only need a few minutes inside and about the same amount to cross back through the tunnels. I don't see it taking longer than twenty to thirty minutes, from start to finish."

Gryph put together a rough idea for deployment on the spot. "Chief and I will assist Daedalus with the recovery inside the caves. Phil and Aliyah will be our lookouts at the surface outside of the mausoleum. Lama and Luna can run comms and be our digital eyes and ears from onboard *Hera*. Everything else is situational awareness. This is going to be a very fluid op, but we've all been through much worse with much less. We can nail down the details and pack the gear we need after breakfast tomorrow. We'll have to wait until dark anyways before we sneak into the tunnel. If all goes well, we should be rolling into the Old City this time tomorrow. In the meantime, I suggest we get some sleep while we can. We'll be staying onboard until we depart for Hebron in the evening. There's no need to find alternate accommodations. We brought our own flying five-star hotel. Why downgrade?" Everyone laughed at the absurdity and accuracy of the comment. It was certainly no hardship utilizing *Hera* as their mobile headquarters. Plus, the jet would be well protected and guarded with all the other planes at Ben Gurion International Airport.

"Works for me. I'd be too freaked out to break into a crypt in the middle of the night," Dallas said. "That kind of shit gives me the creeps. I'm cool to hang back here with Luna. But right now, I'm going to follow orders and hit the sack." He grabbed a bottle of water off the table.

"A working breakfast will be served in the dining room at eight o'clock tomorrow. Just leave your order on your doors, and the chef will have your food prepared for the start of our meeting," Daedalus said.

"Sounds like a plan. I can hear a pillow calling my name somewhere," Chief said. He and Dallas both headed for the front of the aircraft for a few hours of blissful sleep.

Aliya and Phil finished their drinks a few minutes later, then went to their respective rooms.

Gryph and Daedalus were the last two people left in the jet's parlor. "Is there anything I need to know about these caves or the keys?" Gryph asked. "We're going in blind as it is. Any additional information or context you can provide would be very useful."

"I haven't been back to these tombs since the night I hid the key at their graves. I did, however, bring along some items from my Library that I think we may need to reach the Ark. Some of them will help guide us on our way, and some may have to be sacrificed to grease the wheels, as the saying goes. I don't really know what we'll need, so I came as prepared as I could. I suspect you've put together your provisions in similar fashion, planning for as many contingencies as you can think of. But if you're asking if there's information I'm keeping from you that would jeopardize the safety of the team or the success of the mission—absolutely not." Daedalus was firm and definitive and Gryph believed him.

"Okay then, Daedalus. We're putting our trust in you. As I see it, we have just under twenty-four hours to finalize plans and gear-up and sneak into a subterranean tomb in the middle of the night to recover an artifact that hasn't been seen in thousands of years, all inside a territory teeming with Hamas militants and religious fanatics while a global catastrophe looms in the background." Gryph said, pounding back the rest of his tequila, "What could possibly go wrong?"

CHAPTER TWENTY-THREE

Laeiszhalle Concert Hall, Germany
February 11, 8:50 p.m.

Private security teams wearing fashionable black suits stood just inside the three arched doorways in front of the centuries-old Laeiszhalle Concert Hall. The Hamburg police force, known as the German Landespolizei, patrolled the area in front of the ornate neo-Baroque structure. There had been a steady stream of Porsches, Mercedes, and BMWs of every shape and size dropping off black-tie-attired guests over the last half hour.

The invite list for the fundraiser was restricted to ultra-high-net-worth individuals, high-ranking politicians, influential activists, and celebrities who were sympathetic to the cause. The last of the guests were making their way to their seats. The doors would be closed and secured. Any latecomers, turned away.

Basileus watched from a private balcony high above while the guests he'd invited settled in below. The small chamber orchestra finished tuning their instruments and took their positions at the conductor's direction.

A man wearing a black hooded robe walked spiritedly toward the center of the stage, turned and smiled at the audience in front of a spot lit microphone perched on a dark wood lectern. Beautiful, intricate towering cylinders extended from the Walcker/Beckerath pipe organ soaring to the magnificent building's roof. The vertical piping climbed to the highest reaches of the gold and ivory theater. Elaborate embellishments covered the acoustically sensitive walls, affording the theater a regal ambience. While the room could normally seat two thousand people when sold out, tonight the number was closer to four hundred. Even with such immense size and splendor, the atmosphere exhibited a warm and intimate aura.

"Meine Damen und herren. Ladies and gentlemen. Willkommen im Laeiszhalle. Welcome to Laeiszhalle. My name is Brother Jacob. We have a very special evening planned for you tonight. Our generous patron and climate champion will give some remarks after the performance. Please make yourselves comfortable, and remember, all phones and recording devices must be put away until you leave the building. Our staff has been instructed to remove any individuals who are found breaking this golden rule. Please understand this is for our protection, as well as yours. And remember, the good Lord is watching us all, and he never misses a thing." The monk wagged his finger at the crowd in a playful gesture as he finished his disclaimer. Laughter from the audience demonstrated that the message, while stern and direct, was softened by the delivery and charisma of the clergyman.

"This evening is just for you, our VIP guests. Let tonight's program bring some light to our souls. Choose to be in the moment and focus on the beauty of the performance over the impulse to share our intimate evening with others. Instagram or Facebook are closed for the night." The crowd roared with laughter as Brother Jacob bowed his perspiring bald head toward his adoring fans and exited stage left. The posh attendees gave the holy looking man a round of applause as he walked off the large, gilded stage.

The tuxedo-clad conductor flicked his baton, and a trio of flutists broke into a medley of bird sounds while percussionists tapped on strange looking drums at the introduction of what could only be described as an eco-themed symphony. An eclectic mix of wind, wood, and percussion instruments played by masters of their craft created an auditory rainforest composition. Ten minutes into the piece, the lights dimmed into a pastel gray as the sounds of a rolling thunderstorm flowed from the stage. The deep bass from the thunder was pierced by the trill notes of a tribal pan flute emerging in the background. The entire set was an homage to the environment and the elegance of nature's soundtrack. At the conclusion of the unique performance almost an hour later, the audience was on its feet, cheering and whistling.

Basileus had been making his way down to the stage level as the music flowed into its final movement. He already slipped into the robe of the Brotherhood wearing the large, drooping hood over his head, obscuring his features. The black mask he wore made any attempt to discern his identity utterly impossible.

When the applause died down, a low murmur washed through the crowd as the musicians put their instruments down. The lights suddenly dimmed, this time to almost complete darkness, forcing anyone left standing to quickly take their seats.

The lights on the stage went out completely, save for the spotlight on the lectern that Brother Jacob had addressed the crowd from before. The self-styled monk reappeared under the arc of light and was met with another warm chorus of applause.

"Magnificent, wasn't it?" he said, eliciting another standing ovation for the musicians. "Mother nature is beautiful on so many levels. It's such a shame that we have mistreated her for so long. Earth is our home, yet we treat it with such indifference." A fresh round of applause showed the audience's solidarity and support of his remarks. "We are blessed to have someone very special with us tonight. Someone who is a true champion of our planet. Someone who prefers not to seek the limelight but instead chooses to redirect that radiance and illuminate this most noble cause—through all of you!" He swept his hand across the room at everyone in the building. "It is only with your help and influence that we can truly make a difference."

The crowd erupted again, but this time it was self-congratulatory, and the loudest chorus of cheers yet. The talking heads, celebrities, and politicians would never miss an opportunity to pat themselves on the back. Even with the lack of press and exposure, they could still rely on one another to inflate their giant egos. While it was true many in the room genuinely cared about the fragile state of the planet, the reality was, they were much more concerned with the size of their bank account, upcoming projects, or latest polling numbers.

"Without further ado, I'd like to introduce—" Brother Jacob was interrupted by a commotion in the seats in front of him. Two large security guards were forcibly removing a man and woman for trying to record his remarks. The ultra-low light in the auditorium was a tactic deployed by Dima making it easier for his men to identify any suspicious lights coming from the audience. He had spotters in the rafters scanning the crowd for the telltale cell phone glow. The well-known Hollywood couple were being removed from the scene efficiently, but without any regard for the embarrassment the actors may have endured. Their phones were snatched up and pocketed by the burly guards. Another digital glow jumped to life across the room, but that encounter devolved into something much more aggressive. That particular hip-hop mogul wasn't giving up his phone or his seat and, as such, was forcibly removed from Laeiszhalle, kicking and screaming. In fact, that was all part of the deterrent. For the rest of the evening, no one dared look at their phone, not even to check the time.

"Sorry about that bit of unpleasantness, everyone. Many thanks to the rest of you again for following our simple request. There are those who would like to disparage and manipulate the good work that we do and, as such, we must do everything in our power to protect our privacy—and yours. Without further ado, It's my pleasure to introduce my friend and mentor, a true leader in our fight for this beautiful planet of ours, Basileus Aristaeus." The crowd rose to their feet and went wild in anticipation of their mystery speaker.

Basileus strode confidently across the stage toward Brother Jacob, greeting him with a warm embrace. Brother Jacob walked off stage as the spotlight faded to black. The lights behind Basileus rose in intensity, bathing the tall flutes of the massive pipe organ that the Laeiszhalle was famous for in a soft yellow glow. He laughed silently at the fictitious last name he used. Aristaeus meant "excellence" in Greek and was also known as the god of agriculture. He found it too ironic to pass up. Basileus wasn't his first name either; he kept his real identity a secret. Basileus was more of a title than a name anyway. It meant king or emperor. The blend of the two made him Emperor of Excellence, or an excellent king. Either way, he found the name to be apropos.

He waited until the applause died down and remained silent until not even a whisper could be heard in the darkened space. "Many thanks to all of you who have taken time from your busy schedules to gather here tonight for this most worthy endeavor. As Brother Jacob said in his introductory remarks, our planet is in grave danger. I fear the situation is far worse than the so-called experts would have us believe. There are entities out there that seek to silence us. They seek to further line their pockets while they rape and pillage the planet with impunity. It is for these reasons that I am forced to conceal my identity. Not because we fear these terrorist organizations masquerading as oil and mining companies. No, we stay hidden to thwart those who seek to put profit before our planet. It's only with your help, my dear friends, that one day I will be able to shed this mask and cloak."

"God bless you Basileus!" a well-known British actress shouted from the front row, like a groupie at a concert. "Keep fighting for us!" A rumble of support and cheers echoed from the crowd. Basileus bowed in thanks. She'd performed her part beautifully. In fact, he would be seeing her later in the evening at his hotel, as had been pre-arranged. The two of them met in London ten years earlier when she was barely twenty-one and, by chance, working as a flight attendant on one of his jets. He made a few well-placed calls and helped her on her way to stardom. She would be forever loyal.

"The time has come for humankind to face certain unavoidable truths. During the last one hundred and fifty years, we as a species have done more damage to this planet than in all our previous time on Earth combined. We throw plastics and waste products into our oceans, destroying entire ecosystems. We've poisoned wildlife with countless oil spills, killing hundreds of millions of animals, fowl and fish. We treat our stratosphere like it's an open-air sewer."

Despite the dim lighting, Basileus could see heads nodding in agreement as he spoke. "The toxic pesticides we spray on genetically modified crops have decimated the honeybee populations worldwide, creating a massive decline in pollination rates. We've destroyed the coral reefs in our beautiful oceans trawling with fishing nets and by our negligent use of phosphates. We have brought about irreversible warmer ocean temperatures due to greenhouse gas emissions. These massive living reef structures survived for millions of years, and we wiped them out in a century. They're not hurt, or sick. They're dead. Gone forever." Basileus paused for dramatic effect, and bellowed, "Forever!"

There were gasps from the seats, followed by hushed but excited chatter. The pedigree, power, and money the invitees had were some of the reasons they'd been selected, but it was their radical fervor when it came to saving the planet that made them especially important. They had been assisting with his secretive plans without even knowing it, like puppets on a string. Happy to assist with any environmental initiative without question if it got them great press. Their compassion was an inch deep and a mile wide.

Basileus raised his hand, signaling that he had more to say. "There are over one billion cows on Earth at present, and that number grows each year. Did you know their flatulence contributes to almost thirty percent of all methane emissions?" A smattering of laughter rippled through the aisles. "Not to mention the chemicals and energy used to breed and consume these poor animals. All for our insatiable appetites. For cheap burgers or thousand-dollar gold-foil-wrapped steaks sprinkled with copious amounts of salt from celebrity restaurateurs. This madness must stop now!"

The crowd jumped to its feet again, and Basileus quieted them once more. "The clock has run out. Drastic measures are required if we have any chance of righting the wrongs we've inflicted on this majestic blue rock we call home. We cannot stay silent anymore. Shout it from the rooftops. This is an emergency, not a mere setback. The time will come in the not-so-distant future when the people of the world realize their collective mistake, only it'll be too late for all of us. Our priority is to spread the need for urgency and put an end to these harmful practices once and for all. By whatever means necessary."

Basileus continued discussing some new initiatives he had planned, putting the crowd into an even deeper frenzy, now that they were captivated by him. He concluded his remarks and received a final thunderous standing ovation. Truth be told, he held almost everyone in the room in disdain. They would go back to their privileged lives thinking that coming to listen to the rant of some eco shaman would absolve them of their responsibility and culpability. It may help them sleep better, but Basileus knew the truth. He rationalized away his own use of those same luxuries as necessities in the battle for the very life of the planet. A god could do no wrong. Basileus almost convinced himself that he was nothing less than Zeus incarnate. His grasp on reality long since faded away.

After the concert and speeches, Dima drove Basileus back to the hotel. The evening's events were a monumental success. Now it was time to unwind. He posted men throughout the hotel and had two standing guard directly outside the doors of the presidential suite, which Basileus occupied. Dima was staying in the adjacent room but would be patrolling the building all night. His men were excellent at what they did, but he only trusted himself.

Basileus was finishing a drink inside his palatial room, reflecting on the evening's events. The reception he received was even better than he had hoped. He would continue exploiting such people to spread his message so more of the survivors in his new world would have a like-minded consciousness. Putting his vision for the planet's health first before anything else.

Basileus had witnessed the unspeakable things people did to each other in war. He watched as famine wiped out millions of people over the years. Tribal and religious disputes raged for millennia and didn't look like they were ending anytime soon. He profited greatly from other people's misfortunes but never tried to influence the outcomes of those calamities directly, though often playing on both sides of the disputes. He felt this neutralized his preference in those conflicts and simply left the outcome to fate. But Earth had no real protector. If he was to rule the world, he had to be the one to save it.

One of the sentries posted outside his suite knocked and then opened the door. "Sir, your guests have arrived. Should I send them in?"

"Yes. Let Dima know they're here and that I'm not to be disturbed until morning."

"Yes, sir." The guard had trouble containing his smile at the last instruction. He could only imagine what the next few hours would be like for his boss.

A moment later, the same guard reappeared with the famous English actress from earlier in the evening. She slipped into the room with a stunning brunette in tow. The two women had their fingers intertwined and did a little twirling dance across the room until they literally fell into Basileus's lap, knocking the trio onto the large bed. The guard sighed as he closed the door, laughter erupting inside. He sulked outside, pondering why his life felt like he was always the nail at a convention of hammers. *It must be good to be a king of men like Basileus,* he mused. He took up his post outside the door and settled in for a night of self-loathing.

On the other side of the door, the mood was much more upbeat. "It's been far too long, my love," the gorgeous film star said as she kissed Basileus on the lips. "I hope you don't mind… I brought a friend along to play." She wasn't going to hear any protest from him. The two women began undressing their tuxedo-clad host while simultaneously unsnapping and unzipping their couture dresses. As the threesome tumbled into the sheets together, Basileus smiled. *It really is good to be king.*

μέρος τρίτο
PART THREE

CHAPTER TWENTY-FOUR

Bet Shemesh, Israel
February 11, 1:04 a.m.

G ryph was running through his mental checklist before they exited the vehicle and laid boots on the ground. The Daedalus crew had been snaking through deserted roads for the last hour and just pulled into the town of Bet Shemesh. This small desert metropolis of 125,000 people was about a half hour drive from Jerusalem and the last major stop before they would cross into Arab-controlled territories in Hebron.

"We're five minutes out from the edge of the city," Chief said to the five passengers in the back.

A Wolf Armored Vehicle, known as a Ze'ev in Israel, was transporting Gryph, Ali, Phil, Daedalus, and a newcomer to the ground mission inside its bulletproof cab. Solo Daniels, the probationary pilot who'd helicoptered them into New York on their first day, had also piloted *Hera*. Having Solo take command of the massive business jet was the final step in completing his recruitment process. He'd performed every assignment flawlessly. Solo was now the official pilot of the Daedalus crew, responsible for managing all flight operations going forward. The ex-fighter pilot had flown some hairy combat missions during the war in Afghanistan and was already an Air Force Silver Star and Air Force Cross recipient. Daedalus recruited him immediately after his last rotation. Gryph felt it would be smart to bring him along and see how he performed in the field under pressure. He didn't anticipate any serious action during their current incursion, but he could always use an extra pair of eyes and ears. He knew Solo was a decorated and experienced pilot and military man, but he wanted to see if he was as cool and in control on the ground as he was at forty thousand feet.

They maneuvered their way through the city, traversing the narrow streets until they reached the outskirts of the Israeli town, bringing them even closer to the Arab security patrols. Their armored vehicle kicked up dust as it tore down a long gravel road before reaching a dead end by way of a heavy metal gate. The yard they were stopped at was ringed by a thick metal fence, topped with rusting strands of concentric razor wire. The gate in front of the Ze'ev rolled open just wide enough to allow the vehicle to pass through. They inched slowly forward, realizing they were surrounded by armed soldiers on all sides. When their vehicle cleared the gate, it closed immediately behind them. The remote location of the yard afforded them roads that were devoid of cars or foot traffic. Their rendezvous point looked like a car dealership, a junkyard, and a mechanic's shop rolled into one. The first stage of their advance from *Hera* to that point had proceeded like clockwork, but that was the easy part. Everything would get more difficult from here. Their IDF escort dared not proceed much further in the Wolf. Any incursion by the Israeli military could be perceived as an act of aggression if they were confronted by Arab security patrols. They couldn't afford to become the spark that ignited the next powder keg of the Arab/Israeli conflict, needing to be much more discreet going forward.

Gryph and the rest of the crew exited into the cold chill of the desert night. Daedalus stayed within the confines of the Wolf as Gryph went to ask the whereabouts of their rendezvous for the next leg of the insertion. Suddenly, two black SUVs raced up to their position. Powerful headlights illuminated the group in front of the massive Ze'ev. The windows on all sides of the SUVs were tinted, obscuring the people inside. Small green flags flew from the vehicles' roofline. It wasn't the welcome wagon Gryph was expecting. Had they been double-crossed already? The flags were unmistakably Hamas. Chief grabbed his Sig Sauer well before the SUVs came to a full stop.

Aliyah walked past the hulking SEAL. "It's all good, Chief. Be cool." She marched directly toward the pair of tinted SUVs.

The two drivers exited the vehicles at the same time but left their engines running. Gryph instinctively reached for his weapon, keeping it at his side, knowing the situation could go downhill quickly. *And this was supposed to be the easy part*, he thought.

Ali's silhouette was bathed in the harsh glow of the bright xenon headlamps. She walked closer to the SUVs with her arms out wide, making it obvious she was unarmed. It looked like she was performing some sort of macabre roadside sobriety test.

Phil positioned himself so there were no obstructions between him, Ali, and the two new arrivals. He grabbed the rope dart he'd tucked into his waistband at the small of his back. The deadly weapon was essentially a razor sharp eight-inch dagger tied to the end of a thin tensile rope. Phil could throw the knife from twenty feet away with a flick of his wrist. He knew they couldn't draw any attention to themselves, and gunfire would surely do that. This method of dispatching someone was entirely silent and just as lethal. He would aim for the neck, severing arteries and bone. They wouldn't even be able to scream once impaled by his knife.

Phil adjusted his grip on the blade as Aliyah and the driver drew to within a foot of each other, then the strangest thing happened. The driver of the vehicle mimicked Ali's wide-armed, weapons-free approach. Suddenly, Aliyah pounced on the driver, who, in turn, picked Aliyah up and spun her toward the still-running SUV. Phil dared not throw the dagger while the target was spinning around with Ali, but he'd be able to drop the man as soon as Aliyah freed herself from his grip.

"David!" Aliyah shouted. "It's been too long. How are you?" she asked when he put her down and released her from his bear hug.

Phil put the blade down and let out a sigh of relief. David, whomever he was, had no idea just how close he'd been to catching a knife in the jugular. Emotions he hadn't been expecting flooded his thoughts during the tense moments when he thought Ali's life was in danger. He had a duty to protect the team, but protecting Aliyah felt like something more than duty. Phil chalked it up to the effects from the quick adrenaline spike and refocused on the scene in front of him. But he still wasn't 100 percent convinced that it was just his job. For those brief seconds, it felt like something more.

"Everyone, this is David. He and I worked in Mossad together for many years. He's the big brother I never had."

Daedalus exited the Ze'ev with the driver and joined the larger group. A quick round of introductions were made, and the Mossad agent began to explain the details for the next phase of their escort.

"You can't roll into Hebron under IDF protection without alerting anyone. If you need to go in and out undetected, the only way to do so is under a Hamas flag. I'll have my associate, Yehuda"— David pointed to another Israeli commando wearing Hamas army fatigues—"escort you on your trip until you're all back here safe. He'll deal with any locals if they come asking questions. Yehuda will be in the lead car with Aliyah. I'll follow close behind with your Commander Oake. The rest of the passengers can fill the empty seats. I was told you only need a short time at the tombs. The faster we get out, the better it will be for everyone. Any questions?"

"Why do we need two SUVs?" Gryph asked. "We could all squeeze into one. Wouldn't that be less conspicuous?"

"I was instructed by my superiors to ensure this operation goes exactly as planned. We have a saying here. In English, it would translate to, 'One is none, and two is one.' I've been in many situations where a back-up vehicle has saved the day. Hopefully, it'll prove redundant, but I want Aliyah and the rest of you to make it in and out without issue. Also, these Hamas guys never travel alone. Sending only one vehicle in would seem more suspicious than two."

Gryph smiled. "We have the same saying back home. I guess preparedness is a universal concept for success." He was glad the IDF team Aliyah selected were as detail oriented as he was and prioritized their safe undetected extraction. "How long will it take to reach the tombs from here?"

"About thirty minutes," Yehuda said. "We can drive very fast with the vehicles flagged like this. Even the local Hamas representatives will want nothing to do with this convoy. The only people who roll around with these flags are the most ruthless and feared of all Hamas factions, the al-Qassam Brigades. Everyone gets the hell out of the way."

"Comms check, boys and girls." Dallas's voice sounded through each of their earbuds with incredible clarity, momentarily interrupting the conversation.

Gryph pressed the tactical microphone taped to his throat. "Got you loud and clear."

The rest of the team checked in one by one. The sub-vocal communications system they were using had been developed at the Workshop. The microphones and earbuds were nearly invisible but provided incredible sound. The encryption they were using ensured their conversations remained secure.

Phil and Solo grabbed the large black gear bags and transferred them from the Wolf to the SUVs. Phil removed a few Heckler-Koch MP5 submachine guns and requisite ammo from the bags before stashing them in the rear of the two blacked-out Hamas transports.

Solo retrieved a small, matte-black, metallic cube from his bag and set it on the ground beside the idling SUVs. The young pilot pulled a controller from his pocket and entered a series of commands. Seconds later, the cube began to vibrate and hum on the desert floor. The IDF soldiers backed away from the shaking box as the cube began to dissolve and transform, finally morphing itself into a stealthy flying machine.

"What is that thing?" David asked.

"It's a nano surveillance drone that'll follow our convoy as we make our way to the tombs. The feed will give us the opportunity to observe any incoming threats giving us a bird's-eye view of the action on the ground. It's programmed to be fully autonomous and will follow the signal I'm sending from this transponder. It can't be detected by conventional radar either. Pretty cool, huh?" Solo held up the small device for everyone to see.

With the drone buzzing overhead, they had a clear view of the first few miles of road leading out from the city. There was little to no vehicular traffic detected, so Solo gave the team the green light to proceed ahead. Gryph, Daedalus, Solo, and David piled into one of the SUVs while Aliyah, Chief, Yehuda, and Phil sped off in the other. The Ze'ev they rode in on would remain in the yard until they returned.

It didn't take more than a couple minutes before all traces of development disappeared behind them. There was nothing but desert and dark skies in every direction. The two vehicles drove in a tight formation as they raced along the dark, deserted, two-lane highway that was only weakly illuminated by the cloud-covered moon. Twenty minutes of uneventful driving later, the lights of Hebron appeared like distant fireflies in the night. The pinpoints glowed larger through the windshield of the SUVs as they approached the first buildings that fronted the ancient town.

There were very few lights on inside any of the dwellings as they drove through the city. The late hour ensured traffic and peering eyes would be kept to a minimum. It didn't take long before they arrived at the Tomb of the Patriarchs.

The large edifice of the tombs stood in stark contrast to the surrounding buildings. The structure's base was a wall constructed from stone blocks rising twenty feet high and transitioned to columns soaring another fifty feet. A minaret, typical of many mosques, towered above it all.

The SUVs pulled into a pair of parking stalls situated in the far southwest corner of the public lot. It would be less than a two-minute walk to the cemetery they were planning to break into. A large thicket of olive trees provided a natural break between the parking areas and the adjacent memorial gardens in the graveyard. The mature olive tree canopies spread their foliage over the corner of the area where the two vehicles were idling. Power was at a premium in that part of the region, and fortunately for them, the parking lot lights were dark for the night save for a few small lights positioned much closer to the building.

"We're here. Everyone out," Gryph said from his throat mic, and the team poured out of both SUVs. Some were holding MP5s, while others were hauling the gear bags. "The IDF team is going to remain here with the vehicles. The rest of us are headed to the cemetery. There shouldn't be anyone out here at this time of night, but keep alert just in case."

Chief took the point position, and the rest of the crew followed in a modified diamond formation, Daedalus in the center. Gryph was surprised at the ease with which Daedalus moved with the team. He was sure that sometime during the secretive man's past he'd trained with some type of militarized force.

A minute later, the cemetery came into view. It was ringed by a small stone wall. The area they needed to cover seemed much larger in person than on their surveillance photographs. They took cover behind a low barrier separating the sacred tombs from the balance of the memorial gardens. Fortunately, it was just as dark over there as it was by the SUVs. They dared not use any flashlights which would reveal their presence.

Phil unzipped the duffel bag he'd been carrying and pulled out a black aluminum case. A moment later, he had it open and began handing out what looked to be some kind of futuristic goggles. They were ultralight, high-tech heads-up displays (HUDs), with thick padded straps to keep them securely in place.

"Holy shit! These things are amazing! It's like night vision meets X-Box with these bad boys on," Chief said. "I've said it before, and I'll say it again. You have the most badass gear I've ever seen."

The HUDs gave the users the ultimate tactical advantage, not only providing low-light/night-vision clarity, but they did also so with rich colors, not the washed out green and white images many previous iterations were limited to. The lenses also provided digital zoom capabilities, activated by sliding a finger up or down the side of the goggles. A navigational module with an overhead map of the area was superimposed in the top left of the user's field of view, including the current position of each member of the Daedalus crew. Their locations were represented by small floating green triangles. In the opposite corner of their displays was a screen showing the camera feed from each team member. A similar swiping motion would allow the wearer to choose the feed they wanted to see. HD cameras were built into the exterior of the HUDs, providing the livestreamed content. Time, temperature, and heart rate were also displayed for the wearer and broadcast back to the team onboard *Hera*.

The location of the mausoleum and the hidden entrance was identified by a bright red dot on their displays. It would be damn near impossible to get lost with the advanced technology they had at their disposal. *It almost feels like cheating*, Gryph thought. Daedalus mapped out the area with Gryph and Aliyah on the flight over. He was certain he could pinpoint the crypt from the satellite imagery. The clarity the colorized night vision provided made traversing the old boneyard much easier. This allowed them to avoid trampling on any sacred resting places as they journeyed toward the small stone structure Daedalus had tunneled through all those centuries ago.

They followed the path their navigation systems sent them on and quickly reached their destination. The crew found themselves gathered in front of a mausoleum constructed from the same Jerusalem stone and architectural style as the famous tomb that towered in the background.

"As far as I can tell, you guys are alone out there. Solo's eyes in the sky show no activity anywhere," Luna said. While Dallas was operating the communications and infosystems for the group, Luna was monitoring the drone Solo released earlier and had been watching their proceedings from a couple hundred feet up. The optics onboard the mini aircraft were as advanced as the ones on the HUDs they were wearing, giving Luna and Dallas a complete aerial view of the operation. The feed from the drone could be sent to the HUDs if the situation warranted. The team back aboard *Hera* were watching the separate live feeds on a bank of high-definition monitors and could forward any of those images to the team if asked.

The mausoleum was twelve feet wide and about the same in depth. The block walls making up the perimeter of the crypt rose eight feet high and were topped with a domed roof soaring another eight feet, giving the overall structure a height of over fifteen feet. While not excessively tall for a mausoleum, it was easily the largest one in the cemetery. A dark, worn metal door, standing five feet tall was perched above a single step at the base of the crypt. An intricate stone archway curved over the entry and terminated on either side of the doorway, creating a slight overhang that Gryph and Daedalus gathered under. Ancient runes were carved into the stone crypt. They had weathered over time and were barely visible now.

"This is the place. I remember the last time I was here quite clearly," Daedalus said. "I can't believe it's been so long. I know it's a cliché, but being here now, it seems like it was only yesterday, and at the same time, a lifetime ago. This is a surreal experience, even for me."

"I'm glad you're enjoying this trip down memory lane, but you guys have some graves to rob and a world to save, so let's get cracking, boys." Giving Dallas the opportunity to provide running commentary while monitoring communications wasn't something Gryph had considered earlier, but there was nothing he could do about it now. Besides, he was right. They needed to get moving.

The door to the crypt was secured with a combination of heavy chain and padlock that looked to be at least fifty years old, if not more.

"What are we using to get this thing open?" Aliyah asked. "That lock looks like it's seen better days, but that chain is still pretty solid."

Chief reached into the bag Solo had brought to the site and retrieved a pair of wrenches. The experienced demolition expert slipped the tools through the padlock so that one side of each of the jaws were through the padlock's loop and the rounded edges of the wrenches were set back-to-back. He squeezed the wrenches together in his powerful hands, putting tremendous strain on the tired iron. An instant later, the old lock blew apart. Other than the muffled sound of the broken metal clanging onto the ground below, the night remained still.

"Not bad, Billy," Gryph said with a chuckle. "Cute little trick." He slipped the chain from the door and, much to everyone's surprise, the door creaked open for a few inches, as if fate was either daring or inviting them inside.

"That's some spooky-ass shit. Did you guys see that door just open by itself? You wouldn't catch me going in there. No fucking way." Dallas was glued to his display.

"Dallas!" Gryph said. "Keep the commentary to yourself and the channel clear unless something goes sideways. The whole stone wall has shifted over time. The front of the building has pitched forward a few degrees. The door was succumbing to gravity, nothing more."

"Sorry boss. My bad."

"Alright. Game time, everyone," Gryph said. "I'm going inside with Daedalus and was originally planning on bringing Chief in with me, although I'm not sure he'll be able to fit through that door even though I want him watching my six. Chief, you'll have to stay topside with Ali and Solo." The big SEAL didn't look upset when told he didn't have to go crawling through the crypt.

"Phil, you wait here while I go in with Daedalus to find the entrance," Gryph said. "We'll need somebody to stay somewhere between this entry and the caves themselves. I'm not sure what side of the cave I'll need you on yet, so be ready to back up either position quickly. This shouldn't take us long, let's get at it."

Solo cleared the remnants of the lock and chain from in front of the portal, and Gryph was able to pull the timeworn door open all the way. The mausoleum before them was pitch black. Stale air and dust wafted from the small opening. None of them were overly superstitious, but something about crawling into a crypt seemed extremely unnerving.

Gryph motioned to the open doorway. "Age before beauty," he said to Daedalus. The older man nodded and slipped into the opening without a second thought. Gryph had no fear of ghosts or spirits, he did however have a healthy fear of enclosed spaces. His phobia wasn't as debilitating as it used to be, but the current surroundings and situation were compounding the problem. He dove through the opening behind Daedalus before he allowed his mind to run wild with a succession of frightening scenarios.

Phil looked back at Aliyah, Billy and Solo. "Is it just me, or did those two guys seem way too okay with crawling in there?" All three of them shrugged in response. The trio were just happy it wasn't part of their assignment.

"Think of the stories you'll be able to tell your kids," Chief said as Phil crouched down and peered into the black void.

"Yeah, sure. But only if I make it through this alive first." With those final words, Phil disappeared through the rectangular opening swallowed by the darkness of the mausoleum.

CHAPTER TWENTY-FIVE

Cave of the Patriarchs, Hebron
February 11, 2:09 a.m.

The three men huddled close together on the other side of the small metal door. The HUDs provided a clear view of the interior of the mausoleum. Heavy stone coffins were stacked from floor to ceiling. Each of the limestone pieces had an inscription detailing the lineage of the body or bodies that lay inside. Daedalus ran his fingers along the epigraphs. He remembered walking that path so many nights ago. The ancient stones were a testament to the longevity of the long-lost visitor who now finally returned to retrieve what he buried there lifetimes ago.

It made him wonder what type of monument would be erected for him when he was finally dead and buried. Would he lie in an unmarked, anonymous grave, with no one to remember him? Or an elaborate edifice like this… where he'd still be forgotten. He pushed those thoughts aside, knowing they would only serve as a distraction, and he needed to be clear and focused.

"What do we need to do to gain access to the tunnel?" Gryph asked Daedalus, who seemed oblivious to the question, lost in his own world. Gryph was struck by the fact that the entire mission could end before it even started if they couldn't find the secret way into the Cave of the Patriarchs. Even if the tunnel was real, it could very well have collapsed after all this time, and they'd be finished.

"You know, it's not as spooky in here as I thought it would be," Phil said. "These heads-up displays help a lot. It doesn't look like we're creeping around in the middle of the night. Everything is bright and vivid. Not that it's a warm and cozy space, but it's not the haunted bone pile I was dreading either."

"Caretakers come through these mausoleums every few years to clean out any debris, dead animals, or insects that may have burrowed their way in and built nests," Daedalus said. He walked to the back of the mausoleum and stopped, placing his hand on top of a large stone coffin laying against the rear wall. Unlike the other tombs on the sides of the stone enclosure, this coffin sat solitary, with no others stacked above it. "We're going to need to remove the lid from this one here," he said, hovering over the long stone box.

They were now faced with their first daunting task. The lid to the massive limestone coffin was at least a foot thick and looked like it would take all three men considerable effort to get it off.

Phil unzipped the duffel bag he'd brought inside and removed a telescoping pry bar and a fluorescent-orange wedge that looked like an oversized door stop. "Let me see if I can get under the lip with this," he said as he scraped the pry bar around the coffin's lid, delineating its edges. Small pieces of stone and dust rained down over the sides of the deep stone box and onto the ground below. He quickly completed the maneuver to all four sides, clearing the old seams of sand and mortar.

Phil grabbed a hammer from the duffel and pounded the leading edge of the pry bar under the front right corner of the lid, extending the telescoping handle out fully. "We're gonna need to put all our weight on this end to get that lid to budge. Once we get it slightly lifted, I'll jam this orange wedge under the lid to keep it from closing again. It'll be easier to reposition the lid after the initial seal is broken, and the wedge will give us an easy pivot point after."

Phil's plan was simple enough, each man quickly took up a position on the bar. "On the count of three, put all your weight on the end."

Dallas had been monitoring the activities inside the tomb and pushed the feed from Phil's HUD, allowing those on the outside to follow the progress as well.

"Okay, everyone ready? On three." Phil, Gryph, and Daedalus each grabbed hold of the long bar and steeled themselves like one would do in a gym before attempting an ultra-heavy deadlift or bench press. "One... two... three." They jumped in unison to gain every ounce of momentum as gravity pulled them back down on the thick metal bar. To everyone's surprise, not only did the lid move easily, it flipped up violently against the back wall of the crypt and came crashing back down onto the coffin. Dust exploded inside the tiny space, momentarily obstructing the view from the camera feed.

"Holy shit! Are you guys okay?" Dallas asked. "That sounded like an explosion."

It took a second for everyone inside the mausoleum to realize what had just happened. As the dust settled, they saw the top slab had broken into a few manageable pieces and was haphazardly resting across the top of the coffin.

"We're okay," Gryph said. "The top slab looked a lot heavier than it was."

The trio dusted themselves off, then inspected their handiwork. The good news was that there were only a few pieces to move now. They positioned themselves around one of the larger pieces and slid it into the corner, careful not to drop it over the edge.

Phil jumped back as soon as the first large section was slid out of the way. . . The bad news.

"Whoa! There's somebody in there. I thought there was going to be a secret passageway or something. There's a legit dead guy in there." He backpedaled away from the coffin as he announced the discovery of their unexpected occupant, which was entirely unnecessary since the whole team saw what made him jump via their HUDs.

A threadbare white burial shroud was wrapped loosely around a body. All that remained of the relic was a brittle pile of yellow bones and a thick matting of cobwebs. A familiar skull shape was pressed against the time-worn fabric at the top of the body. Both the cloth and the bone had almost decayed into oblivion with the passage of time.

"We need to move quickly," Gryph said, ignoring the commotion beside him.

Gryph grabbed the leading edge of one of the other broken lid fragments, and Daedalus took the other side. The old man's strength was incredible. Gryph was straining hard, even with Daedalus shouldering most of the weight. As soon as the pair finished pushing the remaining pieces of the lid to the side, Daedalus reached in and removed the bones from the coffin, gingerly placing them on top of one of the large stone fragments.

"We'll lay him to rest once again when we're on the way out, but I'll need both of you to help me remove this." Daedalus said as he dusted the macabre grime from his hands.

Gryph and Phil peered into the empty coffin. Only small bits of cloth and cobwebs occupied it now. "Remove what? It's empty," Phil said.

"It has a false bottom. There's something hidden beneath it." Gryph was already leaning halfway inside, looking for some type of release mechanism. "We need to remove this base, too."

"Correct again, Commander." Daedalus was impressed.

"How could you possibly know that?" Phil asked.

"This coffin is easily over four feet high. The body was close to the top, so it had to have been resting on a platform. And Daedalus said he needed help removing the rest of it. Just made sense to me."

"Maybe for you, Gryph, but for the rest of us mere mortals, no offense to Daedalus, it wasn't as obvious," Phil said.

Gryph noticed a series of small iron loops protruding from the inside edge of the platform they needed to remove. He reached inside and tugged on a few of them, hoping it would trigger a trap-door or something, but nothing budged.

"We may have a problem, guys. The false floor of this coffin is also stone, just like the lid. We're gonna need something to lift it out, but I don't think Phil's crowbar is going to cut it."

"Daedalus, how did you seal this place up by yourself? Those slabs must weigh a ton." The question came from Aliyah over their comms. She'd been watching the proceedings from her feed.

"I didn't seal any of this up. That task was completed by others once my assignment was complete. This is the first time I've seen this coffin with anything inside of it. The last time I was here, there was only a tunnel and stairs that led down from the coffin's base."

With no clear direction on how to proceed, Daedalus would have to improvise. "Captain Daniels, can you bring me the aircraft cable spooled up in the bag? I have an idea."

Phil offered to get the high-tensile cable from Solo outside, using any excuse to get away from the open coffin.

"I'll need one of my silver briefcases as well," Daedalus said.

"How are we looking outside, Chief?" Gryph asked. "Did our little accident with the lid wake the neighborhood?"

"All clear out here, bro. Just whistling Dixie past the grave-yard… in like, you know, an actual graveyard."

"You guys realize you can use those headsets to see each other's POV? That's kind of the point of it, you know?" The not-so-subtle message was delivered in a lighthearted tone by Luna, who'd been monitoring the mission from the aircraft with Dallas.

"You're right, Luna, but it'll take a while to get used to all the features on these," Gryph said. "I'm an old dog already, and these are some really new tricks." The casual ribbing deflated some of the tension hanging in the air.

Solo handed the requisite equipment over to Phil, who returned to the stone coffin with the cable, along with a selection of clips and connectors in one hand and the silver briefcase they had seen Daedalus handling since their first day at the Workshop, clutched in the other.

"So, what's the plan?" he asked as he handed the gear to each of the two men.

"Good thinking, bringing the carabiners too," Gryph said. "We can attach them to the bolts I saw on the bottom slab and loop the line through them. We'll have to somehow rig a hoist above it once we secure it with our cables. We can't afford a repeat performance while removing this section. If it comes crashing down into the tunnel below, the whole thing could cave in, and we'll be screwed before we even get a foot inside."

Daedalus flipped open the silver case. "Leave the hoisting to me. Just get those lines connected, and make sure they won't slip out." Daedalus started working on a digital keyboard mounted inside the case while Gryph connected the long strands of heavy-duty aircraft cable to the military-grade connectors Phil had brought. They were the same clips used by the Army to tie down Humvees to the bed of military cargo planes. They were more than strong enough to carry the load from the stone.

Daedalus finished inputting his last set of commands, then spun the silver case around just as Gryph was about to ask what he had planned next. "We should move back toward the door while ICARUS assembles the bots."

"You brought the nanobots with you? That's brilliant. I've been wondering what you had inside those cases for a while," Aliyah said over the headsets while watching the flurry of activity on her display from outside the crypt.

Daedalus was about to confirm Ali's assessment when a high-frequency buzz filled the small space. It grew in volume and intensity until it sounded to the three men inside like they were in the heart of a beehive. A blur of metallic black smoke poured from the case and cascaded over the open coffin. The nanobots looked like ants swarming over an invisible anthill, each on a mission that had yet to be revealed. Less than a minute later, a series of crisscrossing structures rose above the open coffin, and the room fell back to eerie silence. The smell of static electricity lingered in the confined space.

"Okay, let's connect the cables to the rigging ICARUS created." Daedalus raced back to the coffin. Gryph and Phil were too stunned to move.

"Did that look as cool in person as it did on the display?" Chief asked. "I love those nanobot things."

"Yeah, it was pretty amazing in here too," Phil said. "A bit scary with all that tech flying around in such a small space, to be honest, but it looks like ICARUS constructed a gantry to help us hoist the false bottom out." A thin black rail, which had materialized only moments before in front of their eyes, ran lengthwise down the center of the coffin and was perched a few feet above it. The upper structure was supported by thick nanobot struts secured to both sides of the coffin and anchored to the floor.

"Slip the cables you've rigged over the open end of the rail until they're spread out evenly, then stand back," Daedalus said.

Phil and Gryph completed the task in short order and stepped back to the middle of the room where Daedalus had retreated. He pulled the nanobot controller from his jacket and sent the final instructions to the mechanized gantry suspended over the freshly desecrated grave.

The intensity of the static smell in the room blossomed again, a soft groan emanated from the stone box. Loud creaking and snapping sounds drowned out the soft buzz from the nano-fabricated gantry. A large crack erupted from the coffin area. Everyone instantly worried the old stone had split and was now literally lying in the way of their success.

The three men ran toward the coffin to determine the extent of the damage but stopped when the edge of the slab, still rigged tight with bolts and cables, rose into view over the coffin's lip. The gantry itself rose in height too, hoisting the slab with it until the concrete cover was suspended three feet above the opening. It was like watching a stone cork being pulled free.

They all looked down into the open pit to see a deep void below the coffin's previous location. There appeared to have been a small cave-in on the right side of the pit some time ago, but the large opening still allowed full access to the bottom via a crude rock staircase protruding from the wall on the opposite side of the cave-in. The primitive staircase looked to drop at least twenty feet straight down.

"You're sure that nano-crane is going to be able to keep that slab suspended?" Gryph asked. "If one of those slips while we're under it, we'll either get squashed like a bug or buried alive. We can't really exit the other way either, even if the underground path to the caves is still clear after all this time. How do we explain to the Arabs who protect this site to ignore the American commandos sneaking into the mosque from the eternal resting places of their ancestors? They wouldn't take kindly to that at all. It would probably be a worse fate than the lid crashing down on us. Not to mention igniting an international incident or religious jihad we spark in retaliation."

"Not to worry, Commander," Daedalus said. "These work like the nanobot safety netting we have protecting the roofline in the Workshop. Even if this stone were to shift, the gantry would adjust to compensate. This big slab would stay safe even if an earthquake struck directly underneath. As for the weight, I could suspend something a hundred times heavier than this chunk of rock, and we'd remain safe. I swear on my life."

Phil and Gryph looked at each other and both knew they weren't going to back out at this point. It was Phil who sprang into action first. He swept his legs over the edge of the coffin and let them dangle below him. His arms straddled the top edge like a gymnast on parallel bars. In one motion, Phil swung from the lip of the coffin to the stone steps projecting from the wall that ran all the way down to the bottom.

"I'm pushing the feed from Phil's camera to your displays now," Dallas said, and a new image burst to life revealing a tunnel leading away from the bottom of the stone steps where Phil was currently standing. A noticeable slope fell away in the earth, evidence they weren't done with the descent just yet. Gryph and Daedalus worked their way to the bottom, albeit with less speed and grace than Phil exhibited on the way down.

The path ahead appeared to be a natural fissure in the rock created when the caves were first formed. They could see places along the roof that had been reinforced using the same marble pavers the staircase used, only much larger. The crude building materials and long-forgotten construction methods had withstood the test of time.

"Phil, you stay here on this end of the tunnel," Gryph said. "If anything happens to us inside the caves, or if the tunnel collapses and traps us, bring Aliyah and Solo down here to dig us out. Billy can handle himself alone up there and keep people off our backs until we're all out safe."

Phil nodded, silently relieved that his journey underground stopped there.

Gryph turned to Daedalus. "I'm going in first. I want to have a clear line of sight to the other end of that opening the whole time. There's no point in you following until I'm all the way through. Phil might need your help on this end with the nanobots, and there's bound to be some spots where we may have to fight to get through. We can't have you getting trapped and blocking the way behind and me blocking the way forward. Plus, you're the only one who knows where to find the key once we get through."

He darted into the cave before Daedalus could even begin to argue. Gryph found that he could almost walk upright in the first section of the passageway, deeper down portions of the tunnel began to shrink considerably. After a few yards of easy progress, he had to resort to squeezing through the tunnel sideways. He referenced the GPS navigation on the HUD as he progressed. The measurements showed he only had about seventy feet to go, unfortunately the passageway in front was quickly narrowing to a small shaft. It was a good thing he left Chief up top. The big man never would have made it through the first narrow section.

"Dallas, can these optics determine if the path forward is clear or obstructed? It's getting kind of tight now, and I don't want to crawl toward a dead end or have something collapse on top of me."

"Yeah. Give me a second, I'll fire up the sonar modules for you." Dallas activated the feature on Gryph's device. "Okay, Gryph, tap the lens to toggle the screen into active sonar mode. That should give you the info you want."

Gryph tapped his finger on the screen, a blue topographical grid was overlaid across the surface of everything in front of him. The sonar feature provided measurement and distance calculations, which were automatically displayed on the HUD. Gryph crawled headfirst into the skinny opening, focused on the image he was being shown. He could clearly see the aperture on the other side. The way was clear, but the last fifteen or twenty feet of the tunnel looked too narrow to pass through.

Gryph didn't have any real vices in life, except for coffee and maybe his particular line of work and the assignments it brought. Fear was something he respected and even used to his advantage at times, but he very rarely let it control him. The glaring exception to this was his irrational fear of being buried alive. Granted, most people would be terrified of that thought as well, but Gryph couldn't shake the feeling that it was really going to happen to him. Nothing terrified him more. He couldn't remember any event from his childhood or his military career that would've triggered such a fear. He wasn't afraid of dying in battle. As a soldier, he accepted that would likely be his eventual fate. The thought of being buried alive sent shivers down his spine. Gryph shook the thought from his head and focused on the next twenty feet. It was going to be a tremendous struggle physically, but even more so mentally.

Biting back the bile in his throat, Gryph dove into the tightening crevice; his mind running through a succession of the horrifying possibilities that lay ahead.

CHAPTER TWENTY-SIX

Deep inside the caves
2:36 a.m.

Gryph remained laser-focused on the end of the tunnel. A small outline of the opening on the other end was visible through his HUD. If he could see the way out, he figured he would be fine. A continuous view of the exit was the only thing keeping him from full-fledged panic.

The first half of the crawl wasn't as bad as he thought it would be. The last half, however, was a nightmare. The tunnel narrowed dramatically the farther in Gryph went. It reached the point where he could only move forward by extending his arms in front of him and wriggling his hips and shoulders just to get any forward progression at all. He could still see the opening ahead on the sonar, but the next ten feet of the tunnel narrowed to a pinch point so small, he wasn't sure that he'd be able to make it through.

Determined, he pushed forward by clawing at the hard ground with his fingers, which were already bleeding and raw from pulling himself through the first half of the confined space. The bulky combat boots he was wearing were proving to be a very poor choice of footwear, and had long since been of any use assisting his progress. The final section was the smallest he faced yet. Gryph had to turn his face to the side to be able to slide his head through. The passageway was barely wide enough for his head, not even a foot in height. The repositioning of his head meant he also lost sight of the exit for the first time, at the worst possible moment, too. Sweat and dirt trickled into his eyes, stinging them. Not being able to wipe the irritants away was making the difficult journey even more maddening. After clawing and wriggling like an overgrown inchworm, and gaining only a few more feet, Gryph realized he was completely and utterly stuck.

He had unwittingly pushed himself too hard into the tapering space. The earth surrounding him was now packed tightly around his body, and even the limited movement he had before was gone. Gryph worked his arms and shoulders against the packed soil, but it was no use. Dirt and dust were constantly getting into his mouth and lungs. He was finding it harder to breathe. He tried unsuccessfully to expand and contract his chest, slow his breathing, and calm himself. He had less than ten feet to go, but for Gryph, it may as well have been a hundred. He struggled with all he had to get loose, but it only wedged him in tighter. His heart was banging out of his chest. He knew he was on the verge of passing out.

"Gryph, you're going to be okay, brother. Just try to control your breathing. We're coming to get you right now," Chief said over his earpiece, after watching Gryph's vitals spike on the HUD, but Gryph knew if he were to be pulled out now, he wouldn't be able to endure such torture again. The earth around his chest not allowing him to inhale even half of a regular breath. He'd been stuck for the last few minutes, unable to move forward or backward. With every shallow breath he took, Gryph sucked in more dust and dirt.

"Guys, I'm stuck, and I'm not sure what to do. I can't fit my chest… through this last pinch… point… no matter what I try. I can't see anything. My face is mashed… against one of the… walls." The message came across in short gasps as he fought the panic in his chest, constricting his air supply even further. His camera showed nothing but the jittery motion against the dark rock wall.

"Dallas, can you push any type of image to these HUDs?" Phil asked.

"Uh, yeah, I guess. What did you have in mind?"

"Can you find a live feed or a loop of a beach somewhere and send it to Gryph's screen? Turn all the other info and overlays off."

"Sure, hold on. One sec." A few ticks later, Gryph's HUD was awash in turquoise water and powder white sand. The effect was like being in a virtual reality simulator. The wide-open spaces and clear blue skies that appeared in front of Gryph's eyes calmed his nerves, his breathing became much less erratic. Luna added a gentle soundtrack of ocean waves to complete the sensory fake out.

It brought Gryph back from the brink of panic. He took as large a breath as the confines of the tunnel permitted and slowly exhaled until he expended every last ounce of air in his lungs, flattening his torso as much as his body would allow, and made one last ditch effort to claw his way free.

He dug his fingers deep into the packed ground pulling and writhing forward with all his might. He imagined he was swimming against an incredibly strong current that was trying to hold him in place. Eventually, inch by inch, he worked himself free from the pinch point until his entire upper body broke free. Gryph pulled himself the rest of the way through until he rolled out onto the cavern floor on the other side. He felt like he'd been birthed by the very earth itself, but he'd finally made it through.

A huge cheer erupted over the comms. The entire crew had been holding their collective breath as Gryph powered his way through the last few feet of the small fissure.

Gryph lay panting on the ground and took a moment to let the adrenaline fade away, shaking off the effects of being trapped. He took in his new surroundings. "That was some creative thinking, Phil. An ocean view was genius. I don't think I would have made it through without that. I owe you one."

"No, you don't. Not at all. You did the impossible, Gryph." Phil was just happy he hadn't volunteered to go in. "You sure as hell wouldn't catch me crawling that far inside. Any sane person would have turned back long before. You were buried alive in there, dude." Gryph hadn't told the team about his phobia, but he had been thinking the exact same thing while lying there, trapped.

Now that Gryph had made it through safely, Daedalus was next up to embark on the same harrowing journey.

"What Gryph accomplished by flattening his body and crawling without any air in his lungs was astounding, even to me. Any other man would have blacked out with that much physical exertion. Bravo, Commander."

"Uh, not to rain on anyone's parade, but how the hell is Daedalus going to get through there now? He's even bigger than Gryph is." Dallas wasn't wrong. "We may have another problem, too."

"What problem would that be?" Daedalus asked, already frustrated and antsy after watching Gryph's passage.

"Assuming you or Gryph find what we need down there, how is he going to come back out? There's no way he's going to be able to do that all over again. No offense, Gryph, but you're crazy to even try it."

Daedalus was an experienced mountaineer and had crawled and climbed through almost every inch of the spaces inside the Workshop and Labyrinth while originally mapping his underground base. On many of those expeditions, he had to traverse through spaces almost as tight. He wasn't bothered by the extreme confines of the tunnel after watching Gryph's torturous attempt. However, he wasn't sure he could fit through it even if he wanted to, fear or no fear.

"I happen to agree with your reasoning, Dallas," Daedalus said, "but I'm sure I can pull him back through on his way out this time. He just has to hang on for the ride."

"But if Daedalus isn't following him in, how is Gryph going to know where to look for the key?" Aliyah asked from far above.

"That won't be a problem," Daedalus said. "We can use the HUDs. The video feed from Gryph's camera will serve the same purpose as me being inside the cave with him."

As if on cue, Dallas broadcast the feed from Gryph's camera, illuminating the interior of the tomb for the whole team to see.

The cave was much smaller than they were expecting. The tunnel Gryph emerged from was at the rear of the cave. As luck or the intent would have it, he'd been deposited into the lower of the two caves. Adam and Eve were purported to have been buried in the lower sections. The biblical forefathers and their wives were buried in the cave directly above. Now all Daedalus had to do was reveal the exact location of the key that would unlock the pathway to their next destination.

Gryph panned around the ancient tomb. A low ceiling and a small outcropping of jagged rocks were the only things visible. He walked a few yards to a spot where the top of the cave rose to its apex. Directly below the elevated roof section were two distinct outlines on the ground. Each one was twelve feet long and five feet wide. They were ringed by a series of small, uneven rocks, with a larger headstone, two feet in diameter, embedded into the earth. There were no ceremonial artifacts that he could see, nor any visible inscriptions on the walls.

"It looks like you found the graves right where Daedalus said they'd be. I can't believe we're looking at the final resting place of Adam and Eve. I know I've said it before, but this is so surreal." Luna was speaking in hushed tones like golf announcers do on TV, even though she was more than fifty miles away. "Only a handful of people have ever stood where Gryph is now since the beginning of recorded time. Thank you for letting me be a part of this."

On board *Hera*, Dallas looked up to see Luna wipe a tear from her eye. He placed his arm around her and flashed a genuine smile that she returned with a toothy grin and a warm embrace.

"Okay, Daedalus, it's up to you now. What am I looking for?" Gryph wanted to grab the key and get the hell out of there. He'd already been down there far longer than expected.

"Uh, guys, not to make a bad situation worse, but we've got company coming in from the front gate," Chief said. The small team outside the mausoleum saw the telltale sign of flashlights bobbing up and down in the distance. There was no way they'd be able to talk their way out of the situation, not the way they were dressed and armed. They really didn't need this wrinkle in the plan right now. Especially when with other, more immediate concerns.

Unfortunately, the pair of flashlights was coming directly for them. Chief realized the guards were following the pathway that ran the perimeter of the graveyard. The good news was the route they were taking was predictable. The bad news. . . it would lead the patrol right to where they were standing. He estimated they had less than a minute or two before the guards would be on top of them.

"Gryph, I'll quickly guide you to where the key is hidden." Daedalus said. The ancient man took in the scene fed by the camera on Gryph's goggles through his own high-tech optics. None of the interior looked familiar to him though. The last time he was inside the cave, he was working by candlelight. The meager illumination back then cast deep shadows on the walls that couldn't even begin to illuminate the space the way the night-vision goggles did. None of it looked like it had when he was there, but the layout of the cave itself wasn't important. He knew exactly where he left the precious artifact.

"Here they come," Chief said as he watched the two guards come around the last corner. He and Aliyah stashed the gear bags inside the mausoleum and hid behind the stone building for cover as the patrol approached the square building. They already pulled proprietary energy pulse weapons from their holsters. Billy found the little beauties inside the Workshop armory, along with a wide array of conventional and next-generation weaponry. The electric shock weapons would dispatch the two guards without making a sound. By the time they came to, the Daedalus crew would be long gone. The electrical charge was also designed to cause short-term memory loss through temporarily stunned neurons. The two guards wouldn't remember a thing about that night, never mind the specific part of the cemetery they were in when they were attacked.

Meanwhile, twenty feet below the surface, the search for the key continued.

"Gryph, I believe the grave on the left side is the resting place of Adam, the one on the right is Eve. You'll find what we came for under the stone marker at the head of Adam's grave." Everyone watched Gryph make his way between the outlines of the first man and woman said to have walked the earth. He took a knee as he reached the tops of the two graves. Although Gryph wasn't a religious man, he offered a silent prayer, asking forgiveness from the first couple for intruding on their eternal slumber.

Up top, the two guards stopped just short of the mausoleum. Chief was ready to explode from behind the stone wall. A second later, he and Aliyah heard the familiar scratch of a lighter, followed by the deep pungent smell of tobacco.

She heard the two guards complaining in Arabic about the bitter cold and their overall miserable existence, but the men came no closer to the lethal pair hidden right around the corner only a few feet away.

After the impromptu smoke break, the security guards reversed course and headed back toward the exit.

Momentarily pausing his search to watch the scene unfold outside the mausoleum on his HUD, Gryph was relieved to see the situation resolve itself. None of them would hesitate to use force, even deadly force if warranted, they'd prefer to avoid conflict if possible. So far, it was shaping up to be one of those lucky nights. With the potential crisis averted at the surface, he went back to completing the task at hand.

Gryph placed his hands on either side of the flat stone marker closest to him, lifted it from its place quickly, before unceremoniously dropping it after spotting a yellowish-green colored scorpion scurry out from under the boulder and disappear into a small crevice in the cave wall. The Palestine yellow scorpion, also known as the Deathstalker, was a highly venomous species found in those parts. While not lethal to healthy adults, its venom would still cause a severe reaction. The last thing Gryph needed was a medical emergency.

He was much more careful the second time when lifting the headstone out of the way, hoping to avoid any other multi-legged, venomous visitors from making an appearance. Thankfully, he scared off anything else after dropping the marble block. Everyone's HUDs received the images of Gryph picking up a sharp, pointed stone from the ground, carefully working away at the sand that had been compressed by eons of time and weight of the burial marker. Gryph dug down at least half a foot and still hadn't uncovered anything.

"Uh, I'm not sure if you're seeing this clearly or not, but there's nothing here." Worry erupted in the pit of Gryph's stomach. If they couldn't recover this first key, they were finished.

"It has to be there. Try the headstone next to it. Perhaps I've mixed up the sides after all this time." Daedalus's voice didn't sound as convincing as before.

Gryph replaced the soil and returned the first headstone to its former position. He gingerly lifted the adjacent marker, fully prepared to drop it on anything that could bite or sting him, but nothing ventured out from under the rock this time. He set the headstone aside and grabbed his rudimentary stone tool once again. It took only a few passes before his makeshift shovel hit something hard. He reached down and cleared the remaining debris away with his hands so as not to damage whatever precious artifact lay below.

"Got it!" Gryph exposed an edge of the object that was wrapped in layers of thick cloth, looking relatively intact. After exposing the full artifact, he switched back to the stone tool and began to break the earth up around their prize. Less than a minute later, Gryph removed a tapered box measuring about two feet long and slightly less in width. He re-packed the sand and debris he'd disturbed back into the hole, replaced the grave marker, and backed out between the outlines of the two original biblical figures.

"Okay, I'm coming back out now. I'm keeping the box in front of me while I crawl out. Daedalus, meet me at the pinch point with the rope. Secure the box first, then pull me the hell out of here."

"I'm already on my way, Commander." Daedalus had started his trek through the narrow cavern as soon as Gryph exposed the first signs of the box.

When Gryph reached the pinch point, he saw Daedalus lying on his belly on the other side, ten feet away. "I don't know how you did this the first time, Daedalus. No one here to help you, using only a candle for light. That must have been terrifying."

"Like you, Commander, I was driven by something greater than myself. But I have to tell you"—he cracked a wide smile— "I don't remember the opening being this small." The two men burst out laughing. The light-hearted moment relieved a lot of the stress that had been building inside Gryph since he first slithered into this mess.

"Pass me the rope, and I'll sling it around the box for you to extract. Once you've got it, toss the rope back to me and pull me out," Gryph said. Minutes later, the man who'd buried the box eons ago once again cradled it in his arms. He removed the rope from around the box and fed it back through to Gryph, who kept a long spool slung over his shoulder. Daedalus backed his way out of the tunnel until he was safely inside the mausoleum at the bottom of the pit below the empty stone coffin. He placed the box on the ground, then coiled the rope tight around his arm. "Let me know when you're set, Commander," he said.

"Ready when you are." Gryph wiggled headfirst into the opening of the tunnel, inching his way into the pinch point until Daedalus was ready to pull him through.

Gryph grabbed the rope with an iron grip and gave it a tug to remove the slack. "Okay, pulling you out now," came the reply from Daedalus.

What the extraction lacked in drama, it made up for in efficiency. The force of Daedalus pulling was more than enough for Gryph to clear the tight space in one swift movement. Once Daedalus was certain Gryph was free and moving easily on his own, he scrambled up the stone staircase with the box tucked under his arm. A minute later, Gryph was at the bottom of the pit inside the mausoleum. He looked up to see two smiling faces leaning over the lip of the stone coffin, twenty feet above.

"Welcome back to the land of the living, Gryph." Phil was relieved to see his boss back safely and none the worse for wear. Phil reached in to help him out of the last section of the limestone sarcophagus, after Gryph climbed up the ladder. The two men brushed themselves off, sending fresh plumes of dust into the mausoleum.

"What are we going to do with this thing now?" Gryph motioned to the broken slabs suspended above the open grave.

"Leave it to me, gentleman. Step back." Daedalus keyed commands into the silver briefcase again.

The complex lattice structure that had been keeping the heavy marble slabs high above the work area began its controlled descent with the fractured lid in tow. The nano structure deposited the slabs perfectly into place onto the stone crypt. Only two small cracks appeared on the surface of the tomb where the broken pieces met. Daedalus filled the fissure with sand and rubbed it in with his hand to obscure the breaks. No one would ever come this near, let alone look close enough to notice.

The three men finally exited the tomb and into the wide expanse of the night. Gryph had never felt happier to be outside with nothing above him but sky and stars. "I'm going to rank that in the top three things I never, ever want to do again."

Chief and Solo replaced the chain on the door. The lock was beyond repair, but they would remedy that when they put their mystery box back when they were done with it. The lock and chain only had to pass a cursory inspection until then, and that remote corner of the cemetery looked like it saw very few visitors anyway. Everyone came for the Cave of the Patriarchs tour.

"Let's get this back to *Hera* before we open it," Daedalus said. "I don't want to risk destroying whatever's inside out here in the elements."

"What do you mean 'whatever's inside'?" Dallas asked over the comms. "You don't know what's inside the box? I thought you said it was a key."

"It could very well be a physical key, Dallas, or it could just be a metaphor for opening the next stage in the quest. I buried the box at the request of the king, but have never laid eyes on its contents. We'll know the truth soon enough. Let's get out of here so we can all find out."

"You don't have to ask me twice," Gryph said. "Everyone, move out."

They piled into the SUVs and raced back into Israeli-controlled lands, transferred everything back to the Ze'ev armored vehicle at their junkyard rendezvous point and made their way back to Ben Gurion Airport a little after 4:00 a.m.

Daedalus sat quietly in the back the whole time, cradling the ancient box on his lap. No one had asked, but everyone had the same question on their minds. What were they going to find inside this box, and how would it lead them to the long-lost Ark and the manna they needed to save the world?

CHAPTER TWENTY-SEVEN

Onboard Hera
February 11, 1:09 p.m.

Chief, along with the rest of the crew, went straight to bed after returning from their late-night recovery mission. However, he was the only one still sleeping. The exhausted team all caught a bit of much needed shuteye when they got back to the jet. The long drive back from the tombs allowed much of the adrenaline from their excursion to fade and permitted them to get a few hours of sleep, albeit in fits and starts.

Gryph, Aliyah, and Phil were congregated in the parlor onboard *Hera,* which was still parked in a private hangar at Ben Gurion. Luna and Dallas were working at the command center inside the massive fuselage, attending to a multitude of tasks and equipment that supported Aliyah's tests. The oddly cute pair told Gryph they were hoping to do a deep dive on the nanobot technology while the rest of them were working on whatever the box held. The science behind the little mechanized army both intrigued and confounded Dallas.

Luna's vast knowledge of computers, networks, and digital communication protocols allowed her to understand and digest some of the complex nano systems she and Dallas were attempting to unravel. They were like two peas in a pod now. Gryph made a note to discuss Luna's skill set with her the next time they had an opportunity to chat privately.

Solo went back to his captain's quarters to get some rest before piloting the jet to wherever the next leg of their quest took them. The destination hadn't been relayed to him by Daedalus as of yet.

More perplexing, Daedalus had not been seen or heard by any-one since they arrived back on board his flying palace. He'd retreat-ed into his palatial suite with the ancient box, closed his door, and remained there ever since.

Now that everyone was awake, they were all eager to continue with the mission, but none of them had a clue as to where they were going or what they were supposed to do once they got there.

"Someone want to wake up Chief. If we don't get him up, he'll sleep until dinner," Gryph asked.

"Take it easy, brother. I was just taking a power nap." Everyone in the parlor turned to see Billy K wander toward them. "By the way, you gotta try these mini chocolate croissants they baked for us. I could easily eat a dozen of 'em. Like, no problem." He left a trail of flaky crumbs in his wake until he plopped down into one of the sumptuous leather recliners beside a window. The sun shone through the portal, illuminating an even bigger pile of the buttery pastry on Chief's massive chest. He closed the window shade in a futile effort to keep the crumbs more obscured.

"I'm gonna knock on Daedalus's door. We've been cooling our heels long enough." Gryph got up and marched toward Daedalus's room. After a short walk through the massive jet, he found him-self at the two large, lacquered doors outside his boss's suite. As he raised his hand to knock, the door opened, leaving Gryph in an awkward pose. He lowered his arm. "Uh, good morning, or af-ternoon now, I guess," he said, glancing at his watch. "I was just coming to see if you've made any progress with the key. Any idea where we need to head next? The team is anxious to get moving."

"Unfortunately, I haven't made much progress, Commander. Let's join the others and I'll explain." At that moment, Gryph no-ticed the pallor of the man's skin and the dark circles under his eyes. He was certain Daedalus hadn't slept a wink. Through the doorway, Gryph watched Daedalus retrieve the box from the top of his desk, he noticed the lid was no longer secured in place, but under the box instead. Unfortunately, from his vantage point, he couldn't see the contents of the interior. *No matter*, he thought. *The mystery will be revealed in a minute anyway*. Gryph still caught himself trying to sneak a peek as they walked back to the rest of the group, to no avail.

"Sorry to have kept you all waiting this morning. I had hoped to have made better progress by now, but I'm afraid I'm no further ahead than I was when I first opened this box last night." The mission's success hinged on Daedalus's ability to determine their next step, and he was concerned that this setback would deflate the team, leaving them feeling as dejected as he did.

"So, are you gonna share your toys or what?" Chief asked, tearing another one of the delicious pastries in half. Flakey crumbs tumbled from his lips once again.

"Excuse me?" Daedalus asked, confused.

"I mean the box. Specifically, what's tucked away inside of it. My boy Gryph here climbed through his own personal hell to get that. Are you gonna let us see it or what?"

Daedalus set the box on the table so they could all see it clearly. He placed the lid beside it. The thick cloth that was wrapped around the exterior of the wooden box when Gryph found it was now loosely covering the contents. Daedalus reached to pull back the time-worn fabric.

"Please tell me Gryph or Ali figured it out already." Everyone turned to see Dallas and Luna entering the parlor.

"No, unfortunately not, I was just about to show them the key, Mr. Hayle." Dallas knew the resumption of the formality in his boss's response was a not-so-subtle cue to back off.

"So, it's an actual key then?" Aliyah asked.

"The artifact inside may very well be a key, Ali, but how it works, I'm not certain. I've been up all night trying to decipher its code." Daedalus flicked his hand in frustration toward the box. Confused looks were passed around at the mention of an unsolved code.

"Dallas and Luna have been running the possibilities through our quantum computer via remote link back to the Workshop, but nothing yet. Maybe it's missing something, or there's another step I wasn't told about. Or maybe…" Daedalus was beyond exhausted and was crashing. "Let me show you. Maybe you'll be more successful than I was." Daedalus pulled the cloth away with a flourish, like a magician during his big reveal.

Inside the box lay a model of an unorthodox candelabra. Three arms extended upwards at steep angles from each side of a thick center post. The lower arms were staggered on the center support ensuring they would finish level with the others at the top. The candelabra appeared to be made of solid gold. The relic's front face was adorned with an array of multi-colored jewels running in neat little rows across the whole surface. The value of the artifact, even without its hidden purpose or pedigree, would be immense. The stunned silence was broken by Chief letting out a long cat-call whistle. "I've seen a lot of different kinds of keys in my life, but that one takes the cake."

"That thing would be worth a fortune to a private collector. I might know a guy who—" Dallas stopped mid-sentence when he saw the look Gryph was giving him.

"Daedalus, you said you were working on deciphering this last night and that Dallas had the quantum system back at the Workshop doing the same," Gryph said. "And you still haven't uncovered anything?"

"Unfortunately, no." The admission seemed to darken Daedalus's mood even further.

Gryph lifted the artifact out from the box. "Wow, it's a lot heavier than it looks."

"I've printed out pictures from every imaginable perspective." Daedalus passed around glossy photographs showing the artifact from all sides, including the top and bottom. Gryph inspected the candelabra closely, then handed it to Aliyah. He picked up a few of the photos being passed around and compared them to the physical item.

"I know what this is! It's a replica of the menorah that was used in the ancient Jewish Temple," Ali said. "The real menorah stood at least five feet tall, though. This is only a model. It's funny, biblical scholars have debated for ages as to whether the arms on the menorah were straight like this one are or were curved as shown on the relief on the Arch of Titus in Rome. I guess this puts that argument to rest, not that we could tell anyone about it. I'm not sure they'd believe us even if we did."

Phil leaned in closer to get a better look and was astounded by the artifact's beauty. "Was the original menorah covered with jewels too?" he asked.

Aliyah passed the menorah to him for a closer look and said, "No, not at all, actually. It too was made entirely from gold—just like this one seems to be—but the original, while very intricate, didn't have any jewels on it."

He brushed his fingers across the multitude of diamonds, sapphires, and rubies. "You're right, Gryph, this thing is crazy heavy. It's gotta be solid gold, for sure." He gave it one last inspection, then passed it over to Chief. Phil grabbed a couple of the close-up photos to examine further, not quite sure what he should be looking for.

"Make sure you don't drop it, Billy boy," Dallas said. "Those fat fingers of yours are probably still greasy from the five pounds of croissants you shoved down your gullet." Chief just continued his examination, not giving Dallas the satisfaction of a response.

"I'm pretty sure you're not going to be able to figure this one out, big guy," Dallas said. "I've focused the brute force of the Workshop's supercomputers on cracking the code on the front of that thing since last night, and we still have nothing."

Chief had already tuned Dallas out and was lost in the intricate details engraved into the handcrafted masterpiece. He opened the window shade behind him again. Sunlight danced across the menorah. The jewels sparkled brighter as an explosion of color radiated over the menorah's golden arms.

"Dallas, what makes you think there's a code on the front?" Gryph asked, hoping to regain some of their momentum.

"I didn't. Daedalus told me that's what he thought it was. He figures the jewels contain some kind of hidden message or map to find the key. He didn't tell you any of this yet?" He looked around for a response but, getting none, rambled on. "Okay, well, Daedalus thought he could figure it out himself. I don't want to blow sunshine up his ass, but judging by the nanobot engineering and coding I've seen, he's about as smart as they come. I guess he's not as sharp as he was when he was young. Like, a thousand years ago." He burst out laughing, but no one else seemed to be in the mood for it.

"Wow, tough crowd. OK. Anyway, I told him I reconfigured the quantum computer array at the Workshop, and bet him a grand I could break the code in under an hour. I fed the AI engine the images we took and put it to work. I was wrong, though. ICARUS has been running since last night, and still hasn't broken it."

"I couldn't locate a cipher or anything that was left behind for us to unlock this puzzle. And I fear that may not be the worst of our problems." Daedalus said, as he lifted the lid to the wooden box that had, until then, remained face down on the table. The tapered top was wider at one end than the other, accommodating the menorah as it widened at the top. He flipped it over, exposing the side that faced inside the box, and handed it to Gryph. Aliyah and Phil crowded in to get a closer look. Billy stayed seated and was still toying around with the menorah in his hands, enthralled by the colors of the sunlit spectrum firing across his massive frame.

Gryph held the lid up for everyone to see. Two images were carved on its underside. The picture at the bottom entailed two intersecting curved lines that formed the profile of a fish. The other image, directly above, showed an arrow with a small circle on the shaft where the feathers or fletching would be attached. It was pointing directly at the fish.

"The ichthys, that fish on the bottom, is one of the earliest Greek symbols for Christianity." Everyone looked up from the box lid to see Luna peering overhead. "Many denominations have incorporated that symbol as a representation of Christ. Some simply refer to it as the Jesus fish."

"That's true," Gryph said. It had been his first thought as well. "It could be exactly that. It could also be a symbol representing food or a body of water." He wanted to avoid definitively attributing meaning to anything at that point, even if Luna ultimately proved to be right. Bias that set in early could potentially lead the group astray. Gryph wanted to ensure they wouldn't exclude possibilities this early on. "Anyone here have thoughts on the arrow?" he asked. "What about the placement of the images in relation to each other? There could be some significance to the fish being below the arrow. Anything else you see that we're not contemplating yet?"

A few conversations struck up at once as the lid was passed around the small table. Theories introduced by some were expounded upon by others in a collaborative way. Gryph loved seeing everyone so focused and determined. Everyone was buzzing, happy to be working on something again.

"Hey, guys, this menorah thing is so cool. I remember I had a puzzle kind of like this when I was a kid," Chief called out from his seat by the window, apparently not wanting to be left out of the conversation.

"Yeah. I'm sure your mama let you play with her immense collection of priceless jewels. Or maybe you mean the vast array of complex puzzles you were stimulated with as a child. Whatever, Sailor Moon." Dallas chuffed his head in Chief's direction.

"We need to identify some of the frontrunners here, Gryph," Aliyah said, not wanting any further distractions. Her brilliant mind was already rushing in a hundred directions at once. "I think Luna's on the right track with the iconography of the fish. It makes sense that the symbol they used as a clue would be recognizable throughout the ages. Now, if the fish represents God or Jesus, how does the arrow shown on the box fit into this?"

Phil decided to get up and see what Chief was up to. He'd seen all there was to see on the lid and hadn't the slightest idea what any of the symbols meant or how that would lead them to the key. Billy was so preoccupied playing with the menorah that he didn't notice Phil watching him from behind. "Uh, Gryph? I think you're going to want to see this." Phil said over his shoulder to the rest of the group.

"Maybe the arrow represents an attack on Christianity," Luna said. "Although it could just as easily mean that—"

"Guys, you *really* need to check out what Chief has done with the menorah. Like right now." The casualness in Phil's voice was gone, replaced by a much more urgent tone.

"I told you he was going to break it." Dallas still wasn't letting up. He walked over to where Chief was seated to see the suspected damage firsthand.

Everyone shifted over toward Chief. The refraction of sunlight exploded off the menorah, sparkling over the walls and ceiling. Billy spun his chair around to give the group a clear view of the ancient relic.

"Holy shit. What did you do?" Dallas's eyes were wide with disbelief. A similar look of astonishment washed over the entire Daedalus crew as soon as they saw what Chief had accomplished with the surface of the menorah. The jumbled mix of colorful jew-

els that ran up and down the arms and base of the intricate candelabra were now organized in neat little rows of the same color. A
single color of gem sparkled on each of the menorah's six arms.
Its base was a solid row of emeralds. The center shaft consisted of
two vertical rows of flawless ice-colored diamonds. Six rubies sat
like flames atop each of the branches that extended from the center.
The ruby "flame" above the center stem was still missing from its
position, but Chief was working on rectifying that.

"How did you do that?" Gryph was just as flabbergasted as
anyone else.

"It was a fluke, bro. I was counting the number of jewels on this
thing and felt one of them move when my fat greasy fingers passed
over it." Billy shot a smug look at Dallas as he parroted the previous barb. He wasn't sure what he enjoyed more, the progress he'd
made with the menorah, or the fact that Dallas was choking on a
big slice of humble pie.

"I lined up two emeralds at the bottom and started from there.
Like I said, I did puzzles like this as a kid. You know, those mixed-
up tiles in a plastic square you slide around until a picture appears
at the end? I knew there was no picture at the end of this rainbow,
but figured they could be organized into groups."

"That's incredible, Chief." Aliyah was smiling ear to ear. "How
did you know what color was supposed to go on each branch?"

"Funny you mention that, Doc. Before I figured out these little
things moved, I noticed there was a small engraving on the top of
each arm matching the shape of each gem. If you look closely, each
colored gem is cut a bit different from the others. I'm just about
done, though. I have a little more work left to get the last ruby into
the top center position. Then I think it's finished."

"What happens after it's fully aligned?" Phil asked.

"There's only one way to know for certain," Gryph said. "Don't
let us take up any more of your time, Billy. Finish it." Everyone
crowded closer to watch this massive man, with sausage-like fingers manipulating colorful little stones on a toy candelabra. He had
to move some stones from seemingly correct positions to get the
last gem into the right stack. Three steps forward, one step back.
Slow perhaps, but progress was being made.

"I think that diamond needs to slide down, not the sapphire you just moved," Dallas said, peering over Chief's shoulder.

"Yo, can somebody get this guy off me? This was going much easier without everyone breathing down my neck."

"Sorry Chief's," Gryph said. "Let's take a few steps back, give him some space." The perimeter quickly expanded. Chief spun his chair back around, giving himself an additional layer of privacy.

"So, what do you think the arrow on the box means, Gryph?" Aliyah asked while waiting for Chief to complete his puzzle.

"You know, something has been bothering me about that ever since I saw it. I can't quite put my finger on it yet."

"We know you have a knack for piecing these kinds of things together," she said. "We've seen you do it a few times already. Can you just be quick about it? We're kind of in a rush." She couldn't keep a straight face. Gryph chuckled and shook his head.

"Hooah!" Chief roared. Aliyah was so startled she nearly jumped out of her skin. Everyone turned to see Billy K holding the menorah in one hand and an elaborate skeleton key in the other, a rare smile across his face.

"Chief, you never cease to amaze." Daedalus felt a wave of excitement wash over him. They were finally getting somewhere.

CHAPTER TWENTY-EIGHT

London, England
February 11, 7:03 a.m.

Basileus had already gone for a quick five-mile run and was finishing his breakfast when the BBC chyron flashed at the bottom of the television. He sopped up the last of his eggs with a piece of multigrain toast and knocked back his second double espresso of the morning. He unmuted the flatscreen on the wall and was already smiling before he'd heard a single word.

"This is investigative reporter Nina Stewart broadcasting from Hawke's Bay, New Zealand, for the BBC. For those viewers who may not be aware, we've been tracking an aggressive type of agricultural blight that has been killing livestock and decimating crops across the globe. Until today, these areas remained relatively small, both in terms of geographical size and number of livestock lost. But what we've discovered here in picturesque Hawke's Bay is nothing short of a nightmare."

The camera panned from the striking brunette reporter to the scene over her shoulder. Thousands of sheep were seen rotting in yellow blanched fields. "You can see that crow and buzzard carcasses are intermingled with the larger mammals. It appears nothing escaped the wrath of this pestilence. Authorities I've spoken with all say they are baffled by the occurrence. This outbreak is by far the most severe to date. The affected area is over ten thousand hectares. For our US viewers, that's about twenty-five thousand acres. A massive area. Everything is just… dead. There doesn't seem to be any risk or transmission of this disease to the human population, but the CDC is keeping close tabs on the situation. They feel that—"

Basileus turned the TV off. He'd heard all he needed to. The release of the toxin had gone according to plan. February was the middle of the summer in New Zealand. As per usual, the crops and animals were healthy and maturing well. Everyone was saying it was sure to be another bountiful season. The harrowing effects of his toxin were sure to stand out when growing conditions were supposed to be ideal—how could it not? This attention grabber would plant the seeds of panic for what was yet to come. The doom and gloom would be in full effect on social media in a matter of hours. News traveled fast these days, and bad news traveled even faster. It was just the opening salvo in an information war. By the time he was done, chaos would abound, but he didn't care. He'd be safe and secure in his massive bunker while civilization crumbled around him.

The reporter had been a lover of his. In fact, it was none other than the fearless reporter, Nina Stewart, who'd joined Basileus and the famous actress after the event in Germany the other night. Nina flew straight to New Zealand on the first flight out the morning after their tryst, to deliver the breaking news report. It was already 9:00 p.m. in New Zealand. The news would slowly trickle out as everyone on the east coast of the States woke up. He knew exactly what Nina was going to tell the public. He'd written the script himself. She'd been a journalism major and aspiring model when they first met. A well-placed email to an executive board member secured her a job with the BBC. She was more than happy to return any favors to her generous benefactor. Basileus had hundreds of people who would do anything for him.

"Dima!" he yelled from the expansive French chateau inspired kitchen. The echo of his voice rang off the stone and wood finishes that lined the well-appointed space.

"Coming, sir," came the immediate reply. Dima had been eating breakfast in his room. Hot black coffee, a handful of almonds, a banana, and a long drag from his cigarette. *Breakfast of champions,* he mused. He stubbed out the smoke and was in the kitchen standing opposite Basileus a few seconds later.

"The story just broke in New Zealand. People are going to start looking for answers. This should flush Daedalus and his team out into the open again. Have you heard anything about the hacker working with them? Were you able to trace the woman from the internet café? Where are they now?" The inquiries came rapid fire. Dima's heart rate increased as the questions piled up. The only thing worse than Basileus getting bad news was Dima having to deliver it himself when he was the cause of it.

Dima shifted nervously on his feet, his gaze falling to the floor as the questions came to an end. He straightened and looked Basileus in the eye. "The woman was easy to track down. Her name is Luna. She owned the cybercafé that my men shot up. We searched her personal records and found her address from a utility bill. I've had someone watching her place around the clock, and sure enough, her and the ninja showed up. She must have had to grab a few things the day after the attack. She came back to her place empty-handed but left with a small rolling suitcase."

"Excellent. Did your men follow them? Where did she go?"

"They did follow her, but they lost them somewhere in midtown Manhattan." Dima could see the anger building behind Basileus's eyes. Losing someone in New York was like losing a needle in a stack of needles. "They must've noticed the tail and ducked into a building to shake them loose. They were on foot when he last saw them, not in a car or anything, so they couldn't have made it far."

"That's twice they've escaped your people. Ask your men exactly where they were when they last saw them. See if the location is close to where they slipped by you last time. At least we can try and pull the net tighter still. No one just vanishes into thin air, certainly not twice in a row."

"Yes, sir. I'll call my men as soon as we're finished here."

Basileus turned and walked away, frustrated they were being led in circles. When it was obvious there were no further questions coming, Dima relayed the only good news he had, hoping to end his briefing on a positive note, however slight it may be. "There's one other thing that may prove useful. My agent reported that he got close enough to overhear them saying something about flying out in the morning."

Basileus was still walking away from Dima but stopped when he heard this new tidbit of information. "How did he get close enough to overhear details of their conversation and yet lose them when all he had to do was keep them in sight?" He didn't try hiding the suspicion in his voice.

"Sir, he was using a laser microphone and recorded as much of the conversation as he could. When they left her apartment, he stayed back a safe distance to ensure he wouldn't be detected. I was told he lost them when they turned a corner down an alley. One moment they were there, and the next they were gone as I just explained. The tracker told me he was very sorry."

"And what did you say to him in response?"

"I didn't say anything. I pistol whipped him and almost broke his jaw. He'll need some serious dental work before he'll be able to chew steak again." He laughed nervously.

"Why didn't you kill him?" Basileus's tone was even and calm, as if he were asking for simple directions or if it would rain tomorrow.

"He's... Well, he's my cousin, Yvgeni, sir. I'm the only family he's got left. I promised his father I'd look out for him. I swore an oath on his deathbed."

"You broke his jaw and knocked out his teeth. That's how you look out for him?" Basileus turned back to face Dima. His eyes narrowed, and a serious look blanketed his face.

"*I almost* broke his jaw," he said. "I could have put a bullet in his brain. I'd say that's me looking out for him." Dima told his cousin as much when he picked him up off the floor, bleeding, and whimpering.

Basileus smiled. "And here I thought you'd gone soft on me, my sweet Dima."

Dima learned long ago of his boss's manic mood swings and erratic behavior, acutely aware that any little thing could set Basileus off. As of late, the number of triggers had grown by the day. "I may be getting older, but soft? Never, sir. I'll be dead before I go soft."

"Ah, my friend, don't forget that I hold the key to your immortality. Soon you will be brought before the Brotherhood and take your seat at the table of eternity. However, we must not fail now. We have never been so close, but also never as exposed. Any mistakes going forward bear life-or-death consequences—for everyone. Am I clear?"

"Yes, sir. Understood. I will not let anything stand in the way of your success and me taking a seat by your side. We'll successfully distribute your cleansing seeds to the four corners of the Earth. Your plan will finally bring healing to the world. It will be a privilege to be part of your new kingdom."

"I know you will, Dima. And we'll have all the time in the world to wait for the Earth to heal and for you to see the beauty and splendor that she once was, before humankind poisoned and destroyed her. Fifty years, maybe one hundred at most. Earth will heal quickly and devour the last remnants of mankind. From the soil, man was created, and back into the soil he will go."

Dima remained silent. He'd heard this diatribe more times than he could count. "Will there be anything else, Basileus?"

"Yes. I still want to know where the woman and her friends were flying off to. These people aren't flying commercial. They'll need to bring weapons with them and will have to maintain a flexible schedule. Check all outbound departures between five and ten o'clock on the morning they presumably left. There'll be quite a few to analyze. Look for flights that were added to the departure schedule in the last thirty-six hours. Scrub any planes with regional flight plans filed. They won't be flying if it's somewhere relatively close by. Too risky. Let me know if you find anything else that seems out of the ordinary. Report back to me this evening. That will be all." Basileus exited the kitchen, leaving Dima alone to complete his new tasks.

Dima nodded; happy he'd escaped the meeting relatively unscathed. He had never seen Basileus as on edge as he'd been over the last few weeks. His boss was acting irrationally and was prone to violent, uncontrolled outbursts. He'd given himself 50/50 odds that Basileus was going to put a bullet through his forehead when he told him they'd lost Daedalus's men again. He was afraid of being in the wrong place at the wrong time. But truth be told, he was sick of Daedalus and his team making him and his operation look bad, potentially keeping him from the seat at the table that he'd rightfully earned.

He walked back into his bedroom, poured himself the last dredges of lukewarm coffee from a half-finished pot, fished out his phone, and placed a call to his contact at Teterboro to hopefully obtain Daedalus's flight info. His informant there would help track down information from the other airports as well, if need be. Teterboro saw almost 500 flights a day, and the most likely departure point if they were in the city. Regardless, he would cast a wide net and see what came up in the catch. Dima figured he'd still have time to filter through all the information, condense it, and get it to Basileus before dinner.

Once they found Daedalus and his team, Dima mused, he'd take great pleasure in twisting a knife into each one of them, especially that skinny bitch who killed his friend in the café. He'd have a little fun with her first, then gut her like a fish. A belly wound was one of the most painful ways to die, and he looked forward to watching her suffer. An eye for an eye and all that. What were a few more lives when they were on the brink of taking billions?

Dima tossed another handful of almonds into his mouth and chased them back with the rest of his coffee. He shrugged on a heavy leather bomber jacket, picked up his Walther P99 pistol from off his dresser and holstered it opposite the identical piece already secured under his left arm. Having just hung up with Teterboro for the second time that morning, he was assured receipt of the flight plans he requested within the hour.

Keeping Basileus happy was always his highest priority, and finding Daedalus's destination would certainly bring Dima into Basileus's good graces once again, but finally locating and killing the annoying interlopers would undoubtedly secure his entry into the Brotherhood, and all the benefits that came with the appointment.

Dima walked out of the opulent manor and closed the heavy door behind him. He shook out a smoke from his pack of Marlboros. He lit the cig and drew a deep drag into his lungs, paused, then exhaled a long plume of smoke into the morning air and up into the rafters above. The enormous, heavy timber-and-stone archway overhead extended out from the mansion, protecting anyone underneath from rain or snow, although it was useless against the cold bite in the air this particular morning. His breath clouded in front of him as he marched along the garden path toward the carport. The sound of his heavy boots echoed off the hard, stone surfaces until he was fully out from under the port cochere. Dima took one last drag before flicking the balance of his smoke into the gravel. Amber sparks rolled across the stones, extinguished immediately by the cold wind.

He walked up to a detached building and used his key fob to gain access to a solid, secure door. A flash of green on the LED access point followed by a soft chime confirmed his credentials, a moment later he was inside, surrounded by millions of dollars' worth of engineering perfection.

Basileus had a stable of luxury vehicles parked inside the enormous garage, masterpieces in a variety of makes and models. The only thing they had in common, other than their eye-bulging prices, was the color. They were all finished in a stealth-like flat black. Dima's eyes cross the expanse of Porsche's, Lamborghini's, and Ferrari's. All beautiful machines, but he decided that morning he would take the Rolls Royce Ghost into the city. He had access to all Basileus's cars. It made being an errand boy feel less demeaning.

That morning, he took a nice quick drive through the country for the first twenty minutes or so. The car hugged the curves across the rolling landscape with the power and luxurious ride that only a Rolls could deliver. Then the first wave of traffic hit, and it got worse the closer he got to the city limits. Even when the congested traffic morphed into a sea of stationary metal, he reveled in the way people looked at him while driving the Ghost. He was in no real rush to move. Strangers on the sidewalks and those behind their meager steering wheels stared at him, green with envy. The vehicles all around gave the Rolls a larger cushion of space as the cars and trucks jockeyed and inched forward under a drizzling cold, gray sky. Dima figured it was just a glimpse of the way he would be treated by everyone once Basileus's plans were carried out. There would be a new pecking order, and for once, he'd be on top.

Dima was nearly at his first destination of the day when he felt his phone vibrate in his pocket and simultaneously ring through the car speakers. He answered the call using the hands-free button on the hand-stitched, leather-wrapped steering wheel. His phone had been synched to the Rolls long before, having played the role of chauffeur for Basileus often.

The voice on the other end was his contact at Teterboro and judging by the heightened pitch in the caller's voice, he was very excited about something.

"You said you'd take care of me if I found anything that stood out or seemed unusual. Well, I think I found something, and called you right away."

"If it's helpful, I'll be sure to send something extra special into your account this month." Dima was hoping this was the lead he desperately needed. Realistically, he would've happily paid anything for the information. US currency would be worthless soon enough, and it really wouldn't cost him anything. The clock on his success was ticking faster, and he needed some good luck. Quickly.

"That's very generous of you, sir. You've always been more than fair with me. I really appreciate it. So, anyway, I ran all the flights that departed that morning, then filtered out the ones you asked me to—no local flights, only recently filed flight plans, etcetera—and there's only one flight that stood out to me. Not so much the flight, but the plane itself."

"I don't understand. The plane stood out how?"

"A brand-new Boeing Business Jet took off from Westchester County Airport in White Plains, New York, three days ago. Only this was no regular jet. The guys on the ground I spoke to said that model isn't even available to the public yet. They wanted to get a closer look 'cause all of us in the industry, well, we're fanatics about anything aviation related and such."

"Get on with it already. I don't give a shit about your hobbies."

"Right, sorry, sir. The ground crew reported that it was impossible to get close to the plane. They said the jet had a large security detail keeping everyone away. They figured it was a Saudi prince or something. Anyway, the flight plan was registered just the day before, and the flight manifest listed only seven passengers plus the crew. Pretty big plane for just seven people. But these days, people take a fifteen-passenger jet with only one or two people on board all the time. Still seems like an expensive trip on a really rare aircraft, if you ask me."

"Were your men able to see anyone as they boarded?" Dima was finally getting a good feeling about this.

"They didn't see everyone, unfortunately, but my friend did report seeing an Asian guy with long black hair getting out of one of the cars that drove right up to the security perimeter. The other passenger in the car was described as a pro wrestler by one person and someone else said he could have been an NFL lineman. Either way, both reports said he was huge and that he and the Asian loaded a bunch of hard-side cases into the plane before getting onboard. The security detail cleared the area before anyone else arrived. They didn't see anything after that."

"Were there any women traveling with the group?"

"Not sure. They only saw the two people exiting the vehicle."

Dima hadn't realized it until that moment, but he was smiling ear to ear. It must be the ninja from the café and some new member of their squad. From the sounds of it, the big guy must have been additional muscle. It had to be them.

"Were you able to track their intended destination?"

"Yes, sir. Their flight plan showed a direct flight from Westchester to Ben Gurion Airport in Tel Aviv. I've received confirmation that they landed there as planned. I'm not sure if that's what you're looking for. Like I said, no reports of a woman on the tarmac, but the plane and the route stuck out from everything else that morning. Just wanted to inform you immediately. What should I do next?"

"You've been very helpful," Dima said, much kinder and gentler now. "As a token of my appreciation, how's an extra ten thousand sound?"

"Ten grand? Holy shit! Thank you so much, sir."

This unique air traffic control contact had been found totally by chance. Dima and his thugs had gone to make some "inquiries" at a flophouse that Dima had been using for drug distribution. He found out that the duo running the house were skimming cash and product. Dima and his enforcers shot both dealers moments after they kicked in the door. Dima delivered a double tap to the head on the more senior of the two. One of his other men dispatched the second thief in the same manner. Efficient and professional. The assholes didn't even have time to wonder why they were there.

Dima moved through the house and interrogated everyone inside to determine who else was in on the skim. Two more inquiries and two additional dead bodies later, they found the pathetic air traffic controller hiding under a blanket, whimpering in a corner. The crybaby was afraid it was a police raid and the end of his promising career. He was just a junkie riding out his trip after making a purchase in the house. Wrong place, wrong time. Dima spared his life, figuring he would be a useful tool in his toolbox. The air traffic junkie always provided priority clearance for Dima and his boss whenever they flew out of the private charter terminal at Teterboro. Dima figured snooping around to look for Daedalus's jet was an even easier task. If he reported the controller to the authorities, his life would be over. The air traffic junkie was always more than happy to oblige, especially for the cash bonuses.

"I'll tell you what, I'll throw in another ten grand," Dima said, "if you can tell me where they're planning on going to next."

"You've got to be kidding. I'll get on it right now, sir, and call you back as soon as I hear anything." The line went dead. He was happy the junkie was taking his request seriously. The $20,000 would keep him as high as a kite for months.

The good news Dima received would certainly go a long way in appeasing Basileus for his earlier mistakes. He would present this update just before dinner, proving once again he could still deliver, even under a tight timeline.

Dima ended the call and pulled the Rolls up to a nondescript storefront. The area was well known for its posh boutiques, hip nightclubs, and chic restaurants, which were famously impossible to get into. The Ghost's oversized wipers efficiently wicked away the drizzle that kept accumulating on the clear glass courtesy of the perpetual rain that plagued London. The rhythmic sound of rubber streaking across the glass had almost lulled Dima into a trance when the side door burst open.

A leggy blonde with a barely-there skirt and far too much make-up unfolded herself into the passenger seat. She leaned over and kissed Dima on the mouth. He could taste the cigarette she must have just finished on her tongue. She was his lunch date and something fun to play with before he had to run the balance of his errands later. Dima figured he'd go back to her place to ravage her after they ate lunch, and only then, head back to the estate to deliver the good news to Basileus. The woman was a thoroughbred, and he couldn't wait for the ride.

"So, where do you want to go for lunch? Pick any place you like," Dima said. "I can walk into any restaurant and get us the best table in the house—no questions asked."

The blonde pursed her collagen-filled, bee-stung lips and pondered which hotspot would look best on her Instagram page. Before she could provide Dima with an answer, his phone rang. He instantly recognized the number shown on the call display. *That didn't take long*, he thought.

"Keep your mouth shut, and don't say a word," Dima said to his lunch date before answering the call.

"Tell me you found out where they were going to next?" Dima asked before the caller even had a chance to say hello.

"Well, yes and no."

"Don't play games with me? Need I remind you that you stand to do very well if you tell me what I need to know and very badly if you don't."

"I'm sorry, sir. I didn't mean to offend you. I wasn't playing games. I meant to say that yes, I know where they are, and no, they haven't gone anywhere yet. Their jet is still parked at Ben Gurion. They haven't left. Or at least their plane hasn't. Also, there's no flight plan on file for their departure."

Dima clenched his fist and punched the air triumphantly, but kept his voice calm and steady. "Good job. I'll send you everything I promised in a couple hours." He hung up without another word, even as the junkie was still thanking him profusely.

"Lunch is canceled. Get the fuck out."

"What? What are you talking about? I got all dressed up and everything for you, Dima." He couldn't stand her whining even at the best of times, and was in no mood today. He wanted to get back to the estate immediately. The disappointment was written all over the woman's face. She leaned in close and whispered seductively in his ear. "I'm not wearing any panties, baby." She licked her cherry red lips as she pulled away from his ear.

"I'm not going to ask you again. Get out before I throw you out. I have important shit to do. Buy yourself something to eat. You're too skinny anyway." He threw a few one-hundred-pound notes at her as she reached for the door. She scooped up the cash and tucked it in her clutch as she stepped onto the curb. Dima closed the passenger door with a touch of a button, another cool feature on the incredible vehicle.

"Call me!" was the last thing Dima heard her say before the door closed, and he squealed away from the curb.

He pressed the first entry on the speed dial and waited for the call to connect.

"What is it, Dima?" Basileus didn't sound like he was in a good mood, but Dima was hoping to remedy that. It was the best lead they had on Daedalus since they'd ambushed and killed his team in the field earlier that year.

"I found them, sir. They're in Israel." Dima could barely contain his excitement. "They got there a few days ago. Their private jet is still sitting on the tarmac there." He relayed a condensed version of how he came by this information, leaving out the part about his clandestine drug house and the story of how he met the junkie working in air traffic control. That sideline wasn't something Basileus was aware of, and Dima preferred to keep it that way. He wouldn't have need for the extra cash once Basileus's plan was complete, but until then, it had provided him with a steady stream of income, independent of his work with Basileus. When he finished giving his summary, Basileus remained silent for almost a minute. Dima dared not interrupt. He knew Basileus was deep in thought, and any sound from him would be met with fury.

"Dima, get my jet ready to depart for Tel Aviv as soon as possible. Bring your best team. If you need more men, send another jet. Spare nothing. We're going to defeat this threat to my plan once and for all."

"Yes, sir. I'll have my team ready to leave before dinner. We'll be airborne before dark. Anything else?"

"Yes. There is something else," Basileus said.

"What's that, sir?"

"Welcome to the Brotherhood. You've earned your seat, Dima. You've finally found Daedalus and his team. Now let's go kill every single fucking one of them."

CHAPTER TWENTY-NINE

Onboard Hera, Tel Aviv
February 11, 2:19 p.m.

Chief stood triumphantly with the key in one hand and passed the heavy menorah back to Daedalus.

"How the hell did you get that key?" Dallas asked. "I've got to admit, I didn't see that one coming."

"I didn't either. I was sliding the last few gems into their slots, and when I tried to push the last ruby into place where the center flame would go, instead of sliding into place, the top of the key popped right out of the middle slot."

He handed the key to Gryph to inspect. It looked to be made from solid gold too. Gryph realized many of the same symbols from the box were also engraved onto the spine of the key. Everyone squeezed in to examine the new clue, effectively blocking out the overhead light and making it all but impossible for Gryph to examine it with any accuracy. Aliyah tried in vain too but couldn't get a good look because of the group crowding around Gryph.

Aliyah ducked her head and twisted her shoulders through the mass of bodies and plucked the key from Gryph's fingers. The unexpected loss of the object startled him until he realized what had happened. He just grinned and shrugged. Aliyah was a genius in her own right and would have as much of a chance of unlocking the secret surrounding the key as he would. The pack instantly dispersed once the key was gone from Gryph's grasp and migrated around Ali. With some breathing room now, he went back to examine the painting on the lid. Something was bubbling to the surface from his subconscious, but he couldn't quite put his finger on it.

Aliyah backed away from the group and stood up to examine the golden key under the overhead LED light. Luna moved in close to catch another glimpse, while still giving Aliyah enough room to inspect the key without feeling intruded upon. She appreciated the gesture and extended the object for Luna to see better. The golden key was incredibly intricate when viewed under bright light.

"It has the same fish and arrow symbols as the box," Luna said, seeing the engraving up close. "These clues must be here to show us where to go next. There's no way they would repeat these symbols on the box *and* the key if they weren't trying to tell us something."

Gryph was watching the interaction between the two women while inspecting the lid. Suddenly, he sat back. "That's it! That's what I was missing." He grabbed the lid off the table and rotated it in his hands. A broad toothy smile broke out across his rugged face.

"What are you talking about?" Aliyah asked. "What did you miss?"

"Just goes to show how easily bias can set in. I couldn't quite grasp it at first, but I knew something was off the whole time. It must have been why I was pushing so hard not to accept anything as a definitive conclusion before we thoroughly examined every option and disqualified the ones we thought didn't fit."

"I'm glad this is clear for you, Commander," Daedalus said, "but I'm still not following."

"Yes, sorry. It's still swirling around up here." Gryph pointed to his head with a twirling motion. "But it's starting to come into focus. I'm not sure I have it all figured out just yet, but I'm convinced we've been looking at this backwards—or upside down, to be more precise."

Aliyah opened her mouth to ask him a question, but Gryph finished his thought first. "I think Luna was right on the money when she identified the first icon as the Jesus fish, but we made a significant error that I didn't catch at first, and it had nothing to do with the fish, although I did swallow the mistake hook, line and sinker. Pun intended."

"Gryph, leave the jokes to me, okay? That was terrible." Dallas cringed at the pun, intended or not. "Stick to making your gourmet coffee and saving the world." Gryph tried to ignore the jab but was having trouble concealing a grin.

"We went off the rails right at the start," Gryph said. "As I said earlier, I think Luna was right about the fish representing Christianity, but we got the arrow all wrong. It's not an arrow at all."

"What do you mean? It sure as hell looks like an arrow to me." Dallas felt the need to defend Luna's initial interpretation of the drawing even though she didn't seem to take any offense to what Gryph was offering. Gryph certainly didn't mean to point fingers. That wasn't his style.

"It looked that way to me too, Dallas. That's likely why it took me so long to figure this out. I should have pushed for other ideas at the time, but it doesn't matter now. I'm certain it's not depicting an arrow."

"How can you be so sure?" Daedalus asked.

Gryph held the cover up for everyone to see. "The lid is noticeably wider at one end than the other. The top of the menorah is also wider than its base. It'll only go back into the box one way. You can't put it in upside down, it wouldn't fit."

"Of course! I see what you're getting at now," Aliyah said. "I can't believe you caught that though."

"Can someone tell me what the hell it is you two brainiacs are talking about?" Dallas said. Everyone else seemed to be as lost as he was, although not as vocal about it.

"Phil, pass me the menorah please." Phil handed it to Ali, and she laid it above in the box. "Like Gryph said, the menorah only fits one way." Aliyah rotated the menorah over the box to prove her point.

"So what?" Dallas said.

"If it only fits one way, then we know which end is the top and which is the bottom," Gryph said. "No one would construct a box for such a valuable item and assume someone would store it upside down, right?"

"I guess so."

"Okay, then there's definitely a top and a bottom, and we know which end is up. The lid matches the profile of the box perfectly." He loosely placed the lid back on the box, showing everyone the perfect fit once oriented correctly. "So, if this is the top of the box"—Gryph pointed to one end— "then this must also be the top of the lid."

"If that's the case," Aliyah said, anticipation building in her voice, "then the 'arrow' isn't pointing down at the fish. The fish, representing Christ or God, is actually located at the top of the image, and the other symbol is below it. That also makes sense theologically. Nothing would be put above God. We were looking at it upside down."

"If it's not an arrow we're looking at, what is it?" Luna asked.

"Go ahead, Gryph," Aliyah said. "You saw it first."

"The arrow, as we've taken to calling it, is likely a combination of two icons that were also used as early Christian symbols. When all of this is read together, it's about as obvious as a big red X on a treasure map. The triangle is a common symbol in early Christianity. It symbolized many different things: a rock, a temple, or even the eye of God watching over humanity. The three sides of the triangle represent the Holy Trinity in Catholicism. There are a few other representations, but notably for us, it was also used as a symbol for a church."

"So, the triangle is one icon, by itself and the other symbol is a cross?" Luna asked.

"Not just any cross, Luna," Gryph said. "An inverted cross."

"Like devil worshippers?" Dallas said in a fearful whisper while looking around at everyone, as if saying it aloud would somehow summon Lucifer right then and there.

"No. In fact, quite the opposite. The inverted cross is known to represent none other than Saint Peter himself. After his capture, he asked to be crucified upside down, feeling unworthy to die as Jesus did."

Dallas shook his head in confusion. "Okay, but I still don't see how a fish, a triangle, and an upside-down cross get us to X marks the spot."

"Oh, I get it!" Luna shouted. Her eyes were wide with excitement. "There's only one place on Earth where those symbols make sense together." Gryph smiled. He knew Luna just figured it out too. She closed the loop for the rest of them. "The Church of St. Peter at the Vatican. That's the preverbal X marks the spot for us. The uppermost symbol, now that we know there's an *up,* is the fish, alluding to God above. Right below is the triangle representing the rock, his tomb, or the Church itself. And finally, underneath that, St. Peter's inverted cross." Luna said it matter-of-factly. She could see a few others in the group weren't all the way there yet. "St. Peter is buried under the high altar at his namesake church, St. Peter's Basilica at the Vatican. Another scriptural fact for those who may not be aware, Jesus was said to have given St. Peter two keys, one silver and one gold—the gold key being able to open the gates of heaven. Our recent clue includes a gold key too. There are far too many coincidences to ignore now. That must be where we need to go, St. Peter's Basilica or somewhere close by it."

"You don't think the gold key we released from the menorah is the actual gold key of St Peter, do you, Gryph?" Chief asked.

"No, I think those were more metaphorical, Billy. I'm not sure how a physical key would unlock the spiritual kingdom of heaven. But it must unlock something valuable."

"Do you think Luna's right?" Aliyah asked Gryph. "Are we going to the Vatican next?"

"I do. Although I didn't even think about the two key reference. I was more focused on what I saw carved into the lid, which led me to the same conclusion, but the two keys, that just re-enforces it for me. To be completely honest, I'm not sure what we do when we get there. That's going to be a whole other problem. The Vatican is its own little world, complete with its own police and military. Some of the best in the world, actually. It's also known for its vast and secretive collection of artifacts. Finding the lock that matches this key could prove to be very challenging, to say the least."

Daedalus was following the back and forth, nodding as the dots were connected, and announced. "I know what we need to do now and who we need to see at the Vatican. Unfortunately, we need to go back to the Labyrinth first. There's something I need to retrieve for this next part of our journey. Something I could not have possibly anticipated beforehand."

"Don't tell me you have the matching silver key back at your Batcave," Dallas said.

"No. I do have many other priceless treasures locked away in my vaults, but the key you're speaking of isn't one of them. How-ever, we must head back right away. Once I've secured what we need, we'll depart for Italy and continue our search. We have no time to spare. Basileus has already begun to release his toxin. I fear we may already be too late."

Gryph picked up the sleek handset on the wall that would connect him directly to the cockpit. "Captain Daniels. We need to depart for New York ASAP. How long until you can get clearance for takeoff?"

"Let me check with the tower, Commander. I'll be back to you in a moment."

"We should secure this box and the contents," Phil said. "We wouldn't want anything getting damaged before we even get a chance to use it."

He was amazed at the progress they'd made in such a short period of time, and the deductive reasoning displayed by the group was otherworldly. However, his role with the team was managing logistics, and as such, his task was to ensure they had what they needed, when they needed it. In this case, he felt it was his responsibility to guarantee they didn't break or misplace this ancient artifact and ruin whatever faint hope of success that remained.

"Phil's right," Gryph said. "Let's get this packed up and put somewhere safe. We'll need it again later."

Solo's voice came over the speakers above the group. "Sir, your friends at the IDF already notified the tower that we have priority clearance for takeoff. We'll be next in line whenever we choose to taxi out to the runway. I can have us wheels up in twenty minutes if that works for you."

"It's good to have friends in high places," Daedalus said, smiling for the first time in days. "Commander, get us airborne as soon as you can."

Phil stashed the artifacts in a safe spot onboard while everyone else settled in for the long flight home. Once they were airborne, Gryph decided he was going to see if he could get Daedalus to reveal what it was that they had to fly all the way back to New York for, only to turn around and head right back across the Atlantic for Italy. The curiosity would drive him crazy.

True to his word, Solo had them in the air twenty minutes later at just a hair before 4:00 p.m. Tel Aviv time. He notified the cabin that they would be back in New York in under twelve hours. With the seven-hour time difference, they'd be back on US soil around 9:00 p.m. EST.

***

Dima received an encrypted WhatsApp message from his contact inside the Teterboro air traffic control tower, relaying the updated status on *Hera* to Dima, who was currently in a jet with Basileus cruising at 42,000 feet and already more than halfway to Tel Aviv. Upon reading the message, Dima felt his heart drop into his stomach and his destiny slipping away. He jumped up from his seat, marched into the cockpit, and told the pilots to abandon the flight plan they were on and head straight for New York. Unfortunately, as the pilots informed him, they had nowhere near enough fuel onboard to fly that kind of distance and would have to land and refuel if that was indeed their new destination.

Dima stormed back from the cockpit and collapsed into his seat. Had someone tipped Daedalus off that they were being pursued? Something or someone must have spooked them. He begrudgingly picked up the receiver that would connect him to his boss's private stateroom.

"What is it, Dima? I'm trying to get some rest before we land."

Dima swallowed hard. "Basileus, we have a problem."

CHAPTER THIRTY

Onboard Hera
February 11, 12:30 p.m. EST

Shortly after takeoff, Gryph suggested that most of the team stay onboard to work on their respective tasks while Daedalus went back down into the Labyrinth to retrieve whatever it was he thought he needed. Phil and Chief would accompany him, providing transportation and security for the quick retrieval.

While the guys were preparing for the quick trip to the Workshop, Aliyah got back to work inside her traveling laboratory. She had all her equipment powered on and was running her latest batch of tests before the plane had even taken off. She still had a lot of work to do designing the antidote, assuming they could find the elixir in time.

Gryph walked up to the large room that Aliyah had converted into her lab and knocked on the doorframe, not wanting to startle her again. She turned to see who it was just as she inserted a tube into a complex-looking device that began to whir and beep as the analysis of the sample began.

"How's it going, Ali? With all the running around we've been doing chasing down these artifacts, I haven't had a chance to check in on your progress."

"I actually do have good news on that front. I think I was able to isolate the mechanism responsible for the alcohol production in the toxin. It's a fairly complex piece of bioengineering, but thankfully, as we suspected, it wasn't designed with any defensive capabilities other than the protection provided by the elixir's regenerative properties."

"That's better than good, that's great!"

"Well, I'd hold off on popping the champagne just yet. Without the elixir, we won't know that we'll be able to neutralize the toxin. I've had some success so far disabling the alcohol-producing effects using a cell I created to mimic the toxin. I'm hoping this latest iteration will be the one," she said, pointing to the machine currently analyzing the sample.

"I have no doubt you'll figure it out," he said. "What are the next steps once you have the antidote dialed in?"

Aliyah sighed. "That's a whole other issue. Once I get the antidote to work, I need to merge it with the elixir and find a method to distribute it using the nanobots. If I can get the antidote operational, we can deploy our microscopic army to areas the toxin has affected, and hopefully the elixir will keep our antidote alive long enough for it to break its bond and neutralize the alcohol production inside the toxin's cells."

"That sounds easier than it probably is, huh?"

"It's a simple idea, but yes, there's a lot of technical wizardry that goes into it. Dallas and Luna made great progress on the nanotech already and have been passing along their insights so far. They've both been a tremendous help."

Gryph was originally a bit skeptical about having Luna working on the team, but the fact that she seemed to keep Dallas engaged and focused on his work was an immediate benefit he was grateful for.

"The other issue we're going to have to face is acquiring enough elixir to produce the quantity of antidote we'll need. Each affected geographical location needs to be treated. The upside is, I don't think we'll require a lot of the elixir for our little cocktail to be effective. I've designed it to move from cell to cell, sniffing out any alcohol production, then stamping it out and moving on to the next cell until the area is entirely cleared of the toxin. When the toxin has been neutralized, the antidote will 'starve' and snuff itself out. That's my rough plan anyway."

"Sounds like you have it under control—or as best you can under the circumstances. I guess the only thing left to do is to secure as much elixir as we can and get it back to your lab ASAP."

"That sounds a lot easier said than done, too." Aliyah laughed. She knew they still had a long road ahead and needed quite a few things to fall into place for them to have any chance of stopping the oncoming plague.

"I don't want to take up any more of your time. You have more important things to do. Let me know if you need anything."

"To be honest, a cup of your magical coffee would be heavenly right now."

"I'd love to oblige, but I left my beans and press back in the Labyrinth. Tell you what, I'll have Phil and Billy K pick it up on their way back with Daedalus's secret. Sound good?"

"That would be perfect. Thank you. By the way, do you have any idea what he went back for? He seems to have a bit of everything stored in the Library."

"I've been wracking my brain trying to come up with some ideas too, but I'm not even clear about what we do when we get to the Vatican. Too many possibilities to zero in on any specific one. Whatever Daedalus thinks they have stored there, it had better work. We don't have any time left for a plan B."

Hours later, *Hera* touched down in New York, after a smooth flight back across the Atlantic. A strong tailwind put them down an hour ahead of schedule. The gleaming jet taxied to its private hangar, where she would be expeditiously refueled and restocked with any provisions consumed on the previous flight. They hadn't yet notified the tower of their departure time or intended future destination. Solo would file the appropriate paperwork once Daedalus and his team were back on board. He figured they could be airborne within an hour of his call to the tower.

Phil, Chief, and Daedalus piled into one of the SUVs they had left in the New York hangar just days earlier and immediately departed on their errand to the Labyrinth. Aliyah stayed onboard to continue refining and perfecting the antidote with Luna and Dallas.

The techno-pair were engrossed in programming the delivery system for the antidote in anticipation of getting their hands on the pure source. Over the course of the past few days, Daedalus and the two lovebirds had designed a nanobot for the antidote's distribution that, which magnification, looked very much like a spider with a pair of scuba tanks for a body. The theory was that the antidote would be loaded into the tank-like structures and released only when the spider bots detected any abnormally high alcohol levels.

The digital army of spiders would then crawl through the affected area, releasing its crop-saving payload as it went around before reclaiming the antidote when the task was complete. The bot army would then relocate to another affected area until the toxin was neutralized. The speed at which they could complete the task and move on to the next area was astounding. The remediation would only take a few weeks at most if all went according to plan. Unfortunately, they knew such things rarely did.

Daedalus was spending a significant amount of time with Dallas and, as of late, Luna, educating and training them on these microscopic wonders. The ICARUS AI software did most of the heavy calculations and design, but a significant amount of tuning and correction by human hands was required to get it to work perfectly. Everyone was pushing forward, eager to get to Rome and on to their next clue. There was nothing more to do until Daedalus and his secretive cargo from the Labyrinth were safely back on board.

CHAPTER THIRTY-ONE

New York City
February 11, 9:01 p.m.

Phil was piloting the white Lincoln SUV through the streets of New York. After clearing some heavy congestion in the Lincoln Tunnel, and light traffic in the city, the trio rolled up to the large, secure gate (at street level) protecting the underground Workshop far below. The vehicle went through each of the requisite security checkpoints again as they descended to the lowermost level. Chief had kept an eye out for anyone following them from the airport but didn't see anyone, or anything, suspicious—which was suspicious to him in and of itself. The ex-SEAL was in a perpetual state of paranoia, a trait that had kept him alive in situations that would likely have proven fatal otherwise.

Daedalus was the first one to exit the vehicle. "I'll need less than thirty minutes. If there's anything else you require, get it squared away quickly, and bring it back on board."

Phil had been given specific instructions for the location of another priceless object tucked away in the Workshop: Gryph's coffee system and his private stash of roasted beans. Since he was back, he decided to pack a few more personal effects as well. While they hadn't run into any serious trouble in Israel, he knew their luck wouldn't hold out forever. Basileus and his goons weren't going to just roll over and quit. They were coming for Phil and his friends. And when they did, he would be ready.

Phil set to packing away some of his own martial arts weapons about the same time Chief was making his own private trip to the armory deeper inside the Labyrinth. Chief also had a sinking feeling the next part of their journey would be the most perilous. As such, he wanted to grab a few odds and ends. He knew from experience that missions grew more dangerous the closer they came to completion. The fact that the hit squad from Luna's café had yet to materialize again gave even more credence to the nagging suspicion in his gut.

The overhead LED lights flickered on as soon as Chief opened the door to the armory. Rows of flat-black automatic weapons in every shape and size lined the walls. Boxes of ammunition, piled three feet high were stacked neatly on pallets running down the center aisle. Explosives including: RPGs, C-4, incendiary grenades, and more were stored at the back of the room. Knives, crossbows, and tactical gear had a section of their own on the other side of the room. He remembered the first time Daedalus opened the doors to the weapons superstore. Not many things surprised Billy K, but the contents of that room made him do a double take.

The SEAL teams that Chief led and trained had access to the most advanced weaponry on the planet. The specialists and engineers who created these state-of-the-art pieces would customize them to each SEAL team member's individual specs. However, the firepower that was stockpiled inside the Labyrinth's armory made the Navy's weapons look downright primitive by comparison.

Chief walked toward the ballistics door at the rear of the armory to grab a few more hard-shell tactical cases that were stacked by the partially open door. A two-foot-thick steel-and-concrete blast door led to a cavernous shooting range beyond. It was there that he'd taken the opportunity to increase his expertise and hone his skills with these new weapons. He'd spent a few hours each day inside the range, familiarizing himself with the proprietary weapons, loving every second of it.

He packed the hard-shell cases with items he hadn't brought on board when they flew out to Israel earlier in the week. He was in and out of the armory in less than ten minutes. He returned to the lab entrance, to see Phil already waiting, his own errands apparently completed too.

Chief had overheard Gryph asking Phil to grab the coffee and brewing gear. Judging by the small case that Phil had placed on the counter, he'd found it just fine. It was a good thing too; Billy was a huge fan of Gryph's coffee and had been for a long time. He also noticed a black tactical bag slung over Phil's shoulder. *Seems like everyone did a little stocking up while back home*, he thought.

Chief strode over to Phil just as Daedalus emerged from the Labyrinth carrying a small package of his own.

"I'm ready to go. Did you two get everything you needed?" Daedalus asked. Both men nodded in response.

Chief glanced at the case Daedalus was carrying as they were leaving the Workshop. "Want me to carry that for you, boss?" he asked, even though he was carrying two hard-shell cases already.

"That's okay, Chief. Thanks anyway, but I'll keep this one with me. Please take no offense though. When I open it, you'll understand."

"No offense taken. You know, I was pretty handy back there with the menorah thing. I'd be happy to take a stab at this one too later if you want." He winked at his boss, "I'm on a roll."

"I appreciate the offer, Chief, but this one isn't a puzzle. Nothing to solve this time around. It will hopefully be a simple transaction. I'll trade the contents of this box for access to the Vatican's secret vaults and, hopefully, the elixir."

Daedalus had possessed this specific artifact longer than almost any of his others and never thought he'd have to part with it. Under the circumstances, however, he had no choice. "I suspect that's where they'll want to store this little treasure once I hand it over."

Phil was beyond curious about the contents now. "Who do you have to give it to when we arrive?"

"There's only one person I can trust with this exchange. I've sent word to a cardinal that we're on the way."

"Do we need to be worried?" Chief asked. "I mean, about who we trust?"

"Not from the Vatican officials or the Swiss Guard protecting the city. From them I anticipate a warm, albeit suspicious, reception. It's what happens after that worries me. Let's get back onboard, and I'll bring everyone up to speed."

The three men walked to the SUV and packed the new gear in the rear compartment. However, the box Daedalus brought never left his grasp. He held it securely on his lap, watching the city race by as they made their way back to the airport.

***

Far too many hours and miles behind, Dima sat alone at the front of his plane. He was seething mad, having been thwarted by Daedalus again. Basileus had been furious when Dima told him the jet they were tracking suddenly departed without any notice. Unfortunately for Dima, that was just the warm-up. Basileus flew into a white-hot rage after he was told they'd have to reroute and refuel for the flight to the States, putting them even further behind.

Dima hadn't seen Basileus so angry since... well, ever. He was sure Basileus would've had him tossed out of the jet at 40,000 feet if it wasn't for the fact that opening the door would kill everyone onboard. There would be no sleep or a relaxing Cuban cigar and expensive single malt scotch on this flight. He would be counting the minutes until they touched down. It was already feeling like the longest trip of his life, and it wasn't even close to over yet. He knew one thing for sure: he was going to kill the bastard who had tipped off Daedalus and put him in this position. He'd take his time with them, too. For the first time in hours, a smile creased his lips as he contemplated all the terrible ways he could exact his revenge.

***

Back in New York, Phil pulled into the hangar and brought the Lincoln to a smooth stop in the same spot as earlier. Daedalus exited the passenger seat and walked briskly toward *Hera,* anxious to get out of the cold and continue their journey. Phil and Chief unloaded their gear from the SUV and caught up with their boss a few double-time strides later. Gryph appeared in the doorway of the jet high above them.

"You guys get everything we need?" Gryph yelled down, really only concerned with Daedalus's response. He could clearly see the box and bags Phil and Chief were carrying.

"Yes, Commander, I believe so. Please let Captain Daniels know we can get underway for Rome immediately." Gryph left for the cockpit to relay the instructions as the three men boarded the plane via the steep stairs.

***

A few hundred yards away, perched high in a nest of concrete and glass, a pair of eyes peered through high-powered field binoculars at the Boeing Business Jet readying for takeoff. This specific set of eyes belonged to a flight enthusiast and Director of Air Traffic Control at Westchester Airport, home to *Hera* for the last few months. Hours earlier, the director had received a message from a friend he met at one of the many aviation clubs to which they both belonged. This friend, who worked at Teterboro Airport, was asking for information on the very jet the Westchester Director was staring at right now. As if on cue, the phone in the air traffic control director's pocket vibrated.

He held the binoculars steady in one hand and answered the WhatsApp call on his phone with the other. "Hey, bud, I'm looking at your jet as we speak. It's lit up like a Christmas tree. She's a thing of beauty alright."

"Yeah, it's quite a beast. What are they doing now?"

"Actually, they're pulling out of the hangar right now."

"Did you happen to see anyone exit or enter the jet after they landed?" Teterboro was hoping for juicy information and another handsome payday.

"I didn't see anyone specifically. But I saw an SUV pull away from their hangar area shortly after they landed, but it was dark already. The SUV just got back a little while ago, so I guess…" He paused as he checked the clock on the wall and his notes with their landing time. "They were gone less than a couple hours, tops." He also passed along the new flight plan they had just filed with the tower moments ago. "I hope that helps. That's really cool that you're working with the FBI's anti-poaching task force. I'm glad I could help."

"Yeah, that's great. Thanks, man. I really appreciate it. Someone's got to look out for those poor, defenseless animals, you know? Anyway, thanks again. I have to make a few calls. Talk later."

The Teterboro controller disconnected the call. His cover story seemed to have done the trick. He had noticed earlier that Westchester's profile picture on WhatsApp was an image of him cuddling with his multitude of pets. He guessed correctly that the animal lover would bend over backwards to help him, if he thought he was saving animals from poachers. The bit about helping the FBI was the cherry on top. International poachers, a rare luxury jet, the FBI chase… it was too much to resist.

The Teterboro spy tried to reach Dima on his phone, but the call wouldn't connect, He left a message saying he'd try him again in thirty minutes. The little break would give him time to daydream about his upcoming payday and the bonus that was sure to accompany the divulgence of this new information.

μέρος τέταρτο
PART FOUR

CHAPTER THIRTY-TWO

Onboard Hera, heading east across the Atlantic
February 13, 2:10 a.m.

"Aw, Dallas, you're adorable," Luna said as she licked the pink frosting off the cupcake Dallas just handed to her.

"It's an early Valentine's Day thing. I just didn't want it to pass by without getting you something. And with these idiots, who knows what mess they'll get us into this week?" A large silver serving tray was covered by a dozen pink cupcakes. Little red candy sprinkles adorned the thick cream cheese icing. "With all this flying around everywhere, I have no idea what day or time zone we're running on anymore, but I just wanted you to know I was, uh, thinking about you. That's all. No biggie."

"Aw, you're even sweeter than this frosting." She leaned over and gave him a kiss on the mouth, leaving a smudge of red sprinkles on his lips. Their faces were still only inches apart when Gryph walked into their mobile control center.

"Sorry to interrupt. I just finished brewing a fresh pot of coffee with the beans the guys brought back. Either of you care for some?"

Keeping the team well caffeinated was a strategy Gryph used early and often. At this early hour, it was mission critical.

"I'd love one, Gryph, thanks," Luna said as she wiped the sugar from her lips.

"Me too," Dallas said "The stuff they have on board is shit compared to the stuff you make."

Gryph poured some of his steaming black magic into two matching mugs and passed them to the tech wizards. "How's everything coming along with the nano integration? Ali told me you guys made some real headway there."

"Yeah, it's been a lot to digest, but I think we have a pretty good understanding of the engineering behind the bots now," Dallas said. "Daedalus may be a bit of a freak, and I'm still not sure what to make of all his bullshit claims, but the guy knows tech. He's a whole other level of smart. Like Elon Musk-level genius."

"Okay. Let me know if there's anything you two need—other than a little more privacy, that is." Gryph smirked as the pair blushed at the comment.

"We're okay now, Gryph, thanks for asking," Luna said, trying to change the subject as she took a cautious sip from her cup. "Damn, this is amazing coffee. And I make the stuff for a living."

Phil was reading the latest Reacher novel while reclining in a buttery-soft leather chair. "You should try the cupcakes, Ali. They're delicious."

Aliyah plucked one of the remaining few treats from the silver tray and took a bite. "I think this is the first thing I've eaten in hours. I've been staring at my screens non-stop for days, it seems."

"It's a good thing you came out now. Another few minutes, and you'd be fighting for crumbs," Gryph said. "Chief was popping them into his mouth like they were peanuts. I had to stop him after the fourth one and remind him that Dallas arranged this for Luna." Everyone chuckled and could relate to the quick boost that hot coffee and a sugar kick had on a fatigued body.

Aliyah had been working with and observing Dallas and Luna all week long. "Those two have been inseparable," she said to Gryph, out of the couple's earshot. "Dallas asked me what he could buy her for Valentine's Day once we landed. I told him to *do* something sweet instead, that it would mean more to her. Who knows where those two will end up at the rate they're going?"

"I hope everyone enjoyed the cupcakes," Dallas said as he and Luna walked back into the parlor. "I had the chef make them especially for Luna."

"Yeah, so we heard," Chief said, rolling his eyes but grateful for the tasty snack, nonetheless.

"I hope you saved one for me." Heads turned to see Daedalus enter the parlor with his mystery box in hand.

"Absolutely. Help yourself, sir," Luna said as she presented the tray to her gracious host.

Daedalus took a seat at the large table and set the box on the highly polished surface. "I'm sure you're all wondering what this is and where we're going." The eager expressions on everyone's faces were answer enough. "Thankfully, I have the answers to both of those questions, although I fear those won't be the last questions I'll have to answer before we're finished."

Dallas and Luna took seats at the end of the table, and Phil slid into the empty seat beside Aliyah. No one wanted to miss the grand opening of this mystery box.

"As to where we're going, you've masterfully solved the riddles pointing us to the Church of St. Peter at the Vatican. However, when we land, we're heading to the Apostolic Palace first. The person we need to see about accessing the secret vaults will meet us there."

"Is that the cardinal guy you were talking about earlier?" Chief remembered the little tidbit of information Daedalus had divulged while they were departing from their recent trip from the Workshop.

"Yes. Cardinal Mott has been coordinating the details of our visit and will greet us when we arrive, along with a mandatory Swiss Guard security detail that will take us to meet the pope. From there—"

Dallas's eyes almost popped out of his head. "Hold up. Did he just say the pope? Like the dude with the white hat pope? Are you fucking kidding me?"

"Dallas!" Luna shot him a disappointed look for his crude reply. It seemed wrong to drop the F-bomb in the same sentence when discussing the pope. She wasn't Catholic, but it seemed sacrilegious to her anyway. Dallas sat back, arms crossed, not wanting to pick a fight with Luna, clearly astonished he was the only one who thought this plan was the craziest one yet.

"As outrageous as it seems, Dallas, that's exactly what we're going to do." The looks Daedalus received from around the table told him he needed to provide additional details for more than just Dallas in order to get the team behind this plan. "I understand the concern that you all may have with my ability to get an audience with the pope and, furthermore, garner his favor and take us to the archives to reveal the lock that matches our key. I would be just as hesitant to believe such a claim if I were in your position—if not for the fact that I have this to offer as a trade." He pointed to the small wooden box on the table.

Before anyone could ask about the contents of the box, Daedalus slid aside the simple metal bolt holding the box shut and flipped the lid open to reveal a small mound in the center of the box, covered by a white cloth with a thick red stripe running down the center. "It's been hundreds of years since this saw the light of day. It's funny, even the thought of me handing it over to someone else would have been entirely out of the question only weeks ago."

Daedalus picked up a corner of the white cloth, pulling it free from the box and holding it up. The remainder of the fabric unfurled, revealing that the thick red stripe was just one portion of the design. Another red stripe bisected the vertical near the top, forming a large red cross. Everyone's gaze dropped back down from the cloth to the box's contents.

Luna gasped, and her hands flew to her mouth in shock as soon as it was uncovered.

"Is that what I think it is?" Gryph asked, his voice calm, but his eyes remained riveted to the box.

"Judging by Luna's reaction and the look on your face, Commander," Daedalus said with a mischievous grin, "I'd say you have a very good idea as to what you're looking at."

"Again, I'm glad someone knows what this is all about," Dallas said, frustrated he was behind the curve once more. "Anyone care to enlighten the rest of us? All I see is a cheap tarnished cup. I'm not sure why the pope would bend over backwards for us over an old, tin— Wait. No way!" The lightbulb went off above his head. Dallas jumped up from his chair. "That's the fucking Holy Grail, isn't it? Holy shit, man, that's got to be the most priceless object in your entire collection!" He shook his head. "I knew I should've asked for more money," he mumbled, leaning in for a closer look.

"Yes, Dallas, this is the Holy Grail. The very same cup that Jesus used during the Last Supper. I believe the Catholic Church would do anything to add it to their collection, including arranging our little meeting with the pope and providing information and access for our special key."

A silent reverence fell over the room. The group mesmerized by the historical significance of the artifact they were staring at.

"I came into possession of the Grail almost two hundred years after it was used by Jesus for the last time. His earliest follow-ers accumulated a vast trove of his personal effects, which were kept safe for generations among his most ardent disciples. It was a tumultuous time. War and corruption were rampant. These relics were in danger of being plundered and lost, and I was entrusted with safeguarding some of those sacred items, including the Grail."

"Why did they trust you with such important things?" Aliyah asked.

"I had already built a small fortune for myself. It's amazing how being immortal can tip the scales in one's favor. I had power and connections, the two elements that have always been the keys to any kingdom. Not much has changed over the last couple millennia in that regard, I suppose. Anyway, I was the safest person they could ask at the time, and not only because I wasn't part of the Roman Empire. I also happened to be a friend and confidant to the family of one of Jesus's closest and earliest followers. By that point in my life, I had already helped the guardians of the Jewish Temple hide some of their treasures. You bore witness to uncovering one of them earlier this week." Daedalus paused in contemplative thought. "I'm not sure why fate chose me to be a protector of these exceptional items, but choose me it did. The Library of Alexandria I've secured inside the Labyrinth is my true life's purpose. The accumulation and protection of these antiquities has been the primary reason I have kept myself going all these years. This is one of the few times I've had to relinquish anything from the collection, but never anything as consequential as this."

"Desperate times call for desperate measures," Gryph said. "Let's hope this is the last thing you'll have to give up."

"The cardinal I mentioned earlier will be expecting us early this morning. He understands what we require and what I'm offering in return. For those of you who want to accompany me to the Apostolic Palace where the pope's residence is located, feel free to come. I can't guarantee that His Holiness will meet with everyone or that you'll all be able to join us when we go looking for our lock, but we've been stuck on this plane for a few days now, and if you wanted to do a little sightseeing, however brief, this would be the time."

A few hours later, *Hera* touched down at FCO, Leonardo da Vinci-Fiumicino Airport, Rome's largest. A fleet of four black Mercedes Maybach sedans waited for them just outside the private VIP terminal. Also waiting on the tarmac to greet them were representatives from the pontifical Swiss Guard, an officer from the Gendarmerie Corps of Vatican City State, and a lieutenant from the Polizia di Stato, also known as the Italian State Police force. They certainly weren't traveling discreetly anymore. Meeting with the pope, the spiritual leader of almost 1.3 billion Catholics around the world, on less than a day's notice and then requesting access to the most sensitive locations in all of Catholicism was bound to draw its own security response, something even Daedalus couldn't bypass entirely. Gryph and Daedalus made quick introductions with the militarized welcome wagon before everyone piled into the waiting luxury limousines.

Light and warmth from the midday sun fought to penetrate through dense cloud but was tempered by the cloudy sky. Still, the temperature outside required only a light jacket to ward off the chill and dampness in the air. Minutes later, they were racing toward Vatican City. The procession of police and government vehicles made the ride to the Apostolic Palace a breeze. They passed the requisite checkpoints without so much as slowing down and parked in designated security spaces.

The Daedalus crew walked the short distance from the cars to the Apostolic Palace's grand entrance. The papal residence was perched three stories above, on massive white columns, and was clearly visible from St. Peter's Square. A massive bronze door, patinaed green by time and the elements, was being protected by two Swiss Guards dressed in their traditional red, orange, and purple uniforms, complete with red plume hats and formal armor. While their attire may have appeared strange compared to more contemporary military designs, there was no doubt when it came to the degree of lethality and rigorous training methods which made the Swiss Guard one of the most respected armies in the world.

Once they'd gathered outside the soaring arched doorway, one of the guards who accompanied them from the airport broke from the group and spoke a few quick words in Italian to his brother-in-arms protecting the doorway. The two guards moved hastily from their position and cleared the passageway for Daedalus and his guests.

"I guess that means we're good to go?" Chief asked rhetorically.

"I think you're right, Chief," Gryph said. "Let's go meet the pope."

CHAPTER THIRTY-THREE

The Apostolic Palace
February 13, 10:10 a.m. CET

Every inch of the ceiling above the long hallway before them was adorned in depictions of angelic figures in flowing robes and other religious iconography. Gold-gilded frames enveloped masterpiece after masterpiece along the underside of the giant barreled ceiling.

Phil had been in awe since they walked through the large door. "This place is giving me some serious Sistine Chapel vibes," he said as they made their way past an enormous room known as Clementine Hall. The famous room was adorned with Renaissance frescoes and other exceptional works of art. It was primarily used for official receptions and occasionally for rituals, including serving as the private visitation area for Vatican officials to view and pray with the body of the pope upon their death.

"The Sistine Chapel is much more beautiful than Clementine Hall, signor." The unsolicited opinion came in perfect, albeit heavily accented English from one of the Swiss Guard escorts as they made their way closer to the papal residence. "It's definitely something you should see during your time here with us."

The Swiss Guardsman turned his attention to Gryph. "Commander Oake, perhaps this would be a good time for my men to escort some of the members of your party on a private tour of the Vatican while you conduct your business with His Holiness."

"As I'd informed the Cardinal before my arrival, I'll need to keep my security team with me at all times," Daedalus interjected. "Each of these people play a critical role in my being here."

"Yes. I have been informed. Cardinal Mott has arranged a private audience with His Holiness. It will then be his decision as to who follows past that point. The Pontiff's word will be final, and any argument whatsoever will result in you and your associates' immediate removal from the country."

"From the country? That's a bit harsh, don't you think?" Chief grunted to Gryph. The SEAL hadn't left the Commander's side since they departed the aircraft.

"Vatican City is also a country unto itself, Chief. What they say goes. Period. And don't let the funny looking uniforms throw you. These are the elite of the Swiss Guard. I'm sure these guys are almost good enough to give us a run for our money—and we're pretty good at what we do." He winked at Chief as they continued through one magnificent hall after the next.

After ascending a narrow spiraling staircase, they were finally ushered into the papal library. It was a plain room compared to the immense body of artwork they had just traveled through, hundreds of books adorned the walls.

Seated at a simple wooden desk was one of the world's most powerful men and, thankfully, one of the most peaceful among them. Beside him, Cardinal Mott stood acting as liaison between the Holy See and the Daedalus crew.

The pope appraised the small group at the entry to the library. He smiled warmly at them, uttered what appeared to be a blessing, then made the sign of the cross, and beckoned everyone to come closer.

Cardinal Mott explained to the pope that he'd known Daedalus for some years now and the man was a renowned collector of rare and priceless artifacts. He added that on more than one occasion, Daedalus recovered important pieces of art that had been stolen from the Church during World War II. He added that Daedalus never charged for his services, or taken credit for the art he's recovered.

Daedalus winced a little at that last statement. While it was true that he'd recovered many stolen artifacts for the church, not every item made its way back to the Vatican. Some were stored deep in the Labyrinth, and Daedalus didn't have any moral dilemma about that. He knew those items would never leave his possession to be sold on the black market, so what difference did it make whether they remained in a Vatican vault or in his? The artifacts were safe and sound in either location. It wasn't something that kept him up at night.

They had debated earlier on how to present their current predicament to the pope and the collective assessment was that telling the truth, or a slightly modified version thereof, would be best. They would simply leave out certain facts which would further complicate an already complicated situation.

Daedalus explained to both pious men about the toxin that would destroy the planet's food supply and what the human fallout from such a disaster would look like. He also told the pope of the test runs that already took place, and concluded with the media report on the BBC from the other day, emphasizing the imminent threat.

When it came to explaining the key found in the jeweled menorah, Daedalus twisted the truth by saying the location of the menorah was a secret passed down in his family from one generation to the next, without disclosing the actual name or location of the cave.

"I've always wondered whether it was just a myth, or if any of those stories were based in fact. When we went to the cave a few days ago and finally unearthed the menorah, there was no doubt left in my mind that this was very real. With the assistance of one member of my team"—Daedalus motioned to Chief— "we were able to discover this hidden key inside the ancient candelabra."

Billy beamed with pride at the acknowledgement. Daedalus passed the golden key along with the high-definition pictures they took of the menorah to Cardinal Mott, who glanced at the items before handing them to the pope.

The pontiff took the key with great reverence and spent a half minute turning it over in his hands, inspecting every facet of the relic before moving on to the pictures.

"Thank you very much for the opportunity to see such incredible items from so long ago. I hope that once you have completed your tasks, the key will be returned to its origin, or perhaps left here for safekeeping." The pope had yet to pass the key back to Cardinal Mott.

"Well, that's the issue, Your Holiness," Daedalus said, "We believe our key fits inside a special lock that's located somewhere inside the Vatican. You see, another member of my team"—he nodded to Luna— "deciphered the clues on the box the menorah was housed in, and those clues led us here." He continued to expound on the inverted cross, the symbol for St. Peter, and the other clues directing them to that very spot or somewhere nearby. A few pictures of the menorah and its box were passed back to the pontiff for his reference.

"I can see how you would assume the location of the lock that you are seeking would be located somewhere near St. Peter's Cathedral based on what you've just described, but I'm not sure how you can be so certain?"

Gryph answered on behalf of his boss. "I wasn't completely sure we would find what we were looking for here either until you took hold of the key, Your Eminence. I'm something of an expert in reading people. Please don't take any offense at my observations, but I saw the expression on your face register recognition and surprise, in that order. You've seen these symbols somewhere else, haven't you?"

The Swiss Guard escort looked mortified by Gryph's accusations, but held his tongue in deference to Cardinal Mott, whom he thought should have said something to quell the American's arrogant tone. It was not his place to interrupt, but he was boiling inside.

The pope remained silent, his face stoic as Gryph continued. "You still haven't denied seeing anything like this before, Your Holiness. You've asked only how we could be certain this is the right place, but I believe you've just resolved that uncertainty for us. Will you confirm that the lock we're looking for is here? We're not on a treasure hunt looking for fame and fortune. We're fighting for the survival of humanity. If the lock we need is in the Church itself or in your secret vaults, we need to find it, and open it as quickly as possible."

The pope pondered what he had just heard for a few moments before he spoke. "I am a man of God and very much believe that the truth will set you free—"

"John 8:32," Luna said. "Oh gosh, I'm so sorry, Your Holiness. It's like a reflex for me. I hear scripture, and it just sort of pops out.

I know you're aware of the source." Luna's cheeks flushed with embarrassment.

"Bless you, child. It warms my heart that there are those who still understand the importance of Bible study, and you know yours well." He turned to Gryph. "To answer your question, yes, there's something here I recognized. But the lock you seek is in a place that you are not permitted to enter. Only a select few cardinals and I can access these sensitive sites. I'm sorry you have come all this way for nothing. Please accept my sincerest apologies."

With that, the meeting was apparently over. The Swiss Guard couldn't wait to escort these rude Americans out of the palace. The holy soldier moved toward Gryph, and a fraction of a second later, Chief was in front of Gryph, face to face with the elite Vatican warrior. Before the situation escalated into a full-out battle, Daedalus spoke up. "Your Holiness, I believe I have something that may allow you to grant me access for this noble purpose."

The pope raised his right hand slightly toward the Swiss Guard, still engaged in a standoff with Chief. The guard immediately heeded the command and moved back to his position along the group's perimeter.

Daedalus reached into the large leather bag he'd brought from New York, grasping the holy relic he had kept in his collection for centuries. He placed the box in front of the pope and unfastened the latch. He lifted the lid and moved the red-and-white striped cloth to reveal the metal chalice inside. One did not need Gryph's expertise in deciphering body language to see that he had the pope's undivided attention. The pope didn't, or perhaps couldn't, speak for a moment. "Many throughout the ages have purported to be in possession of the Grail," he said. "While little is known about the Chalice of Christ, the Church does have some intimate knowledge that would prove its providence without question."

"I have no issue submitting to your test as long as the Grail stays with me the entire time you're authenticating it," Daedalus said.

"That will not be an issue, Signor Daedalus. We can do it right here, right now. It will not be an invasive process."

Gryph had been closely watching the interaction between the two men. Judging by their expressions, both seemed to be telling the truth.

"How do you propose to verify the authenticity of an object that has been lost for time immemorial?" Daedalus asked.

"The cardinal speaks very highly of you, Signor Daedalus," the pope began, "and that carries a great deal of weight with me. Furthermore, the key you have brought today, along with the slightest chance the Grail could finally be returned to the church, have tipped the scales in your favor." The pope's kind blue eyes passed over everyone standing in the library. "What I tell you now is not ever to be spoken of again. Are we agreed?" Silent nods from everyone prompted the supreme pontiff to proceed.

"The Church has amassed many relics, holy items, and knowledge over the past two-thousand years. The Crusades, brutal as they were, happened to be very efficient in capturing many lost treasures."

"Probably because they stole everything after they were done with their rampage," Aliyah whispered to Phil a little too loudly.

"That is actually the truth of it, signorina," the pope said, overhearing the comment. "They plundered as they went, taking everything back to Rome. Once it arrived here, it remained safe and in one secure location, even to this day. Not scattered to the four corners of the Earth, lost forever." Aliyah was mortified. She was hoping the ground would open up and swallow her. She didn't think her quiet musings would be overheard. At least the pope didn't seem to take offence to the remark. But still, she knew better and cringed inside. *When in Rome... don't insult the pope.*

"Many of the artifacts that were attributed to Christ were collected by his earliest followers and disciples," the pope said. "These holy relics were kept safe by the families of those followers, putting their lives at great risk. These relics were then retrieved from the families who had been hiding them during the Crusades and finally brought back to the Church in Rome some thousand years ago. But not everything had been recovered. Some things were thought to have been lost to the sands of time forever. Other parties may still be in possession of artifacts from our sacred history; passed down through generations, somehow evading capture or destruction."

A silent acknowledgment rippled through the Daedalus crew. Surprise registered on their faces upon hearing a corroboration of the fantastical story Daedalus had told them only hours earlier, and from the pope himself, no less.

"What those Crusade collection periods also garnered for the Church were a cache of treasures from those living alongside Jesus during his ministry and the years immediately after his resurrection. The disciples Peter, John, Matthew, and Thomas had the most diverse and largest collection of personal items that we have catalogued and secured safely in our vaults. We send some of these relics to churches around the world, bringing more sanctity and holiness for those who worship there. The bones of Peter the Apostle lie under St. Peter's Basilica for that very reason."

The pope gestured to the Grail, which was resting in the box. "May I?"

"With the understanding, Your Eminence, that once you confirm what I already know to be true, you will take us to the lock matching my key and allow us to continue our mission. The Grail will remain with you when we leave. The key and menorah will be returned to the cave. I give you my word."

The pope didn't hesitate. "I accept your terms, Signor Daedalus. But I must ask, surely you know the Grail is said to have the ability to heal and provide everlasting life. Why would you ever part with such a priceless treasure?"

Daedalus smiled politely. "The idea just doesn't appeal to me anymore. Please proceed with your inspection." He slid the box closer to the pontiff.

The pope handed the golden key back, and then with a flourish, Daedalus pulled back the cloth concealing the simple metal cup inside. He unfurled the fabric fully, revealing a large red cross emblazoned across its surface. The holy man used the cloth to take the cup out of the box in reverence to its sanctity.

"The cups that each disciple used at the Last Supper were found among the breadth of recovered belongings," Cardinal Mott said, as the pope inspected the chalice. "These cups likely survived the early years after Christ's crucifixion because of their discreet size and unassuming nature. Each was given the same marking from the metalsmith who fashioned them. A circle surrounding a triangle was stamped into the base of each goblet. Vatican scholars had long ago theorized that these vessels may have been purchased for the

Passover holiday, in accordance with its stringent dietary laws and restrictions. The Last Supper, as you may or may not know, was a Passover Seder. It is conceivable that the utensils and dishes were purchased or perhaps even donated in a single transaction, creating an identical lot. In any event, we have confirmed through our research that these precious items were, in fact, the very cups used at the Last Supper."

"Only a select few clergy at the Vatican are chosen to study the Grail and its secrets," the pope said, apparently complete with his inspection. "Cardinal Mott happens to be one of those selected for that noble pursuit and is our resident expert."

The pope passed the cup to Cardinal Mott for his examination. It didn't take long for tears to well up in his eyes. A silent prayer spilled from his trembling lips as he examined the ancient vessel. "The markings are clear and precisely where they should be, Your Holiness."

Neither the pope nor Cardinal Mott had disclosed five of the cups already in their vaults were found wrapped in the same white and red cloth as Daedalus's, when they were brought back to the Vatican a thousand years ago, but none in as pristine condition as this. Cardinal Mott's hands trembled as he placed the Grail back into the pope's hands. He kissed his fingertips once the relic was out of his grasp. "I believe it's authentic, Your Holiness. The Grail has finally found its home."

"I believe you are correct, Cardinal Mott." The pope placed the chalice and cloth back into the box, closed the lid, then turned to Daedalus. "This has earned you the right to accompany me to my private vault, Signor Daedalus. It is located underground and away from the other Vatican archives. The entry is not even a ten-minute walk from here using the restricted passageways that cross under Vatican City. We will not be seen or disturbed that way. Cardinal Mott, please join us as well."

The Daedalus crew, along with the pope, Cardinal Mott, and their disagreeable Swiss Guard envoy, made their way under Piazza Del Marco, otherwise known as St. Mark's Square, the largest walkable open-air plaza in Vatican City.

After a short walk through a complex web of tunnels, the group came to an abrupt stop. A vault-like door was being protected by a pair of Swiss Guards, looking more menacing than any they'd seen thus far. They were armed differently than the other guards too, both carrying Heckler and Koch MP5s across their bodies. The guards couldn't believe their eyes when they saw the supreme pontiff and his guests striding toward them. The room was hardly ever accessed and never by so many people—and certainly never by women.

"Is everything alright, Holy Father?" one of the guards asked in Italian, certain the pontiff was being held against his will.

"All is well, my son. These kind people are simply returning something lost to us long ago. I'm here offering assurances that they are returning it somewhere safe." He smiled and made the sign of the cross. The two guards returned the sign in kind and stepped aside to take a knee on either side of the doorway, bowing their heads in a show of respect and humility.

The pope removed a key card from a pocket concealed in the folds of his robe and placed it against a reader placed off to the side of the doorway. A green light flashed on the device, and the locking mechanism clicked open. The group walked into a small room that didn't have much to see except for a bookcase and small table that must have been used to examine the many priceless manuscripts and artifacts stored somewhere else in the facility, because this room looked empty.

The pope walked to the end of the room and rotated a simple coat hook hanging on the rear wall. A moment later, the bookcase at the end of the room slid three feet to the left, exposing a secret door. The pope didn't reach for the key card this time. The concrete-and-steel blast door could only be opened by retinal scan, and only one set of eyes on Earth could open the two-foot-thick slab standing in their way.

The pope completed the scan, and the pressurized door hissed open, rolling on mechanical rails, revealing a antechamber that kept the room under constant temperature and humidity control. A light flickered high above, centered in the room, illuminating a large golden cross inlaid into the white marble floor.

"The lock you are searching for is inside here, my friends. This room will also be the new home for the Grail. Your treasure is in good hands, Signor Daedalus. I promise you that."

The trio walked through the doorway first and into the inner-most sanctum in all of Vatican City.

"Oh… my… God." Luna's eyes bugged out of her head.

"Yup," Gryph said. "That sounds about right."

CHAPTER THIRTY-FOUR

*The Secret Papal Archive Room at the Apostolic Palace
February 13, 11:27 a.m. CET*

The L-shaped room looked deceivingly small from the doorway, but once inside, a substantial interior area was revealed. The view from the door allowed them to only see the bottom leg in the L. The longer section was only exposed once one walked inside the secret chamber.

"This private vault is kept separate from the other Vatican archives and vaults, both those known and those hidden from official record," Cardinal Mott said with a sly smile. "It was deemed too dangerous to keep these special items with the balance of our collection in the event of fire or theft. This vault is only known to the sitting pope and three others at any given time, known as the Four Keepers. When one of the Keepers passes away, a successor is chosen by the pope to replace them. Needless to say, it is highly… unorthodox to have persons other than any of the keepers present. Under the circumstances, the Grail, and your quest to protect the world from this terrible threat takes precedence over our protocol."

The pope took up a position in the front of the small group and crossed himself before venturing any further inside. "Please remove your footwear, for the floor you walk on is sacred ground. There are objects in this room that have been touched by the divine. The items stored here can never be seen by the masses, some for the public's good and admittedly, some for the protection of the Church itself."

So much for "the truth shall set you free," Gryph mused. Everyone removed their shoes and proceeded with great reverence into the vault. Gryph wasn't a religious man, but he had to admit to feeling a sense of sanctity. No other word could describe the palpable aura inside the vault. A twelve-foot golden crucifix dominated the far end of the room. The corpus, the proper name for the body of Christ on the cross, was life-size and incredibly intricate in its detail. Another solid gold inlay was set into the floor and spilled out from the base of the crucifix, creating a golden mirror image.

"I can see why you chose this room as the new home for the Grail," Daedalus said, surveying the antiquities secreted away in the private papal vault.

"For millennia we have been protecting some of the most important religious artifacts that the world has ever known," the Holy Father said. "Some groups allege we are in unlawful possession of their belongings. Others assert that we possess some items that we simply don't have. In any event, our efforts have been successful in keeping all these magnificent treasures from being lost forever." He turned to Daedalus. "As a collector, you must see the logic in keeping these priceless historical artifacts safe from human greed. In many instances, these groups would rather see these items destroyed than in anyone else's possession. It's precisely why much of this has been kept here to this day."

Daedalus couldn't agree more with the sentiment. The Library of Alexandria was safe because he held the same view. "It's true," he said. "Priceless treasures which stood for thousands of years were recently destroyed by ISIS in one catastrophic wave of destruction. Any religious artifacts returned to their origins in the Middle East within the last hundred years would have ended up as ash or rubble. Everything looks safe and secure right here. You'll hear no argument from me."

Luna had yet to pick her jaw up off the floor. She'd been in a stunned stupor since she first laid eyes on the contents of the secret vault. She caught Aliyah staring at a massive and absolutely gorgeous tapestry hanging on a golden rod along one of the walls. Luna walked over and stood beside her. "You know what that is, Ali?" The thick mosaic backdrop featured a mixture of blue, purple, crimson, and white. Gold threading was spun into figures of cherubs across the breadth of the fabric. It was thirty feet tall and at least twice as wide.

"It's called the Parochet," Aliyah said, her voice barely above a whisper. "It's the Aramaic word for the giant curtain that hung in the Jewish Temple in front of the Ark of the Covenant containing the Ten Commandments and the jar of manna we need to complete the antidote."

"It's also a well-documented fact that General Titus, before he became emperor of Rome, plundered the Second Temple after slaughtering the Jews in Jerusalem. He used the Parochet to wrap up and transport the Temple treasures he stole." Aliyah's head was swimming with all the biblical stories she had read as a young girl. Back then, she often imagined what it would have been like living in those times. Now she was mere inches from something no Jewish person had laid eyes on in over 2,000 years.

Luna laid a comforting hand on Aliyah's shoulder. She felt her take a deep breath and watched her new friend wipe a tear from her eye. "I'm not sure if I'm angry that this has been kept from my people for so long or happy that it has at least endured to this day. Maybe the pope was right." Aliyah wondered aloud.

"They seem to have a wide variety of faiths and practices represented down here, including some that have been written off as myth or legend," Luna said. "I think I just saw the actual Chinon Parchment." She pointed to a sheet of parchment the size of a dining room table. It recorded the hearings and orders of the Roman Catholic military order, including a detailed account of the trial of the Knights Templar.

The two women took their time taking a mental inventory as they made their way over to Gryph and the others. They passed by a thick marble pedestal supporting a crown of thorns, laying under a glass dome. Adjacent to the crown was a five-inch-long iron spike resting on a white silk cloth under an identical clear cover. A thick, rough-hewn timber, over eight feet in length, was nestled in a matching gold box near the base of the crucifix. An iron spike matching the one being displayed on the marble column was still clearly embedded in the wooden beam. A dark discoloration was visible on the wood around the protruding spike. It seemed pretty obvious to everyone what the objects were. Luna was in awe being so close to such hallowed relics.

Their attention then shifted to a remote corner of the room seemingly designated for objects that didn't quite belong with the sacramental items housed in the vault. The most shocking of all the oddities—in a room that was full of shocking oddities—was a large skull which looked humanoid in nature, but was certainly not human. Luna and Ali both seemed to see it at the same time and displayed identical looks of horror. The elongated skull and small face looked eerily similar, if not identical, to the alien-shaped heads Hollywood had made famous.

The pope noticed the two women and the object of their attention. They were so transfixed by what they were seeing, they didn't notice his approach until he was almost beside them. "As I said, there are things down here we keep for the protection of the Church and for the protection of man."

"But if you know there are such things as… aliens—" Luna said.

"Who says these are not of our world?" the pope said. "The Lord has made many creatures since he created the Earth. Perhaps this is simply one that had gone extinct long ago. But I don't disagree, they could raise questions that are unanswerable at present. Some of those questions could undo the very fabric of society. It could even test the faith of some members within the Church itself. Therefore, it was deemed too sensitive for any place, except for this room, where faith is always in abundant supply." He smiled and gestured toward the end of the room and, ultimately, the end of their unsanctioned sightseeing tour. "Please, let's join the others." He was being a very gracious host, but exposing every secret the room contained was not part of their deal.

The group assembled in front of a large glass cabinet. Several books were placed on each shelf. A few were thick leather bound tomes, accompanied by at least a dozen smaller journals. A few scrolls were bound together with a crimson band, resting in a box on the lowest shelf.

Dallas noticed a small blue light blinking opposite the scrolls. "Cardinal Mott," he said, "not to state the obvious, but why would you need a security system in this room? Seems kind of redundant once you're here already, no?"

"The lights aren't for conventional security purposes, signor. Those are indicators that confirm that the case is sealed properly.

The documents inside are protected by a mixture of inert gasses keeping decay and aging at bay. The entire preservation system is computer controlled and monitored twenty-four seven. These artifacts are rarely removed or handled. The gasses keep them in pristine condition."

The group followed the pope to the front left corner of the room and stopped in front of a beautiful golden cabinet. An ornate jeweled box was mounted above a set of deep drawers. Cardinal Mott grasped a thick gold knob and opened the top drawer, revealing twelve gold partitions across the interior. Identical silver cups appeared in each of the twelve slots.

"These are the cups from the Last Supper that we have reclaimed over the years," Cardinal Mott said. "You can see that each one is the same size, shape, and color. Furthermore, they all carry identical markings. The same marking the Grail you brought has stamped into its base, signor," he said, turning to Daedalus.

"There are twelve spaces inside the drawer, one for each disciple. But where would the Grail fit?" Daedalus asked.

Cardinal Mott slid open an almost imperceptible seam in the jeweled box situated above the drawers, exposing a gold-and-diamond-studded cradle fitted for a goblet that he was sure matched the same dimensions as those found in the drawer below, identical to the one they had brought from New York. Glass sheeting protected the contents of the drawer, the telltale blue light blinking away.

"I'm satisfied the Grail will be safe here with you, Your Holiness. I'll be happy to leave it with you—as soon as my key opens the lock you said we could find in this vault."

"Ah, yes, of course, Signor Daedalus. But to be clear, I never said your key would be able to open it. I only told you that I believed we possessed a similarly styled lock."

"All disclaimers aside, Your Holiness, I'll need to at least try it before I can hand over the Grail for your... safekeeping."

The Swiss Guard looked like he was going to have an aneurysm. This man was bartering with the pope as if he was buying souvenirs outside St. Mark's square, but he held his tongue. It was not his place to interfere with the pope's affairs, only to keep him safe. However, these people were pushing their limits.

"Of course, my son. Try you must. Let us pray that your journey was not in vain." They walked from the golden cabinet to another enormous table, not far from the skull that had spooked the two women earlier.

"Jesus Christ!" Dallas blurted. "What the hell is that?" He pointed at the skull, then clamped his hand over his mouth, realizing what he'd just said. "Oh my God, I'm so sorry, sir. My bad. Sometimes I just—"

Luna squeezed his other hand as hard as she could. "Dallas, stop talking. Literally, not another word."

The pope forced a smile and brought everyone's attention back to another intricately jeweled box, nestled among other fascinating items. He picked up the mysterious cube and showed it to the group. "This is the object I was referring to when I said I recognized the symbols from your key. I had prayed many nights beseeching the Lord to enlighten me and reveal the significance behind this wondrous cube, hence the reason I so easily recognized the pattern and design from your pictures. I could never gain any true insight into its meaning." He looked at the cube affectionately, as if being reacquainted with a long-lost friend. "I am truly blessed that the Almighty may have delivered both the answer and the key collectively through you, Signor Daedalus—and your friends, of course."

The pontiff waved his hand at the artifacts in front of them. "This table is designated for relics with purposes that have not yet been determined. Others are puzzles that remain unsolved or unopenable. When certain objects came into the possession of my holy predecessors, they were placed in the papal vault for the Four Keepers to study in… shall we say, a more private setting. Just as Cardinal Mott does for us here as it pertains to matters of the Grail."

He moved the cushion on which the cube was resting toward the edge of the table closest to where Daedalus was standing. "This puzzle box has no slot for a key that I can see, but the pictures of the menorah and the key you sent ahead to Cardinal Mott match the design on this cube. As I said, I cannot guarantee your key will work, but the coincidence was too great to ignore."

Daedalus and Gryph examined the jeweled cube and compared it to the pictures they had taken of the menorah. The pope was right. The rows of multi-colored jewels on the cube were fashioned in the same style as the ancient candelabra. Even the types and shapes of the gemstones used were identical.

"I agree with your observation, Your Holiness," Gryph said. "It seems as if the menorah, the key, and this mysterious box were created as a set, or intended to look as such. What can you tell us of its origin?"

Cardinal Mott was eager to hear the answer to this question, too. The pope had introduced him as the resident Grail expert, but it was unlikely he could be an expert on everything stored inside the papal vault.

The pontiff returned to his discourse on the cube. "The limited text passed down with this magnificent piece referred to it as Solomon's lock. Another reason why I found your key and lock request so compelling. Its purpose remains a mystery, but the text made cryptic references to the Temple treasures hidden somewhere in Israel."

Discreet, hopeful looks were shared in rapid succession.

"If there's a chance your key can unlock this cube, then I urge you to try opening it now. From what you've told us, nothing less than the fate of the world is at stake." The pope's lips moved silently, and he made the sign of the cross and backed away from the table, leaving the Daedalus crew crowded around their riddle to solve.

Dallas was a set-in-stone atheist, but was pleasantly surprised that the leader of the Catholic Church was being so cooperative. *The pope is a pretty solid guy*, Dallas thought. Lord only knows what the pope thought of Dallas.

"Chief, I was wrong earlier," Daedalus said. "I told you we wouldn't need you to solve any puzzles this time around, and yet here we are again. It seems you're our resident puzzle expert now, so would you please take a look at the cube? Maybe this can be solved in a similar manner as the menorah."

Billy K may not have shown it, but he was bursting with pride inside. His physical size and expertise in combat were the traits he was most often called on to use in the field. Having someone this high up the food chain requesting his help for nonviolent problem-solving skills was a rare occurrence—and he was savoring every second of it. The fact that Dallas had to stand silently under Luna's scornful look made it all the more delicious.

"Hey, Phil, you were good luck for me last time. Come over here. You've been too quiet." Chief set to work examining the cube, touching each one of the jewels as he ran his thick, calloused fingers up and down each side of the box.

"I'm all good here, Chief, just admiring the scenery. You do your thing." Phil had been quiet and extremely reserved since they first made their way through the Vatican, to the papal apartments and their final trek into the vault. Something was bothering him. Aliyah had noticed a shift in his demeanor earlier too, but she was dealing with her own distracted feelings after seeing the pilfered artifacts of her ancestors hung like hunting trophies on a wall, not to mention the disturbing image of the skull that would likely haunt her to the end of her days.

Phil had positioned himself with a vantage point that suited him just fine. He would leave the puzzle to Chief. Contrary to what Billy thought, Phil wasn't feeling lucky at all. In fact, he had a sneaking suspicion their luck was just about to run out.

Chief rotated the cube in his hands for a few minutes before he abruptly stopped. "The menorah had a stone in it that I was able to twist and slide away to create a space to start shifting the jewels around. I don't remember which one it was though. I pressed it by accident and got excited when things started moving around and, well, you know the rest."

Dallas couldn't hold it in any longer. "Why are we entrusting an object so important that it needs to be protected in the pope's private vault to a SEAL demolitions expert? He literally has the fate of the world in his hands. He just got lucky last time, that's all. He admitted it himself. Even a blind squirrel can find an acorn every once in a while. And another thing, why is he all of a sudden the only puzzle sol—"

"Got it!" Chief exclaimed.

Everyone turned away from Dallas's tantrum and crowded around Chief, leaving the hacker extraordinaire embarrassed and alone. Even Luna walked away from him.

"It was a diamond this time. I rotated it a bit and felt a click, then I pushed down, and was off to the races." Chief showed them the new gap he'd made in the jewels, allowing him a free space to move the stones into alignment. "The shapes of the stones are carved into each row, like the menorah had," he said, moving the gems around the priceless puzzle. However, after five minutes, he was certain he'd made little to no progress and was feeling the weight of everyone's eyes on him, adding to the pressure. No one had said a word while he was working on the cube, giving him complete silence to concentrate, but that somehow made it worse.

"I have an idea," Dallas said.

"That's good 'cause I'm fresh out," Chief said, looking deflated. "I can't figure this thing out with everyone watching, and you guys can't go anywhere. So, we're stuck."

"You already did the hard part, Billy boy. Getting the first gem to move was what we really needed," Dallas said without a hint of sarcasm or malice.

"Can you elaborate?" Gryph asked, not knowing if this was going to be just another one of Dallas's punchlines or if he'd actually figured out a solution. The tone in Gryph's voice made it clear that this was not the time for jokes.

"I can model the cube's gem layout and have the AI work out the solution for us. It'll give us step-by-step moves that we can follow until all the gems line up. It's a simple thing for me to program. Honestly, it's probably less than fifteen minutes of work." There was no arrogance or bravado in his voice, just a thoughtful contribution to solving a problem.

Will wonders never cease? Gryph thought.

"I'm going to have to get back to the surface to do it. There's no signal whatsoever down here. I can use my sat phone for the connection to the Workshop. If I can see some sky, I'm good to go." Dallas and Luna proceeded to snap hi-res pictures of every side of the cube to upload via the sat phone once they were topside.

Aliyah told Gryph that she wanted to get some fresh air and would accompany them up. Gryph felt more comfortable knowing Ali was going with the programmers anyway. She was a one-woman security force in her own right and was more than capable of protecting the pair while they were working on the cube's digital solution.

In reality, the walls were starting to close in on Ali. It wasn't claustrophobia. She needed a break from the enormity of what she'd just seen. The rest of the Daedalus crew decided to stay put in the vault and with the Grail.

"Remember, don't mess with the cube until we're back," Dallas said. "We're using the current positions of the gems as the starting point. We'll have to download the solution to my phone and come right back down, so we can't adjust for any moves you make once we leave here. Billy Boy, that means you. Hands off. You did your part, now let me do mine." The trio walked out of the vault under the protection of yet another Swiss Guard escorting them up top for the satellite connection they needed.

Those remaining behind sat in silence for a few minutes, each man contemplating everything they'd learned in the last hour and where it would lead them next.

Something had been gnawing at Gryph since they arrived though, a question he couldn't leave unasked. The problem was, he couldn't think of any good way of getting it answered without calling out the pontiff directly. He figured this was as good a time as any, hoping the pope would understand and not take any offense with his inquiry. After all, he was in the forgiveness business.

"Your Holiness, we very much appreciate your cooperation and the openness you have shown since our arrival."

"Of course, my son. I'm happy to play whatever part I can to preserve life on Earth. And, of course, to see the Grail returned to the Church."

"Well, that's the thing, Your Holiness. You've allowed visitors inside these walls for the first time in history, and we've seen things down here that are quite... let's just say extraordinary." Gryph could have chosen a host of other adjectives, but that was the most benign of the bunch.

"You have been entrusted with secrets that go as far back as recorded time, and yet you've been the most gracious and transparent host that anyone could have hoped for. You seem very approachable and easy to speak with, too. I guess I just wasn't expecting that. But that's probably why you're the pope." Gryph chuckled. "You may be a role model for over a billion people, but we"—Gryph motioned to his friends— "well, we certainly are not. Are you not concerned that once we leave, one of us will tell others about this room and what we've seen"?

The pontiff smiled his biggest, kindest smile yet. "No, my son. You promised you wouldn't divulge any of the secrets I have shared with you. I simply trust you will keep your word."

"You trust us? That's assurance enough for you?" Gryph still wasn't convinced.

"It truly is. Besides, who would you tell, Signor Oake? What would you say? That you met with the pope in a secret room that no one at the Vatican has ever heard about to exchange a puzzle box for the Holy Grail? And with a group of men *and* women, no less? Who would believe such a fantastical tale?"

Gryph laughed. The pope was right again. Who would ever believe them? The story was so improbable he could barely believe it himself, and he was there. "That's probably the only excuse that really makes sense. Thank you for being so forthright with me again, Your Holiness."

The pope smiled and winked. "The truth shall set you free."

Everyone shared a laugh and relaxed a bit—everyone except Phil. He remained rigid in his seat, his eyes fixed straight ahead. Something was definitely wrong, and somehow he was the only one who'd noticed.

CHAPTER THIRTY-FIVE

*The Secret Papal Archive Room at the Apostolic Palace
February 13, 1:05 p.m. CET*

Dallas was waiting impatiently for the download with the puzzle's step-by-step instructions to finish. As anticipated, the programming didn't take him long to work through, but much to his dismay, the connection on the proprietary sat phone was running significantly slower than he would have hoped. Heavy clouds rolled in overhead, darkening the sky in concert with his mood. Watching the progress bar inch closer to the 100 percent mark was getting him more anxious by the second. It wasn't just the mission that had him on edge. It was what happened when he exited the vault that put him on high alert.

"We're being set up," Phil had whispered to him when he left the vault. "Watch your back." Dallas was going to stop and ask what the hell he was talking about, but Phil had warned him off with a subtle shake of his head.

Dallas relayed Phil's warning to Luna and Aliyah as soon as they were outside and out of earshot of their accompanying Swiss Guard. The two women had been keeping an eye out for trouble while Dallas worked his magic with ICARUS back in the Workshop.

"This connection sucks ass," he said for the umpteenth time. "We've been up here way too long. We need to get back. Those guys could be in trouble."

"Gryph and your friends can handle themselves just fine, Dallas." Luna tried to offer some measure of comfort, but she'd be lying if she said Phil's message didn't unnerve her too. Aliyah looked up and nodded vacantly at Luna's half-hearted reassurance. She hadn't stopped pacing since they surfaced from the vault and was well on her way to wearing out a small patch of grass in a corner of the courtyard they were staged in.

Aliyah hadn't said much since they left the pope's secret room, lost in her own thoughts. She had been happy for the break from the oppressive vault, but was eager to get back now, knowing her friends could be in trouble. She was certain that if Phil felt something was amiss, he was likely right. The storm clouds brewing above mirrored the feelings rolling through her mind, as small droplets of rain began to splash on the garden's travertine border.

"Finally!" Dallas punched the air as the download indicator reached 100 percent. "Let's get this back down right away."

They started toward the door that they had emerged from earlier making their way back down the convoluted passageways and into the secretive chamber which, until that day, was known to only a handful of people on Earth.

Dallas walked through the doorway first and saw his friends still huddled with the pope and Cardinal Mott at the far end of the room. Phil had remained in exactly the same spot, wearing the same stone-cold expression. No one seemed to be any worse for wear.

"You guys miss me?"

Gryph ignored Dallas's question. "Were you able to figure out the solution to the cube?"

"Yup. Took me less than ten minutes to program it, but almost twice as long to upload the pictures and download the instructions. The connection on the sat phone was pure shi—," he said, catching himself at the last second while glancing nervously at the pope. "Sorry about that. What I meant to say was the download speed wasn't as fast as I hoped it would be. That's what took us so long." Dallas explained.

"Let's see what you've got for us." Gryph motioned for the sat phone.

Dallas opened the instructions. "Okay, first we need to find the side of the puzzle box that matches this image's starting point." Dallas showed Gryph a close-up view of the cube on the screen. It took a few rotations until they located the jeweled face that matched the image. "Now we just push the 'play' button and follow the instructions until we reach the end."

"Okay Chief, you're up," Gryph said. "You're the one who figured out the original combination, so you may as well see it all the way through." Gryph slid the cube over to his brother-in-arms and moved out of the way so Chief could sit beside Dallas and get a clear look at his screen.

The improbable duo had to pause the playback and go back a couple of times, but otherwise Dallas and Chief made quick work of the digital directions. The stones were all aligned save for the last few gems that Chief was deftly moving into the correct positions. As they got closer to the solution, everyone in the vault moved nearer to the pair until a small semicircle had formed behind them, watching breathlessly as the intricate puzzle was finally being solved.

Chief slid the last gem, a diamond, which upon closer inspection was slightly larger than the others, into the center position. Each side of the cube now matched the computer simulation.

"Okay. What next?" Gryph asked.

"On the menorah, I pressed the last stone when all the colors lined up, and the key just popped out." He pressed on the center diamond that he had just slid into place. A loud click emanated from the gold box. Chief froze. Everyone else tensed.

"The top panel has a little gap in the middle that definitely wasn't there before, guys." Chief still hadn't moved a muscle, but he could clearly see the new fissure in the center of the golden cube.

Daedalus pulled the key from the menorah out of his pocket. "It would seem we have finally found the lock for our key." He held the ancient key aloft for everyone to see, letting it hover an inch above the opening. It looked to be a close fit. "This would be a really good time to pray," he said. The irony of the present company and location not lost on anyone.

He slipped the key inside. The close fit proved to be perfect when the key disappeared into the slot. He twisted the mechanism almost a full revolution before the key unlocked the cube. The box unfolded like golden origami. The age-old secret was now only moments from being revealed. The pope crossed himself and said an inaudible prayer. Cardinal Mott leaned in for an even closer look, his eyes wide with amazement.

The deconstructed cube had flattened and segmented into six square sections flat on the table. Four gold square plates ran vertically, flanked by one square on each side of the second position, forming a golden cross. A multitude of symbols and ancient lettering were etched into the inside face of the cube, hidden from view until now. The cube was finally open for all to see.

"It looks like another puzzle," Daedalus said.

"Of course," Dallas said, reaching his breaking point. "It can't ever just be the end. We always have something else to solve, somewhere else to go. I'm sure it's just like all the other times too. No clue where we're going or what we have to do, right?"

The semicircle of people had tightened again as soon as the words "another puzzle" were spoken. Aliyah took a seat beside Chief, who was still seated directly in front of the deconstructed gold cube.

At first glance, the central intersecting square seemed to be the most intricate of them all. Hebrew letters were carved into the golden surface. There were ten letters across each of the rows and ten columns in total, creating a grid of one hundred letters on the center square.

"Looks like an ancient word jumble," Phil said. "Can you identify any of that?" he asked, turning to Aliyah. Her nose was all scrunched up as she scanned the grid of letters.

"You might be right. I don't see anything that makes sense to me though. It's all just gibberish."

"It could be a coded cypher," Daedalus said, "but we'd need another key to unlock the translation. Dallas, you can run this through ICARUS when we get back to the plane. Maybe it can crack this code for us."

Dallas nodded. "Yeah. No problem."

Luna started taking photographs of the newly exposed interior face to upload to ICARUS for when they had a signal again. She was hoping to have the same success with this new puzzle as they had decoding the gems to open the box initially.

"Unfortunately, that might be the easiest part to solve," Aliyah said. "At least with the letters, we have a couple of ideas to explore and some massive computing power to help. The rest of this is going to take some really creative thinking to solve."

The other squares posed an additional problem. "Any idea what the markings on the rest of the cube mean?" Aliyah asked.

The top square of the flattened cube was engraved much like the center panel directly below it, but instead of a mix of letters, a large triangle was etched onto the upper portion of its surface, with three small squares engraved directly below it running along its base. The left side of the cross was the least detailed of the six. Three wavy horizontal lines stacked upon each other were the only things depicted on the square. The right panel, directly opposite, had a series of shapes cut into its surface, but unlike the Hebrew lettering, which was organized into ten neat rows and columns, the shapes engraved on this panel appeared to be placed in random locations in relation to each other. The two panels didn't seem compatible. The rest of the engravings were just as perplexing.

"I'm afraid this puzzle isn't going to be solved easily or quickly," Daedalus said. "Your Eminence, I'd like your permission to take this with us. There could be additional clues embedded here that will only reveal themselves after we analyze it further." He saw the sympathetic look on Cardinal Mott's face evaporate and harden upon hearing the request.

"Your Holiness, first we must catalogue and protect this treasure," the cardinal said. "How can this be allowed to leave the protection of your vault?"

Uneasy looks passed between the members of the Daedalus crew. They had to take the cube with them regardless of the Vatican's response, but knew they'd never make it out of the subterranean maze if the entire might of the Swiss Guard were deployed to protect Vatican City's most important person.

"What do you suggest we do, Cardinal Mott?" the pope asked. "We gave our word that we would help if they were able to unlock the cube—which they have."

"May I gather some of my cataloguing and photography equipment before we go any further with this?" the cardinal asked respectfully. "I think we can all agree that documenting this rare event is a prudent course of action for everyone. I promise I won't be gone long."

"I think that's a fair solution. Go with God, Cardinal Mott. We can all examine this incredible new discovery further while we await your imminent return." The pope crossed himself once again. Cardinal Mott mirrored the sign, then hurried out of the room. Gryph knew waiting for the cardinal's return would be the most efficient method for them to leave the Vatican grounds with their new puzzle, even if it meant a slight delay.

They weren't making any headway on the cube, so the pope used the opportunity to speak about a few of the more benign items in the collection, passing time until the cardinal returned. He gave no further explanation or comment on the more extreme oddities in the room. Those questions would undoubtedly remain unanswered.

Daedalus was growing more impatient by the minute. This secret vault, while certainly a surprise, paled in comparison to his own collection. He had seen all that he needed to already. It was time to leave and continue their mission. No more stories needed to be shared, no further elucidation from their hosts was required.

"Your Holiness, I would like to thank you again for your graciousness and hospitality," Daedalus said as he stood up. "My colleagues and I must attend to our urgent business and allow you to continue with your important work. I'm sorry that we've taken up so much of your precious time already. It has been a very surreal encounter, to say the least, and has been a great honor for us all. We will send you detailed files on the cube for you to review and will return the artifact once we have completed our mission. Could you please have your guards escort us back to our vehicles?"

"It is I who should be thanking you, signor. The Grail has finally been brought home. We will forever be indebted to you for this kindness. But won't you please stay until Cardinal Mott returns? I'm sure he would like to say goodbye in person before you depart."

Gryph was impressed by the pope before, but his admiration grew by the second. He knew the pontiff was stalling for time until the cardinal returned, but the sincerity and warmth he exhibited to the team seemed genuine, even if he had ulterior motives. *This pope would have made an excellent operative*, Gryph thought. Highly intelligent and an ability to lead and inspire, he could accurately assess a situation and think quickly on his feet. The killing part would probably be an insurmountable issue though. In an alternate reality, maybe…

"I appreciate that, but we really must be going, Your Eminence," Daedalus said. "Cardinal Mott knows where to reach me and why we're in such a hurry. I'm sure he'll understand. Again, I'd like to ask your permission to take the cube with us until we find what we're looking for." The pope's brow furrowed at the thought of losing the artifact forever. The Vatican didn't even have a single picture of the interior markings yet.

Daedalus understood the pope's hesitation. "I've sworn an oath to return the key, and I give you my word that this will be returned here to you as well."

The pope was discouraged that his guests wouldn't stay longer, but he didn't want to press the subject. He didn't doubt that they would return the artifact as promised, and he finally had the Holy Grail. However, he knew the Vatican needed some record of the etchings before they could let the cube out of the vault. Just as he was about to articulate his concern to the group, the problem solved itself.

"Your timing is impeccable, my son," the pontiff said to Cardinal Mott, who just walked back in seemingly empty-handed. The pope reiterated their guest's request to leave as soon as possible, but also his concern about the cube leaving the vault without being documented first.

"I thought you left to get some specialized equipment," Phil asked. It was the first thing he'd said in almost an hour.

"Yes. That was my intent, signor. However, after I left, it dawned on me that it would take a significant amount of time to set up and calibrate the equipment properly. It would be overly burdensome to you and your mission. I turned back after being outside for only a few moments. I apologize for any delay I may have caused you. I think we can take a few simple pictures in the meantime, as you suggested, and will await the return of the original and your tidings of good news."

He slipped a phone out from beneath his black robe and snapped a few quick pictures of each of the panels and a few close-ups of the flattened cube from above. "I think this is all we require for now. A much more detailed examination will be conducted upon its return. May your journey further enlighten us as to its divine secrets." He turned to the Swiss Guard. "Please escort our guests back to their vehicles. Provide a papal escort to the airport as well. They have urgent business to attend to." He grasped Daedalus's hand with both of his. "Goodbye, my friend."

"Goodbye, Cardinal Mott."

The pope stood to bid farewell to his guests. "May the Almighty God bless you all. I will pray for your success."

The Swiss Guard led the Daedalus crew out of the secret vault and back to their cars parked in the secure lot. The fleet of Maybach's were waiting to make the trip back to the airport. Gryph told everyone to hold up before they got too close to the cars. The Swiss Guard remained at the perimeter of the building fifty feet away, safely out of earshot. "Phil, what has you so spooked?"

"There's something off about the cardinal, Commander. I caught him discreetly snapping pictures of us when we first arrived. He continued to take them while we were walking to the papal apartments and then again when we went to the vault."

"Are you sure he was taking pictures of us?" Daedalus asked.

"One hundred percent. I think it took him some time and effort to get a clear shot of each one of us, but I kept my eyes on him the entire time. I clearly saw him sneak a picture of Dallas and Luna as soon as we were getting settled in the vault. I'm not sure if he got mine or not. I tried to stay out of his sightline."

"I've known Cardinal Mott for more than a decade," Daedalus said. "I'm not sure why he would do such a thing."

"I don't know either, but I know what I saw. I'm getting quite good at spotting it too. Just ask Dallas." Everyone knew Phil's sharp eyes had spotted the trench coat guy taking pictures of Dallas inside Luna's café.

"Your friend didn't want us to know he was taking our pictures," Phil said. "That alone is suspicious. It's even more bizarre when it's coming from a senior cardinal inside the Vatican. He's supposed to be a religious scholar, not a spy."

"Okay," Gryph said, as they continued walking toward the waiting vehicles, "everyone stay quiet about all of this until we're back on-board *Hera* and we get a better handle on who—and what—we're dealing with."

Gryph pulled out his phone and relayed instructions to Solo, got a quick reply, and hung up. "We're in priority flight sequence. We'll be able to taxi out as soon as we have a destination."

He took a deep breath, held it for a moment, then exhaled it twice as slowly. A cardinal in the Vatican was spying on them, they had an entirely new puzzle to solve, and the toxin was spreading around the world while they were chasing still their tails. The knot that had been forming in Gryph's gut tightened. He felt their chances of succeeding slipping away.

CHAPTER THIRTY-SIX

Leonardo da Vinci-Fiumicino Airport
February 13, 3:18 p.m. CET

Basileus hadn't left the confines of his Dassault Falcon jet for the last twenty-four hours. It was parked inside a VIP hangar, making it easy to watch the steady stream of aircraft taking off and landing from Italy's largest airport. He'd been eating, sleeping, and directing his illicit operations ever since Dima's contact in New York passed along *Hera's* latest flight plan. His patience finally was rewarded. He'd been able to watch Daedalus's jet touch down in Rome by arriving there hours earlier. He now had *Hera* in his sights from a hangar not even a hundred yards away. A lion crouched in wait.

Basileus was furious when Dima first told him they'd lost Daedalus mid-flight and ordered an immediate retreat to London to regroup. He couldn't believe Daedalus was going to slip through his fingers again. Basileus refused to chase after his quarry like a cat would a mouse, choosing instead to hunt from the shadows. *More akin to a lion stalking its prey*. The Daedalus crew would come right to him, like gazelles in the grass, alert but not yet alarmed. And when they did, he'd pounce.

A few rows in front of his boss, Dima was deep in thought, replaying recent events in his mind. He was anxious to get moving and inflict a world of pain on Daedalus's team. They were the last thing standing in the way of his immortality. He wouldn't rest until he put each and every one of them in the ground. He could still feel the remnants of the adrenaline rush that fired through his body earlier, when his mole at Teterboro reported the news that Daedalus was headed for Rome. It was the sliver of hope he needed. Basileus had the pilot redirect their London-bound jet for Italy while they were still flying over Europe and managed to land in Rome a full eight hours before Daedalus even touched down. They hadn't moved since.

Swarms of blue lights flashed off the corrugated aluminum jetways and the terminal's tinted glass. A symphony of light and sound, all in anticipation of the Boeing Business Jet and its special guests' imminent arrival. Dima knew he wasn't going to get close enough to inflict the damage he'd been salivating over due to the extra security personnel that had descended onto the scene. He figured they'd have to follow the group to wherever they were headed to stage his final assault.

Curiously, just as Dima started gearing up and readying his kill team to follow the passengers and their escort, Basileus instructed Dima to have everyone stand down and stay put while the Daedalus crew simply walked away from their plane. There was no need to follow their targets now. Their destination was obvious. The security contingent that flooded the tarmac to greet them was a dead giveaway.

Basileus explained to Dima, if it was just the city and state police providing the escort, their intended destination would be nearly impossible to determine without following close behind. It was a risky gambit with that large of a security contingent to be sure. The arrival of the Swiss Guard was the red flag—or more accurately, the large, red-plumed hat which gave it away. Their presence meant they were going to one place only. The Vatican.

Basileus knew they only had one chance to strike and trying to intercept them on the way to, or inside Vatican City, wasn't it. He knew that attempting to force their semi-militarized convoy from the road without vehicles and soldiers of their own would be a suicide mission. A full-frontal assault inside the Vatican was even less likely to succeed and would produce the same fatal result. All were non-starters.

Fortunately, he'd correctly discerned where Daedalus was going and knew they'd have to return to the jet sooner than later. The lion would have patience and wait until the troublesome group finished their little errand at the Vatican and left Rome for their next destination. The jet's newest flight plan would be easily available from their sources. They would simply follow close behind, having already fueled the jet for their own immediate departure. Once airborne, Dima would have time to coordinate an advance strike team to join their offensive and ensure no one slipped away this time.

The Russian realized the logic in Basileus's strategy, even if it meant having to keep his emotions in check for a little while longer. The reward in store for him would definitely be worth the wait. He did as he was told and ordered his onboard team to stand down. They didn't seem as bothered by the wait as Dima was, but none of them had the carrot of immortality dangling in front of them either. They were mercenaries who were just looking for the big payday. They didn't care about an extra day or two on the job. This gig was going to set them up for life. Little did they know that the stack of US cash they put their lives on the line for wouldn't be worth the paper it was printed on in the coming weeks—if they even lived long enough to see it.

Dima saw the way the Daedalus crew handled themselves in the café and knew not to underestimate them again. He also knew that most of his men would be killed and would be catching a one-way flight home in the cargo hold, zipped up inside a leak-proof vinyl body bag. The handful who made it back alive would be dead within a year anyway. None of that mattered to him. As long as he made it back and Daedalus was dead, the losses were acceptable. The birthing pains of a new world order.

Basileus retired to his private bedroom and left instructions to be notified immediately when there was any new activity around Daedalus's plane. If they lost him again, everyone's heads would roll. The rest of the men treated the next few hours like an extended coffee break. Some engaged in idle chitchat, a few of them bragged about their previous experiences and exploits. The embellishment was being laid on thick. Others just had a bite to eat and nodded off. Eat when you can, sleep when you can. Some rules were universal.

It was after 3:00 p.m. when the procession of blue lights returned to *Hera*. The motorcade snaked across the tarmac, halting traffic, both ground and air, until the parade stopped at the base of the jet. A light drizzle had been falling on and off for the last hour. Rivulets of precipitation trickled down the windows, distorting the detail of the arriving passengers.

Dima jumped up from the wide leather seat he was sitting on as soon as he saw the blue strobes flash through the windows and ran toward Basileus's suite, slowing mid-stride at the sight of his boss already making his way back from his room. Dima was afraid Basileus would think he hadn't notified him quickly enough, and he braced for the onslaught, but before he could profess his innocence, Basileus spoke. "I saw the lights just now, as well. The chase begins anew."

Dima spun on his heel, thankful to avoid another incident, and headed back to the center of the plane to join his men. "I've already put a call in to get their flight plan. We'll have it before they take off, sir."

"That's alright, Dima, I already know where they're headed. The captain has already filed our flight plan to Tel Aviv, with instructions to depart immediately after their plane." Basileus pointed out the window at the massive fuselage, still bathed in flashing blue lights. Fluorescent-striped workers scurried like mice below, attending to tasks facilitating an imminent departure.

"How do you know where they're going? They haven't even filed the paperwork yet." It never ceased to amaze Dima how his boss was always two steps ahead of everyone.

"It was just as I figured when I saw the Swiss guard. Their destination was the Vatican. What I didn't anticipate was their private audience with the pope. They apparently bartered their way into the archives with a unique artifact in exchange for some information. It seems that newfound information is now sending them to Israel."

"I don't understand. How do you know those details, sir." Dima was more confused than ever.

"I was briefed by a cardinal who sits on the high council of our Brotherhood. His identity hadn't been revealed except to a select few. He came to me after reading your report on the original attack on Daedalus's team in the field. The cardinal recognized Daedalus's unusual name immediately." Basileus paused and smirked. He was the proverbial pot calling the kettle black. "This was the first time we learned that our secret test sites weren't such a secret anymore. It was pure coincidence that the cardinal was already an acquaintance of Daedalus. Only since he meddled in our affairs were we even aware of his existence. It's fate that our paths have intersected in this way."

Dima was sure the little tidbit of information the cardinal delivered had bought him a ticket to immortality, too.

"Cardinal Mott called me an hour ago," Basileus said. "He snuck away briefly from the group to inform me of their intended destination. He'll call me back for details once we're underway."

As if on cue, a fleet of Maybach's came into view and rolled to a stop at the base of Daedalus's jet. Security vehicles flanked all sides of the incoming convoy. Basileus watched his enemies exit the luxury cars through a pair of high-powered Zeiss Victory binoculars. He needed to see Daedalus up close and personal.

Instead of faces emerging from the car, he saw flashes of bright reds, yellows, and white explode around the vehicles as soon as the doors were opened. A gaggle of multicolored umbrellas sprang to life, covering the occupants from the moment they stepped out onto the tarmac. From his elevated position, the only thing Basileus could see clearly were the tops of the annoying umbrellas. Based on the number of canopies, he calculated there were six or seven people at most. *A very manageable number indeed*, he thought.

Basileus watched the procession make their way to the steps leading to the jetway. The first man to climb the steep staircase must have been the new soldier they recently brought in. He was carrying a black case in one hand and an umbrella that barely covered his massive frame in the other. He was huge, just as Dima had described. While Basileus couldn't see his face, he wouldn't need it to recognize him again; his imposing size made him an unforgettable figure.

The features on the next person up the staircase were similarly obscured. At first, all Basileus could see was a mane of long black hair whipping wildly from under a white-and-yellow umbrella, Vatican state colors. But fate decided to smile on him once more. The umbrella was suddenly lowered and retracted into its smallest compact shape. The man bounded up the steps, and Basileus finally had a clear look at one of them. Unfortunately, the only other memorable features, other than his long hair, were the dark sunglasses he wore and the black case he was carrying, which looked identical to the one the giant man had just brought onboard.

Next up the stairs was a man and a woman under the protection of a single red umbrella. The couple was unremarkable, other than they fit the description of the hacker and the woman from the internet café to a T.

"Sir, what are we going to do when we land?" Dima asked, interrupting the surveillance operation. "Do we have any weapons or vehicles that'll be available to us in Israel?"

Basileus pulled back from the window, pinched the bridge of his nose, and sighed. "Can't you see that I'm trying to watch them? Your questions can wait. But yes, I have contacts in East Jerusalem who will provide both. Now be quiet." Dima dropped his gaze to the floor and shrank back into his seat.

Frustrated by the interruption, he turned back to the window. He blinked away the dryness in his eyes and peered through the binoculars again. As the steps came into focus, he caught a fleeting glimpse of a woman exiting the platform into the jetway. He was about to express his extreme displeasure with Dima for distracting him from getting a good look at her when he noticed the cars below *Hera* begin to pull away. The last two people were on the way up the stairs together. Unfortunately, they too were both hidden under a single large umbrella. Basileus panned all the way to the top of the stairs before the duo got there and steadied his gaze, waiting for them to appear in his field of view.

One of those two people would be the infamous Daedalus. None of the other individuals he'd seen so far fit the bill. He wasn't sure how he would determine which of the two was Daedalus until the first man reached the door. The one holding the umbrella collapsed the canopy and shook the rain off the fabric before bringing it onboard.

Umbrellas are held aloft for leaders, not the other way around, Basileus thought. That answered the question as to which one of them was Daedalus. Curiously, the two men paused at the top of the platform, neither making a move to enter the jet. Their backs were both turned to him and Basileus had a sinking feeling that Daedalus would slip inside while remaining concealed, proving his elusiveness once more.

The sinking feeling in his gut morphed into a fit of terror when the man holding the umbrella walked into the massive jet, leaving

Daedalus exposed against the wind and rain at the top of the elevated platform. He watched Daedalus take a few deep breaths before boarding. Basileus had a picture-perfect view of Daedalus and kept his eyes fixed on the man until he vanished through the door of his flying palace.

Basileus dropped the binoculars to the floor and felt the blood drain from his head. If he weren't sitting down, he would have fallen over. Dima noticed the sudden loss of color on his boss's face and rushed over to him. Basileus didn't even notice Dima approach. "Sir, are you okay? You don't look well. Can I get you something?"

Basileus's lips opened and closed but emitted no sound, like a fish out of water gasping for air that would never come. His eyes were fixed and cast downward, remembering faces and events from long ago.

"Basileus, should I get a doctor? I think you might be having a stroke."

"It can't be." his voice a hollow whisper.

"What happened? What should I tell the pilot to do?" Dima didn't want to make a mistake if there had been a new development and endure his wrath yet again.

Basileus just sat there, dazed and confused. The entire world shifted beneath his feet. He could see Dima talking to him, but couldn't hear anything except a high-pitched droning. A headache exploded behind his eyes, likely brought on by the effects of the vertigo he was feeling.

Hid boss stood up and tried to shake the confusion from his head. "I'll be in my room, Dima." He took a few tentative steps toward his suite, then stopped. "Instruct the pilot to follow them as planned. We've already been granted clearance to leave right behind their jet."

Without further explanation, he turned and walked into his suite, leaving the door slightly ajar. Basileus leaned his head on the wall beside the door and took a deep breath. A cold bead of sweat trickled down his back. Why did this have to happen to him now? He couldn't allow this to derail the plans already set in motion. He already knew they would have to keep a close watch on Daedalus for them to be victorious, but now his world had flipped upside down and inside out. Basileus had a disconcerting feeling that they were the ones now being hunted.

Dima was worried about leaving his boss alone. He'd never seen even a moment of weakness in Basileus's countenance before. "Are you sure you're okay?" Dima asked through the partially open door. "You look like you just saw a ghost."

Basileus pushed off the wall and opened the door fully, putting himself face to face with his trusted bodyguard. "You know what, Dima? I think I just may have."

He closed the door, sloshed an obscene amount of forty-year Macallan into a crystal glass, and poured it down his throat. The amber liquid burned on the way down, but did nothing to thaw the icy fear that was now coursing through his body.

CHAPTER THIRTY-SEVEN

Leonardo da Vinci-Fiumicino Airport
February 13, 6:27 p.m. CET

As soon as the cabin door closed behind Daedalus, the boarding process was complete. Their request for an expedited departure had been granted, the Vatican having seen to their VIP status. There were only two Alitalia flights ahead of them in the queue. A pair of Airbus A330 aircraft, with their distinctive green-and-red tail liveries, were already rolling out to their assigned runways. Solo steered behind the parade of jumbo jets, watching each of the aircraft take their turn racing down the long strip of asphalt, gaining enough speed to launch their hulking mass into the air.

"We're up next," Solo's voice rang out over the intercom system. "Grab a seat if you haven't already." *Hera's* quad GEnx-2B engines roared to life as they hurtled down the runway approaching V1 speed, also known as the "commit to fly" speed. Seconds later, the nose of the Boeing Business Jet reached skyward and on to their next destination.

Dallas had his palms down on the large, lacquered table everyone had once again gathered around. Exasperation tinged his voice. "How is this cryptic box supposed to lead us to a hidden location that has the stuff we're looking for?" Another puzzle to solve. Another location to infiltrate. The wild goose chase seemed to have no end.

Gryph's response was measured and calm. "There are a few things we need to work on to figure that out, Dallas. Remember, this puzzle was meant to be solved, and we're all going to work together to figure it out. Just like we've done before. We'll keep solving problems until there are no more left to solve. This is the literal end of the world if we don't succeed. There are no alternatives here."

Daedalus nodded in agreement. "I wholeheartedly agree, Commander. I'm very thankful the Vatican doesn't actually know our intended destination, for now." For the first time since the start of the mission, Daedalus hadn't retreated to his private room when they got back onboard *Hera*. As soon as the cabin door closed behind them, Gryph and company had convened around the large conference table in the living area to discuss next steps, and for once Daedalus joined them without delay.

"Well, I've only had a little bit of time to examine this," Gryph said, gesturing to the golden cube, which was now flattened across the polished table, "but there are a few things that jumped out at me right away."

"Uh… question." Luna raised her hand. "Why are we thankful that we've kept the destination secret from the Vatican 'for now?'"

"Because we'll need a head start to find the hidden Temple treasures and recover the manna for our antidote," Gryph said. "Then we just have to wait."

"Wait for what exactly?" she asked.

"For Basileus and his men to come to us." There was a menace behind Gryph's look that Luna hadn't seen before. Devoid of feeling or compassion. Like a shark. She was certain Gryph and the other apex killing machine shared the same primal instinct. It made the hairs on her arms stand on end.

"I know we still need to get back to the puzzle issues, but I'm totally lost now," Dallas said, always feeling two steps behind. "Gryph, explain to me what the Vatican and Basileus have to do with each other again?"

"I'm pretty sure Cardinal Mott is bent. He either works for Basileus, or they're somehow forcing him to betray us. Daedalus thinks it's the latter, but either way it doesn't matter. We've been compromised."

"How did you find out… Wait. Why do you think the cardinal is working with Basileus?" Dallas had a whole slew of new questions that were all competing to be the first out of his mouth.

Daedalus answered this time. "Divine providence. Fate. Luck. Whatever you want to call it. The real tipoff was courtesy of our own Captain Daniels. He'd been in contact with the control tower, providing periodic updates on our timeline while we were at the Vatican to ensure we didn't lose our priority departure status. I called him as soon as we drove away from the Vatican to let him know we were on the way to the airport. That's when he relayed a very concerning message back to me. He told me that he'd radioed the control tower to inform them we'd be departing within the next hour. The tower confirmed his request and then serendipitously added, '*our friends would also be granted clearance to take off right after us, as they had requested earlier.*'"

"What friends?" Phil asked.

"That's what Captain Daniels wanted to know as well. The tower provided him with the tail number for the other jet. He thanked them for the courtesy toward our *friends*. Since then, I've made a few quick inquiries of my own. I tried tracking the jet's registration, but it's registered to an offshore company that, unfortunately, proved to be untraceable. It was just a shell company owned by another shell company and so on, like a Russian nesting doll. With enough time, I would get to the eventual owner, however, Captain Daniels was able to obtain their recent previous departure and arrival locations from their registration number. It was this worrisome bit of information that proved both useful and chilling."

Chief leaned in. "Okay, I can think of a bunch of reasons why their previous takeoff and landing info would be useful to us, but I'm not sure why you're worried."

It became obvious to all that Daedalus and Gryph were working on this problem during the drive back, because Gryph answered for Daedalus.

"It's concerning because they've been shadowing our flight path for the past week. There was a slight deviation a couple days ago, but I think they may have been caught off-guard by one of our surprise departures. They've been playing catch-up for a bit but have otherwise been our shadow. It's likely why they put in a standing order with air traffic control to follow us out of Rome. They couldn't afford to have us slip away unannounced again. Flight records show that they were already parked on the ground waiting for us when we landed in Rome. They knew when and where we were going to be ahead of time."

"Wait! They're following us right now?" Dallas shot a panicked glance toward the back of *Hera*, as if it had a big rear window he could see through.

"I would hope so," Chief said. "It'll make it a hell of a lot easier for us to kill 'em. I'm tired of chasing these clowns." He got a few odd looks, but couldn't care less.

"Gryph, you said they were on the ground already when we landed in Rome," Phil said, still trying to piece this together. "I don't understand how they beat us here if they were supposed to be following us."

"I believe that's where our Cardinal Mott comes into play. I think the covert pictures you saw him take of us were sent to Basileus when the cardinal stepped away from the vault to get his equipment and came back empty-handed. Whether he wanted confirmation it was us, or he was seeing us for the first time, I'm not sure. But Daedalus made sure they got a good look at him before we boarded. There's no mistaking us now. He basically dared them to follow."

Phil shook his head. "I still don't see how that got them here ahead of us."

"Cardinal Mott was the only person who knew I was coming to Rome ahead of time," Daedalus said. "I believe the cardinal notified Basileus that I would be coming to the Vatican to meet him. As soon as they were tipped off, Basileus and his henchman flew to Rome to lie in wait for us."

Gryph could see the previous events tumbling around, his mind piecing them together until a clearer picture emerged. "We were already back in New York while they were trying to catch up to us from Israel. After they lost track of us, they headed back to their home base in London, but picked up our scent once again." Before anyone had a chance to ask how he knew that, Gryph continued. "The tail number flight records we requested also showed all of their flights originated and terminated at a private terminal outside of London."

Everyone let that sink in. Gryph wondered if they'd been under watch this entire time or had they stayed a step ahead by sheer blind luck. Either way, he wasn't in control of the situation, and that wasn't something that happened to him often, but it was something he was certainly going to remedy.

"I realize we need a plan to deal with Basileus and his goons when we land," Aliyah said, "but we need to figure out where this puzzle is sending us first, and that's not going to be easy." Everyone had been so engrossed in the conversations about Basileus that they were oblivious to the fact that Aliyah's eyes hadn't left the golden riddle on the table.

Everyone quieted down, their collective attention fully on the golden cube they had been chasing down, via one puzzle after another, for the better part of a week.

"I've already had a good look at it," Gryph said to Ali. He only needed to see the puzzle once. "Tell me what you see." Commander Oake was already formulating a theory as to where the cube was leading them to.

She centered the puzzle in front of her and began to describe it in clinical detail, not unlike conducting a post-mortem on a cadaver. "This puzzle seems to be made from solid gold, just like the menorah and the key. Now that it's laid flat, it looks like a golden cross. It's been unfolded into a row of four squares vertically bisected by a row of three squares across."

She pointed to the golden square at the top of the long row. Everyone shuffled tight for a closer look. "An equilateral triangle has been carved into the top square with three smaller squares etched right underneath it. If you look really closely, each point of the triangle has a different shape etched beside it. Moving down one square, we have what Phil called his ancient *word jumble*. It looks just like it sounds. A ten-by-ten grid of Hebrew letters that make no sense. Below that, the third panel contains only random shapes in random places, each with a small golden protrusion projecting approximately five millimeters from the surface. The upper right panel is similar to this one and also features the little protrusions. The panels with shapes don't seem to line up directly with the word jumble square either. It's like they're part of a different puzzle."

She paused while she let that thought roll around in her head, allowing it to gain a little more traction. Then she pointed to the panel closest to her. "The bottom square has a line etched down its center from top to bottom, bisecting the square in two halves. A series of five hash marks run down the middle of each side, ten in total. And finally,"—Aliyah took a deep breath, reaching the end of her summation— "the top left square has three wavy lines on top of each other, stacked closely, all located near the bottom of the panel." Everyone was now on the same page and had a clear idea of what they needed to decipher. Unfortunately, no one seemed to have the slightest idea what it meant or how to solve it. Aliyah sat back, ran her fingers through her hair, and shrugged.

"Well, that sounds a little past *what the fuck* to me." Dallas was once again angry and dejected.

Luna glared at Dallas and shook her head in disappointment. "Like Gryph explained to us before," she said, "we solve problems until there are none left to solve. Let's just focus on the puzzle."

Gryph gave a respectful nod to Luna. Without her assistance, Dallas would have been unmanageable. "Ali, do any of these markings or letter sequences mean anything to you?"

She studied the complex puzzle and ran her fingers over the surface of each face of the cube. "Nothing jumps out at me yet. You?"

Gryph smiled. "You really don't see it?"

"Whatcha putting together there, boss?" Chief asked.

"We've done a lot of the problem solving together already. Admittedly, the word jumble is a new wrinkle, but I think I see where this is pointing us. However..."

"Why is there always a 'but' or 'however' when we're about to get good news?" The anger in Dallas's voice had faded, replaced by juvenile whining.

Gryph wasn't sure which one of the two he hated more, the shouting or the whining, as usual, he chose to ignore both.

"*However,* I'm sure we'll need to solve the word jumble to pinpoint exactly where we need to go. My guess is that once solved, it'll point us to the Ark's location."

"You seem to have noticed something that we're missing, Commander," Aliyah said, half smirking, her brow still furrowed with deep lines of concentration. "Care to enlighten the rest of us?"

"I think the box that we found the menorah in, and this golden cube have a lot in common," Gryph said. "The symbolism and the orientation are really the same clue all over again, which makes perfect sense. If someone was fortunate enough to possess all three pieces to the puzzle—the menorah, the key, and the cube—then the solution for one would be intuitive as a solution for them all. Quite ingenious if you ask me, because if someone were to stumble across just one of the puzzles by chance or theft, it would lead them nowhere. With that reasoning, I think Ali was correct in deducing that the panel with the image of the triangle is the top of this map."

Dallas threw his hand in the air in exasperation. "You just called it a map! How do you know it's a map if we don't even know how to read any of it yet?" Luna shot him another annoyed look. He put his hands up in mock surrender and fell back into subdued silence.

"We may not be able to read it yet," Gryph said, pointing to the top square, "but let's assume for a moment that the meaning of the triangle is the same as it was on the box from the menorah."

"The triangle again?" Aliyah asked. "There's no inverted cross under it this time, only these three small boxes. I'm not sure what that's supposed to symbolize though. What do you think it means this time around?"

Luna, who was fully engrossed in the puzzle, interjected. "Does anyone have thoughts on what the panels with shapes are for, or how to unscramble the word jumble? They must be part of the key to solving the puzzle. They wouldn't be placed here randomly."

Gryph jolted upright in his chair. "What did you just say?"

"What? That they wouldn't be there randomly?"

"No. Before that."

"That they must be part of the key to solving the puzzle?" She spoke haltingly, growing more confused by the syllable.

"Yes! That's it. Luna, you're brilliant." Gryph jumped up from his seat. "It's a good thing you kept that key with you. I had a hunch we were going to need it." He extended his hand toward Daedalus, who fished the key out of his pocket and placed it in Gryph's palm.

"I think this key is the key to solving our puzzle—pun intend-ed." Gryph waited for a response to his corny joke and realized he was the only one who understood it. "Nevermind. It'll make sense in a minute."

He took his seat and pulled the unfurled cube across the table toward him. "I've studied the pictures of the key and noticed little

holes bored out below each of the jewels on the spine. The significance of which I had previously overlooked."

"What do you mean?" Aliyah asked.

"The holes on the key serve a purpose other than being decora-
tive. Gryph rotated the key to line up one of the shapes engraved on
its shaft with the corresponding shape on the corners of the triangle
located on the upper panel. "Notice how the end of the key finishes
at a point." Gryph moved the key into the final position. "When the
key, triangle and the center panel below are all aligned…"

"The key points directly to a letter on the word jumble!" Luna
exclaimed.

Gryph placed the key on another corner of the triangle and let
the other end of the key swing freely toward the word jumble below until it came to rest on another single letter in the word jumble.
He repeated the procedure for the last angle until three Hebrew
letters were assigned to the three boxes etched directly below.

"Incredible." Aliyah was stunned. "Absolutely incredible. The
Hebrew letters the key points to are Aleph, Vet, and Nun. Together they spell Ehven in Hebrew. It means stone." Aliyah looked at
Gryph and rolled her eyes. "I get the pun now. 'The key is the key
to solving our puzzle.' Your coffee is much better than your jokes."

Gryph smiled, feeling the momentum shift back toward them.
"It's confirmation enough for me that the key is used to read the
map. And since we know the key seems to connect shapes to letters, we just need to line up the key over the word jumble, and see
what we can decipher."

"You think the solution to the puzzle might lead us directly to
the stone?" Ali asked excitedly.

"No!" Luna gasped and clamped her hands over her mouth, her
eyes wide above her fingers.

"You're talking about *that* stone, aren't you?"

Dallas was watching the back and forth like a tennis match.
"Can one of you armchair geologists tell us what the hell you're
talking about?"

"They mean the Foundation Stone," Luna said.

Dallas sighed deeply. "Okay. I guess I'm the only dummy here.
What is that, and where are we supposed to find it?"

"The Foundation Stone was what the Ark of the Covenant rested on inside the Jewish temples, it's currently centered under a seventy-foot-tall dome constructed of gold-leaf-covered lead known as the Temple Mount, the Dome of the Rock, the Noble Sanctuary and more. It's written in other Jewish texts that it was the first piece of land to emerge from the seas when God created dry land in the story of Genesis. It is also the rock where the biblical Abraham was prepared to sacrifice his son and the same spot where his grandson, Jacob, wrestled with an angel after watching them ascend and descend from heaven on a ladder. Islamic teachings explain that their Prophet Mohammed ascended to paradise from that exact location, too. It's one of the holiest sites on Earth for many religions because of its prodigious history." When Luna finished, she noticed everyone's eyes were on her.

Chief nodded. "That's pretty impressive. Not gonna lie."

"Our Bible camp went to Israel on a prayer trip when I was seventeen," she said. "I tend to remember facts and figures. They just sort of file themselves away in my head after I hear them. Anyway, I was fascinated by the beauty of the dome and the significance of what lay below it and wondered how all religions preach peace and love but choose to fight one another instead. How'd they get it so terribly wrong?"

"Take it from me, Luna, and I've seen a lot in my life," Daedalus said. "It's not religion. Many people use religion as a scapegoat for much of the suffering in the world. But the truth is much simpler— it's us. People have weaponized religion as an excuse for all manner of evil. But if it wasn't religion, we would have utilized something else. Conquest and envy are tightly woven into our DNA. Many wars have been fought over land, resources, food, power, and even advantageous military positions. These have nothing to do with religion. Righteousness may have provided the excuse and the context they needed, but a person's belief in God is rarely the real cause, contrary to some opinions."

"Thanks for the sociology lesson. How exactly does that help us?" Dallas didn't need a civics lecture right now.

"It doesn't, Mr. Hayle. Except as a reminder that people are capable of doing terrible things to each other for no reason other than it suits them at the time. We shouldn't lose sight of the evil we're fighting here or the catastrophic trouble we would incite by damaging any of these holy sites, especially the Dome on the Rock. If that, in fact, turns out to be where we're headed."

"Okay, we're getting way off track here," Gryph said. "No one is talking about damaging anything. Let's work through the rest of this puzzle. We can do this if we just focus and work the problem. As cliché as it sounds, it works. Leave the speculation for another time."

Aliyah had been listening to the discussions, but her eyes hadn't left the cube. "You know, looking at this from the paradigm of it being a map, I think I can see what Gryph is getting at now. This could be a symbolic representation for a path to the Ark."

Phil's eyes widened in shock. "Ali, a minute ago you were stumped. Now you seem to be able to read the map. What makes you so sure?" He didn't sound doubtful, just bewildered by the sudden change.

"I simply took a step back from it. If you look at it as one whole message instead of multiple intricate puzzles, the simplicity of it kind of jumps out at you. I had to make a few big assumptions, but it seems to fit." She saw Phil and Dallas were waiting for her to expound on what she had worked out. Gryph motioned for her to continue, certain she was on the same path he was.

"I know I just described it in detail before, but simplified, I see the triangle equating the rock or Foundation Stone. The bottom panel looks like it represents the Ten Commandments. Two stones split in two. Five inscriptions per side depicted by the hash marks. Five commandments per side."

"Weren't the tablets rounded at the top though?" Luna asked. "These are perfect rectangles. Wouldn't they carve them into the right shape if they were truly representing the Ten Commandments? Are you sure that's what it's supposed to mean?"

"It's a common misconception that they were round. Similarly with the original menorah. Its arms are often shown as rounded, not angled like the one we uncovered. According to the Torah, the tablets fit into the Ark perfectly. There were no gaps from rounded tops. If this map is the real deal, the person who left it for us would have known they were squared off, not round. I know it requires a leap of faith, but it fits. Literally."

"What about the wavy lines?" Daedalus asked.

"I'm not entirely sure, but I think those could depict a water source. Maybe coming in from that side, again only taking this at its most simplistic face value," Aliyah said.

"I agree with everything you've said so far," Gryph said, "but I don't think it necessarily depicts a *source* of water. I think it may be the opposite. Maybe a drain or sewer trough of some kind."

"It's true that it could just as easily flow outward. What makes you think it's a drain and not a supply though?"

"The Temple was situated on a hill. As you know, it's referred to as the Temple Mount. Any water brought to the site would have to be carried in. It wouldn't be gravity fed, as it was the high ground. The wastewater from the site would easily flow downhill from the elevated position and out through a drain. We need to see if we can find any records that would indicate there was something like that in place two thousand years ago. That may not be so easy."

Luna was typing furiously into her phone while Gryph was talking. Just as he finished speaking, she broke in. "I did a quick Google search and found out that there was, in fact, a drain shaft that exited from the west side of the Temple. It says here that the opening was about two feet square and was accessed once every seventy years to clean out the blood and grime from the temple sacrifices. It doesn't say exactly where it ended up in the Temple or where it emptied out to though."

"Well, at least that fits our narrative somewhat," Gryph said. "We've already identified the Foundation Stone and the drain culvert to its left on the puzzle, and of course, the Ten Commandments below. We're making good progress now. Keep going."

It didn't take long for them to work the key around the shapes on the side panels, convert them to letters and then to words. When they were finished, they sat back, awestruck.

"Well, that's about as X marks the spot as we're going to get," Daedalus said. "Ali, I think we're going to need to call in some favors."

Finally, they had a location. Now all they needed was a plan.

CHAPTER THIRTY-EIGHT

Ben Gurion Airport
February 13, 8:08 p.m. Israel Standard Time (IST)

The team made short work of converting shapes to letters and letters into their next clue on the flight over to Israel from Rome. The cryptic solution implied that an access point to the treasure room was hidden far below the Foundation Stone, with access gained via an ancient drain system. Where exactly they would find that drain was anyone's guess, but some kind of plan was better than no plan at all.

Luna was able to refine her search for their sought-after drain and came up with a bit of good news quite quickly. "This is fascinating. You guys should really read it sometime." She looked up to see a few *"That's great, but can you get on with it?"* stares, so she did. "There was a complex system of cisterns and pools all connected via common drainage canals cut out or carved into the walls of the ancient city of Jerusalem deep underground. You can still walk through large parts of it today on a variety of historical walking tours. It says here that many of the ancient openings were sealed up with rock and plaster thousands of years ago, having long since gone dry. Take a look at this. A picture's worth a thousand words."

She flipped her screen toward her new friends, revealing images from a website about an Israeli tour company specializing in Old City and Western Wall tunnel tours. The pictures showed men and women of all ages and sizes decked out in freshly ironed jeans and sensible shoes making their way through what looked like a maze of narrow, stone hallways. The flattened stones, Luna explained, had been previously submerged and were now polished smooth after thousands of years and millions of gallons of water flowing over them.

"That's just great!" Dallas said. He was growing more bitter about this never-ending mission by the minute. "What are we supposed to do with that? It's at least a hundred yards of identical looking rock in either direction." Luna ignored him and continued scrolling through the images on the website.

"No, not identical," Gryph said. "Flip back a few pictures."

She swiped right a few times until Gryph stopped her. "Right there. That's it!" Her screen was frozen on an image of three women standing in front of a section of underground wall that had been filled with stone and was oriented much differently than the others. "Why's that section of wall so special that they thought to include it on the website?" Gryph asked.

"The caption says that spot is the closest you can get to the Holy of Holies from the Western Wall. It's still quite far away, but it's directly across from the room where the Ark of the Covenant was located in the temples. It looks like a passageway that was already filled in, but there were dozens that crisscrossed all throughout the Temple Mount and down toward its ancient perimeter walls. The Western Wall being the most intact and well preserved of them all."

"Luna, can you find any pictures that show another aqueduct that may have been sealed up or filled in?"

"Let me check." Luna sat down and went to work on her digital expedition.

"Ali, can you make a few calls to your friends at Mossad and get us some private time in the tunnels tonight?" Gryph asked. "We won't be there until late, and while I doubt we'll have to contend with any tour groups, we don't want to be stopped by the police or IDF while we work. I'd rather not utilize any of my new contacts for this. Who knows how many moles Basileus may have planted. Your requests will be just as effective and will keep us off Basileus's radar."

Aliyah stole a glance at her iWatch, thankful its time zones automatically adjusted for their crazy travel schedule. "No problem. It's almost half-past eight now. I'll make a call and tell them to expect us just after eleven tonight. That'll give us enough time to gear up and drive over. I'm sure it won't be a problem having the place to ourselves until just before sunrise, but no longer than that. The morning prayer sessions begin for Jews and Muslims at that time. We need to be in and out of there before then, no matter what, or our cover will be blown, and all hell could break loose."

"We'll have to make sunrise work then. Call in the favor."

She walked over to a seat by the window where there was less background conversation and embarked on coordinating that night's security clearances.

As Aliyah made her call, Luna told the others what she had found online. "Looks like you were right, Gryph. Cisterns were constructed all along the Western Wall that utilized the stone footings as integral parts of their construction. The Jerusalem we see now was built right over the top of the ancient one, with pieces of the old still poking through in spots. Anyway, it says these cisterns were fed by the Gihon Spring, which was also known as Saint Mary's Pool. It was the major water source for the area and one of the reasons Jerusalem was populated originally. A large reliable source of water in the desert made it a very hospitable place to pitch your tent, so to speak."

"Does it say anything about the drain we need to find?" Dallas asked, his impatience growing in his tone.

Luna gave him a side-eye glare. "I was just getting to that." She was getting really tired of his attitude and was going to let him know it as soon as they were alone. "Fortunately for us," she said, "quite a few tunnels and passageways have been discovered and mapped out over the last decade or so. Most of them seem to be too far from our location to qualify, but a few lead straight from the Western Wall toward the Temple Mount, and one in particular looks like it could be a winner."

Luna tapped her phone's screen a couple times and brought forward the information she had dug up earlier. "In 1867, an early explorer named Charles Warren discovered something within the Temple Mount area that he called the Blood Channel."

She switched images again and expanded an annotated drawing of the Temple Mount compound to the full size of her phone's screen. "He hypothesized that the blood and gore from the daily sacrifices that were made at the Temple went down a drain at the base of the altar, then traveled through this Blood Channel and merged with others before it flowed out beneath Robinson's Arch on the far west side of the Temple Mount. Look here on my phone." Luna zoomed in even closer on the image. "This Blood Channel runs parallel to the temple, never beneath it. That makes sense since the sacrifices were made in the courtyard of the Temple complex, not in the Temple itself. I'm not sure how we get beneath the foundation stone, seeing as the drain never crosses under it, but it gets us nearby. I'm not seeing anything else that would lead any closer to the Temple Mount than this."

"There must be some physical connection between the Blood Channel and the Temple's treasure room," Gryph said. "We have between now and before sunrise to find it. We'll split up when we get inside the Blood Channel to look for any—"

"Sorry, that won't work," Luna said before Gryph got too far ahead of himself. "One source online says that the Blood Channel opening was less than two-foot-square. Another source that backs up that claim stated that only small children were sent inside to clean it out because adults couldn't fit. Besides, we don't even know if the channel is intact the entire way. Any portion of it could have caved in or been sealed shut a long time ago."

Gryph thought for a moment. "You know what, Luna? The solution for that issue actually resolves another problem I was wrestling with earlier."

"That's great because I was thinking we were up shit creek. Care to share?" Dallas asked.

"Nanobots." After speaking his simple one-word reply, Gryph saw a light flicker behind everyone's eyes. While the team may not have had a crystal-clear idea as to how Gryph envisioned the bots being utilized, they knew the technology and solutions provided by the invisible army would only be limited by their imaginations.

"That's brilliant!" Daedalus immediately saw the benefit of using his micro-creations for the task. "I've used the bots for search and recovery purposes previously. Dallas, Luna, and I can start modifying the program for the tasks that lay ahead."

Gryph stood up. "Chief, you, and Phil need to put together the firepower we'll need when we run into Basileus and his thugs. And don't pack lightly. If they show up, they don't leave. Got it?"

A mischievous grin spread across Chief's face. "You know me, boss. I'm the type to bring a grenade to a knife fight. I brought a bunch of cool toys from the Workshop that I've been itching to try outside of the test range. Phil and I will make sure we have enough firepower to send them straight to hell. Twice over."

Gryph laughed. "One is none and two is one."

"Amen, brother," Chief said as he and Phil left to assemble their deadly arsenal.

A couple of hours later, Gryph noticed the blue lights from their IDF escort through the windows long before the vehicles arrived at the base of the jetway stairs leading up to *Hera*.

"Time to put this plan into motion," he said. "Our ride just showed up. Let's get moving." The Daedalus crew packed up everything they felt they would need for this last stretch of the mission, deposited it into the Ze'ev armored vehicles parked near the nose of their plane, quickly piled inside before racing out into the cool desert night.

***

A pair of binoculars in the control tower were trained on the stairs that led from the hulking business jet to the militarized convoy below. The set of eyes behind the field glasses counted seven bodies as they made their way down to their vehicles. They were all carrying heavy bags and tactical cases. Wherever they were going, they weren't traveling light.

The phone in Basileus's pocket chirped and vibrated, announcing an incoming call. He pressed the screen to accept, then placed the phone to his ear. It took a moment for the caller to realize his call had been answered.

"Eh, yes, shalom. Hello. This is Yuval from Ben Gurion airport." The heavily accented Israeli voice was slightly muffled. "I was told to call this number when a 'special jet' landed here, and it landed a couple minutes ago. The passengers just left the plane and drove away in IDF cars and battle trucks."

Basileus said nothing, then disconnected the line. He was watching the same scene unfold from the window of the Dassault Falcon. His own jet, having landed only moments before, had been directed to the same VIP terminal as *Hera*. They made it to their gate just in time to see the cabin door to the Boeing jet open and its passengers spill out. "Dima, get your men and your guns. Tonight, we go hunting."

Dima flashed a wicked grin, revealing a set of tobacco-stained choppers. "We'll kill them all this time, Basileus. I promise. We'll show no mercy." The stone-cold looks on the mercenaries lent credence to the bodyguard's prediction.

"I would expect nothing less. I've arranged transportation for us," Basileus said. "It'll be here soon."

Dima wasn't sure why they weren't in more of a rush to get off the Falcon. "Basileus, how are we going to track them from here if they're already driving off with the Israeli police?"

"I have people posted at the airport exit watching for their convoy to drive by. They'll follow them and tell us where we need to go. This allows us to keep a safe distance and the element of surprise."

Dima was concerned to hear that Basileus had other operatives in play who weren't known to him, and it must have shown.

"Dima, do you really think that I would leave everything up to you and not take matters into my own hands? This project is far too important." Dima could feel his men's eyes boring holes into the back of his head. Such an insult normally elicited a quick and violent response from the Russian. His lack of action showed the level of fear and respect he had for his boss.

Basileus fished his phone from his pocket and read a message he'd just received. "Our transportation will be here in five minutes."

"That was very smart, sir. I'll make sure we're ready when you give the word to move out." Dima wasn't going to let his ego mess up his chance at immortality. He was too close to his goal, but was seething inside. He was supposed to be the man in charge. He had earned that position of trust, and Basileus had promised him acceptance into the Brotherhood. Now some other asshole was trying to worm his way into Basileus's good book. Dima wasn't okay with that. Not by a long shot.

Basileus looked over Dima's shoulder at the team his bodyguard assembled. Scars, sneers, and everything sinister stared back.

"There are seven of them," Basileus said. "When you find them, kill them where they stand, then bring me their heads."

A few strange looks were exchanged. Some of the mercs laughed nervously amongst themselves until they realized he was dead serious. "I'll pay a million-dollar bonus for each head delivered back to me. Literally." Basileus added for good measure. A wave of greed-fueled bloodlust washed over the hired killing crew. They'd all seen and done worse before. For an extra million, they wouldn't think twice.

CHAPTER THIRTY-NINE

Western Wall Security Checkpoint
February 13, 11:04 p.m. IST

Strands of dark clouds crawled across the face of the moon, throwing shadow and light across the ancient stone structures, far less potent than the artificial illumination that was blinding their vehicle now. The harsh glare of the high-wattage lights surrounding the convoy was in stark contrast to the pinpoints of starlight fighting valiantly to sparkle in the sky high above.

An IDF soldier in full battle gear carrying an M4 carbine approached the lead vehicle's driver's side door. Credentials were extended by Aliyah's friend, David, the Mossad agent they'd met days earlier, who was currently seated in the passenger seat. Information was exchanged in rapid-fire Hebrew. Credentials were returned, and the soldier stepped back and nodded to his men. The gate barring their path was moved aside by two similarly attired and armed soldiers. Cameras were placed high and low and visible everywhere. The exit process would be the same, but in reverse, as this was some of the most secure real estate on the planet. After clearing the checkpoint, the convoy rolled forward.

Phil's voice popped into everyone's ears. "Comms check, everyone." Each of them responded via their sub-vocalized mics, having already secured them into place on the drive into the Old City from Ben Gurion Airport. They had already donned their HUDs to further obscure their identities from the multitude of cameras pointed at them.

The procession of vehicles came to a final stop. Aliyah's voice was in their ears now. "This is us, gang. Pack out everything we'll need. We won't be able to come back for anything."

"Copy that," Gryph said, followed by the other five in quick succession. Dallas and Luna were working in the field for this op. Their talents could be required on the fly, as no one was certain they'd be able to send or receive a signal from deep underground. Truth be told, the pair felt safer with Gryph and friends than on-board *Hera* alone, knowing they were being watched by Basileus.

They stepped out of the Ze'evs and transferred their gear into backpacks that they could carry easily through the tunnels. Daedalus, Phil, and Chief each carried a nanobot briefcase. The latter two also carried a black beach-cooler-size crate between them. Everyone was wearing dark next-gen ballistic bodysuits no thicker than a pair of jeans, only much less comfortable. The high-tech suits of armor could stop a .40 caliber bullet fired at close range while instantly dispersing the force of the impact to other areas of the suit, minimizing the acute compressive force and, with a bit of luck, prevent a fractured rib or two. Needless to say, any type of blade trying to slice or puncture vital organs wouldn't be able to find a way through.

David escorted them through a wide steel door that sat adjacent to a long row of airport-type metal detectors. Stanchions were placed behind each machine to queue visitors into manageable lines. All but one sensor was powered down. Not many people were entering the compound at that time of night, in great contrast to daytime hours when throngs of tourists, students, and locals would have to pass through the magnetic sentries on their way to the Western Wall or to the Souq, the open-air market that wound through the Old City's narrow cobbled passageways. The metal detectors were the last line of defense before the Wall in case the first few checkpoints failed to deter anyone dumb enough to try and smuggle a weapon through.

David stopped before what looked like a large circular fountain at the center of the plaza. The Western Wall was bathed in a soft yellow glow off to their right.

"The cameras up here are all live and recording, but the ones inside the tunnels happen to be down for maintenance tonight," David said with a wink. "Remember, we won't be able to see what you're doing down there, so if you run into any trouble, you'll be on your own. We prefer not to get any more involved than we already are."

"We appreciate your help once again, *achi*," Aliya said, using the Hebrew word for "brother." "If we can ever repay the favor, just ask." She rose on her tiptoes to give him a hug and kiss on the cheek, then turned back to the Daedalus crew. "The entry to the tunnel system starts there," she said, pointing to the bottom-left corner of the courtyard fifty yards away.

Dallas was pecking away on his tablet. "I'm activating our GPS and synchronizing a series of remote beacons we can place throughout the tunnels, relaying our position to one another and connected to *Hera* and ICARUS, once we get too deep for a 5G signal to reach us." A tight cluster of dots burst to life on their displays. Above each dot floated their first names and other digitized stats. "You should be able to see each of our positions on your screens now. I've also added relative elevation from sea level. We may have to split up down there, but hopefully this is enough info to keep us from getting completely fucking lost."

White chairs speckled the main floor of the plaza. The constellation of uncomfortable plastic seating orbited loosely around a scattering of large wooden lecterns, typically used to place the Torah scrolls on while they're read aloud for those in close enough proximity to hear.

Thankfully, only five men were at the Wall at that time. Three were seated in the chairs, and two others were standing, swaying their head and shoulders back and forth in a rhythmic movement of meditation and prayer. All of them, whether seated or standing, were looking directly at the Wall, their faces less than a foot away from the stone their ancestors placed there to protect their Temple over 2,000 years prior. The Western Wall section of the ancient Temple's outer perimeter fortification was purported to have been constructed using funds donated to the Temple treasury exclusively by the poor. Auspiciously, it was the only part of the ancient Temple that had survived to this day.

"Yes!" Dallas yelled, far louder than he should have. More than loud enough to elicit frowns and stern looks from the trio of seated men. Oblivious to his intrusion on their peace and quiet and itching to tell the group what he was so excited about, he continued without missing a beat. "Luna found the most amazing resource online. Some local archaeological society posted a shit ton of AutoCAD drawings on their public server. We downloaded the whole thing before we left the jet then dumped it into ICARUS, along with a bunch of other drawings they stored on their site. It just finished processing, cataloging, and geo-referencing the whole thing and sent it to our private cloud." He was getting more animated as he spoke.

The three men seated at the Wall must have realized the contemplative peace they sought would be unattainable with the new interlopers present. They stood up wearily, their age making the simple task much more difficult and painful than it should have been, and reluctantly shuffled off toward the exit.

"Are you guys listening? This is going to make finding everything so much easier. We'll have a super-detailed augmented reality overlay of the ancient temple structures wherever we look. All the recently discovered pathways, empty cisterns, and yes, you guessed it, drainage routes." He was grinning from ear to ear.

"That's awesome! Great job, Lama," Gryph said. The compliment seemed to have Dallas standing a little bit taller. Luna looked to be a little more relaxed as well. Having Dallas play the part of "Debbie Downer" was starting to take a toll on her feelings for him. She saw such potential if he would only stop making an ass of himself every time they faced a setback and put others before himself for once.

The crew arrived at the entry point to the tunnel system, where the Western Wall intersected with the floor of the courtyard. Walking the first few paces into the covered walkway, they were greeted by a rat's nest of cables snaking across the floor, the walls, and along the cavern-like ceiling. The cords were connected to an eclectic mix of high-pressure sodium lamps and a smattering of modern LED lights, each throwing competing tones of light over each other. A few large fans sat off to the side, ostensibly to provide some fresh air into the tunnel system when they were powered on. At that hour, however, their blades were still; extension cords coiled and draped neatly over the tops of each fan.

The lack of air movement added a stifling effect with their gear and goggles on. The earthy smell from the stone walls and floor, coupled with the lack of fresh air, gave Gryph flashbacks of getting stuck in the cave system in Hebron. He slowed his breathing and centered himself. This would be hard enough without getting in his own head.

After walking a few more paces into the tunnel, they found themselves flanked by a series of mismatched bookshelves crammed full of prayer books and loose sheets of paper. More plastic chairs littered the walkway. The bright orange glow from the sodium lights faded from the entry as the group ventured deeper into the tunnels. After only a minute or two of travel, they were enveloped in a much different environment.

Phil ran his fingertips along the surface, peering in between the gaps and cracks in the ancient stone wall. "Ali, what's with all the little papers jammed inside the wall?"

"The Western Wall is the last vestige of the ancient Jewish Temple, the holiest site in all of Judaism," she said. "People place notes in the spaces between these stones to petition God to answer their prayers."

"Is that something for only Jewish people to do?"

"No. Not at all. People of all faiths are welcome to place a note and try to connect to a higher power."

"Does it work?"

"There are many stories of miracles coming to fruition after praying here and placing notes in the Wall. My own... well, they mostly went unanswered."

Phil picked up a scrap of paper that had been left atop a stack of chairs and penned a note of his own, then placed it into a crevice in the wall. He shrugged. "I figure it can't hurt. Plus, we need all the help we can get." It wasn't hard to guess what he'd wished for.

"Hey, Dallas!" Chief bellowed from the rear of the group. "How 'bout some of those fancy directions you promised?" They arrived at an intersection with multiple paths all branching out from where they stood.

"Heads-up overlay coming online now." As the last syllable left Dallas's mouth, their displays bloomed to life.

"Holy smokes! You weren't messin' around. This guidance is awesome! It may be worthwhile putting up with you after all."

Chief laughed at his own joke. He was obviously impressed. Dallas, not so much.

Bright green, red, and blue lines appeared over the surface of everything on their displays. As their focus changed from one area to the next, the lines updated in real time.

"Think of it like Google Maps, Temple version," Dallas said. "This'll show us the entire network of roads and alleyways that have been buried and lost for over two millennia. The green lines indicate streets and pathways that are still accessible today, like the one we're walking through now. The red lines show previous walkways, roads, and such that have been identified by the archaeological society but aren't accessible today, at least not completely. Hopefully, one of these leads us to where we need to go. The blue lines represent anything water related. The cistern pools, drains, culverts, basically anything that held water at one time is shown in blue. Any questions?"

"David told us the cameras are off inside the tunnels," Gryph said. "We should be far enough inside by now to be invisible to anyone watching. Chief, unpack whatever you need, and take point. Phil, keep an eye on our six. We don't need any surprise visitors, at least not until we have what we're looking for. The rest of you, grab your weapon of choice, and keep it close. If Basileus shows up tonight, you won't have time to secure it. Best to do it now."

Chief popped the lid on the crate that he and Phil had carried down. A wide assortment of lethality was available. Glocks, Sigs, and H&Ks were passed out. Dallas pulled a chrome-plated Desert Eagle 10 mm from the crate. The Israeli-made hand cannon gleamed, even in the low light. "I'm taking this one for sure." The pistol looked massive in his hands.

"First off," Chief said, "get your finger off the trigger." Dallas slipped the 10 mm behind his back, like a kid trying to protect a toy from being taken away.

"Dallas, listen to me. That's a hell of a lot of gun. It's also a very tough one to shoot straight. It's got a wicked kick to it. Try this one instead. Trust me, bud. I shoot these things for a living." Chief extended a matte-black Glock 22 to him. "It's a .40 caliber. It'll leave a big hole. Just line up your target with the laser sight that's under the barrel, pull the trigger, and the bad guy goes down."

He produced an extended clip containing fifteen hollow-point rounds. "The Glock's safety is on the trigger itself, so just point and shoot. And remember, keep your finger *off* the trigger until a bad guy is lit up in by the laser dot. If you shoot me in the ass by accident, you may as well put that barrel in your mouth before I get to you. We clear?"

Dallas didn't respond, but he brought the Desert Eagle back out from behind his back and swapped it for the Glock. Chief noticed that Dallas kept his finger out of the trigger guard this time and had it pointed down the barrel taking that as, '*Yeah, we're clear.*'

The Daedalus crew, now armed to the teeth, ventured deeper into the tunnel systems. The elevation dropped away slightly as they progressed along the length of the massive wall. They had been following a green line that looked to extend almost the entire length of the wall. The Blood Channel they were searching for was supposed to be close to the midpoint of the ancient stone perimeter, the exact spot their GPS indicated they were currently standing on.

There was very little differentiation in the tunnel's appearance. The paths and stones looked similar to one another. Their current location proved to be no different.

"Okay, so now what? It says it should be right here," Dallas said.

Daedalus chuckled. "Were you expecting a flashing neon sign, Mr. Hayle?"

Dallas's face flushed red, but the HUDs obscured most of his embarrassment. "No, I guess not."

"It may not be a neon sign," Gryph said, "but there should be something that'll point us in the right direction. This junction has red and blue lines that lead from this spot toward the Temple Mount, unfortunately, I don't see any infills or previous penetrations that we can follow. Any drains here must have been filled in centuries ago."

"Remember, much of this structure goes deep underground," Luna said. "Maybe the channel runs below the wall."

Aliyah nodded. "That could be, or maybe it's not located exactly halfway. We could be only a few feet away. We should look around this whole area. We're close."

"Sure, but what are we searching for?" Phil asked. "Everything looks the same to me."

"Let's take a really good look around for anything out of the ordinary here before moving on," Gryph said. Their bright LED flashlight beams bounced over the walls, looking for anything that looked like a marker for the entrance they were seeking.

Daedalus didn't take part in the search. Instead, he flipped open one of the nano cases and went to work. He was down on one knee, entering commands into the briefcase, when Dallas came over beside him. "I couldn't find anything different. All these stupid stones look identical. What are you planning on doing with the bots if we don't know where to send them yet?"

"I'm sending reconnaissance bots up the blue and red lines that branch out from here toward the Temple. If the Blood Channel really was on one of those paths, the bots will have a good chance of finding it."

The stone surface reflected sound well, and the others heard everything that Daedalus said, even without the aid of the subvocalized mic taped to his throat.

"I've programmed this first batch of bots to look for micro erosion caused by running water. It would have created a unique pattern, distinguishable from the surrounding stone."

"That's genius," Gryph said. "How are you going to get the bots onto those paths? This wall doesn't seem to have an opening we can exploit."

"I can make a hole, boss," Chief said, grinning. "Brought some C-4 along. We wouldn't need a lot."

"No way, Billy," Gryph said. "This wall has stood for thousands of years. We're not going to be the ones who bring it crashing down. We need another way."

"We don't need to cause any damage to the Wall for what I have planned," Daedalus said, without looking up from his case. "Remember, these are nanobots. They can penetrate the mortar by working their way through the microscopic cracks in the wall and reassembling on the other side, or hopefully inside our long-lost Blood Channel. No damage done."

"Very, very smart," Dallas said, nodding along.

"I've programmed them to follow the blue and red lines to the Temple," Daedalus repeated for good measure. "Once they pick a track to follow, they'll scan their surroundings and send all that info back to our displays to interpret. Little digital canaries in the coal mine, if you will."

Daedalus finished entering the last of the commands, then stood up and backed away from the case. The space filled with a low buzzing sound, and the smell of petrichor once again filled the air. A black mist rose from the case, slowly at first, until a thick, steady stream poured out. The bots wafted into the air, spreading across the wall like a fungus. Less than a minute after being released from the case, the nano army had already begun to fade into the limestone. A minute later, there was no trace of them left on the surface. The buzzing was gone, not even an echo, though the air still carried a tinge of static electricity due to lack of air movement.

Luna stood there with her mouth open. "I've only seen that happen on a screen before, never in real life. That was the coolest thing I've ever seen."

"He has an entire crane made from the little buggers back at the Workshop," Chief said. "Amazes me every time he fires it up."

"I've marked the bots in yellow on our displays to measure their progress," Daedalus said, bringing the conversation back to more pressing matters.

The red and blue pathways showed little yellow flecks peppered along the ancient pathways, slowly creeping up the colorful lines toward the Temple Mount.

"How long do you think it's going to take for them to find anything?" Phil asked.

"Depends on what you mean by *anything*," Daedalus said. "The only thing we actually need to find is the Blood Channel. Then figure out how to locate the Ark from there. I suspect the bots will uncover a treasure trove of information while they search the area. Their usefulness is unlimited."

"'Unlimited' is a pretty big word," Dallas said.

"Uh, guys," Luna said, her voice rising over the discussion, "are you paying attention to this? Check out the bots. Something's happening."

Their HUDs showed the yellow specks consolidating on a singular track. The blue line beneath was barely visible.

"The nano programming is set to locate any type of shaft approximately two feet in diameter that displays any water or erosion patterns," Daedalus said. "They must have found some matching criteria. The bots will now coalesce to cover the entire surface area to form a digital mesh over the object, rendering it for us in precise detail. That's what we see happening right now."

A thick yellow line flowed from their position and terminated at the site of the ancient Temple. The annotation from the swarm's discovery indicated that it had identified an aqueduct measuring just over two feet wide and slightly less in height. It also bore the telltale signs of previously running water. The location and the direction also seemed to fit the ancient narrative.

"Can we get a look inside somehow? Confirm if there's anything unusual that would indicate we're on the right path?" Gryph asked.

"Way ahead of you," Dallas said as he manipulated the bots into surveillance mode, enabling them to capture a high-definition video feed from inside the abandoned trough. "I have the playback set to start from the other side of the wall. It'll work its way down the blue line toward the Temple site. The bots will laser scan the interior as it travels inside the shaft, looking for anything we can use to find the next clue."

The image on their HUDs switched over to the interior of a stone trough. Small pebbles and rock fragments were scattered throughout. The smooth limestone finish was unremarkable. The bots were working their way through the channel for a few minutes, revealing more of the same. Two locations closer to the Temple compound had incurred significant structural damage. The resulting cave-ins would make the route impassable if not for the nanobots' unique abilities. There was no way that anyone, not even a child, could have been able to crawl through the Blood Channel now.

"We're already under the Temple compound itself, and I haven't seen a damn thing that would make me think this drain goes anywhere special," Dallas said. "Why can't we just catch a lucky break for once? Why does everything have to be so hard all the time?"

The enthusiasm shown earlier had evaporated.

"Stop!" Gryph shouted.

Dallas flinched at the command. "Take it easy, Gryph. I was venting. It's just so frustra—"

"Not you. Stop the playback. Go back five feet. Left side of the wall near the top."

Dallas obliged and zoomed into the spot Gryph had noticed while he was throwing his tantrum. "No way! Is that…" He was too stunned to finish.

Gryph smiled. "Looks like our lucky break to me."

CHAPTER FORTY

Western Wall Plaza
February 14, 1:01 a.m. IST

"Dima, tell your men to keep their weapons holstered and their mouths shut," Basileus barked from the front passenger seat, then returned his attention to the highly guarded security checkpoint to which they had just rolled up. "But be ready to attack if this doesn't go our way."

Their lookout from the airport had followed the Daedalus crew to the Dung Gate, the closest checkpoint to the Temple Mount and the Western Wall. The unflattering moniker was given to the location from the time it was used as a refuse dump during the Temple era and the accompanying odors carried on the prevailing winds. Currently, it served as the most practical way to access the pair of holy sites by foot, taxi, or bus.

Basileus rolled down the window of the Mercedes Sprinter van. The night air was crisp and clean. The fetid use of the Dung Gate had been snuffed out long ago. Now only its name betrayed its malodorous past.

"Good evening, officers," Basileus said in flawless Hebrew. "Our friends passed through here a couple of hours ago. They arrived here in IDF vehicles but required some additional technical support and told us to meet them here. Could you help us locate them? I'm not sure exactly where they are now though. We got a little turned around on the way over here and are running quite a bit behind schedule. Any help would be greatly appreciated."

A young IDF soldier glanced at the driver and peeked his head through the open window at the gaggle of passengers in the back. A couple of them raised their hands in casual greeting. Others stared at the floor, trying to look bored, hoping the angle and poor lighting would help conceal the battle scars chiseled into their faces.

"Your friends didn't tell us to expect anyone else. We have no way of confirming your arrival with them, sorry," the soldier said, still not taking his eyes off the van's interior.

The men in the back shifted slightly, hands silently reaching for concealed weapons. Dima shook his head imperceptibly at the escalation. They were sitting ducks inside the van. A firefight there would do nothing but get them arrested or killed. They needed to bide their time for a few more moments.

"I completely understand your position, officer, but they are completing some very important and very secretive work for your government," Basileus said. "That's why they arrived with the military escort." He wasn't sure what Daedalus was up to, but he was hoping to glean a nugget of information from the guards as to their whereabouts before the firepower behind him was unleashed. "I would hate for there to be an incident on the Temple Mount because we were unable to reach our friends in time."

"What do you mean by an *incident*?" the soldier said, now a little less sure of himself.

A female guard came over to the van's window to confer with the young IDF soldier, her rifle in a low ready position. The men seated in the back bristled and reached for their weapons. Dima waved them off again. The guys were itching to spill blood. Dima was fine with that, but not yet.

"Okay, I'm really not supposed to divulge the reason we're here tonight, but under the circumstances, you aren't really leaving me much choice," Basileus said. "Our friends are trying to stop an imminent terror attack. I'm not sure of all the details yet, but our friends called us for assistance and said we needed to hurry."

The two IDF soldiers retreated from the vehicle and spoke quietly to each other. The younger of the two soldiers approached the window again. "I understand the problem," he said sheepishly, "but without clearance, we cannot let you proceed to the tunnels." Basileus feigned disappointment, though he could barely suppress his smile. A location at last. Now they were getting somewhere.

"Listen, I've done what I was asked to do. If you won't let us through, then any innocent blood spilled in the attack will be on your hands, not mine. Be sure to file your security report confirming that we were here, and that we explained why we needed access but were refused entry. We'll be filing ours right away. You know the expression, 'shit rolls downhill?' Well, I'm not going to be the one at the bottom of that steaming pile when it stops. You are!"

Basileus allowed the soldier to think about that for a moment. "You must really like working traffic duty because I don't see anything else in your immediate future, except maybe a dishonorable discharge for letting hundreds of innocent Israeli citizens die because you wouldn't let us help our friends."

He turned in his seat to address the passengers in the back, loud enough for the IDF guards to hear. "Okay, guys, seems like we're going home. If the Israeli army cares more about protecting a roadway checkpoint than their own people, I'm sure as hell not going to put my own team in harm's way for them. Turn around, let's head back."

The driver shifted the van into reverse, the bright white reverse lights illuminating the guards who had taken up a position behind the vehicle.

"*Regga, Regga,*" the young soldier said, Hebrew slang for "Hold on a sec." He motioned for the gate to be removed from in front of the van. "Please don't take any offense, sir. I was just following protocol. We are grateful for any help that saves lives."

"I completely understand. I just hope we're not too late," Basileus said. "Do you have any idea where into the tunnels they went?"

"We're not sure. We heard only that they were going down. We can't even tell you where they are now. The cameras inside are all down for maintenance tonight. You'll have to start at the beginning, but it could be hard to find them. There are a lot of passages, and it's easy to get lost. Make sure you call out for your friends, so they hear you coming."

Basileus smiled. "We'll be sure to do that. You've saved many lives tonight." *Not a total lie,* he thought. Two more minutes of that by-the-book bullshit and an all-out firefight would have blazed from the rear of the Sprinter. The van was waved through the security checkpoint and finally settled into a parking stall designated for tour buses. The Benz inched higher on its frame as the lethal contingent of men exited the vehicle.

"Grab the bags from the back," Dima said. "Let's get moving." The rear door was flung open, and two black duffel bags were retrieved from the rear. Boxes of ammo peeked out from one of the unzipped bags. The other contained an assortment of handguns and a half dozen FN P90 submachine guns.

The team made their way to the same entry point at the base of the wall. "Where to now, Basileus?" asked Dima.

"In there." He pointed to the well-lit cavern to their left. "Walk softly and keep an ear out for any sign of them. When we find them, they'll be trapped like rats."

***

One hour earlier

Dallas was stunned. "This drain line would have been impossible to find without the nanobots."

"And very likely why this secret pathway has remained hidden for so long," Aliyah said.

Gryph thought he spotted an irregularity on one of the large blocks that made up the sidewall of the drain channel when the laser scan passed by. Sure enough, when the playback was reversed, the distinct shape of a menorah was visible on one of the stones. He asked Dallas to zoom in on the image to confirm.

"This wouldn't even be visible to the naked eye," Dallas said. "The only reason it showed up at all is because of the laser scan. The original etching of the menorah on this block has long since faded away. What we're seeing is a ghost of the engraving."

"Is that the only block with a symbol carved into it?" Phil asked.

"So far it's the only one we've found. I have another set of bots looking for any other anomalies, but nothing so far. I'm bringing the large swarm back around now to get another look at this area."

They watched the nanobots concentrate around the stone with the familiar menorah shape. The bots enveloped the entire limestone block, crawling through mortar and the microscopic spaces in between, revealing the stone's true shape and dimensions. A new close-up image of the faded menorah was displayed in a small window on their HUDs. A true-to-life, low-light image from inside the Blood Channel filled another.

"Lama was right. The menorah was invisible to the naked eye," Phil said while looking at the interior of the stone without the laser filter. He was impressed that Dallas had thought to deploy a laser scan that could pick up the infinitesimally small details they would have otherwise missed. "In real life, it looks just like all the other stones beside it."

The readings from the nanobots showed the block to be 1.026 meters long, 0.67 meters high, and 0.84 meters deep. An almost four-by-three-foot chunk of solid limestone with a depth of almost a yard. It was a very heavy slab and would be difficult, if not impossible, to move.

Gryph knew the stone had to be the key to the next chamber. He didn't know how it all fit together yet, but had a hunch. "Dallas, have the bots measure and compare the stones on either side of the one we just found."

"Yeah, no sweat. I can redirect them now." The swarm received the command and scattered from its position on the menorah stone and enveloped the limestone blocks on either side.

"Is there any way to configure nanobots to generate a GPR signal under that block?" Gryph asked. This type of radar would provide a bird's-eye view revealing any hidden structures or voids directly under the area they were investigating without having to disturb any physical property.

"Yeah. But ground-penetrating radar won't be as quick to program as that three-dimensional measuring trick we just used. You'll have to give me some time to figure that one out. By the way, the sizes of the adjacent stones should be up on screen any second." As data on the neighboring slabs poured in, Dallas went right to work on the GPR assignment. His brow knotted in concentration as he pored over the tablet, trying to devise a method to reprogram the bots and quickly deploy them per Gryph's suggestion.

"Well, isn't that interesting," Aliyah said, when the measurements finally entered their collective field of view. "The limestone slabs on either side of the one with the markings are nowhere near as large. I don't know if that has any significance, but it could be that someone didn't want that specific stone easily moved from its position."

"I was thinking the same thing," Gryph said. "Which means there could be something worth protecting beneath it."

"That's why you wanted the GPR scan? To see if there's a hidden room under the stone or something?" Chief asked his friend.

"I didn't really know what it would show, Billy, but I was hoping it would reveal some kind of anomaly." With the difference in measurements shown on the scan and the discovery of the menorah engraved into the stone, everything started to finally fall into place.

A string of barely audible curses spewing from Dallas signaled the hacker extraordinaire had yet to solve his GPR assignment. "I'm trying to reverse engineer the program that we used on the roof of the cavern in NY," he said. "The bots in the Workshop created a mesh to make us look invisible to GPR. That function is native to their original programming. I'm getting close to flipping that around to use it as a GPR signal itself, but I still need a few more minutes."

"Don't get me wrong, guys, I hope our treasure is under there," Phil said, "but what are we going to do even if we do find it? The Blood Channel has two impassable blockages that we saw already. None of us could wiggle our way through that path without getting stuck. Especially after witnessing what Gryph went through in that cave back in Hebron."

"We'd have to knock a hole into this wall to get started," Chief said, rubbing his hands together as he began to appraise the ancient structure for tactical demolition.

"We're not using explosives on anything down here if we don't have to, bud," Gryph said. "Let's wait and see if we discover anything here first."

The next twenty minutes felt like double that, but Dallas finally completed the reconfiguration. "The extent of my greatness is totally lost on you guys. Just call me Captain Nanobot. These little fuckers are now capable of ground-penetrating radar." He took a little bow.

"Good job, Lama. We never doubted you for a second," Gryph said. "Let's see what the radar reveals."

Dallas activated the GPR, sending the signal deep into the earth and decoding it as it bounced back to the bots, creating a 3D image of the composition below the area in question. The GPR results flashed onto their HUDs, replacing the previous images.

"Does it get old being right all the time, Gryph?" Phil asked.

The scan exposed a shaft that descended directly below the largest stone, the one with the menorah marking. The GPR showed a straight vertical drop for the first eight feet under the block. Then it angled down and away, running for another twenty. The shaft finally poured out into a small rectangular chamber. The four walls were identical in size and perfectly square, proving this final buried room was built, not naturally formed. Whatever secrets the chamber contained, they had been hidden away and protected with great effort.

"Let me guess…" Dallas already anticipated what the next order from Gryph would be. "Send a swarm down the tunnel and take a peek in the room?"

Gryph smiled. "You got it, Captain Nano. Let 'em loose."

CHAPTER FORTY-ONE

Inside the Western Wall Tunnels
1:36 a.m. IST

"Don't touch that!" Dima hissed.

The massive, tattooed arm, connected to an even bigger man, recoiled just before contacting the miniature electrical device. A small black cylinder the size of a soda can had been hanging on a wooden support only a few yards into the tunnel entrance. A blue LED light flashed intermittently, indicating it was active.

"I was just checking to see what it was," the mercenary they all called Tiny, who was anything but, hollered back over his shoulder. "Chill the fuck out, man," he muttered under his breath. Tiny wouldn't dare say anything like that loud enough for Dima to hear. The merc was enormous, deadly, and not altogether there, but he wasn't suicidal.

"What do you think it is, sir?" Dima asked as his boss walked up to the device. They were walking in a diamond formation inside the pathways, with Basileus—the high-value principal—securely in the center of the pattern. The protective shape collapsed as the group gathered around to investigate the device.

"Looks like a wireless speaker to me," Tiny said, trying to be helpful. "Finders keepers?" he asked only half-jokingly.

Basileus scowled at the giant and then returned his attention to Dima. "It's a signal booster."

"Are you sure?" Tiny looked confused. "My buddy has one that looks just—"

Tiny was cut off mid-sentence by the metallic snap of the slide on Dima's trusty Walther P99 pointed at the giant's temple. "Say something stupid like that again"—he slid the barrel down a few inches— "and I'll blow your fucking jaw apart. I don't want to hear your voice again. Nod if you understand." Tiny responded as instructed and stepped away from the pair.

Basileus plucked the signal booster from the metal spike it was hanging from and held it in his palm like he was appraising a piece of fruit. "This device was left to ensure our *friends* down here would be able to stay connected while they were deep underground." He raised the booster above his head and smashed it against the ground. It shattered on impact, sending shards of plastic and circuitry across the ancient floor. "There will be no calling for help now. Let's keep moving."

"You heard the man!" Dima barked. "Move your asses."

The men re-established the protective formation around Basileus and proceeded deeper into the tunnels. Their hunt was almost at an end.

CHAPTER FORTY-TWO

Inside the Western Wall Tunnels
1:46 a.m. IST

The Daedalus crew watched in silence as the procession of na-nobots scurried along the secretive path. The swarm covered the newly discovered route quickly and had just reached the final chamber at the end.

"You know, I've been wrestling with how to deal with the Ark of the Covenant if we actually find it," Gryph said. "The nanobot deployment solved a lot of issues but has also created a couple of new challenges for us as well."

"Great, a new problem," Dallas moaned.

"We've been on a problem-solving roll lately," Phil said. "We can definitely work through a few more."

"No, it's not that," Dallas said. "I wasn't talking about what Gryph said. I just started having trouble with the signal from the boosters I placed along the way. Our upload and download speeds are practically non-existent now. I'm going to reset the network and see if that fixes it. The HUDs will be offline while it restarts, though it should only take a minute or two." The crew slipped the goggles down around their necks as soon as the displays went dark, starting their reboot sequence.

"Okay, getting back to what Gryph just said. What did you mean this solved and created some issues for us?" Phil asked.

"There are stories and myths about those who died shortly after being exposed to the Ark and its powers. I'm not one to give much credence to curses and such, but based on what we're seeing here, I don't think anyone has been in its presence since it was hidden away, so those stories are probably just that—stories. However, I wouldn't be surprised if there were some protective elements that the Ark inherently possesses or may have been put into place as a final line of defense."

Aliyah nodded. "I remember reading when I was younger that in Temple times, the Kohen Gadol, the Jewish high priest, would make his annual trip on Yom Kippur into the Holy of Holies, the inner sanctum of the Temple where the Ark was placed. Other priests assisting in the service would tie a rope around the *Kohen Gadol's* waist in case he died performing the once-a-year service and would have to be pulled out. Quite a few high priests died during, or shortly after they were in direct contact with the Ark."

That ominous thought hung like a pall in the air.

"That's yet another reason why the bots are better to breach the room than any of us," Gryph said. "There's also the religious and cultural sensitivity of the object itself. We're talking about something that was supposedly carved by the finger of God. We must be respectful and extremely cautious as well. I think it's better that it remains undisturbed by human hands."

"That makes sense," Aliyah said. "The last thing we need is another ancient malady to contend with. I appreciate the sentiment toward keeping the Ark... I don't know, pure, I guess."

"I'm all for keeping a safe distance too, but I don't see how that's a problem for us," Phil said. "But we don't have anyone on the inside of that room to collect the samples and bring them back out."

Gryph tilted his head to Dallas. "I was hoping Captain Nano over here could help us out with that."

"Yeah, well, I can't do jack shit without that relay up and running. I daisy-chained the boosters together throughout the tunnel to get us a signal down here. I can't reprogram the bots without ICARUS, and that's all running in the cloud. No booster. No signal. No dice."

"How are the bots working right now if they aren't connected?" Chief asked.

"They're autonomous once they have their programming set from the aluminum cases," Daedalus answered. "Any previous tasks or skills can also be utilized again because the programming is stored within the nanobots themselves. Like cached memory.

Prior programmed assignments like measurement, GPR, crane towers, and the gantry hoisting systems are all available without an outside connection, but we can't encode any new tasks until the signal issue is fixed. They're currently in autonomous search mode. We should be able to see what they've discovered hidden in that room as soon as the main system comes back online."

"Guys, we have a much bigger problem than the drop in signal." Dallas's eyes were fixed on his tablet. "I equipped each of those boosters with a fiber-optic lens to double as a surveillance camera. I figured with those assholes on our trail, it might be a good idea."

"What did the camera feeds record?" Gryph asked, already having a sinking suspicion as to the answer.

"A whole mess of bad dudes. The surveillance recorded a few of them before they destroyed the booster, but without that connection, I can't get the bots reprogrammed."

"Can we replace it?" Gryph asked.

"Yeah. They probably destroyed the first booster they saw, the one closest to the entrance. It's unfortunately the most important of the three that I daisy-chained throughout the tunnel. Without that first signal at the entrance, there's nothing to relay further. I may not need all three boosters to get a signal down here, but it's that first one that will make or break it."

"Did you happen to bring any spares along?" Gryph asked.

"Yeah, I brought a couple, actually. I keep hearing the 'one is none, two is one' line you and Chief have been spouting and figured it was a good idea."

Gryph was happy that some of their good habits were rubbing off on Dallas.

"They haven't found or destroyed the second or third boosters yet," Dallas said, "They must be moving through the tunnels pretty slowly, but you guys would run directly into them on the way out to replace the booster at the entry. So, replacing it isn't so simple."

"No, actually, it is that simple," Daedalus said with resolute determination. "We're going to make them pay for what they've done already and ensure they can do no more harm in the future. Give us the boosters, Dallas. We'll get the signal back up and running and you continue gathering the samples we need from that treasure room."

"Okay then," Gryph said. "Phil, Daedalus, Chief, and I will head out to replace the booster and deal with Basileus and his hired guns. Ali, you're the last line of defense here. Keep Luna and Dallas safe until we get back. Although it seems Luna can hold her own too."

Dallas was relieved he wasn't asked to head back to the entry point with the others. "I can work through some ideas to secure the manna while you're gone," he said. "I can't upload anything yet, but I can get the program ready for when the system comes back online using the tablet in the briefcase."

Without any further prompting, Chief unzipped the gear bag he had brought along to grab a few last-minute add-ons to his weapons cache before they headed out. He would leave behind enough goodies for Aliyah and Luna to use in case any of Basileus's men slipped past them.

Phil had already removed a few pistols and ammo from his go bag and reached in for one more weapon. The last item he pulled from the bag was a hand-forged katana sheathed in a sleek black scabbard. The razor-sharp sword was over two hundred years old and was his favorite weapon. The HK45 tactical pistol he wore on his hip was there because he was also smart enough and experienced enough to know that one never brought *only* a knife to a gunfight, no matter how sharp and strong the steel. Other weapons, both martial arts and conventional, were secured into holsters, slings, and various pockets.

Chief looked like he was ready for World War III. His massive frame sported a collection of brute automatic firepower. He had an Airtronic PSRL rocket launcher strapped to his back. Spare ammo was stuffed into every pocket and flap in his tactical vest. The butts of matching Sig P226s peaked out from the holsters on both his hips. An HK MP7 was slung across his chest. Gryph was similarly armed but left the rockets for Billy.

Phil was more than a little surprised when Daedalus chose to wear only a pistol tucked behind his back and a similarly styled longsword to his own across his left hip.

"Interesting choice of weapon, sir, considering all you have at your disposal, that is." Phil wasn't sure why the man felt he needed a long blade over an automatic gun. "Swords—katanas in particular—have been somewhat of an obsession of mine since I was a little boy," Phil said, eyeing Daedalus's blade.

"May I?"

Daedalus smiled widely. "Of course, Master Wu. It would be an honor to share it with someone as knowledgeable about these magnificent weapons as you." He unsheathed the blade enough to expose a few inches of steel, then offered it to Phil for inspection.

Phil was gobsmacked when he got a closer look at the sword. He recognized the famous katana instantly. A shot of adrenaline surged through his body.

"There's no way. Is this…?"

"The Honjo Masamune." Daedalus bowed his head slightly as he said the name. "I brought it onboard *Hera* when we first left New York. It's been on the jet ever since."

Goro Nyudo Masamune was born in Japan in 1264 and rose to fame as Japan's greatest sword maker. His blades were used by the samurai warriors of the time, and no doubt played a large part in their legendary success. The Honjo Masamune was widely regarded as the greatest katana sword ever forged by Masamune. The blade was named after Japanese General Honjo, who used it in the battle of Kawanakajima in 1561, more than 200 years after the sword was created. This Japanese national treasure was relinquished by the Japanese royal family in 1945 as an example for all Japanese citizens that even nobility would fully comply with the order to surrender all their weapons to the allied forces at the end of World War II. Swords, katanas, and other ceremonial blades were included in this roundup.

"The Honjo was said to have gone missing on its voyage across the Pacific in December 1945," Phil said, "along with a cache of other notable blades." The martial arts master had an encyclopedic knowledge when it came to such edged weapons. Phil carefully returned the one-of-a-kind sword to Daedalus. A more detailed inspection would be in order later.

"The ship actually made it all the way back to the US with the Honjo onboard," Daedalus said with some amount of pride in his voice. "I know this because I met the ship as it docked. The captain of the vessel and I had an… *arrangement,* and I've possessed the Honjo ever since."

Everyone kept busy making final adjustments and additions to their personal armory and didn't pay much attention or seem that impressed with the history of the katana, as impressive as it looked.

"I'm not sure you guys understand the pedigree of that katana." Phil looked down at his hands, still somewhat shocked and in awe from the item he'd just held. "The Honjo Masamune is the Holy Grail of swords. Even just being able to see it in person would have been a fantasy bucket list item, never mind actually grasping it. This trip keeps getting more unbelievable by the day. Thank you for allowing me to see it, Daedalus."

"If you guys are finished measuring swords, can we get moving now?" Billy K said, itching to flex his trigger finger.

"Chief is right," Gryph said. "We need to find a place along the main path where we can stay hidden but still establish a clear line of sight to the threat coming our way. We need to be hyper-aware of staying out of each other's crossfire or catching a ricochet off one of the stone surfaces down here. This isn't easy terrain for close-quarters combat."

"There were a couple areas we passed with empty cistern pools we could hide inside until they pass us, as long as they don't search too thoroughly," Chief said. "We can flank them from the rear after they walk on by and then light 'em up."

"Solid plan, Billy. I was thinking something along the same lines. I also spotted a few narrow alleyways jutting off the main pathway that would serve the same purpose as your cistern idea. I guess we'll decide as we come up to them. Unfortunately, we're going in blind this time. The HUD routing features won't work until we get that first booster replaced."

"Actually, I think there's a way you could use them now," Luna said. "You could follow the path we came in on, but in reverse. Those directions are still in the HUDs' memory. While you're right, we can't program a new path or show you areas that we weren't in previously, at least you won't get turned around and lost on the way out. When you get the boosters back online, the HUDs will guide you right back to us from wherever you are."

"Luna, you're brilliant." Gryph was thankful for the assistance and insights Luna had brought to the team. Everyone slipped the

HUDs back over their eyes. Getting lost and surprised by Basileus's group was not something they could let happen.

"Everyone ready?" Gryph asked before he gave the final order to move out.

"You better be," Dallas said. "The second booster just went out."

CHAPTER FORTY-THREE

Inside the Western Wall Tunnels
1:53 a.m. IST

Dima kicked away the remnants of the booster he crushed under his boot. This relay had been suspended from a steel spike protruding from the wall, similar to the first one.

"I was concerned that it would be a challenge to locate our *friends* inside this maze of cobbled passageways." Basileus laughed. "How considerate of them to leave us these digital breadcrumbs to follow."

The tunnel forked into two different paths from where they stood. "Do we split up and cover both routes at once or stay together?" Bough #1 asked.

Dima had brought the sadistic siblings along for this mission, much to their delight. They'd beaten Brother Marcus to the brink of death again in a futile effort to squeeze out any last tidbits of information, but he hadn't divulged anything new.

The brothers left him chained to the cell floor and on death's door when the call came from Dima to join the rest of the hastily assembled hit squad. The cruel siblings rushed out from the castle dungeons, salivating over the coming carnage Dima promised the mission would bring. Now that they were in the tunnels, Bough brother #1 had taken the point position after Tiny's earlier run in with Basileus and Dima.

"We'll split up here. I'll go down the path on the left with Basileus. Both Bough brothers will come with us."

Dima knew the element of surprise was fading with every minute. They'd been taking a slow and cautious approach, but they needed to cover as much ground as possible now. One booster going down could be relegated to a glitch. But two boosters down? They'd send someone to investigate soon.

"The rest of you, follow Tiny through the right side of the tunnel," Dima said, pointing to the two meanest looking SOBs on his revamped crew. The first man was Eastern European with an affection for white power tattoos. The other was a six-foot-five Nigerian who was built like an NFL linebacker with the height of an NBA point guard. Neither looked as if they had ever smiled a day in their miserable lives. They were an odd pair considering the wide chasm of ideology between them, but money was the great equalizer.

Gesturing to the other route. "These paths might come together again somewhere up ahead, so don't shoot at anything until you're damn sure it's them coming out from the other side, and not us."

"Dima, are you making me take point again 'cause I was joking around about the speaker before?" Tiny said, not very comfortable with the narrow passage that lay ahead and the threat that may lie beyond.

"No, you fat fuck. I'm making you take point because your gigantic body will stop any rounds from hitting the men behind you. Now get moving before I shoot you myself."

For a moment, Tiny looked as if he was going to say something, but knew it was futile. A few of the mercs snickered at the insult, but none would have said or done anything different if they were in Tiny's size fifteen shoes. The big man hung his head in defeat and took a couple of hesitant steps into the tunnel. The hired gunmen split into their designated groups and set off in search of their targets.

"If anyone spots another booster on their side of the tunnel, smash it, then radio the rest of us immediately, so we can all converge on your location. If we keep following the boosters, we'll be able to locate these assholes faster," Dima said. "Keep your eyes open and your mouths shut. We're getting close to them now."

The two groups trekked deeper into the tunnels, taking slow, deliberate steps, attuned to any shift in shadows or sounds. After a few minutes of silent progress, Bough #1 brought his meaty right arm up, halting the procession behind him. His brother sidled up to him. The fraternal twins were inseparable. Dima joined the Boughs at the front.

"What is it?" he asked.

"I'm pretty sure I heard something scraping along the ground up there, but the path we're on curves to the right about ten yards ahead," Bough #1 said. "I can't see anything beyond it."

The trio peered ahead into the low light, straining to see or hear anything out of the ordinary. After an uneventful twenty-second wait, Dima twirled his finger in the air, signaling for everyone to continue their search, when suddenly he also heard the unmistakable sound of boots plodding softly on stone. His hand immediately clenched into a fist that drove the soldiers back into a crouch. A flurry of silent hand signals passed through Dima's team from front to back, ensuring everyone knew that all hell would likely break loose as soon as they cleared the bend in the tunnel.

Meanwhile, Basileus's other strike team in the opposite tunnel from Dima's had also come to a grinding halt.

"Tiny, what the fuck is going on?" asked the thin, wiry mercenary who'd just joined the huge man at the front of the pack. The ex-soldier was a late addition to Dima's team and was easily distinguishable by his heavily tattooed face and body. A pair of brazen SS lightning bolts took up most of the real estate on the back of his shaved skull. A large swastika rested in the center of his forehead. The balance of his inked skin looked like the top of a high school detention-room desk. The xenophobe wouldn't be landing a job at Starbucks anytime soon.

"Shut up, Adolf," Tiny spat back, bestowing the racist a fitting nickname. He hadn't bothered to ask the guy for a name when he boarded the plane. Tiny may have shown deference to Dima, but he wasn't going to afford this piece of shit the same courtesy.

"Something moved up there by that intersection." Tiny stabbed his chunky finger toward a dimly lit path that veered right from the main corridor. "I saw a shadow, or something move against the wall in that alleyway over there."

"Well, I don't see anything now, chicken shit. Why don't you just imagine there's an all-you-can-eat buffet around the corner instead? That'll get you moving." The comment elicited a few chuckles from the peanut gallery behind them. The Nigerian stayed silent. He had no choice but to work with the racist, but if the hate-filled man decided to talk shit to him, he'd already resigned himself to decapitating the little Nazi puke right where he stood.

"Bunch of comedians, huh? Fuck all y'all then." Tiny stepped aside. "Skinny Hitler here can take a look then. I'm not moving. I know what I saw."

"Yeah, no problem. Move your fat ass out of the way and let a real soldier show you how it's done. I'm not letting you or any other of these other *deports* fuck up my million-dollar payday."

Adolf squeezed by Tiny and soon found himself standing alone in the center of the intersection. He stared intently down the darkened path to his right and the corridor straight ahead for a good ten seconds each before giving the rest of the squad the all-clear sign to join him.

Adolf figured they had a couple options: continue straight ahead on the main pathway and deeper into the tunnels to find Daedalus, or stalk down the new alleyway on the right and see if anyone was hiding down there, as Tiny had implied. When the Nazi turned around to present the options to his group, he noticed another tunnel running parallel to the one they'd just walked through, emptying into the same large intersection, like standing at the point of a V.

He was about to tell Tiny to do a quick recon down the alleyway and chase another ghost when, out of the corner of his eye, he registered movement down the parallel run. Adolf raised his weapon and pointed it down the tunnel. He slipped the pad of his fingertip over the trigger. A couple ounces of pressure was all it would take to send whoever was about to exit the tunnel into oblivion. The pressure on his fingertip increased as dark shadows crept closer along the stone wall. Adolf tensed and started to squeeze the trigger even tighter before finally relaxing his grip entirely when he saw the first of the Bough brothers emerge from the opening.

"You two hillbillies were about a second from getting blown to hell." Adolf turned back to the dark alley and took a few confident strides. "This whole crew is amateur hour. You're a bunch of puss—"

Before he had a chance to finish the insult, a nickel-size hole was punched through the center of his forehead, obliterating the swastika that had been visible only moments earlier. The round removed a good portion of the back of his head along with the balance of the offensive SS imagery on exit. The mercs who were moving into the intersection watched in horror as he collapsed against the wall in a visceral explosion of brain tissue, blood, and bone.

"Everyone down!" Tiny screamed as the echo from the shot died out.

"Where the fuck did that come from?" Dima yelled, exiting from his leg of the tunnel, and joining the others up ahead.

Everyone in Tiny's group had ducked for cover when Adolf's head exploded. They cautiously rose from their positions, weapons at the ready. Laser dots peppered the perimeter walls as the team scanned their surroundings for the origin of the well-placed kill shot.

"I think it came from the path on the right," Tiny said. "I told that dumbass I saw something, but he wouldn't listen. Serves him right."

The Nigerian spat on the corpse as he walked by. "He talked too much anyway."

With the element of surprise now gone, the balance of Dima's group joined Tiny's at the convergence of the twin tunnels. Their position, a good ten feet back from the alleyway, protected them from any more fire from the path on the right.

Basileus was still in the center of his men, but didn't seem bothered by the gunshot or the death of Adolf. He assumed few, if any, of Dima's crew would survive the assault. He was eagerly anticipating the showdown and putting an end to the last of his obstacles.

Dima pointed to the Boughs. "Get down there and take out the sniper guarding their position. Let me know when he's down." Dima's team was using a standard tactical communications setup. Mics and earbuds would keep his men in constant communication, but they weren't nearly as sophisticated as the devices the Daedalus crew were utilizing. The brothers, eager to spill blood, obliged without hesitation.

The Nigerian crept forward and took the Boughs' place. "Follow those two inside after they take out the sniper," Dima said. "Eliminate whoever's left."

The Nigerian nodded and began a weapons check when all hell broke loose.

Two minutes earlier

"There's an alley on our left that looks like a sweet spot for us to set up an ambush," Chief whispered. He and Gryph had evaluated a few other options as they made their way along the well-worn path, acutely aware that out in the open, every step closer to the entry point was another step closer to confronting their enemy.

They were standing at a large intersection that a pair of parallel tunnels spilled out into. Like the point of a V. According to the history on the HUDs, either one of the two tunnels would lead them back toward the entrance.

"We took the tunnel on the right when we first came in," Phil said. "The first booster we need to replace is about thirty meters down that same path."

"Okay, let's get—" Gryph stopped and held up his index finger. Everyone froze. He turned his head slightly and squeezed his eyes shut, straining to hear the sound again. At first there was nothing. He was about to dismiss it, but then he heard it again, more distinct this time. Voices.

"Chief, this alley is going to have to work. We're out of real estate." Gryph motioned for the other three men to clear the open intersection. "The voices I heard are getting louder and clearer. We have twenty seconds at most before they exit one of those tunnels and dump out into this spot we're standing in."

The four men ran to take up positions down the darkened alley. The same streets had run red with blood throughout innumerable wars over countless centuries, proving the adage that "The more things change, the more they stay the same." Blood would be spilled on those stones again tonight. Gryph was just praying it wouldn't be theirs.

Daedalus, Phil, and Gryph ventured deeper into the alleyway, leaving Chief near the mouth of the opening. He was a legendary SEAL sniper, and there was no one Gryph trusted more with a gun than him.

Chief had a clear line of sight to the center of the intersection and was still able to remain hidden, having been afforded some protection from a natural stone outcropping that jutted into the old walkway. From his position, he could clearly see, and hear, an argument between two men and knew by the sounds of it that one of them, a trigger-happy Nazi-looking asshole would be on his position in less than half a dozen paces and as many seconds.

The best defense is a good offense, he thought, focusing the laser sight from his Sig P226 so the green bead was centered in the middle of the swastika and pulled the trigger. Chief saw the man's head snap back and empty against the cavern wall behind him. A .40 caliber hollow point tended to leave quite a mess. This shot was no exception.

He rushed back down the alley, re-joining his friends, who'd already secured tactical positions behind similar outcroppings. They saw Chief running back toward them and were preparing to lay down a swath of cover fire behind him, unaware of the extent and strength of the incoming threat, but none was needed. There was no one on his tail.

"What happened?" Gryph asked, "I thought we were going to surprise them after they passed by."

"Yeah, that's what I was hoping too, but we were about to have some very unfriendly guests rushing down this alley. I didn't think getting the jump on them would be possible if they took a few more steps this way. And the guy I took out really looked like he needed to be put down anyway. But we gotta move now."

Chief holstered his Sig and switched to the MP7 slung across his chest, extended the retractable butt stock against his shoulder and headed back the way he'd just come. The three men crept out from their positions and followed him into the war zone that awaited them just around the corner.

CHAPTER FORTY-FOUR

Inside the Western Wall Tunnels
2:02 a.m. IST

The Bough brothers edged their way along the side of the tunnel, trying their best to locate the gunman who had dispatched Skinny Hitler moments earlier.

"I can't see anything. It's dark as shit down that way," Bough #1 said as he stepped into the center of the path.

"Maybe that shot didn't come fro—" Bough#2 was silenced by a tight grouping of hollow-point rounds sent courtesy of Chief's MP7. The barrage entered through the front of the unlucky sibling's throat and tore through tendons and arteries. The exit wound was traumatic for the recipient of the bullets and for his twin, who witnessed the slaughter.

Bough #1 felt the warm, sticky arterial blood from his brother pulse across his face for exactly two heartbeats, based on the rhythmic crimson founts pumping feebly from his brother's neck. Bough #1 froze in terror as his brother's head tipped all the way over to the side, hanging only by skin and shredded sinew. His momentary pause proved to be fatal.

Phil let loose a dagger that impaled Bough #1 through the ear as he turned to see his brother bleed out. His head snapped to the side when the five-inch blade pierced the big man's ear canal and embedded itself deep into his brain. He was dead before he crumpled to the ground. And just like that, the sick and twisted Bough brothers were no more.

Chief cocked his eyebrow and gave Phil an approving nod after witnessing the silent lethality and impressive accuracy of Phil's blade. "In hindsight, that was probably a better idea than the MP7 if we were trying to surprise them," Chief said.

Phil smiled and winked. "Same end result, Chief, but unfortunately I'm thinking that was just their opening salvo."

The Nigerian had been much more cautious than the ill-fated Bough brothers, making sure to keep safe behind the bend in the stone path and out of range. The experienced soldier knew he had to go on a full offensive now, bringing the fight to them. He had seen much bloodshed during his days fighting as a mercenary throughout Africa. There was no shortage of work for a man of his skill set. As such, the brutality and gruesomeness of the Bough brothers' deaths didn't even warrant a second glance. He stalked toward the turn into the alleyway, leading with his AK. The classic assault rifle felt like an extension of his body. The firearm was the most widely used and accessible weapon for all of Africa's countless wars, and he was incredibly proficient with it.

The Nigerian had also witnessed the impressive skills his adversaries possessed and wasn't going to walk blindly into their kill box. He was ready to pounce when he heard a commotion behind him. He spun around, leading with the AK as he turned. The hulk of Tiny's large frame came into view at the same time his wheezing reached the Nigerian's ears.

Tiny huffed his way over, sweat pouring from his brow, his XXXL shirt soaked through. "Dima told me to come help. Do you see them yet?" Tiny's breathing was so labored, he could barely get the words out, whether from the sudden physical exertion or the panic setting in because the Daedalus crew was using them as target practice. Likely a bit of both.

The Nigerian shook his head in disgust. *These "killers" wouldn't last a day fighting in my country.* He figured he'd have to defeat this enemy single-handed now. It wouldn't be the first time, and he was determined not to make it his last. If he was the only one left standing, he'd insist on collecting his companions' reward money from Dima, too.

The Nigerian plucked a small metallic sphere off his belt. He drew his arm back to build momentum for a deep throw, but smacked Tiny square in the chest instead, almost bobbling the device in the process.

"Back up, fat man." He could barely tolerate Tiny as it was. The foul breath cascading down his neck from the sweat-soaked mountain of a man was taxing the last of his patience.

Tiny retreated a step, then took another for good measure. The Nigerian pulled the pin on the four-second fuse and threw the grenade around the bend, using the curve in the opposing wall to shuttle the ordnance deeper down the path without having to expose himself further. He started the countdown in his head as soon as he pulled the pin free.

Tiny took a giant step forward and closed the gap between him and the Nigerian as soon as the grenade left the soldier's grip. "Good thinking, man. That'll fuck 'em up real good." Tiny slapped the Nigerian on the back with his sweaty paw, much to the soldier's mounting irritation.

The Nigerian's internal countdown barely ticked to three when the grenade inexplicably rolled right back to where he was standing. Without pausing for even a fraction of a second, he grabbed Tiny by the shirt collar and hauled him forward, causing the giant to topple onto the tiny metal bomb, effectively burying the explosive under his bulk.

The damage from the detonation was thunderous in the closed space, but somehow the sickening wet squelch made by Tiny's body absorbing the shrapnel and blast from the low-yield incendiary rose above the maelstrom. The walls and ceiling shook from the blast, sending pebbles and debris raining down inside the tunnel.

The Nigerian was carried forward by his attempt to jump clear of the explosion and force of the concussive blast rolling through the confined space. He landed face down on the ancient stone path. It took a few seconds for his head to clear and his ears to stop ringing before he could assess the situation. He patted himself down to check for wounds and saw that his hand came back covered in blood. He searched his body for the source of the injury and realized it wasn't his blood at all. Tiny's involuntary sacrifice had painted the walls and everything in the vicinity red, including him.

Gryph was the first to act after the grenade went off. He'd been rushing toward the front of the tunnel seconds earlier when he saw the familiar shape zip around the curve toward their location. He scooped up the grenade as it pinged off the wall and threw it back, all in one fluid motion, like a shortstop snatching a ball from the air and flinging it to first while holding it for only a fraction of a second. He ducked for cover and prayed there was enough stone between him and the explosion to prevent major bodily injury or death. He was pleasantly surprised that nothing but pebbles and smoke rolled his way after the grenade went off.

Phil rushed toward Gryph to make sure he was all right. Gryph flashed the okay sign to let him know he was fine, but kept his focus on the powerful Nigerian, soaked in blood, rising from the floor. He couldn't understand how the man had withstood the blast, lost so much blood, and was still coming for more until he saw Tiny's eviscerated corpse behind him and put two and two together.

While Gryph's mind worked out the human wreckage in front of him, another instinctual part of his brain reacted to the developing threat. He found himself reaching for the Sig on his hip before he even finished processing what was happening.

The Nigerian was less than ten feet away, scampering up from the ground, and would close the gap in an instant. Gryph saw him stretch for an AK-47 that was just out of reach. As the man clambered to gain his footing, Gryph's muscle memory already had his arm up, swinging toward his target. He fired two .45 Parabellum bullets in rapid succession that struck the top of the Nigerian's skull, sending him slumping back to the floor.

Chief arrived at Gryph's side shortly after he fired down the tunnel.

"I'm glad everyone is getting a turn killing bad guys today, but things are getting a bit hairy down here. We gotta keep moving."

Dima seethed with anger, gritting his teeth as he watched his men drop like flies. The threat down that alleyway proved to be more difficult than he had anticipated. He also had a sneaking suspicion that Daedalus was too smart to put all his eggs in one basket.

"Basileus, I think we should press ahead further into the tunnels. They may have split their team up to cover more ground, or to set ambushes for us like this one. The soldiers that Daedalus placed here must be his best, which would mean the rest of his team has been left vulnerable somewhere up there." He nudged his chin to the tunnel ahead.

Basileus considered Dima's plan. "I believe your assessment has merit. We'll carry on further with one of your men. Leave the rest of your team here to keep anyone from chasing after us."

Dima gave his team their instructions and then moved everyone into position. They would provide cover fire for Basileus when he crossed through the exposed intersection. Dima and the third member of their party, his cousin Yvgeni, would cross through with Basileus into the tunnels. Yvgeni's face still bore significant swelling, and the entire left side was an ugly shade of eggplant purple, the aftereffects of being pistol whipped by Dima earlier in the week for losing Phil and Luna in the city. Prior indiscretions were overlooked at that point. Dima had ordered everyone from his existing team onto this mission, wounded family or otherwise.

* * *

The plan was to charge the mouth of the tunnel, laying down heavy fire, providing a path for Phil to escape and replace the booster at the tunnel's entry. Gryph and Chief would eliminate any remaining threat at the point of the V-shaped intersection, then hustle back to Dallas, Luna, and Ali, who were tasked with securing the manna. Before leaving, they would ensure Basileus was silenced once and for all. The plan was solid—until it wasn't.

The tunnel in front of them exploded into a shower of sparks and automatic weapons fire. Shrapnel erupted off the stone walls. Chief had been closest to the intersection and spun back toward his friends when the first shots rang out. He swept his massive arm across Gryph and Phil, knocking them to the ground and out of the line of fire. Chief grunted in pain as the three of them hit the ground hard. Gryph was worried Billy K had twisted an ankle, or worse yet, broken a bone, making their proposed plan and escape much more difficult.

"You okay, Chief?"

"I'll live. But this is gonna need a stitch or twenty." He turned his arm to reveal a deep laceration across his bicep. The skin was flayed open and bleeding badly. A jagged piece of metal was sticking out from the wound. Billy looked at the shrapnel for a moment, then plucked it out with barely a grimace.

Gryph helped his friend tie off his upper arm with a tourniquet and left him to finish wrapping his wound in gauze and duct tape for good measure. The entire process was completed in under thirty seconds. It wasn't the first time the two had found themselves attending to each other's wounds. Chief quickly packed away his small medical kit and picked up his weapon.

"I'm getting sick of being shot at already. If no one has any objection, I'm gonna go kill these motherfuckers. Phil, get ready to haul ass down the tunnel." Without waiting for a reply, he reloaded the MP7 and nodded to Gryph, "Just like old times, bro." In a flash, he was up and charging the path ahead, emptying the thirty-round magazine at any unfortunate souls in his way.

Basileus, Dima, and Yvgeni had barely cleared the intersection under protection of the suppressive fire provided by Dima's men when the intersection exploded with gunfire again. Rock chips and debris nipped at their heels as they raced deeper into the tunnel. Unfortunately, Gryph didn't see them escape, the slight bend in the wall and the incoming rounds preventing him from getting a good visual.

Chief charged into the open intersection after passing by the corpses of the Nigerian, Tiny, and the Bough brothers on his way out. Much to his surprise, he didn't find any further casualties from his onslaught, even though his HK was still smoking after emptying the entire clip blindly into the intersection. He reloaded and took quick stock of the situation. He noticed two things right away. One being a subtle shift in the shadows cast by one of the many safety lights strung along the pathway.

Chief pulled a six-inch metal disc from his front jacket pocket, a little something he had brought along from the Workshop armory. He twisted the top like he was unscrewing a lid on a jar. The rotation caused a loud snapping sound from the disk, morphing it into a multi-faceted spherical shape. A high-pitched whine emanating from the device grew in intensity and volume. Red LEDs flashed all over the surface as Chief reared back and launched the deadly orb into the tunnel closest to him.

"Fire in the hole!" he bellowed.

Chief didn't duck for cover. In fact, he knew there would be no danger in standing right where he was. He had thoroughly tested this weapon at the Workshop under a number of different scenarios. He could only imagine the confusion and terror the remaining mercenaries would feel when the segmented ball rolled to a stop and began to fire its lasers towards any movement within thirty feet of its location.

The sphere rotated and skidded across the ground as deadly lasers, guided by a highly sophisticated targeting program, flashed throughout the assault. It was over in seconds. Pieces of men were piled haphazardly across the tunnel. The impossibly straight cuts that dismembered the unfortunate soldiers were cauterized by the proprietary laser weapon. Bodies simply slid into shards, like shattered pieces of a broken windowpane. The after-effects looked more akin to a macabre art installation than a massacre.

Phil had come up on Chief's heels just as he threw the laser grenade. He couldn't comprehend the damage the flashing red lights he saw from the mouth of the tunnel were causing, but the tormented screams told him all he needed to know. The kung fu master would be able to cross over all that death and chaos and finally get through the tunnel leading to the booster. However, the fact that Chief still hadn't moved yet kept Phil firmly rooted in place.

Chief chose this weapon not only because of its deadly accuracy but also because he worried another concussive blast could destabilize the ancient mortar-and-stone structures, causing that section of the tunnel to collapse, sealing them in. This method would be just as effective without the dangers of being trapped or buried alive.

"No one's making it out of there, dude," Chief assured Phil. "I tested this at the Workshop range with over twenty targets popping up at the same time. It was one hundred percent accurate and hit all twenty in less than three seconds. I'll keep you covered anyway, just in case, but you can go anytime, the disc is powered down now." He tapped the side of his MP7 and motioned for Phil to get moving.

Phil sprinted through the open gap, holding his breath, silently hoping the laser-guided technology was as foolproof as Chief had made it seem. While the distance to cover wasn't even forty feet, it seemed like a mile to him in the exposed intersection. His quads burned, legs pumping as fast as they would carry him across the open expanse until he finally cleared the danger zone by diving headfirst into the mouth of the tunnel. He completed the parkour maneuver, pulling his HK45 mid-roll, and ended in a controlled crouch, pointing the .45 caliber pistol dead ahead. Thankfully, the path ahead was clear of soldiers and hopefully any other impediments to reaching the broken booster. He stood, keeping the sidearm in his grasp, and ran toward the Western Wall Plaza, leaving nothing but shadows and dust in his wake.

Chief saw him make it safely into the opposing tunnel, then turned around to see Gryph approaching.

"Now that Phil is on his way to replace the booster. What do you say you and I take a look at the mess of bodies over there and see who and what we can find? Basileus and his team didn't stand a chance against that laser grenade. It almost doesn't seem sporting." He smirked, not feeling the least bit guilty about the uneven playing field. Gryph just shook his head and smiled.

The pair walked over to the carnage in the adjacent tunnel. Body parts and weapons littered the ground. But something, or rather, the lack of somethings, didn't make sense. The bodies were too few in number. Only three heads were visible in the mess. None were attached to their respective bodies though, and even more disturbing, none of the disembodied faces matched the description of the thugs from Luna's café that Phil had given them earlier.

Gryph looked over at Chief, who'd been rummaging through the bodies for a closer look. "Shit. He's not in this pile either, bro. These are all mercs for hire. None of them is Basileus."

"If he's not here, or part of that first wave of guys we took out, then where the hell is he?" The two friends craned their necks all around. Suddenly, the answer became clear. Gryph glanced down the main pathway that led back to Ali, Dallas, and Luna.

"Shit!" they said in unison and sprinted toward their friends.

CHAPTER FORTY-FIVE

Inside the Western Wall Tunnels
2:11 a.m. IST

Aliyah heard heavy boots pounding toward them. She knew there was no way that Phil had replaced the booster and made it back so quickly, and the signal was still offline. She'd heard the explosion a minute earlier but couldn't determine if the attack was initiated by her compatriots or against them. She reached for her P226, a favorite of SEALs, Mossad operatives and IDF Special Forces. That in and of itself spoke volumes about the weapon's capabilities. Most of the team was carrying the same model.

"Luna, Dallas," Aliyah whispered, "we're about to have company. We need to find cover before they get here." She didn't bother alerting Daedalus. He'd already been alerted by the approaching sound and crouched down, his hand hovering over the hilt of the Honjo katana.

"Huh? We need to find cover until who gets here? What the hell is going on now?" Dallas kept the volume of his voice low but was clearly confused as to what was happening.

Dallas had been laser focused on finishing the programming for the retrieval phase of their operation in anticipation of the signal being restored and hadn't looked up once from his tablet since the other guys left, save for when the explosion rattled the walls around them moments earlier. Aliyah's warning, however, shook him loose from his work and back to the current predicament.

Aliyah didn't bother answering Dallas's question, not because she didn't want to, but because she simply didn't have the answer. "Let's just hope Phil made it out before the blast. It's going to be up to us to hold this position." She was thankful the search for the manna was continuing autonomously on the other side of the wall and out of sight.

"How do you know it's not Gryph and Chief headed back this way?" Dallas asked, panic creeping into his voice. "Maybe they killed Basileus's team in that explosion we just heard." He hoped and prayed that it was the cavalry they were hearing, not Basileus's kill squad looking to go two-for-two against Daedalus's team.

"If it was Gryph, he would have let us know he was rushing back here like that," Daedalus whispered. "He wouldn't want to alarm us. Those boots are getting closer, and I haven't heard a warning from him or Chief yet."

"Daedalus is right. Those aren't friendlies," Aliyah said. "We're going to have to make our stand here." She positioned herself directly across from Daedalus. "Luna, let's hope all that target practice you had with your dad was time well spent."

Luna racked the slide on her Glock, chambering a round. The metallic snap echoed in the stony enclosure. "Don't you worry, Doc. This girl's gonna make her daddy proud."

Aliyah smiled. She had no doubt.

Dallas was still concentrating intently on the tablet, typing furiously a few feet behind the protection of the unlikely quartet. They were now the only ones standing in the way of a delusional madman and his plans for destroying the world.

The footfalls grew louder by the second, devolving into a low rumble as the distance between the two groups closed. Unfortunately, that portion of the tunnel didn't have the same tight twists and turns found in other sections of the underground city, leaving the three of them totally exposed. Whatever was charging around the bend, it was coming straight for them.

One minute earlier

Yvgeni led his small group away from the spray of gunfire erupting behind them, making their escape into the main tunnel just in time. A moment of hesitation longer, and they would have added their names to the scores of others who had perished within those ancient walls.

The three men walked in single file against the right side of the tunnel. Each had a weapon firmly grasped in their hands. Their careful planning would be for nothing if they weren't able to eliminate Daedalus—the last impediment to their goal.

Yvgeni halted the procession upon hearing the all-too-familiar sound of a slide from a semi-automatic pistol ratcheting into place.

"Did you guys hear that?" Yvgeni turned and asked his cousin a little too loudly. "It sounded like somebody—" Yvgeni stopped mid-sentence and hit the ground as a bullet pinged off the wall an inch above where he'd just been standing.

Dima thought his cousin had been killed. The man lay prone on the ground, unmoving. But a moment later, Yvgeni's head popped up. He looked cautiously around. Seeing no incoming threat, he scurried backwards, almost falling over Dima's crouched form.

Dima flattened himself against the wall and motioned for Basileus to stay back and keep low. While he was sure the old warrior could hold his own in a fight, his role had always been that of bodyguard. He wouldn't allow any harm to come to Basileus, even if it meant sacrificing himself in the process. The fact that his boss had the ability to heal any mortal wounds, or so he hoped, may have had something to do with the cavalier attitude Dima displayed when heading into battle for Basileus. This time was no different.

"Both guns," Dima said.

Before Yvgeni could ask what he meant, he saw Dima draw a second pistol that matched the one already gripped in his other hand. He caught the meaning right away and mirrored his fierce-looking cousin's stance.

"Empty both clips. Don't stop until they click. I'll be right behind you."

Dima knew the boy was a dead man walking. If Yvgeni refused the order to go, he'd have to shoot him on the spot. Basileus would be witness to the insubordination and insist on nothing less. But he knew it would be a miracle if his cousin made it through the next twenty feet. He figured he would avenge the death of this *dear* family member, but only after his cousin flushed out the positions of Daedalus's team, hidden in the shadows ahead.

Yvgeni swallowed hard. He was under no illusions. Taking a deep breath, he leveled both guns and charged. Bullets spat from both barrels as he ran. He fired blindly at first, but after a few steps, he discovered the origin of the shot that sailed over him a moment earlier. His eyes fixed on the petite woman standing behind two other figures, looming large despite her slight build. She had her feet slightly staggered, and both arms extended straight ahead in a Weaver stance. *An experienced shooter*, he thought. But by then it was too late.

Yvgeni saw the muzzle flash at the same moment his shoulder exploded. The force of the bullet spun him around, forcing him to drop the gun from his injured, and now useless arm. Yvgeni used the momentum to complete a full 360-degree turn, firing indiscriminately as he came back around.

Dallas watched in horror and disbelief as Yvgeni fired in every direction.

"Get down!" he screamed over the gunfire. He didn't understand why Luna was still standing and facing the shooter until he saw the gun in her hand. He knew her aim was true when the attacker lost his pistol, twisting away after the shot hit him, but the shooter was now spinning back towards them, firing wildly.

Aliyah opened fire at the same time but was forced to duck for cover when an errant bullet came unnervingly close, barely missing her neck. She felt the speed and the air sizzle as the projectile flew by, pinging off the rock beside her. Spinning on her heel, she brought her SIG around again. The second opportunity was all she needed. She fired a tight cluster of shots into Yvgeni's center mass as the Russian completed what may not have been his first, but was certainly the last pirouette of his life.

Unfortunately for Aliyah, Yvgeni kept pulling the trigger as he fell to the ground. One of the last and luckiest shots he would ever take smashed into the side of her knee. The ballistic suit she wore kept the bullet from piercing her skin, but the force of the blow dislocated her knee. She thought there was a good chance her patella was shattered too. A throaty cry left her lips as she grabbed her injured joint, but her reflexive training kept the P226 trained on their would-be killer until his body went limp on the cold stone ground. It was over in under two seconds, the pain from the wound just starting to register for Ali.

Luna lowered her arms, forcing her muscles to relax and release from the shooting stance. She desperately wanted to make her way over to Ali after watching her new friend cry out and buckle to the ground. Luna didn't yet know the extent of Aliyah's wounds, but seeing her still pointing her gun at the dead man on the stone floor gave Luna the reassurance that she was at least alive and alert.

Daedalus had been standing a yard or two behind Aliyah when Yvgeni broke through, shooting. His first instinct was to charge and fight, but he rushed to her side instead after seeing her collapse to the ground. They needed Ali's expertise to complete her work on the antidote once the manna was secured. Losing her meant losing everything.

"I'm okay," she said through gritted teeth when Daedalus reached her side. "My knee is pretty messed up though."

Luna and Daedalus were momentarily distracted by Aliyah's injury and didn't see Dima following closely after his cousin. When Yvgeni ran out into the open, he'd drawn everyone's attention, leaving a small window of opportunity for Dima to peek around the corner and assess the force he was up against. Much to his surprise, he saw only four people. One of them wasn't even facing his direction. The man was armed with nothing but an iPad, casting his terrified face in a cold blue hue. He spied one woman pressed tightly against the wall, but oddly, the man behind her was unarmed. The second woman was a different story though. Brave, albeit extremely reckless, she was standing upright in the middle of the tunnel, her gun still smoking from the shot she just wounded Yvgeni with.

Dima had watched her fire the initial shot and saw his little cousin take the hit in the shoulder. The bodyguard was forced to duck back behind the rocky outcropping as Yvgeni spun back towards him, still firing wildly, almost killing Dima and Basileus in the process.

Dima risked another peek around the curve in time to watch another woman riddle his cousin's torso with bullets. He also bore witness to a lucky errant shot of Yvgeni's hitting the woman who'd killed him just before he died. *Thank you, cousin. You did well.*

Dima took advantage of the distraction that Aliyah's injury created, determined to make good on his vow to avenge Yvgeni's death.

Dallas wasn't distracted anymore though. He saw Dima storming in hot on the heels of the man that Aliyah had just shot. This man, with guns gripped in both hands, was bringing his arms up preparing to shoot. Luna, standing less than a dozen feet away, was distracted by Ali on the ground. Dima had Luna dead to rights.

Dallas dropped the tablet and leaped toward Luna, adrenaline firing his legs faster than he ever thought possible.

"Luna!" he cried, crashing into her, sending her sprawling to the ground.

Rapid-fire shots blasted in the confined space again. Dima was unloading his magazines as fast as his fingers could pull the triggers.

The jarring impact of being bowled over by Dallas knocked the wind out of Luna's lungs, adding to the confusion already fogging her mind. Luckily, the temporary incapacitation, courtesy of Dallas, kept her flat on the ground, unable to rise even if she wanted to.

The deafening explosions from the discharge of Dima's guns finally stopped. Luna somehow registered that he was out of ammo, but she was still struggling to regain her breath before she could crouch down to fire back. Daedalus watched a pair of clips drop from the bottom of the weapons, followed by Dima's well-honed skills at grabbing two fresh magazines.

Daedalus pulled the Honjo katana from its scabbard and spun away from his position behind Aliyah all in a blindingly fast motion, using a combination of Japanese *iai-goshi* sword-drawing technique and a low, sweeping Capoeira spin. The latter was an eclectic martial art known for its acrobatic sequences, especially its rapid movement along the ground.

Daedalus completed the skillful maneuver and was able to draw within a foot of Dima with the razor-sharp steel only inches away from his attacker. He was all that stood between Aliyah and the double-barrel threat aimed their way.

Daedalus struck before Dima finished reloading his second gun. With a flick of his wrist, the Honjo sliced into Dima's forearm. The gun that he'd already reloaded tumbled from his grip. The tendons and muscle on that arm were completely severed and now visible under the thick flap of skin which had been peeled back, barely clinging to his arm. Even the bone had been scored deeply by Masamune's masterpiece of a blade. Dark blood seeped from the gaping wound, pooling and staining the ground at Dima's feet.

Dima lurched back as Daedalus brought the deadly blade around for another strike. The Damascus steel missed his neck by inches, easily slashing a deep cut through the stab-proof tactical vest Dima was wearing, a testament to the razor-sharp edge on the famous katana. Dima's scramble backwards was halted when he collided with Basileus. He helped his wounded bodyguard to his feet after watching the scene unfold from behind the curve in the wall, but now stepped out into the open.

"It's been a long time," Basileus said, staring at the visage of the man wielding the katana in front of him.

The color washed from Daedalus's face. "No. It can't be." The Honjo hung loosely in his hand, the tip only inches from the ground. All of Daedalus's strength was sapped by the enormity of this impossibility.

"You seem just as surprised as I was when I saw you after all these years. The mighty Odysseus."

There were too many questions to ask. Daedalus's mind was twisted in knots. "Hector, my brother, is it really you?"

"Yes, Odysseus. But we're not brothers. Not anymore."

"I don't understand. What quarrel would you have with me?"

"It doesn't matter now. Whether you walk this earth as Odysseus or Daedalus, your time is now at an end. *Old friend.*"

Daedalus firmed his grip on the Honjo's hilt.

"Nooooo!" A blood-curdling howl filled the space. Everyone turned toward the source of the scream.

Luna had recovered from the tackle, finally catching her breath. She was hunched over Dallas's body, rocking back and forth, cradling him in her lap. Even from where they were standing, the blood pooling around his head was clearly visible.

"He was trying to save me." Luna was weeping uncontrollably. "And now…"

Daedalus watched as Basileus whispered something into Dima's ear. The bodyguard nodded and inserted a fresh magazine into the gun he grasped in his only working hand, the procedure made much more difficult with the loss of use in his other arm.

"Your friend is just another body poisoning our planet," Basile-us said callously to Luna. "No one will miss him or remember him. Individually, his death will be as meaningless as yours. Only by sacrificing the masses will I be able to save Earth and secure a lasting future for our species. Maybe you can take some small measure of comfort in that. If not, it's of no consequence to me. You die tonight either way."

The two men locked eyes, hatred burning behind Hector's - resolute determination behind Odysseus's.

"May the gods forgive me, Hector." Daedalus wrapped his hands around the sword's hilt and assumed a fighting stance.

"They might, Odysseus. But I never will."

CHAPTER FORTY-SIX

Inside the Western Wall Tunnels
Two minutes earlier

Gryph raced from the macabre scene of dismembered parts strewn on the ground, Chief following closely in his wake. He was furious with himself for allowing Basileus's men to slip by, putting the rest of the crew in mortal danger.

"Billy, we're not going to make it to them in time." Gryph was in an all-out sprint now. His big friend was moving as fast as he could but could barely keep up through the cramped walkways. They both dove for cover, skidding and bumping along the uneven path of rock and sand, when the first barrage of shots that Yvgeni let loose on his initial incursion rang out just ahead. The echo and rapid-fire concussions of the rounds made gauging the distance and direction to the shooter impossible.

But as quickly as it started, it stopped.

The two men jumped up and continued forward, only to hear four or five more telltale pops. They kept upright this time, flattening themselves against the wall, slowing their progress. They crept along the last few yards as quickly as possible while listening to the balance of the gunfight, not knowing who was firing on whom.

"You have anything in that bag of tricks you brought along that could help?" Gryph asked.

"Bro, I have no clue what we're facing yet. I can't just laser bomb these guys. Our friends are in there. It could be them doing the shooting. We're gonna have to do this old school."

The pair were close enough now to be able to make out distinct voices. Gryph recognized Daedalus, but his words weren't clear enough to discern. Shockingly, the person he was speaking to wasn't Dallas, the only other male voice on their team. That meant Daedalus was seemingly having a casual conversation with the people trying to kill them, and that made no sense.

Luna's guttural cry pierced the air before any reasonable explanation presented itself to Gryph, making the hair on the back of his neck stand on end.

"That's it. We're going in now, Billy. You take care of anything on the left side, and I'll take the right."

As chance would have it, Gryph and Chief still had the element of surprise. Dima was dazed from his severely wounded arm, and the unnerving conversation his boss was having caused the Russian to briefly disregard anything other than the scene unfolding in front of him.

Both ex-SEALs turned the corner quickly but cautiously, blind to the positions their friends were in. They'd overheard the last few comments from Basileus while they were sneaking up behind the madman and his bodyguard.

Gryph had three new questions that needed immediate answers. *Why did he just call our boss Odysseus? Who the hell is Hector? And which one of our friends just died?* The answer to the last of the three questions was by far the most pressing.

Chief and Gryph each took a couple of silent paces forward until they were lined up behind Basileus and Dima. Their progress also brought them into full view of their friends. Neither Aliyah nor Daedalus gave any indication that they noticed the cavalry had just arrived, keeping their faces expressionless and their eyes fixed on the two hostile figures facing them. A few seconds passed, and no one moved. Luna was still crying beside Dallas's body, but couldn't keep her surprise, relief, and fury hidden upon seeing Chief and Gryph sneaking up on the bastards who had shot the man she loved.

"They shot Dallas!" she shouted, pointing at Basileus and his bodyguard. Luna was utterly distraught and not thinking clearly about the repercussions of her actions. All eyes flashed on her for the briefest of moments. Gryph knew she'd made a mistake but couldn't correct for it in time.

Basileus dropped low at the momentary distraction and exploded toward Luna. Daedalus swung the Honjo at him with a lightning-fast strike, but Basileus ducked under the edge of the katana as he ran by. Daedalus/Odysseus was not holding back. That swipe would have taken Hector's head clean off if he hadn't moved out of the way at the last moment.

Gryph fired a shot at Basileus/Hector, *whatever his name really is*, but missed. Mercifully, the round continued down the empty corridor and didn't strike anyone else on his side.

Hector flew past Aliyah in a blur. She was infuriated at being unable to stop him due to her knee injury. It didn't help that the man moved at lightning speed either. Hector moved faster than anyone she'd ever seen. He lunged toward Luna after leaving Aliyah in the dust, knocking her flat on her back and winding her a second time. Hector grabbed Luna by the back of her tactical vest and hoisted her up, putting his body squarely behind hers, making her a human shield and gaining a hostage in the process. He moved a bit deeper into the tunnel, pulling Luna along with him, and kicked Dallas's limp body out of the way with his boot.

It was the first opportunity for Gryph to see what had happened to Dallas. He assumed things were bad after seeing the lack of any physical reaction from Dallas when Hector booted him away. He knew it with certainty after seeing Dallas's head awash in blood.

Chief did the simple math and figured if they took one of his people hostage, he would take one of theirs. Since Dima was only a few feet in front of him and still unaware that the hulking SEAL was standing behind him, Billy K made his move.

Dima had been losing a lot of blood, and his reaction time suffered because of it. He just stood there, dazed. Chief grabbed him from behind in a rear naked choke hold and slammed him into the tunnel wall, knocking loose the gun he held in his good hand and breaking a few of his digits for good measure. The impact of the Russian's skull with the cavern wall opened a wide gash across Dima's forehead. The bridge of his nose cracked and twisted, having been the first point of contact with the stone. Dima's eyes welled with tears, magnifying his already bulging eyes from the choke hold. Even after crashing into the wall, Chief hadn't loosened his grip one bit.

He manhandled Dima until he had the big Russian in front of him, mirroring the stance that Hector had Luna in, a few yards in front of them.

"Let her go, and you can have your *boyfriend* back." Chief's offer was made in a tone that didn't sound negotiable. Dima was turning a deeper shade of purple, blood still pouring from his shattered nose. With the loss of blood from his arm and face, coupled with the lack of air to his brain, he'd be unconscious in a few seconds.

Hector laughed at the proposal. "You're not in any position to make a deal. I alone have the power to give life and to take it away. You may kill my friend there, and I in turn will kill yours. However, I can have him returned to me full of life and vigor while your girlfriend will rot in the ground, never to see the light of day again."

Chief shot a sideways glance at Gryph. *Now what? This fucker just called my bluff.*

Gryph raised his pistol, trying to get a fix on Hector, but he was using Luna too efficiently. "If you kill her, you won't be around to bring anyone back. You'll be dead a fraction of a second after you pull that trigger."

Luna had started to come out of the shock of seeing Dallas lifeless on the ground and realized she had effectively been taken hostage. In fact, it allowed her to tap into some inner reservoir of strength that empowered and emboldened her. Luna wouldn't allow herself to become victimized further. She tried to wriggle from Hector's grasp, but he had a vice-like grip on her. She wasn't going anywhere unless he decided to let her go.

"He'll only get one shot off, Gryph, and his evil plan dies with him too," Luna said. "My life for eight billion is an easy decision." Gryph had been right about her all along. She was a true warrior and was now offering herself up as a sacrificial lamb without hesitation.

"Told you I'd make my daddy proud." She stood a little taller and laughed. "Now shoot this son-of-a-bitch."

Hector was caught off guard by the selfless act Luna was prepared to make. The sincerity in her voice was genuine. She was fully prepared to give up her life to end his. He shoved her further in front of him, keeping his head and torso safely behind her body. While Hector didn't doubt her resolve, he didn't think her friends would try to shoot right through Luna to strike him. It was a calculated gamble, to be sure, but it was a risk he was willing to take.

Shit! Gryph kept his sights trained on Luna, waiting for Hector to reveal any meaningful body part. He knew he couldn't get to Hector through Luna. Not because the shot was too difficult. He'd normally be able to fire a well-placed shot that would kill or incapacitate Hector and would only leave Luna with a small scar, a crazy story to tell, and hopefully minimal collateral damage. The ballistic outfit she wore, however, made that option impossible. The bulletproof suit would deflect anything he fired. The only damage Gryph would inflict would likely be a broken rib for Luna, leaving the coward unharmed behind her.

Dima started to slump in Chief's grip, his face a grotesque shade of dark cherry. The blood vessels in his eyes had broken from the strain. Gone were the frantic whites staring back. Blood-red orbs were half concealed by drooping lids. Dima was on the verge of unconsciousness and certain death in less than a minute if Chief didn't release him.

"Your boy here isn't doin' so well." Chief hefted Dima higher for Hector to see, hoping to draw him out from behind Luna. "And that whole eternal life thing, that's old news, buddy. We have our own stash of the magic juice. You can't do shit to us that we can't fix. Difference is, you're not making it out of here to get to your supply. I'll make damn sure of that. So, I'll say it again. Let her go, and I'll let your guy go. I'd hurry up too, or the only thing left in his future will be adult diapers, applesauce, and *Nurse Ratched*."

Chief was laying it on thick, trying to do anything to get Hector to show himself or let Luna go, a tactic that, unfortunately, didn't seem to be working. The man remained firmly entrenched behind Luna, not falling for the SEAL's ruse.

"No love for the Cuckoo's nest reference either," Billy K said to Gryph, but loud enough for all to hear. "Tough crowd." Chief was cool, calm, and collected, acting as if this kind of thing happened daily. While it wasn't his first rodeo, this encounter was quite unique.

"Hector, this can be settled between us. No one else needs to die tonight." Heads swiveled toward Daedalus. They watched as he sheathed the Honjo and laid it on the ground at his feet. "Let our friend go. No matter how this plays out, it'll eventually come down to you and me. You know that to be true. Let's dispense with the formalities and finish it."

Everyone stood still. Gryph could tell that Hector was weighing his chances of success with the limited options he had left.

"Release Dima now, and you can have your pretty little friend back." Hector pushed Luna a few inches forward but kept his grip firm and his body concealed.

"Okay, Hector, but if that brave woman isn't on the way back to me when I release Dima, I'm going to blow a hole in the back of his head and then come for you next. Understood?"

Hector ignored Chief and looked at Daedalus instead. "Odysseus, you may take her place, but this changes nothing. Tell your people to drop the weapons pointed at me, and the big man with the even bigger mouth to release Dima now."

"At least you still have some sense of honor, *brother*."

Odysseus moved slowly and deliberately toward Hector. He held his arms high, not giving him a reason to renege on the exchange and not allowing Hector any time to change his mind.

Hector responded in kind by letting go of Luna's tactical vest. As soon as she felt the resistance holding her in place disappear, she sprinted toward Gryph. Odysseus and Hector completed their swap at the same time. Chief released the chokehold he had on Dima and shoved the bodyguard away. Aliyah hobbled over to the boys until all four of them were huddled together safely.

During the exchange, Gryph heard a faint chime and noticed a blue LED winking on the ground where Aliyah just scrambled from. Her HUD was back online, which meant Phil successfully replaced the booster. *I only hope the effort wasn't in vain.*

"Your friend, Daedalus, is coming with me," Hector said. Having Odysseus under control and Dima released from Chief's grip seemed to embolden him once more.

"We're going to move farther down the tunnel and out another exit. If anyone dares to follow, you'll find his lifeless body in my wake. I suggest you all go back the way you came."

"That's not going to happen. We're Navy SEALs. We don't leave anyone behind. It's kind of our thing." While Gryph verbally taunted Hector, he didn't dare make a move for his gun. He knew Daedalus would be dead before he touched it. But they couldn't just let Hector take Daedalus with him. They were at an im-passe once again.

While the drama was playing out, Dima scratched and clawed his way back across the stones toward his savior. He coughed and sputtered as his badly damaged neck and punctured lung fought to provide air and blood to his rapidly weakening body. He looked like a wounded animal scampering for its life. Everyone tracked the bloody, pathetic sight as he made his way back to his master's side.

"Now we'll take our leave," Hector said as he shoved Odysseus forward. "I would say 'until next time,' although I'm fairly certain there won't be a next time."

Chief wasn't going to be dictated to anymore. He swung his MP7 level with Dima's head and flipped on the laser sight that illuminated the bridge of Dima's nose. "Take one more step, and he goes down for good this time."

"It seems you aren't taking my threats seriously. Maybe this will change your mind." Hector pushed Odysseus to a full arm's length and prepared to fire a round into the back of his old friend's head.

The echo from the next shot was deafening.

CHAPTER FORTY-SEVEN

Inside the Western Wall Tunnels
2:19 a.m. IST

The ensuing few seconds were absolute chaos.

Odysseus flew forward from the impact of the shot. He reached back reflexively where he thought he felt a round hit his lower back. His hand came back bloody. *I must be in shock,* he thought. *I'm not in any pain.* He expected a wave of agony to wash over him any second, but it never came. Then he realized why. He hadn't been shot—well, not directly, at least. The shot must have hit and injured Hector standing behind him, only smashing into Odysseus after exiting its first victim. The force of the shot was disbursed into the ballistic suit Odysseus was wearing, propelling him forward when it hit. The blood was Hector's, not his.

He looked back over his shoulder in time to see his onetime brother clutching his wounded side and scampering deeper into the tunnel. Suddenly a second shot boomed even louder than the first. Chief had had enough of the cat-and-mouse game. He was the one who fired the second shot, confirming that the laser sights on his MP7 were dialed in perfectly. The center of Dima's face exploded as the round entered the Russian's skull and obliterated the back of his head. *There isn't enough magic juice on Earth to fix that hole,* Chief mused.

Hector was too far into the tunnel and didn't turn back to see Dima fall, but he knew the bodyguard was on the receiving end of the shot he'd just heard. There was nothing he could do for him now anyway. He had his own issues to deal with. He was injured and bleeding badly. He didn't understand what just happened. The shot came seemingly out of nowhere and tore through his lower back, destroying his kidney, before exiting out the front. The wound needed to be repaired quickly, or it would prove fatal. He ducked and weaved when he ran, pulling at the blue sapphire amulet hanging around his neck as bullets pinged off the walls around him. Gryph and Chief kept firing at Hector as he ran through the tunnels, but the rounds didn't connect. Hector's shaking fingers finally found the clasp on the vial dangling from his neck. "You haven't won yet," he spat through bloody teeth and pained gasps, flipping the lid open.

At the same moment, fifty yards behind Hector's escape, Gryph ran over to Odysseus and helped him to his feet. "Are you okay?"

"I'm fine. Really. Feels like I took a right hook to the kidney though. What happened?"

"Lama!" Luna screamed again, this time with joy.

Everyone turned to see Dallas perched awkwardly on one elbow. His other arm, still holding the gun from the round he'd fired into Hector's back.

Luna was there in a heartbeat. She slid to the floor and cradled his head in her lap. "I don't understand. I thought you were... I thought..." She couldn't finish. Tears rolled down her cheeks, as she squeezed him tighter.

Odysseus rushed over to them. "Mr. Hayle, I owe you my life. If you hadn't intervened, I'd be dead. Thank you. . . my friend."

Dallas collapsed into Luna's arms and sighed. "This job sucks ass. I want a raise." He paused and then smirked. "And you're welcome."

Aliyah limped over to inspect Dallas's head wound. "You're one lucky guy, Lama. A few centimeters deeper, and you wouldn't be talking to us right now—or ever, for that matter." She ran her fingers across his head, trying to find the source of the blood. Her quick examination didn't reveal anything until...

"Owww!" Dallas yelped.

"I think I found the point of impact," Aliyah said. "It looks to be from a bullet or a piece of a bullet, maybe even a stone fragment ricochet. It tore across the top of his head, leaving a deep gash too. I can also feel quite a bit of swelling in one spot. That's probably where it made impact before skimming along his scalp, knocking him unconscious. The head is very vascular too. The blood makes the injury look much more severe than it is, but he'll still need to have this attended to by a doctor sooner rather than later. But thank goodness, his hard-headedness literally saved his life this time."

Everyone was thankful and relieved that Dallas would be okay. No one more so than Luna.

"Daedalus, Odysseus, whoever you really are, what do we do about Hector?" Gryph asked. He was grateful that Dallas would make it, but they all needed to refocus and complete the mission.

"Wait. Why did you just call him Odysseus?" Dallas asked, pointing to Daedalus. "And who the hell is Hector? Maybe I got hit harder than you guys think. I really don't feel well." He placed his head back in Luna's lap and closed his eyes to steady the dizziness he was feeling.

"Basileus is actually a guy named Hector, and Daedalus's real name is Odysseus," Luna said. "I'm pretty sure they've known each other for a long time. There doesn't seem to be any love lost between them, at least not from Hector's side. Anyway, don't worry about that stuff right now. Just rest." While Luna was explaining, Aliyah applied pressure to the gash on his head with some gauze pads from Chief's medical kit.

"I'll go after Hector," Odysseus said. "He won't get very far with that gunshot wound, and he'll be leaving me a trail of blood to follow." He picked up the Honjo and handed it to Chief. "Give this to Master Wu for safekeeping." He confirmed the loaded pistol he had concealed in his tactical vest was still there. He shook Chief's hand and clapped him on the shoulder. "The rest of you need to finish here with the nanobots. We need the source of the elixir, or this was all for naught."

They began to hear footfalls growing louder from the tunnel behind them. Odysseus drew his pistol and spun to face the tunnel entry. Gryph and Chief both whipped around, pointing their weapons toward the noise. A voice rang out before the figure came into view.

"Don't shoot. It's me, Phil" He figured that if Gryph had secured the area already, they'd appreciate the heads-up that he was about to rejoin the group and avoid them turning him into Swiss cheese. If he was running into a bunch of unfriendlies, maybe the odd introduction would throw them off momentarily and allow him time to turn and escape without getting killed. If Basileus's assault team took out the rest of the Daedalus crew already, he wouldn't last down there on his own anyway.

Thankfully, the response was from one of his own. "We're clear over here, Phil." Chief's baritone was unmistakable. Phil came around the corner, breathing heavily. He hadn't stopped sprinting since he left them to replace the booster.

"Holy smokes! What happened to Dallas?" It was one of the first things he saw after getting back.

"His head was cut pretty badly. Likely concussed too," Aliyah said. "But he's going to be okay."

Gryph looked down at his injured teammate. Dallas was awake, but was pale and clammy. "Dallas, I know this isn't the best time to be asking, but we're going to need you to hang in there a little longer and help us with the nanobots. Phil got the boosters back up, you and Daedalus are the only ones who can program these things, except he's chasing after Basileus right now, which just leaves you." Gryph used Odysseus's previously known alias to keep things simple for Dallas.

"No," he said and shook his head, but even the slightest movement made him queasy.

"What do you mean? You can't do it while you're hurt? Is it too hard to concentrate right now? Maybe we could—"

"No," Dallas said again, more firmly this time. "I've already finished the coding. I remember completing it and was about to tell Luna I was done, but when I turned around, I must have got hit. Everything just went black. I set the program to execute as soon as the signal was restored. The bots should already be hard at work. Put on the HUDs and check for yourself."

Gryph put his high-tech goggles back on and toggled the view to see the nanobot progress. A huge grin spread across his face. "You're a genius! You did it!"

"What's the plan now, Commander?" Phil asked.

"I need you and Luna to get Ali and Dallas out of here and back onboard *Hera* for medical attention. Ali's knee is busted, and I'm not sure that Dallas can walk on his own either. Luna's going to need a hand managing these two, especially if you run into anyone else on the way out."

"I didn't see anyone in the tunnels on the way back," Phil said. "Same thing with the big courtyard in front of the wall. It was still deserted, but I could hear that explosion and the gunshots clearly, and I'm pretty sure I wasn't the only one. Hopefully it'll be hard to pinpoint our exact location, being that we're so deep into the tunnel system. I think Ali's IDF friends were still keeping their distance and the other authorities at bay. For how long, I'm not sure."

"Okay, that's good news. Let's get them out of here and hopefully Aliyah can convince her friends to buy us a bit more time. Chief and I will secure the manna and bug out of here right after that. Odysseus has his own score to settle. We'll all meet back at the airport on *Hera* ASAP. Any questions?"

Aliyah raised her hand. "I want to see it, Gryph."

"See what?"

"The Ark. I can't leave knowing I'm this close to seeing physical proof of all those stories I heard as a little girl. I can't leave now."

"Everyone can see it," Dallas said feebly, trying to sit up. "Put your HUDs on. I'm going to need a minute here anyway." He tried steadying himself and took a couple deep breaths.

Everyone slipped their goggles back on and toggled over to the nano view. The image on the screen left them breathless.

The enclosure was smaller than Aliyah had anticipated. It wasn't much larger than a typical garden shed, barely enough room to contain the items it held. But this wasn't about the size of the room. It was about the contents it held. Dominating most of the area was a box roughly three feet wide by four feet long, resting under a blue cloth that had decayed badly over the centuries. The majority of the box was exposed, revealing the unmistakable luster of gold. The two ornate angel figurines fixed to the box's lid was the last of the proof they needed. They had found it. The Ark of the Covenant was finally within reach, figuratively speaking.

"I programmed the bots to search for any chemical signature similar to the toxin. Fortunately for us, it's very unique and should be easy to lock on to. As soon as the bots get a hit on the source, they'll morph into collection mode and bring it back to us," Dallas explained, his face gaining a bit of color as he spoke.

Odysseus watched Aliyah wipe a tear from her cheek. "This treasure belonged to your people. It kept them alive and inspired while wandering in the wilderness of the Sinai desert all those years ago. Now, hopefully, we can harness some of that power to save the planet."

"How exactly are we getting the manna from that side of the wall to this side?" Chief asked. "Assuming it's still inside the Ark, that is."

"I programmed the bots to morph into nanotube structures," Dallas said. "Basically, microscopic test tubes. They'll carry the manna internally and then recombine into one large vessel on this end. They're small enough to travel through the rock's pores, just like water soaking through a sponge. Hopefully, they can collect enough of the manna to power Ali's antidote."

"When will we know if this works?" Chief asked.

"Any second." Dallas was perking up at seeing his solution working. "They're locked onto the signature and pouring into the Ark. We should actually be able to see inside now."

The nano view on the HUDs dissolved to black static as the swarm passed through the seams in the gold-plated exterior. It didn't take long for the picture to resolve itself and provide a new vista. A solid block of sapphire occupied most of the interior. Fragments of broken sapphire were also scattered along the bottom.

"I sure hope those little digital buggers didn't cause that damage." Chief looked genuinely concerned.

"No. Those pieces were placed inside intentionally," Luna said, putting everyone's fears to rest. "The Bible relates that the first set of Commandments were written by the finger of God but were shattered by Moses when he discovered the Jewish people had built a golden calf to worship while he was on the mountain receiving the tablets. He went back up the mountain for another forty days, and had to carve the second set himself. Those broken pieces are the remains of the first set, touched by God himself." Luna choked up as she finished the impromptu Bible lesson. "I can't believe what I'm seeing. Thank you again."

"Thank you? You almost died being part of this crazy group!" Dallas exclaimed.

"To be able to stand this close to something touched by the divine, well, it makes it worthwhile to me. Remember, I was selling cappuccinos and high-speed internet last week. I'd trade it for moments like this, risk and all. Any day of the week."

"I think the nanobots found something," Phil said as he watched the swarm run down the face of the sapphire block and pool into a corner. It took a few seconds for the picture to stabilize before they could see the nano swarm's target. A small golden jar resting on the corner of the Ark. The lid to the little jar had been sealed with wax long ago, but had succumbed to the ravages of time. Small sections had become brittle and crumbled away. A thin black stream wriggled up the side of the golden vessel and into the jar, looking like ants invading a honey pot at a picnic.

"As soon as we confirm that the manna is still inside the golden jar, I'm leaving to intercept Hector," Odysseus said. "Make your way back to *Hera* and get airborne as soon as possible."

"Chief and I will wait for the nanobots to complete their task and then bring the payload back to the jet as soon as the collection is complete," Gryph said.

Odysseus looked around at the group he'd assembled. "You've all done more for me than I could have ever dreamed possible, but I must ask one last thing of you."

Gryph didn't like where this was heading.

"If I'm not back by the time Gryph and Chief are onboard Hera, I want you to swear that you'll all leave. The antidote is the only thing that matters now."

The silence that followed stretched on for an uncomfortably long time.

"Well, I sure as shit promise to get the hell out of here as soon as possible—even if it means leaving y'all behind," Dallas said. "Except Luna, that is."

Stunned faces stared back. Then Dallas started to laugh, a full-fledged belly laugh. Gryph, Phil, and then everyone else joined in. Even Odysseus broke down and laughed. A nice memory for them to share.

"That's settled then. Good luck, everyone. And Mr. Hayle... Lama, thank you again for saving my life," Odysseus said with a smile. He turned and ran into the tunnel before anyone could say another word. His hunt for Hector had begun.

CHAPTER FORTY-EIGHT

Inside the Western Wall Tunnels
2:24 a.m. IST

Hector raced through the darkened pathways, clutching his injured body. Blood had been flowing freely from the gaping wound in his back, but the surge had already begun to subside.

He could feel the elixir taking hold. It had been almost fifteen years since his last taste. He learned long ago that only a tiny amount was required to reverse the signs of aging, but if a repair was required for a severe injury, a larger dose was necessary. He also knew that the lifeblood of the gods had its limitations. Repair was possible. Resurrection was not.

Even though it had been less than a minute since he touched the vial to his lips, he could feel the pull of muscle and bowel fusing themselves back together. The pain was intense. It caused him to slow and stumble, but soon he would be completely healed and able to go on the offensive again. The fools had bought into the ruse that he sought a retreat! He would never run from them. He just needed a place to rest and allow the elixir to finish making him whole once more. Then he'd hunt them down, complete his work, and take his rightful place in the pantheon of the gods.

A hundred feet away the Daedalus crew, less their namesake, watched the nanobot swarm into the golden jar they hoped still held some remnants of the manna, as described in the Old Testament.

"Ali, how are we going to know if this batch is still effective?" Gryph asked. "It's been sitting down here in the dark for a couple thousand years."

The image on the HUDs resolved again. "Commander, I think we just got our answer."

A swirling pool of iridescent light danced inside the golden jar. The illumination they saw wasn't amplified by the bots. The glow was organic.

"This is exactly what I observed in the lab, only this is much more intense. If I were to guess, this is even more concentrated than the toxin. We did it. We've actually found the original source of the elixir's power."

"Hey, we still need to extract it and get it out of here safely. This ain't over yet by a long shot," Chief said.

"The bots are already on the way back with it. It'll be an infinitesimally small amount at first, but it won't take long to extract the thirty milliliters Ali thinks we need. Fourteen minutes and thirty-four seconds from now, to be exact." Dallas was getting stronger now, more alert. He'd even made some last-minute adjustments on his tablet while the bots were still in collection mode.

"I've added the bots' progress countdown to the HUDs. They'll all flow back into their case autonomously when they're finished with the collection. Just snap it shut and bring it with you when the timer reaches zero."

"I'll be waiting in the lab onboard." Aliyah was eager to get back to work. "I've already prepared the first array of the antidote to be combined with the manna. I'll be able to run a proof-of-efficacy test utilizing the toxin samples we collected previously to prove our hypothesis. I don't even want to entertain the idea that we're wrong about the antidote."

"And now that Ali has seen the Ark and we've finally found what we've been looking for, it's time for you guys to get back to *Hera*." Gryph needed them back on the plane ASAP and knew their injuries plus the line of BS that Aliyah would have to shovel to get them back on the road and past IDF security would slow them down even more.

"Dallas, do you think you can walk?"

"Yeah, I should be okay. I just need another few seconds, and I'll be good to go."

"Okay. Billy and I will wait here until the bots are done and protect our precious cargo from anyone else who may still be lurking in these tunnels, then we'll double time it out of here and back to the airport, hopefully with Daedalus—Odysseus—in tow."

Dallas stood wearily and placed his hand on the wall for support. "Just think. There's a microscopic army coming through this wall, marching to a set of instructions sent by a supercomputer back in New York. To me... that's my religion. My grail."

"Glad to see you've got your warm and sensitive side back, Lama," Chief said, laughing.

Dallas pushed off the wall and made his way toward the tunnel. "Let's get the hell out of here."

"Keep your HUDs on. It'll be easier to track everyone's egress and physical locations. You'll also be able to keep an eye on the countdown. When you guys get to the jet, tell Solo to request immediate clearance for takeoff. Hopefully, we'll be right behind you." Gryph could see how close they were to the endgame, and was taking as many precautions as possible to ensure a seamless exit.

Ali leaned on Phil for support, keeping as much weight off her bad leg as possible. Luna had her arm around Dallas's waist, while he kept one arm slung across her shoulder. He touched his head wound with his other hand, wincing as he traced the deep gash with his fingers.

Gryph and Chief watched the foursome walk out. Gryph was relieved that their team suffered no casualties, and considered themselves lucky, all things considered. A couple of the injuries sustained by the team were too close for comfort. If they had lost Aliyah or Dallas in that fight, their ability to complete the antidote would have been significantly compromised, if not entirely ruined.

When they were finally out of sight, Chief turned to Gryph. "Are we really going to let Odysseus fight Hector alone? We have over ten minutes before the bots are done. Why don't you stay here and babysit, and I'll go blow a hole through Hector's chest?"

"I was thinking something along the same lines, brother, but I was going to have you do the babysitting. Can't let you have all the fun."

"I'd argue, but you'll just pull rank on me. Totally unfair."

"Then what would you suggest? We draw straws?"

Chief let out a groan. "I'll just wait here with my thumb up my ass, while you get to be the hero again."

"I'm sure you could find something a little more useful to do. Just be ready with the case by the time I get back." Gryph swapped out his empty magazine for a full one and chambered a round. "See you in a few."

Chief began collecting all the weapons and IDs from the bodies that were scattered around the tunnel. *Some guys have all the luck.*

Hector had been resting and allowing his body to heal at the base of a deep cistern after descending a wood ladder to the bottom of the pit. He was hiding in the shadow of a small alcove built into the foundation of the ancient pool. The information placard at the top of the cistern twenty feet above contained relevant details for tourists to reference when they visited. According to the sign, this particular pool was fed by an aqueduct that supplied water to a series of cisterns in the area. This specific reservoir was one of the deepest discovered to date.

The bleeding from Hector's midsection had stopped, but the skin around the wound itched and burned from being stretched closed so quickly. The damage to his body looked more like a bad case of road rash than a gunshot wound anymore. In a few more minutes, it would fade to a bad bruise. By the time he was back on his plane, there wouldn't be any sign of it at all. Hector had been focusing on his breathing to keep the pain from overwhelming him, excruciating as it was. He couldn't afford to pass out and be taken captive. The sound of boots on stone forced him from his meditation. The healing process was not yet complete, and the pain returned with a vengeance.

His eyes had already adjusted to the dim light, allowing him to take in the details of his surroundings. The cistern was shaped like a traffic cone, narrow up top but wider across the base. He guessed that it measured not even six feet wide at the top and was over twenty feet wide at the bottom. The footfalls were getting louder. Hector scanned his surroundings for an exit but found nothing but dark shadows and solid stone in the low light.

Odysseus had been following the trail of crimson splashes and blood-stained stones with relative ease. He figured Hector was just happy to have escaped, knowing the rest of his team had been killed. Covering his tracks must not have been a priority. The bloody trail ended at the top of a ladder. A wet, red stain covered the top rung of the ladder. Hector was down there, hiding in the dark.

Odysseus peered cautiously over the edge, not wanting to catch a bullet in the face. The pit seemed to drop forever and was far too dark at the bottom for him to see anything. If he attempted to climb down the ladder, he'd be riddled with bullets before making it past the third rung. Odysseus thought for a moment and then reached inside his tactical vest and confirmed he had, in fact, brought along the perfect tool for the job.

Hector saw an eclipse-like shadow pass over the opening to the cistern and knew exactly who was up there. He could feel it in his bones. The same shadow he'd lived under his entire life would finally be lifted once he killed the mighty Odysseus. He hadn't even dared to dream of such an opportunity. The frustration would have been too great to bear. And yet here he was on the precipice of that very encounter. Hector also had to face the ugly truth that his enemy would have the advantage of fighting from the high ground if he didn't move soon.

Hector groped along the bottom edge of the cistern, hoping to find an opening to an aqueduct or some connection to another pool that he could follow out. He was about to give up and go out in a blaze of glory, until he encountered a large construction barricade which had been erected to keep the maintenance and archaeological staff away from a hole in the base of the cavern floor.

He peered through the crude opening into an even lower section of the cistern, only to find another ladder descending from there. The bottom of the cone-shaped cistern was actually just the over-flow for an much deeper cistern below. He pulled out his iPhone and flipped on the flashlight, shining it down the second shaft, hoping this deeper passageway would be his way out.

High above, Odysseus was staring into the darkness when it occurred to him that the solution to his problem was literally right in front of his eyes. The HUD's night-vision mode would allow him to see to the bottom of the cistern easily. He triggered the option on the goggles and instantly had a better sense of the situation. He was correct in his original thinking that he'd be picked off while trying to climb down with Hector waiting at the bottom.

He spotted Hector lying in wait in the shadows at the outer edge of the pool, though even with the night-vision function, he was obscured by the construction safety barriers.

Odysseus had to get down there quickly and decided a fireman's slide down the sturdy wood ladder would be the only way. It then dawned on him that he had one more trick up his sleeve. The GPR function on the HUD they used in the caves of Hebron would allow him to see everything below, like sonar for a bat. He switched to GPR mode, and not a moment too soon. The view revealed the last of Hector's body climbing through a small opening at the base of the cistern and into an even deeper pool below. Odysseus knew that climbing down the ladder would be safe now, and wasted no time clambering down.

The second ladder Hector had begun to descend was not the heavy timber kind he used to climb down the first section. It looked more like the type used for mountaineering and exploration. A series of lightweight aluminum ladders were strapped together with bungee cords and secured to the wall with metal pins and clips. This cistern looked far deeper than the first and was much narrower. However, traveling down into the unknown was better than the certainty of getting shot trying to climb out of the pool with Odysseus hovering above. Hector knew he couldn't wait him out either. It wouldn't take long for Odysseus's team to notify the local authorities for backup, and just like that, he'd be trapped like a rat in a pit. The slew of dead bodies in the tunnels would all but ensure he would be taken in for questioning, an option he wasn't prepared to entertain when his plans had just begun to come to fruition.

Odysseus scrambled down the first ladder, keeping an eye on the bottom of the pool as he descended, making sure Hector didn't pop back through the gap and open fire. He made it to the bottom without incident and did a quick sweep to double check there were no surprises that he'd failed to detect from above. Satisfied he was the sole occupant on that level, Odysseus moved towards the opening into which he'd seen Hector vanish seconds before.

"Hector," he called out, "there's nowhere else for you to run. Help me rectify this evil you have let loose upon the world. It isn't too late to turn things around. You trusted me long ago. I beg of you to do it one last time."

His impassioned plea fell on deaf ears. No reply came forth from the darkness.

He toggled the night vision mode and peeked through the hole at the base of the stone wall, figuring he could at least pinpoint Hector's rough position in the narrow shaft. Before he even had a chance to absorb the information provided by the high-tech optical gear, Hector fired a shot that pinged off the wall, missing Odysseus by mere inches. A second and third shot rang out immediately after, but missed wide.

Odysseus examined the previous scan he took with his goggles more closely. According to the GPR, the narrow shaft dropped away eighty feet and ended in a series of large rocks and jagged slabs cluttered at the base of the deep, empty pool. The broken and abandoned stones filled a sixty-foot pit at the base, for a total depth of almost 140 feet to the bottom. And that was from where he stood now. They were already deep below the Western Wall Plaza. Odysseus nodded to himself in the dark. *I know exactly what needs to be done.*

CHAPTER FORTY-NINE

The Cisterns
2:34 a.m. IST

"Hector, I know you're clinging to that ladder. I can see everything you're doing as clear as day." Odysseus was now watching him through the thermal lens on his HUD. He could see Hector's form in pulsating colors, from bright yellows to dark blues. Hector rotated the gun in his hand and extended his middle finger to the opening twenty feet above him, but stayed silent. Without the HUDs, it was pitch black.

"That's not very gentlemanlike, is it?" Odysseus's response was not to taunt, but to prove he could easily see Hector, letting the man know he was facing a fatal tactical disadvantage. Hector holstered his gun. He had been outmaneuvered, but he was far from defeated.

"Hector, please! You still have a chance to right this wrong. Let me help you. What do you want me to do?"

Two thousand years of searing hatred, stoked by the flames of time, erupted into a white-hot fury in Hector's belly.

"Suffer and die, Odysseus! I want you to suffer and die." If vengeance had a sound, his pained howl was it.

Tears streamed down Odysseus's face. "What did I do to make you hate me with such wrath? We were brothers!"

"You have no idea of the torment and pain I've endured because of you, Odysseus. Fated to a torment so painful that even Hades himself would cringe." Hector's voice seethed with rage.

Odysseus was bewildered. What terrible things had befallen his long-lost friend? "Hector, I'm sorry. I don't understand."

Hector had thought about this exact moment thousands of times. He would finally be able to tell his "brother" exactly how he suffered. His only regret was that he wouldn't be able to look him dead in the eye while he did it.

"You may not think back on that fateful night, Odysseus, but I do." Odysseus didn't have to ask for any clarification. He knew the night he was referring to was the one when they last saw each other. "You had the entire fleet at your disposal, but you wouldn't wait for help. It was just you and I against an entire enemy battalion, and yet you had to race off to be the hero once more."

"Hector, I think back on that terrible night often. But I never asked you to join me. You volunteered."

"Of course I volunteered. I was so naïve back then. Foolishly worshipping you like a god. And I bore a heavy guilt for Princess Ianthina's death. If there was a way to save her, like the way you were saved when I poured the elixir into you, I would have done anything to save my queen... and my love."

This last comment shocked Odysseus more than anything thus far.

"Your love? Princess Ianthina?" He laughed at the incredulity of it all.

"She may have loved you, Odysseus. I cannot deny that. But your insane bloodlust for battle would have soon found you dead. And who would be there to console her? Me! I was already her most trusted confidant and messenger. Whom else would she turn to?" Hector's tone softened as he let his mind float back to an imagined destiny. "Eventually, the pain of your death would fade, and the bond between Ianthina and I would grow and then blossom into love. I would become king and she my queen."

"So, now you're hellbent on destroying the world and torturing me with the last pangs of your life because your childish fantasies didn't come true?" Odysseus couldn't believe what he was hearing.

"No, Odysseus. That 'fantasy,' as you call it, was going to be my destiny. But your arrogance that night twisted my fate from becoming a king of men to a prisoner in hell." Hector was no longer daydreaming about what could have been with Ianthina. He was recalling in vivid detail the actual horrors of his own reality.

"Do you remember pouring some of the elixir into my waterskin when we left the raft, Odysseus? You said we should split up and meet by the rock where we left Ianthina's body. Whoever reached her first was to revive her with the elixir, then bring her back to the ship." Even though the instructions were spoken thousands of years earlier, they were still seared into Hector's mind. "You also said that I should return to the fleet if her body wasn't there, because it meant that you would have reached her first and would be on the way back to the ships yourselves already."

Odysseus had a feeling he knew where this was going, and it wasn't good.

"I was captured shortly after leaving the docks, racing toward Ianthina," Hector said. "Our enemy had set up numerous defensive positions, thinking our fleet was about to attack. Apparently, our ships weren't as well hidden in the harbor as we believed them to be. I was surrounded and taken captive. I didn't want the elixir to fall into their hands, so I drank a mouthful, imploring the gods to accept my passage across the river Styx, sealed my flask back up, and tossed the waterskin aside so they wouldn't find it."

That was what Odysseus was afraid had happened. "I was thrown into a dungeon and beaten to within an inch of my life. The soldiers who captured me were there, only to defend against our invading ships. They knew nothing of the elixir. I could have abstained from drinking it, and my life would have ended that night. But it was not to be. You see, Odysseus, it really was my destiny to be king—not just of a country but of the entire world. I have the power and *the will* to cleanse, heal, and restore balance to the planet."

"Hector, the world doesn't have to suffer just because you did. That's madness."

"You're confusing the two issues, Odysseus. I agree that this world doesn't need to suffer. It needs to end. This generation has become arrogant and dismissive toward the plight of our world. They poison our skies and oceans, deplete resources at an unsustainable rate, and have caused the extinction of thousands of plants and animals, forever changing the delicate balance of nature. All of this has occurred in the past couple hundred years alone. The world cannot survive another hundred years with the same moral ineptitude. My dominion over this world has already begun. You're too late to stop it."

Just then, Odysseus noticed a proximity alert blinking inside his HUD. He could see Gryph's icon approaching his location, but he

wanted to hear the rest of Hector's story before they were interrupted.

"You were correct when you said the world need not suffer. But
you do, Odysseus. You must suffer. You must feel the unrelent-
ing agony that I had to endure. After I was beaten, they threw me
into a pit to die. When they came back for my body, I was healed.
They thought I was possessed by a demon or practiced witchcraft.
If I hadn't witnessed your healing on the skiff earlier that night, I
would have thought the same of myself too. They didn't want to
take any chances the second time around, so they impaled me with
spears, arrows, and swords until there was more wood and steel in
my body than bone. I was sure that pit would become my grave,
but hours later I awoke. The blades which had skewered my body
should have killed me, and each edge felt like white-hot metal under my skin, but they didn't. I couldn't die. I pulled every arrow,
knife, sword, and spear from my body before escaping the pit using
the very same weapons to climb out."

Odysseus could feel the stillness in the room shift. He turned to
see Gryph stepping off the bottom of the tall wooden ladder. He
hadn't made a sound as he descended the rungs. Odysseus put his
finger to his lips. Gryph saw the gesture clearly on the HUD and
remained silent.

"I guess curiosity got the better of some of the soldiers," Hector
said, oblivious to the new guest listening in. "Many of them stuck
close to the pit they threw me into, waiting to see if the latest round
of savagery did the trick and finished the demon off. When they
saw me clamber out of that hole, they knew otherwise. Some ran
in fear, but most of them remained behind, eager to rid the world
of the unholy monster they thought me to be. I was attacked again,
but not before I killed most of those would-be crusaders myself.
Ultimately, I was thought to have been killed once more, and my
captors buried my body deep in the ground on the outskirts of the
city, covering my grave with a heavy stone."

If Hector had swallowed a mouthful of the elixir just two days
prior to being buried, then Odysseus knew instantly the source of
the pain and torment that Hector had spoken of earlier. He dreaded
hearing the details, but he knew he couldn't escape it.

"I woke in darkness, my flesh on fire again, intense pressure crushing my body, choking on dirt with every breath. The elixir may repair bodily damage, but it does nothing to lessen the pain. Excruciating doesn't even begin to describe the feeling. I spent almost two months crawling through the earth, moving only an inch a day at first, until I could free an arm or leg enough to move through the packed dirt. I suffocated was dangled in front of death's face more times than I can remember, only to be reborn through the same baptism of pain and suffering."

Gryph was horrified by the tale. He could think of no worse punishment. He didn't need to have a fear of being buried alive for that to have an impact. The experience would be worse than hell for anyone. When even death couldn't provide the escape that a panicked, claustrophobic mind would seek. Hector had been trapped in a nightmare that wouldn't end. Gryph almost felt sorry for him. Then he reminded himself that Hector was actively trying to kill eight billion people, and the feeling soon faded.

"When I finally clawed my way to the surface, I laid on the ground, staring up at the moon and the stars, breathing in the fresh, clean, cool air for the first time in months. I remember how clean the air tasted and how clear the night sky looked. Now that same air is filled with smog and acid rain, the ozone layer depleted to nothing in some areas. The very earth itself birthed me anew, and as such, I vowed to protect my mother. Like the first man created from the dust of the earth and given dominion over the world, it is now my destiny to rule all. I am Zeus reborn."

"Even after drinking such a large quantity of elixir, the effects would have worn off long ago," Odysseus said.

"Ah. That would be true it there was no other source of the elixir," Hector said.

Suddenly, Gryph and Odysseus feared that Hector also figured out that the original source was buried there and got to it first.

But how could he have solved the puzzle without the clues provided by the menorah and Solomon's box? Odysseus wondered. *Was there another map that pointed the way to the Ark of the Covenant?*

Gryph was silently hoping there was still enough manna left for the antidote if Hector had, in fact, already pilfered the golden jar that he saw on the HUDs before rushing out to search for Hector.

Gryph was about to radio Chief to see if the nanobots had been able to secure the necessary quantity of elixir or if Hector had already pilfered it when the answer came from Hector himself.

"I understood and benefitted from the elixir's power, but I didn't know how long the effects would last. Knowing that nothing good lasts forever, I took a chance and returned to the mountain where I was first captured and found my waterskin with the contents still intact. Fate once again interceded on my behalf, Odysseus, setting me on the path toward greatness.

"I continued my search for Ianthina's body after I found the elixir and was relieved when at first I couldn't find her, thinking that you two had made it to safety. Eventually, however, I found her ravaged corpse. Animals and insects had devoured her. Her gnawed-on bones and the thin weathered strips of her dress were all that was left of the princess. I dug her grave with my bare hands and begged her soul for forgiveness."

Odysseus was stunned. He suddenly felt nauseous and dizzy. "When I went back to look, I couldn't find her anywhere." He sputtered, "I thought I went to the exact same spot, but we took different routes to get back there. I wasn't sure. I thought you had found and revived her, so I returned to the fleet and searched the ships and then the waters for you both. I couldn't find either of you, and thought the worst."

"You didn't even try to come back for me!" Hector bellowed in fury. "You called me brother, yet you sailed off, leaving me to the whims of my captors and allowing our princess to rot on the ground without a proper burial. You are no god to worship or hero to admire. You're just an actor and a coward."

Gryph could see Odysseus shaking his head as he listened to Hector berate him, but a SEAL wouldn't leave another SEAL behind either. He couldn't understand how a man like Odysseus, someone with such deep conviction, would have just left his friend behind.

"I searched the island for you for weeks." Odysseus explained, pain tinging his voice. "They must have held you someplace hidden. We lost over twenty men looking for you. They had to tear me away from the search. We eventually concluded that they killed you and threw your body into the sea. You were publicly lauded as a hero of the empire, and the entire country mourned you, Ianthina, and the royal family for a month. None more than me."

Hector let that news sit with him for a moment before speaking. "There was no going back for me, Odysseus. When I crawled out from under the earth after those eternal hellish months, I left the man you knew as Hector dead and buried. Basileus rose in his place."

"Hector, this has to end," Odysseus said, ignoring his old friend's new name. "Surrender to me, and we can work something out."

"I would rather die than surrender. Especially to you." The rage returned to his voice. "You may think you've won, but I have you right where I want you, Odysseus."

Gryph stood close enough to Odysseus to whisper without giving away his presence to Hector. "We've all been listening in on the conversation on the comms, Daedalus—Odysseus, sorry. This guy is a psychopath and a megalomaniac. He sounds like he's about to come unhinged at any moment. I don't like the sound of that last threat. He's not bluffing. We're missing something."

"I'm not going to wait to find out," Odysseus said while reaching into his tactical vest for a metallic black bar the size of a soda can. "I've heard everything from him that I needed to. He'll never come around. The Hector I know is gone." Odysseus tossed the black bar through the opening and waited. Gryph turned away instinctively, but there was no accompanying blast, just a mechanical buzz and the familiar smell of static electricity.

The bar dissolved into a loose nano swarm as soon as it left Odysseus's hands and tumbled through the opening into the cistern below. Odysseus could see Hector twisting around on the ladder, frantically trying to make sense of the metallic cloud churning in the narrow shaft. The darkened cistern and flat-black appearance of the bots made identifying the nano threat impossible. Odysseus and Gryph watched the swarm begin to take shape on the HUD feed. At first, Gryph wasn't sure what Odysseus had planned. It looked like the bots were forming into a series of interconnected poles, but as the structures solidified, they began to take the form of a cage.

It was then that Gryph knew exactly what the ancient Greek had designed.

"You think I'm frightened by your little toys, Odysseus?" Hector laughed, not understanding what was happening above him. "I brought something of my own for you as well."

Gryph heard the ominous tone in Hector's voice, but couldn't see the worry etched on Odysseus's face. Panic and confusion crept into Odysseus's voice when he spoke. "It shouldn't be taking this long. The bots should have completed their final structure by now. The depth and the thickness of the stones must be disrupting the signal strength from the nano case above us."

They watched the cage forming and then collapsing above Hector on the HUD screen, the programming never fully taking hold. The structure faded in and out of physicality. "The weak connection is creating structural lag, just like a video buffering when a mobile phone loses signal," Odysseus said. The upload eventually completed, and the form finally stabilized. A four-sided cage structure hovered above Hector, as if suspended by invisible strings, but was actually anchored securely to the cistern wall. The swarm dropped down in a flash, enveloping Hector in a nanobot jail cell. The tops and bottoms folded inward, sealing Hector inside.

Hector grabbed at the bars. He could feel the thrum of energy course through the strange material. He tried to pull them apart, but they felt as strong as iron. It wouldn't matter. He reached into his jacket and pulled out two small blocks of red putty. He pressed the silver button that had already been embedded in the clay and watched the LED on the Semtex grenade turn from green to red. The powerful explosives would detonate as soon as they contacted any hard surface.

Gryph and Odysseus watched the two cubes tumble from Hector's hand and spiral down into the jagged rocks at the bottom of the cistern. They both looked at each other and realized that was what he meant by having Odysseus right where he wanted him.

As soon as the Semtex cubes struck the broken slabs below, the mass of rocks blasted skyward with earth-shattering force. In response, the bots created a shield at the base of the impromptu jail cell and constricted like a cocoon around Hector. The bots absorbed the brunt of the impact from the flying debris, but didn't entirely shield him from the damage he'd just unleashed. Shards of broken stone exploded through the opening of the upper cistern, pelting Gryph and Odysseus with debris. More concerning were the huge fissures now running up the walls of the cistern in which Gryph and Odysseus were standing. The walls began to crumble on either side of the huge cracks.

At the same time the walls were cracking above, the cage around Hector began to expand back to its pre-programmed form. The emergency life-protection protocol Odysseus designed into the bots had worked flawlessly. That was the good news. The bad news was that a good portion of the nanobot swarm that protected Hector in the blast was now failing. The cage began glitching once again.

Red warning lights flashed inside the HUDs. "The bots are failing. When they dissolve, Hector will plummet to his death."

"Odysseus, if we don't get up that ladder right now, two hundred tons of rock is going to come crashing down on us. We have to leave now." Gryph wasn't sure why Odysseus was hesitating.

"I left him once long ago. I can't do it again."

"You didn't know. I heard the story. You did everything you could. He wouldn't do it for you."

"I'm not doing this for him. I couldn't live with myself knowing I had a chance to save him again, even if he doesn't want to be saved. Never leave a man behind, right, Commander?" How could a SEAL and a fellow soldier argue with that sentiment?

"Commander Oake, you need to leave. That's an order. I don't need help with this. It's my mission alone. Get to safety and complete the antidote. That's all that matters now." Gryph looked him in the eyes. He knew there would be no persuading him otherwise.

"It's been an honor, sir," Gryph said as he shook Odysseus's hand. "I hope to see you onboard *Hera* soon. Godspeed."

Gryph ran to the base of the ladder. Larger pieces of stonework began to fall from above. He had to jump out of the way when a boulder the size of a washing machine crashed beside him. He took hold of the rungs of the tall wooden ladder and began his rapid ascent.

"Commander!" Odysseus called as Gryph was halfway up. "Promise me you'll take care of the Library. I'm entrusting it all to you and the rest of the crew."

"I swear to protect it with my life," Gryph said.

Odysseus nodded and then ran to the opening of the lower cistern, which had now been blown wide open from the force of the Semtex.

"Hector!" he shouted through the dust and noise. He risked a look down, exposing himself enough to be shot at, but no bullets came his way. The air was thick with sand and fine particulate that covered everything in an ash-gray powder. A burning chemical pall hung in the void, burning Odysseus's eyes and throat. Flames licked at the bottom of the pit. Acrid smoke rose through the narrow shaft like toxic breath from the throat of a stone dragon. A pained cry rose from the pit, more animal than man.

Odysseus saw the source of the anguished howl. Hector was suspended upside down from the nano cage. His legs were both twisted at grotesque angles through the digital bars. The bots had taken the brunt of concussive force, but the debris from the blast had peppered Hector's body, tearing it to shreds. His left arm was missing below the elbow. His right was clutching at a vial that dangled from his neck, precariously close to slipping off his head.

"Hector! Don't move! I'll climb down the ladder to get you."

The lower section of the aluminum ladders Hector was on had been destroyed by the Semtex. However, the upper portion remained fastened to the wall, albeit badly damaged. Odysseus put a tentative foot on the aluminum rung, and the ladder immediately began to pull free of its supports. He wouldn't be able to climb down after all. His weight would send the ladder crashing to the jagged rocks and chemical fire below.

Hector sneered up at Odysseus with a face more gristle and bone than the visage of a man. The entire side of his face had been flayed open, revealing a gleaming white jawbone and a row of bloodied teeth. He smiled wickedly as he poured the entire contents of the vial down his throat. Odysseus knew exactly what he had just drank. The last of his flask. Even Odysseus had no clue as to what effect that massive quantity of elixir would bring.

Odysseus couldn't understand what Hector was doing, until it was too late. Hector reached into his jacket and pulled out another red cube, even bigger than the first two combined. Odysseus didn't wait for Hector to drop it this time. He knew another blast would destroy the weakening structure and everyone in it. Hector held on to the belief that a massive dose of elixir would save him from the blast, completely heal him and ultimately become his route of escape.

Odysseus raced over to the wooden ladder just as the explosion from the last Semtex cube obliterated the cistern below, causing the upper section he was standing on to crumble and shatter into the lower pool. He was caught in a veritable 250-ton avalanche of stone and sand.

Odysseus felt a rumble and shockwave under his feet grow to a deafening crescendo, sounding like a mountain was being torn in half. The last thing he saw was a blinding flash of light as the explosion from the Semtex reached the level where he stood. His quick death spared him the pain from the scorching heat of the blast and the weight of the sixty-foot stone wall when it came crashing down around him and into the cistern below.

The general who had battled through the rise and fall of countless empires and safeguarded ancient secrets which were thought to be lost to time was no more. The culmination of his life's work would live on, however. The Library of Alexandria was safe, and new guards stood watch. This wellspring of knowledge had but a single protector before, now it had a team dedicating their lives to defending and studying its secrets.

The world was now under the protection of the Daedalus Protocol.

CHAPTER FIFTY

The Workshop, NYC
February 18, 1:12 p.m.

"Gryph, I'm not going to be able to run this last set of tests unless I can get some more of that coffee into my body stat. I'm going cross-eyed." Aliyah had been burning the candle at both ends for a few days already. In fact, the Daedalus crew hadn't really taken a break since they boarded the plane in Israel and headed back to New York.

Aliyah's knee was in a brace. An MRI revealed that her kneecap was fractured and chipped. Her MCL was strained but not torn. The injury would slow her down for a while, and she wouldn't be skiing moguls that season, but she still considered herself lucky. Things could have been much worse.

She and Luna had been working around the logistics to incorporate the manna into their antidote. They had achieved success early on, the antidote proving effective after only their second attempt. Trial after trial showed the same result. Ali's concoction eradicated any trace of the toxin found in the soil, seeds, and fertilizers already infected by Hector's vast network. They were now in the process of reformulating the antidote to use a smaller concentration of the manna and still maintain its 100 percent efficacy.

"Extra-large, steaming hot, coming through," Gryph rattled on like a barista at a coffee shop. "I'm trying this new blend. I think it could go down as my all-time favorite. Let me know what you think." He set the wide-mouth mug on a rarely seen vacant spot at Aliyah's workstation. She took a careful sip after blowing across the surface of the shimmering dark brew.

"Mmm. If heaven had a taste, it would be something like this." It was quite the compliment, but Gryph couldn't argue with the sentiment. It was ridiculously good coffee.

Phil was working out logistics at the large stone conference table inside the Workshop with Chief and Solo, determining how to best distribute the antidote once they had the formula finalized. Aliyah was certain she could scale up production with some help from Dallas's army of bots, creating enough antidote to neutralize all the toxins produced within a matter of days.

They raided Hector's compound after receiving its coordinates from their contacts at MI6. The meticulous record keeping that the Brotherhood had kept made identifying the locations of the companies Basileus was hiding behind easy. All the shipments of his toxic seeds and fertilizer were immediately halted. The ones already in transit were tracked and recovered. A few, unfortunately, slipped through the cracks and would wreak havoc when applied, but that was what the antidote was for.

They had a happy ending of sorts after finding Brother Marcus in Basileus's prison cell, barely clinging to life. He was taken to Cedars Sinai Hospital for treatment and recovery, but some of his injuries would leave him permanently disabled.

Incredibly, their long-shot plan had worked, and the crisis was over. Large sections of land would still have to be remediated; the soil having been poisoned beyond repair. Nothing that couldn't be removed and backfilled with fresh earth over a short period of time though.

Dallas came tearing around the corner, full of energy and enthusiasm. "I just ran the numbers from your last batch, Ali. I think this is the one. We'll have enough elixir to cure the toxin ten times over. You have some mad science skills, Doc. I'm impressed."

"Mad science skills? Where'd you pick that up?" Phil asked, barely suppressing a laugh.

"Luna keeps me hip, baby."

Dallas had been in a fantastic mood since leaving Israel. Unbeknownst to the rest of the crew, he'd secretly siphoned off some of the manna when the bots first started making their way back from the hidden chamber. He admitted to Luna that he'd "accidentally" collected a microscopic amount of the mysterious substance on his hands while he was "bracing" himself against the wall just before he left the tunnels. The bots released some of the elixir they were carrying back onto Dallas's hand when he made brief contact with the wall. An "insignificant amount" is how he described it to Luna.

It was obvious that he'd been exposed to the manna as soon as he was back on-board *Hera*, however. The wounds on his scalp had already started to heal before they'd even taken off from Ben Gurion Airport. By the time they landed in New York, the scarring had almost disappeared. Luna made him come clean to the rest of the team after he told her the details of how his miraculous healing came to pass. None of them begrudged him his mini miracle. He likely saved the entire mission with his well-timed shot at Hector. Who knows how the standoff would have played out without his intervention? An unintended consequence of applying the manna to the wounds on his scalp was the sudden regrowth of his sandy-blonde hair, something not seen since the '90s.

Luna was inaugurated as a full-fledged member of the Daedalus crew by unanimous vote. Her strong moral character, fearless self-sacrifice, and unique skill set made her a perfect addition to the team. Gryph pulled her aside after she accepted the position and thanked her for agreeing to be part of this new family. They both had a good laugh when Gryph told her she was the only person on Earth who could keep Dallas in check, even though she knew it to be true. She was a good influence on Dallas, something he hoped would continue long into the future.

"Commander, I think we've drafted a great strategy for distributing the first wave of the antidote. We're set to present it to the team when you're ready, sir." Solo Daniels was promoted to a full-time member of the Daedalus crew. His duties would still center primarily around *Hera*, but he wanted to be able to contribute more in the field going forward.

"Thanks, Solo. We'll be there in a few."

"Yes, sir. I'll let the Doctor know."

"That dude has to lighten up a bit if he's gonna fit in around here," Dallas said as he headed toward Phil and Chief for the next briefing.

Luna took the opportunity during Aliyah's quick coffee break to call her dad. There was much she couldn't tell him, so she fibbed a bit and said she'd been recruited by a black-ops government program and that the incident at the café was being relegated as collateral damage from a mission gone bad. Her dad breathed a sigh of relief when she told him she was being generously compensated for the loss of the café by the government. In truth, Gryph had already wired Luna a $500,000 down payment on the compensation he promised before he'd even offered her the job. She deserved the money regardless of her decision.

To say she was shocked when Gryph told her another million dollars would be deposited into her bank account from her insurance company in the next sixty days, along with an extra million from Daedalus's posthumous trust fund, would be an understatement.

There was, however, a sadness that permeated the Workshop despite all the progress they'd made in the last few days. Daedalus not being there himself to see their success prevented anyone from being able to fully celebrate any of their recent accomplishments.

Gryph put down his coffee and fished a vibrating phone out of his pocket. He glanced at the call display and tensed up.

"What's wrong?" Aliyah asked.

"Jerusalem area code." Gryph showed her the screen. "I just hope your friends at Mossad were successful with their 'negotiations.'"

The last of the explosions Hector detonated in the lower cistern caused so much destruction to the lower section of the tunnel, areas a hundred feet away were destabilized and deemed unsafe for passage. Early estimates suggested that the repairs needed to allow them to reopen the tunnels for tourists again could take up to a decade to complete. The vast majority of work would have to be done by hand, as most of the areas were inaccessible to most types of large earth-moving equipment. However, experts figured some of the larger pieces weighed in excess of ten tons each, and there was no practical way to move them.

The topography of the tunnels and cisterns would be altered forever. Maps of this underground city would have to be redrawn, reflecting the destruction and loss.

The lowermost pit, the source of the explosions, had incurred the most damage. The area around the blast was deemed to be beyond repair and highly dangerous. It was now just a 300-foot-deep cratered pit of stone and sand. Whatever would have been discovered down there were considered lost or destroyed. As such, the Department of Israeli Antiquities decided to seal that entire section of tunnel off and abandon it for good.

Gryph was hoping Aliyah's friend was as connected as she said he was. "Good morning, David." It was just after sunrise in Jerusalem. "I'll put you on speaker with Aliyah as well. Go ahead whenever you're ready."

"I have good news for you," he said. "The Israeli government is putting out an official statement saying, and I quote, 'The cause of the blast was due to improper storage of a few large propane tanks that were being used on a recent excavation project. Thankfully, there was no injury or loss of life, as the explosion happened late at night, long after the workers at the dig site had left for the day. Damage was catastrophic, and repairs will take tens of millions of dollars and many years to complete.'"

"Toda," Aliyah said, Hebrew for "Thanks." "I owe you one."

"Yes, you do. Any assistance with the cleanup would be great too. It's a real mess down there."

"Let me see what I can do. Talk soon." She disconnected the call on Gryph's phone.

"You know, I could probably design a quick program to have the bots help clear out some of the tricky areas in the tunnel," Dallas said. "What do you think, Gryph?"

"I think that's a great idea. We have to head back there soon anyway. We still have to replace the menorah in the Cave of the Patriarchs. Odysseus gave his word, and we need to honor that promise for him."

"You're going to crawl through that skinny shaft again? Are you nuts?" Dallas asked.

"No. No chance at all," Gryph said. "I figured you can program the bots to put the box back for us too. If they could extract the manna through a stone wall, I'm sure it wouldn't be hard for you to bury a big box."

Dallas scratched at the fuzz on his newly stubbled head. "Yeah, I may be able to do something for ya. I'm not sure I could watch you go through that again. I still get freaked out thinking about it."

"Much appreciated," Gryph said with a wink. Then he walked over to Phil, Solo, and Chief for the briefing.

"Alright, guys, tell me how we're going to deliver the antidote."

CHAPTER FIFTY-ONE

The Workshop
One month later

The mood was much lighter. The distribution had been completed, and the last of the toxin eradicated. The bots were making quick work clearing out the debris from the tunnels, but it was agreed they wouldn't move anything beyond the capabilities of regular equipment. It would be impossible to explain otherwise.

The menorah was safely underground again, and they even found a way to replace the cracked slab inside the crypt. It seemed the loose ends had been wrapped up. All but one.

"The antidote was a success," Gryph said to his team, who had gathered with him in front of the door to the Labyrinth. "And thanks to Ali's wizardry in the lab, we still have a small vial of the manna left, which is why we're standing here."

He led the group through the door and into the vastness of the Library of Alexandria. "I think we should add it to the collection. Who knows when we might need it again?"

"I was thinking the same thing," Aliyah said, taking a few steps deeper into the vault. Her knee was getting better each week, but moving around was still a strenuous task. "We just have to find a good spot for it."

"About that," Gryph said as he stared into the cavernous vault. "I'm not sure how Daedalus had all this stuff organized before. I mean, if we're tasked with protecting and studying these incredible things, we should probably take a good look around. I, for one, can't wait to see what we're going to find—and where it's going to lead us next."

The group wandered around the Library for almost an hour. There was an endless supply of information to digest, and they soon realized it would indeed take multiple lifetimes to even do a cursory review of the treasures they had in their custody. Solving them would require an eternity. Gryph could see how Odysseus's lifelong thirst for knowledge could only be quenched with the answers held in the Library, keeping him engrossed throughout the centuries.

Just as they were getting ready to leave, Luna shouted out. "You guys, come over here. You need to see this."

Everyone walked over to where she was standing. They were in awe of the object in front of them.

"That can't be real," Dallas said, not believing his eyes.

"I can't see Odysseus keeping anything fake in here. Besides, who would he be trying to impress? No one knows this place exists. It's gotta be authentic."

They all stood in front of the glass case, examining the oddity contained inside. A gold tablet and a larger crystal tablet floated effortlessly, twisting up from the base. The crystal tablet flashed and began emitting a loud crackling sound, startling everyone. Luna reached out to touch the glass exterior. The moment her fingers contacted the glass, the power in the Library went out. Emergency lights flickered to life seconds later.

It took a moment from everyone to grasp the incredulous sight in front of them.

"Well," Gryph said. "I guess that answers where we're going next."

EPILOGUE

The darkness and solitude made determining the time of day impossible. Images rolled in and out of focus. A ladder. A cage. Odysseus. Pouring the elixir into his wounded mouth. A massive explosion of rock and flame. He tried to shake the images from his thoughts, but had no ability to do so.

Panic began to seep into the far reaches of his consciousness. How long had he been trapped? Had it been hours? Days? A week? His mind was too terrified to contemplate that it could have been even longer.

A primal fear flooded his entire being. It all came rushing back at once. He'd been buried alive before and remembered the terror clearly now. Hector could almost taste the dirt again in his mouth. But the sensation was different this time. The unbearable pain and crushing pressure he felt the first time he was buried alive was conspicuously absent now.

At first, the lack of pain brought Hector a sense of relief and comfort. Maybe he wasn't trapped. He began to relax. That calm quickly dissolved into horror when he realized it wasn't just the lack of sensation in his body that he was missing. He became acutely aware that he no longer had any connection to his body, and yet, his mind was still active. It was clearly impossible, but he knew it to be the truth.

Hector had been crushed in the explosion of rock and fire beyond any hope of rejuvenation or repair. The massive dose of elixir couldn't heal his physical body, so instead, it used its power to salvage the one thing it could—his consciousness. Those trillions of electrical connections between the synapses making a person who they were. The manna somehow bridged the space between the physical and the ethereal.

Hector realized his higher consciousness was all that had survived the explosion and was now being sustained by the elixir alone, a facet of this mysterious substance revealed only in death. At the same moment, he understood that his mind had become its own prison. With no physical body to utilize and absorb the elixir, the concentrated power he ingested would sustain his mind for centuries to come.

There would be nothing left of Hector, locked inside his own twisted mind. Alone in the dark, unable to sleep or to quiet his raging thoughts for even a moment. His entire existence would be an endless cycle of insanity.

He knew deep down there would be no relief from this private hell.

That miserable fact was the last lucid thought he had before his mind slipped into an eternity of madness.

FACT VS. FICTION

Thank you for purchasing **The Daedalus Protocol.** I hope you enjoyed reading it as much as I enjoyed writing it.

Some of my favorite authors often add a Fact vs Fiction section at the end of their stories. One last tasty morsel to savor. I've always enjoyed discovering just how much of the novel I read was factual, fantasy, or the author's wild conjecture.

Let's get to it…

Manna from heaven: The description of the manna in *The Daedalus Protocol* is an accurate description of the miraculous food that fell in the desert thousands of years ago. The Old Testament and numerous biblical commentaries described the manna's taste as cakes fried in honey, while others say it would taste like anything the person eating it wanted it to.

The theory that the manna were the spent cocoons of Trehala beetles was posited by Hebrew University in 1927 and again by the British *Independent*, in an article by John Emsley, April 21, 1996. I'm sure there are others, but that's where I got the idea to use the little cocoons as a *natural* explanation of how the manna ended up all over the desert floor. The healing qualities it gained from a meteor shower are purely a figment of my imagination. The timeline of the meteor shower coinciding with the biblical plague of hail is also conjecture. Could *hail that turned to fire* when it hit the ground really be describing a cosmic meteor shower? It sure sounds like it to me.

The Workshop and Labyrinth: The geological formations and types of bedrock that lay under NYC are accurate. The massive bubble keeping the Daedalus crew safe and hidden from the world is of my own design. If there really were large areas of inhabitable space under New York, I'm sure they'd have been rented out by now.

Discoveries of new compounds and elements from outer space: A 15 Ton meteorite was discovered in Somalia in 2019, the ninth largest ever found. It contained at least two new minerals that have never been discovered on Earth and are new to science. There's a whole lot more out there that we don't know about.

Nanotech, Artificial Intelligence and Quantum Computing: While *ICARUS*, the quantum computer inside the Workshop is fictional, the realm of quantum computing and AI is real—and it's already here. Today's quantum computers are more than 150 MILLION times faster than the most sophisticated super-computers in the world. It takes these new quantum's less than five minutes to process information that would have taken regular supercomputers 10,000 years to complete!

With the advent of ChatGPT and OpenAI, it's easy to imagine machines thinking and problem-solving on their own. The nanobot swarm isn't too far off. Nanotech is improving every day and the complex tasks they can perform already are incredible. As the advances in artificial intelligence grow exponentially, it's only a matter of time until the two technologies are combined, and the swarm becomes a reality. Kind of terrifying if you ask me.

The Cave of the Patriarchs: The Cave of the Patriarchs is the burial place of Abraham, Isaac, Jacob, and their wives. Rachel is the only matriarch not buried there. Adam and Eve, the world's first two people, are also purported to be buried there. The site is still under Arab control and has been very well cared for by the authorities in Hebron. I've visited it many times and wondered what the caves really looked like deep under the ground. The secret back entrance through the crypt and the small cemetery nearby can only be found in this book.

Western Wall and Blood Channel: A visit to the Old City of Jerusalem in Israel wouldn't be complete without a stop at the Western Wall and its adjacent tunnels. It's true that people put little notes inside the crevices of the wall to have their prayers answered. The blood channel was a theory put forward by a few archeologists and scholars over the years. According to them, it was used as a drain for the blood and gore from the temple sacrifices. The size and location are described accurately. A connection to the secret vault hiding the Lost Ark and Temple treasures is wild speculation. But it all must be somewhere… you never know.

The Pope's Secret Vatican Vault: I've been to the Vatican and have seen the amazing artwork and artifacts on display to the public. The Sistine Chapel and St Mark's Square are incredible to behold, but I couldn't find any signs directing me to the secretive vault. So, I made this one up. The Parochet (the curtain from the First Jewish Temple) was reportedly seen in the Vatican's possession by a soldier at the end of WWII, during the liberation of Italy. The Vatican has denied the account. Regardless, the Vatican contains a treasure trove of priceless artifacts that the world will likely never get to see.

Don't forget to checkout **TheDaedalusProtocol.com** for information on the release date for the next exciting chapter in the **Daedalus Protocol** series.

ACKNOWLEDGEMENTS

The fact that you've just read **The Daedalus Protocol** proves beyond a doubt that anything is possible.

Writing a novel is a journey filled with equal parts inspiration and perspiration. I am deeply grateful to the many individuals who have supported, encouraged, and guided me throughout the creation of **The Daedalus Protocol**. Without them, this work of fiction would have remained a mere figment of my imagination.

First and foremost, **Thank you to my readers** for choosing to spend your valuable time and money on my book! I'd also like to extend my heartfelt gratitude to my family, whose unwavering belief in my abilities and unending patience provided me with the motivation to keep going when it got tough.

I am incredibly thankful to my dedicated beta readers, **Sonia, Jake, Akiva, Danielle, Bill, Dallas, Tony, Ethan, Nacho, and of course my Mom** and **Dad**. Your invaluable feedback helped shape my manuscript into its final form. Your keen insights, critical eyes, and honest opinions have truly elevated my work far beyond what I could have achieved alone.

A special acknowledgment goes to my earliest editor **Kevin Miller**, who meticulously reviewed every sentence, trimmed the fat, and challenged me to elevate my prose.

To my boys **Jake** and **Akiva**, thank you both for reading and re-reading, (and re-reading) the manuscript, making the story better and cleaner every step of the way. Thanks for keeping me company on those late nights that stretched into early mornings. You always stayed up until the bitter end and got it done. Jake's cover made the final cut, and Akiva's book trailer made the story come to life in video. Your mom obviously raised you right ;)

To my proof reader, **Maxine Meyer**, I offer my deepest appreciation for catching even the smallest errors and ensuring that the final text was as clean and professional as possible. You were instrumental in helping me present the best possible version of my story to the world.

I am also immensely grateful to the artistic mind who brought The Daedalus Protocol to life visually. To **Anthony Chinedu**, my incredible graphic designer responsible for the captivating cover art.

To **Aeyshaa**, whose talents in formatting and layout, coupled with a keen sense of design and typography has made this novel not only a pleasure to read but also a delight to behold in print and digital form.

To **Phillip Nathaniel Freeman**, I couldn't have found a better voice to bring my novel to life in audio book format. He can also be found rocking out with his band, Small Town Titans.

I'd like to extend my sincere gratitude to my friends, both on line and IRL, for their support and encouragement. Your kind words and enthusiasm for this project have motivated me to push through the inevitable moments of self-doubt and creative stagnation. For those of you who find shadows of yourself in the story, I hope you enjoyed you alter-ego's.

Thank you to everyone else who has played part in the creation of **The Daedalus Protocol**, no matter how big or small, I am forever grateful. I hope you enjoyed reading it, as much as I enjoyed writing it.

Visit my website TheDaedalusProtocol.com and let me know what you thought of the first installment in the Daedalus Protocol Series.

Manufactured by Amazon.ca
Bolton, ON

35345147R00266